TALES OF MONSTROSITY
Monsters, Myths, and Miscreants

Marx Pyle, J.C. Mastro, Victoria L. Scott, Anne C. Lynch

Cabbit Crossing Publishing, LLC

Tales of Monstrosity: Monsters, Myths, and Miscreants

Copyright © 2022 by Cabbit Crossing Publishing LLC

This is a work of fiction. Names, places and incidents are either products of the author's imagination or used fictitiously. Any resemblance to actual persons, living or dead is entirely coincidental.

Edited by Marx Pyle, J.C. Mastro, Anne C. Lynch, Victoria L. Scott

Book Cover Design by 100 Covers

Ornamental Break design by Sen R.L. Scherb https://linktr.ee/SenRider

"El Cucuy" Copyright © 2022 by Scott A. Johnson

"Gore Vellye (The Autumn Tumult)" Copyright © 2022 by Anne C. Lynch

"Prey Animals" Copyright © 2022 by Sen R.L. Scherb

"The Devil and Scott" Copyright © 2022 by W.H. Horner

"A Thing of Hope" Copyright © 2022 by Carrie Gessner

"Gnomies" Copyright © 2022 by Kevin Plybon

"Don't Feed the Troll" Copyright © 2022 by Katharine Dow

"Don't Lose Your Head" Copyright © 2022 by Victoria L. Scott

"Eyes Like Burning Coal" Copyright © 2022 by Jeremiah Dylan Cook

"Magicland Mischief" Copyright © 2022 by J.C. Mastro

"Ghouly Girl" Copyright © 2022 by Sophia DeSensi

"Worst Vacation Ever" Copyright © 2022 by Jeannie Rivera

"The Brazen Skull" Copyright © 2022 by Michael La Ronn

"Rebel with a Cause" Copyright © 2022 by Marx Pyle

COPYRIGHT

"An Old Favor" Copyright © 2022 by Marisa Wolf

"The Adventures of Elena and Ned, Gargoyle P.I." Copyright © 2022 by Jeff Burns

"The Greatest of All Time" Copyright © 2022 by Francis Fernandez

"Hexpad Blog: A First-Timer's Guide to the Big City" Copyright © 2022 by Colten Fisher

"The Tiger's Gift" Copyright © 2022 by G.K. White

All rights reserved. This book or parts thereof may not be reproduced in any form, stored in a retrieval system, or transmitted in any form by any means—electronic, mechanical, photocopy, recording, or otherwise—without prior written permission of the publisher, except as provided by United States' copyright law.

CONTENTS

Dedication	VIII
Acknowledgments	1
Foreword	3
By Tim Waggoner	
Introduction	7
By Marx Pyle	
1. Monsters	12
El Cucuy	13
By Scott A. Johnson	
Gore Vellye (The Autumn Tumult)	29
By Anne C. Lynch	
Prey Animals	51
By Sen R.L. Scherb	
The Devil and Scott	67
By W. H. Horner	
A Thing of Hope	101
By Carrie Gessner	
2. Myths	112

Gnomies By Kevin Plybon	113
Don't Feed the Troll by Katharine Dow	135
Don't Lose Your Head by Victoria L. Scott	151
Eyes Like Burning Coal By Jeremiah Dylan Cook	165
Magicland Mischief By J.C. Mastro	183
Ghouly Girl By Sophia DeSensi	213
Worst Vacation Ever: A Frederick Moody Story By Jeannie Rivera	237
3. Miscreants	265
The Brazen Skull: A Good Necromancer Story by Michael La Ronn	267
Rebel with a Cause: An Obsidian Archives Story By Marx Pyle	293
An Old Favor By Marisa Wolf	315
The Adventures of Elena and Ned, Gargoyle P.I. By Jeff Burns	343
The Greatest of All Time By Francis Fernandez	377
Hexpad Blog: A First-Timer's Guide to the Big City By Colten Fisher	403

The Tiger's Gift	425
By G.K. White	
4. Behind The Scenes & Soundtrack	462
Behind El Cucuy	463
Behind Gore Vellye (The Autumn Tumult)	465
Behind Prey Animals	469
Behind The Devil and Scott	472
Behind A Thing of Hope	475
Behind The Gnomies	477
Behind Don't Feed the Troll	479
Behind Don't Lose Your Head	481
Behind Eyes Like Burning Coal	484
Behind The Magicland Mischief	486
Behind The Ghouly Girl	490
Behind The Worst Vacation Ever	492
Behind The Brazen Skull	494
Behind The Rebel with a Cause	496
Behind An Old Favor	499
Behind The Adventures of Elena and Ned, Gargoyle P.I.	501
Behind The Greatest of All Time	505
Behind The Hexpad Blog	508
Behind The Tiger's Gift	511
Tales of Monstrosity: The Soundtrack	514
ABOUT THE EDITORS	517

For all of you monsters out there.

ACKNOWLEDGMENTS

A Kaiju-sized thank you to our amazing Kickstarter backers for supporting this print edition!

Austin Hoffey, Susan Jessen, Rachel Nesbit, Ben Hausman, Mark Rivera, Woody Arnold, Christy Hoke, Kristin Lord, Debbie Beall, Roscoe Beall, Francesco Tehrani, Beth Lobdell, Erik Miller, Chris A. Taylor, Dawn Lumbatis Scherb, Kendall Varnell, Gregory A. Horvay, Noele Clayton, Craft Tyler, Ric Albano, Olivia Havens, Nicholas Kohn, Sergio Oviedo Cardenas, Kelley "Don't blame me for Hamlet" Bard, Heather N Hollis, Roman Sims, Nicolas Mandujano III, A.J. Gragg, Jacob H. Joseph, Kateryna Zvenyhorodska, Melanie Briggs, Winter Hart, Ron Pucherelli, Alayna Almen, Don Witteman, Andrea White, Carolyn, Karen Tan, Frank Lewis, Zachary Oliver Bourne, Christopher D. Shramko, Anna Katrina Velasquez, Bianca Longstaff, C.R. DeVries, Katherine Shipman, Dylan Humphreys, Nina Zumel, Justin Talso, Michele Heidorn, Davin Greenwood, Colby Rodeheaver, Kayla O'Hare, Anthony Hernandez, Sam Fischbeck, Michelle Ho, Nikolai Tys, Robian Ho, James Leonard, Eli Hansen,

Klikke Sietel, Rhel ná DecVandé, Carl Blair, Nicola Jane Wright, Peter Jansen, Colleen Feeney, Mia Karen Sherman, Rory King, Brieann Tabler, Ryan Andrew Holda, Nova Clarke, Brittnay Lomay King, El McAninch, Brandon Belusko, Kyle, Michael Flores, Michael Traver, S.P. Samedi, Matt Selter, Tim Putney-Parret, Didier Schuijren, Devin DeMarco, Kevin Urman, Tiffany George, Curtis Boudreau, Adem K. Boeckmann, Scott Schiffmacher, Kimberly Lucia, Cathy Green, Casey Chowdhary, Kathryn Valentine, Megan Morrison, David Thompson, Benjamin D. Warner, James Robinson, John Lamar, Juan Manuel Aquino, Christina Fernandez, Heidi Ruby Miller, Danielle Kleymeyer, Taylor Cockerham, Shawn Reardon, Bronte Gonzales, Christian Gibson, Rudi Waldschuetz, Michael Pritchard, Darin Bagley, Jeff Hawley, Lucas Lieberman

FOREWORD

By Tim Waggoner

"You talk about monsters like they're your best friends."

"That's because in many ways they are."

I don't remember what my wife and I were talking about when the above exchange occurred between us. Most likely, I was telling her about one horror movie or another. My wife isn't a horror fan, but she tolerantly listens whenever I get excited about a scary book or movie, and she'll smile and nod when I start talking about the differences between *Terrifier* and *Terrifier 2*. I've been in love with monsters all of my life. One of my first memories is sitting on my dad's lap while he read to me from a book about dinosaurs. I couldn't read yet – I thought it was a magic of the eyeballs that I didn't possess – but I learned to recognize dinosaur names by the shapes of their letters. I was fascinated by the idea that the monsters I saw in the book's illustrations had been real – that they've lived, walked, hunted, and killed in the same place I did, only a long, long time ago – and all we had today were fossils of their skeletons. They were like monstrous ghosts from a bygone age. One of my first recurring dreams was of a flying saucer that landed in the street outside our house to disgorge a cargo of dinosaurs (and everything was tinted red for an extra-creepy effect). When I was four, my parents let me watch *Frankenstein Meets the Wolfman* on TV, and I was fascinated that these two monsters not only lived in the same world, but that they could meet and interact. Those two formative events began my lifelong love affair with all things monstrous and monster-related. Until I was an adult, I didn't use the word *horror* much. I referred to scary movies, TV shows, books, and comics as *monster* movies, *monster* books, etc.

As I got older, I began to see that monsters came in many forms, and some of them were indistinguishable from ordinary human beings – on the outside, at least. I came to this realization the first time I saw *Psycho*. I was in high school in the early eighties, and for some reason the faculty had all the students gather in the gym before Thanksgiving break, and they showed us *Psycho*, displayed on an old-fashioned movie screen and shown via an actual film projector (back in the days before VCR's). While we watched the film, the teachers went outside to smoke. I thought it was really strange that the teachers would show us this particular film as a holiday treat – and it's something you couldn't do today without incurring parental wrath – but I loved it. *Psycho* taught me that distortion didn't have to be outward to be monstrous. It could be inward, too.

Why are some of us (and I count you, reader, among our number) so fascinated by monsters, whatever stripe they might be? Monsters are darkness given shape. Death, disease, cruelty, madness, hunger . . . any or all of these can be embodied in monsters, and when monsters appear in stories, we can confront these dark aspects of existence safely and perhaps come to terms with them, at least in some small ways. They stimulate our imagination, too. A story about a bank robber taking a person hostage might be exciting, but a story about a *demon-possessed* bank robber taking a hostage is way more interesting and fun. And practically speaking, monsters create conflict, suspense, and mystery in stories, giving characters a force to contend with which drives the narrative.

But the human obsession with deviance goes far deeper than the need for entertainment or psychological self-exploration. It's deeply ingrained in our DNA. In nature, any physical abnormality could be sign of disease, any wound could become infected and result in death, any mental aberration could be a sign of possession by evil spirits, and any dead body will decay, turn toxic, and spread disease. And don't forget the fear of being prey. When our ancestors heard growling in the night, the thing somewhere out in the darkness might well be on the hunt for them. Malformation, injury, madness, death, being hunted – the fear of these things still lies at the root of horror fiction today. Our species has been on our guard against the monstrous for its entire existence, so is it any wonder that we still are today, only now through our literature, film, and games?

Monsters are awesome. Not only are they fun to watch and read about, they connect us to some of the deepest aspects of what it means to be human. So the next time a non-horror fan asks you (perhaps with a hint of derision in their voice) why you like *those* kind of stories, smile, in your most pleasant tone, tell them, *"Reading about monsters keeps me from becoming one."*

Speaking of reading, you've got some delightfully sinister tales ahead of you in this book, nineteen stories from writers offering individual takes on what makes something – or someone – monstrous. So join us in the shadows, fellow monster lover. You'll be perfectly safe here.

Well, maybe not *perfectly* . . .

INTRODUCTION
By Marx Pyle

Welcome to our anthology of monster short stories, where we've gathered tales of terror, horror, humor, and urban fantasy, featuring all manner of monstrous creatures for your enjoyment.

I can't really compete with Tim Waggoner's excellent foreword. I felt like Tim would be perfect for the foreword, because he reflects, in many ways, this anthology of monster tales. He has written about all types of monsters, and although many of those stories fall under horror, they also can range in tone. Much like one of my favorite TV shows, *Supernatural*, for which Tim has written tie-in books, his stories can be horrific or darkly comedic. Some of his books—like *Nekropolis*, which stars a private eye zombie, or *Shadow Watch*, which stars agents Audra and Mr Jinx (a slightly insane nightmare clown)—are dark, but also very funny at times.

As Tim pointed out so well, we humans are fascinated by monsters in all forms. However, while some monsters have remained popular in modern fiction (such as vampires, werewolves, and zombies), there are many other lesser-known monsters that have not received as much attention in fiction: gorgons, gnomes, trolls, the Dover Demon, the Jersey Devil, and more. Many of you may know of them, but I doubt you would use all of your fingers counting how many stories you've read starring these.

So why are these monsters less represented in modern fiction? Are they just less familiar to a wider audience? Are these monsters too culturally or regionally specific to have universal appeal?

Trolls are primarily associated with Scandinavian folklore, while the Dover Demon is a creature that has only been spotted in a few isolated instances in Massachusetts. Fae, or fairies, are another type of monster that have a timeless appeal, despite being less common in modern fiction. These creatures, which can take various forms including elves, goblins, and gnomes, are often depicted as mischievous and elusive beings with magical powers. They have been a part of folklore and mythology for centuries. While these monsters may not be as well known as vampires or werewolves, they still have a rich history and cultural significance.

In this anthology, we've gathered a diverse selection of monster short stories that showcase the many different facets of these fascinating lesser known creatures. From horror to comedy, these stories offer a unique exploration of the monstrous world. We hope you enjoy them as much as we do!

In the Crossing Genres Anthology Collection, you can always expect a mix of genres, but really what separates most of these stories for this installment—besides the starring monster—is the tone. Some of these stories are downright creepy, while others will make you smile. Much like Tim Waggoner's bibliography.

INTRODUCTION 9

This anthology contains three sections: Monsters, Myths, and Miscreants.

Monsters: This section contains many of the horror, or darker, stories in our collection. We start with haunting stories, and then end on a more hopeful note.

El Cucuy by Scott A. Johnson
Gore Vellye (The Autumn Tumult) by Anne C. Lynch
Prey Animals by Sen R.L. Scherb
The Devil and Scott by W.H. Horner
A Thing of Hope by Carrie Gessner

Myths: This section is a little hard to nail down, except that it tends to have a lot of humor, tinted by a touch of darkness. The section starts with a darkly comedic story about garden gnomes, then takes us to a Troll laboring on a troll farm, followed by a unique online dating story, a hunt for a cryptid, an amusement park with a twist, a ghouly romcom, and then wraps up with kids versus one of the grossest looking monsters in folklore.

Gnomies by Kevin Plybon
Don't Feed the Troll by Katharine Dow
Don't Lose Your Head by Victoria L. Scott
Eyes Like Burning Coal by Jeremiah Dylan Cook
Magicland Mischief by J.C. Mastro
Ghouly Girl by Sophia DeSensi
Worst Vacation Ever by Jeannie Rivera

We love when we can flesh out our story worlds. *Worst Vacation Ever* actually ties into a Frederick Moody novel released just before this anthology, and *Magicland Mischief* takes place in the same world as Mastro's short story from *Dragons of a Different Tail*. You don't have to read any of those to enjoy these stories, but it's good information to know if you find yourself wanting more.

Miscreants: Even though some of the other stories in Monsters or Myths can be classified as urban fantasy, there is no doubt this section is where urban fantasy takes the spotlight, with the first five stories landing squarely under that genre. (Plus, there is a certain fictional drink that makes the rounds in a number of the stories.) We start with a story set in Michael La Ronn's *A Good Necromancer* setting, then check in on the underworld of fae in a story set in my (Marx Pyle's) *Obsidian Archives* world. We then visit noir stories starring a gorgon, a gargoyle, and more. We wrap things up with a tour of a magical city and end on an epic tale.

The Brazen Skull, by Michael La Ronn
Rebel with a Cause, by Marx Pyle
An Old Favor, by Marisa Wolf
The Adventures of Elena and Ned, Gargoyle P.I., by Jeff Burns
The Greatest of All Time, by Francis Fernandez
Hexpad Blog: A First-Timer's Guide to the Big City, by Colten Fisher
The Tiger's Gift, by G.K. White

Like our previous anthology, *Dragons of a Different Tail*, we include bonus content. There is a section with behind-the-scene essays by each author. We hope you enjoy this extra touch.

INTRODUCTION 11

This installment of the Crossing Genres Anthology Collection was made possible by the generous support of our Kickstarter backers. Besides helping us fund this anthology (check out the acknowledgments section for a list of our backers), a few of the backers were able to name characters in the stories and helped us add additional content. That extra connection with our readers made this book even more special.

We hope you enjoy the stories that follow, and maybe find a new favorite monster or two.

One

Monsters

EL CUCUY

By Scott A. Johnson

Someone stared at me in the darkness. In the tiny space between awake and asleep, the awareness hit me and forced off the last vestiges of slumber. I sat upright and peered into my nighttime bedroom. At the foot of the bed, a shadow stood, roughly the size of a child.

"Maria? What's wrong?"

The shadow didn't move, didn't answer. Maybe it was her brother.

"Manuel?"

It wasn't like either of them to sleepwalk, or to just stand at the foot of our bed and watch their mother and me sleep.

The figure shifted, turned to face me. In the dim moonlight that filtered in through the curtains, eyes glowed amber. Just beneath the eyes, the dark shadow split into gleaming white points, teeth that stretched into a wicked smile.

"Do you remember me?"

The voice was quiet, almost child-like, with a razor's edge behind it. There was a familiarity to it, but the same as every other child's voice. High pitched, awkward.

I shook my wife, but she didn't wake.

"Not her," said the voice at the end of the bed.
"Who are you?"
"El Cucuy."

A nervous laugh barked out of my chest. I was too old to believe in fairy tales.

"Bullshit." I lunged for the gun in my bedside table drawer. As I raised it, the toothy smile widened, then the shadow dropped to the floor. I scrambled out of bed to follow it. As soon as it disappeared from sight, my wife sat up and clicked on the light.

"What is it?" She stared at the gun in my hand as I searched the room.

"Did you see him?"

"See who?"

"The kid," I yelled. "There was a kid in here."

"Honey, put the gun down. There's no one here."

But I saw him. I *just* saw the little creep as he ducked down. In the darkness under the bed, I half-expected to see his eyes, the glint of light off his teeth, but there was nothing.

"Come back to bed," said my wife. "It was just a-"

"Mommy!"

My daughter's scream cut through the air. With the gun still in my hand, I tore open my bedroom door and ran down the hall. She stood in the hallway, her face stained with fearful tears. Her hand shook as she pointed into her room.

"El Cucuy," she sobbed. "It was El Cucuy."

My wife gathered her up into her arms and rocked her gently.

"No," she said. "El Cucuy only comes for naughty children, and my children are the best in the world."

I stepped into the bedroom, gun raised. If the kid got into my daughter's room somehow, I wasn't going to let him terrorize her. I clicked on the light.

Everything was just as it should've been. The pink ruffled curtains lay still against the closed window. Her comforter sat crumpled, thrown aside from when she'd gotten out of bed. Dirty clothes sat next to the hamper, and the closet door stood askew, but everything was just as it should've been in an eleven-year-old's room.

"He was there," she said from the doorway. "In the closet. He had yellow eyes."

The eyes at the foot of my bed. The eyes that woke me from sleep.

Do you remember me?

The voice echoed in my mind, scratched at memories as it tried to dig up some identifier from the past. I hadn't heard the name "El Cucuy" since...

The memory slammed into my skull and rattled as it tried to gain focus, but it couldn't. I remembered the stories. Every kid did. El Cucuy, the boogeyman who came for naughty children and dragged them into the dark and ate them. It was a story our parents told us to keep us in line. A story about an evil man who locked his children in a closet until they died. A story we told to other, smaller kids to scare them.

"There's no one here, sweetie," I said. "El Cucuy isn't real."

As if in answer, a second scream cut through the air from my son's room.

I raced down the hall and crashed into the door. It flew open in time for me to see my son's hands disappearing under his bed. His fear-choked screams echoed in the cavernous darkness, which made no sense.

"Manuel!"

The gun fell from my hand as I jumped to grab at my son's arms, but I was too late. The last thing I saw as his frightened face disappeared in the darkness were glowing yellow eyes and the glistening points of smiling fangs.

I flipped the bed, but there was no sign of Manuel among the toys and socks and shoes. It was as if the space under the bed had just opened up, and he was gone.

Do you remember me?

The question floated at the edge of my memory, beat at the door as it tried to break through. I knew the voice. I just couldn't place it.

"Manuel!" My wife clawed at the carpet as she screamed our son's name. Maria stood in the doorway, her face wet with tears. Wide eyed, she sucked her thumb in a way she hadn't done since she was half her age.

"El Cucuy got him," she murmured.

I pulled my wife from the floor and looked her in the eyes.

"Get in the car," I said. "Take Maria. I'll find Manuel."

"Take her where?" she screamed. "Where is safe?"

"I don't know. Just go. Just take her and go."

She scooped our daughter up and ran for the stairs. A moment later, she screamed.

I snatched the gun up from where it lay and ran. At the top of the darkened stairs, my wife grasped my daughter's hands as the rest of the child disappeared into a wall of black. A low murmured laugh came from the darkness below.

"Maria!"

Our daughter screamed as her hands came away from my wife's and disappeared into the black below.

"No no no no!" My wife hit the light switch and bathed the stairwell in a soft glow, but it was empty. There was no sign of our daughter. No trace of the yellow eyes and dripping teeth that took her.

She fell to her knees and rocked back and forth.

"El Cucuy," she sobbed. "It was El Cucuy."

Do you remember me?

The legends were very specific. El Cucuy came for naughty children. He lived in shadowy spaces like closets and under the bed. He terrorized them because he loved their fear. It made them taste sweeter when he ate them.

"Turn off the lights," I said.

She looked up at me, her face a mask of tear-stained confusion.

"He comes in the dark. Turn off the lights."

"No," she wailed.

"Then go to the bathroom. Turn on all the lights. Stay out of the shadows. I'm going to go into the dark to find our children."

"I'm going with you," she said.

We held hands as she flipped the switch that turned the downstairs into an inky mass of black. Through the windows, moonlight let us see the vague outlines of furniture. We felt our way toward the couch and sat. The gun in my hand felt good, cool metal against my skin. Could bullets beat the boogeyman? Did it even matter?

Do you remember me?

As we sat in the darkness, whispers came. Whether my wife heard them or not, I couldn't say, but I did. And I recognized them. My own words, come back to haunt me.

"El Cucuy's coming to get you!"

The little boy in my memory was poor, smaller than the other kids our age. His name was Raul. Everyone made fun of him. Especially me.

"El Cucuy eats poor kids like you," I told him. "He hides under the bed or in the closet and will drag you into the dark while you sleep."

He'd tried to put up a brave front. But I wasn't content with simple taunting. My friends and I followed him home, to the little trailer park at the edge of town. He didn't want anyone to know he lived there. Why would he? We taunted him enough about his ragged clothes and his second-hand shoes.

That night, we'd hidden outside his window and called to him, whispered to him that El Cucuy was coming. We all did it, but I was the one who hid under his trailer. I was the one who, when he came out with a baseball bat to see who was playing tricks on him, reached out and grabbed his ankles. He'd screamed and ran into the woods, and the four of us laughed like hyenas as we ran home.

The next day, he wasn't at school. In fact, we never saw him again. We'd thought it was funny, that we'd scared him so badly that his family had packed up the trailer and moved away. It wasn't until a week later that his body was found in a hollow under a tree in the woods. The people who found him said his face stuck out from the hollow, that it looked like it was screaming, even though he'd been dead for days.

Do you remember me?

I did. The voice belonged to Raul.

"You have to go," I told my wife. "This is on me. I was a mean kid and it's coming back to haunt me."

"What're you talking about?"

I told her the story and hung my head low as I did. I wasn't proud. In fact, I was ashamed that I'd managed to forget. So many years of justifying the actions of a bully, so much time reassuring myself that I was a better person than I'd been. It never occurred to me that debts, even old ones, had to be paid one day.

"You were a child," she said. "That was a long time ago."

From the shadows of the kitchen came a sound like skuttling rats on the tile floor. Two bright yellow eyes lit up in the darkness.

"You remember now?" The voice came from every shadow, every darkened corner.

"Give me back my kids!"

"Come and get them."

A smokey hand made of darkness reached out and beckoned. I handed the gun to my wife.

"Whatever happens," I said. I let the statement hang because I didn't know what else to say.

The icy cold fingers wrapped around mine and pulled me into the darkness. As the shadows congealed, the warmth left my body. El Cucuy stood before me as he truly was.

"Raul," I said. "I'm sorry."

He was exactly as I remembered him, as if the past thirty years hadn't passed. He wore the same tattered pajamas, the same stained shirt, the same battered shoes he did when we were children. His eyes were different, though, yellow and luminous. And his teeth, long and sharp, though I never saw him smile as a child.

"Look what you did," he said.

Around us were doorways of every shape and size. It took me a moment to recognize the ones that went into my daughter's room from her closet, another that came from under her bed. There were small holes where he could watch people sleep, and larger ones where he could reach through and grab them. Every doorway, I came to understand, was a shadow. Every shadow was an open portal to him. From his vantage in the dark, he watched every child and waited.

"Watch now." Raul lifted his hand and the doorways spun by until they slowed at a boy. A younger boy cowered from a verbal onslaught. "Naughty, naughty."

I made to intervene, but tendrils of shadow wrapped around my arms and legs, squeezed my throat and held me in place. All I could do was watch as Raul fulfilled his role as El Cucuy. He waited for the younger boy to cover his eyes, then he reached from some shadow somewhere, in a closet or beneath a bed, and took the older child by the ankles. He didn't even have time to scream before he was dragged backward into the dark. When he flipped over, Raul was no longer the boy he'd once been. He'd grown to gigantic proportions and wrapped himself in a robe of smoke, though his eyes glowed over the mountainous jagged teeth. The boy tried to protest, but El Cucuy opened his maw wide and clamped down on the boy's head. His body jerked as the nerves came to their inevitable conclusion that he was dead.

"Sweet meats," said Raul as the smoke dropped to the floor and revealed him again as the boy I once knew.

"What happened to you?"

"You mean after you and your friends tormented me?"

Tendrils of darkness snaked around his arms and formed into long skeletal fingers.

"Would you like to see? Would you like to know what you did?"

He raised his hands to my face. The fingers of darkness stroked upward on my cheeks until they came to my temples, then pain scorched through my body as they pierced my skin and burrowed into my brain. I tried to scream, but the pain was so much that it stole the breath from my lungs and left me a gasping fish.

My perception shifted. Images, movement, flooded my sight until it became clear that I wasn't myself. I was Raul, many years ago. Voices taunted from outside my room. I knew them, my old friends from school. One was mine. My heart raced as I got out of bed and picked up the bat.

My hands shook and my legs wobbled as I crept down the darkened hallway to the doorway of my trailer. When I reached the bottom step, something grabbed my ankle. The evil laughter that came from under the step was my own, but the fear that shot through my body was no less real. I ran. From my point of view, the trees loomed tall, and nothing looked as it should've. Raul's heart pumped hard in my chest until I was sure it would explode, then I tripped and landed face-down in a bed of dead leaves and mud. The trailer was too far away to see, and the darkness closed in around me. I hugged my legs close to my chest and cried.

It wasn't me. It was Raul, but the sorrow he felt, the shame, the despair was real enough. As ragged sobs choked out of me, another sound caught my attention. A whisper, a soft voice. It called my name.

Raul...

I wiped my eyes and snotty nose on my filthy t-shirt, then looked for the source of the voice.

Poor boy, said the voice. *Poor Raul...*

A single tree rose up in front of me, monolithic in stature and rough like stone. From out of a hollow in its base, darkness as black as shame sank, broken only by a pair of amber eyes.

Come here, said the voice. *They can't hurt you in here. They can't make fun of you anymore.*

I screamed inside Raul's skull to stop, to run away, but the hope in his chest, the desperation was too great. He took a tentative step. When the creature inside the hollow lunged out, it wasn't fear that had him, but grateful relief that his torment was over. As El Cucuy stripped flesh from muscle, skin from bone, a strange sensation grew from the agony. Raul's suffering was a crucible that stoked his anger, turned his despair into hatred. The more the creature hurt him, the stronger his hatred became until it was all that was left of him.

I fell to the floor and gagged as the dark fingers dragged themselves from inside my mind. Tiny barbs hooked my flesh and bone as they slid through, ensuring that even respite came with no relief.

"I'm so sorry," I choked. "I was just a kid. I didn't know."

"You knew," said Raul. "You knew enough about what fear was. You knew that I was afraid, and that was good enough for you."

"Please," I said. "My children. They didn't do anything to you."

"I know," he said. The white of his fangs glinted. "But you did."

I understood. His hatred had patience enough to wait until my children were old enough to expect me to protect them. It had the endurance to let them see their father fail for being such a terrible person.

"Now," said Raul, "I feed on fear. It sustains me, gives me strength. But tonight, I'm not after their fear. I'm after yours."

He swelled, grew to gigantic proportions until all I could see were the burning coals of his eyes and the jagged maw of his teeth, then he swept his arm aside. The darkness fluttered like smoke on the wind to reveal my children. They held each other as tears flowed down their faces.

"What would be worse? Making you watch them die? Or letting them know why they're dying?"

"Don't," I said. "Please. I'm sorry. I'm not the same person I was. I was just a kid."

"So was I," roared the giant shadow. "Did that stop you? Did that foster one ounce of sympathy?"

As he spoke, the shadows around his hands hardened into crude and jagged blades. The children could sob no harder but cried out in raspy voices and pulled each other closer.

"You can't!" I shouted. "They're good kids!"

"But you weren't."

"So, take me instead!"

"That's the idea," said the shadow. "You didn't watch until the end. You didn't see what happened to the one who made me."

The darkness again pierced my mind to show me the death of Raul and his rebirth as El Cucuy. As the boy screamed, the creature that made him, the previous El Cucuy, shuddered and stripped off layers of shadow. As they came away, they congealed and slopped to the ground like tar until all that was left was a pink-skinned man on the floor. In shedding the curse, he'd returned to what he was before.

"His was the first blood I tasted," said Raul. "I was so hungry. The things he did under the sway of the curse called to me."

In my mind, Raul's hunger gnawed at my gut. The man's screams twisted my insides until I couldn't stop myself. It was Raul's memory, but it was me who tore him to pieces, who swallowed the flesh and sucked the blood from his bones. I fell to the floor and vomited.

"You'll be so hungry," he said. "When the curse takes hold, you'll have no choice. Your own children will be your first kill, and you'll have to live with that for eternity."

Before I could protest, El Cucuy swung his shadowy blades and cut into the flesh of my back. The pain stole my breath away, and my body seized. The children called out to me, but their voices were different somehow. In the past, their voices brought me love and happiness. Now their screams stirred something inside me, something vicious and hungry.

"Run!" I gasped. "Find the way out! Momma's waiting!"

El Cucuy continued his onslaught, and from each new wound that opened, smoke oozed like sludge. It coated my skin and seared wherever it touched. My eyes itched, burned, until I could do nothing more than push my palms against them and scream in agony.

El Cucuy's laughter raised in volume and pitch until it became a child's voice, Raul's once again. He fell to the floor exhausted, a look of maniacal rage on his face.

"No!" I screamed. "Run! Find Mama!"

Maria took her brother's hand and ran as I tried to control the hunger inside. It clawed at my insides, twisted my stomach, and made me crave only one thing. The flesh of children. The shadows that wrapped my body writhed like snakes that slithered through the air until they found a larger shadow to bond with. No matter where my children turned, more darkness greeted them until they were backed into a corner. My stomach growled.

"This way! I know the way out!"

I turned to find Raul, false fear etched on his face. I tried to warn my children not to trust him, but all I could do was bellow like the monster I'd become.

"Quickly," he shouted. "You have to trust me!"

Maria grabbed her brother's hand and ran after Raul. Whatever plan he had, it couldn't have been good. I rushed after them, driven by hunger, but focused on the boy who had now stolen my children from me twice.

We passed several doorways, each leading to unfamiliar rooms with children I'd never seen before. Some of them were innocent. Others drew my attention with the scent of mischief and malice.

They approached the doorway that led back to our house, where my wife waited with my gun in her hand. Raul pushed them through, then turned and grinned at me. It was the opportunity I needed. I lashed out with will and rage, and a tendril of shadow caught him around his foot just as he leaped through the doorway.

"Help," he screamed. "El Cucuy! He has me!"

My wife didn't know who or what he was, only that he appeared to be a frightened child with a monster at his heels. She raised the gun and pointed it at me.

I tried to tell her that it was me, her husband, and that the screaming child at her feet was the real monster. But my voice came out as a guttural howl, my words as garbled nonsense. She pulled the trigger until the gun was emptied into my chest. I retreated through the doorway in pain and despair. The last thing I saw of her was her teary eyes and determined face as she flipped the light switch on, and the doorway closed.

My screams echoed in the darkness as I clutched and threw everything my shadowy hands could touch. It was his plan all along. Not just to take my children from me, but to make them fear me, to make me a living nightmare. He'd gotten out, and I could only assume he'd live as a child again, though how I couldn't guess.

I retreated into the shadows and passed by dozens of doorways until the intoxicating perfume of badness became too much to resist.

"Naughty, naughty." The words were the first I'd been able to speak in my new form, and they slid out of my throat in a pool of oil-soaked gravel. The boy who stank of it couldn't have been more than twelve, but the taste of his flesh and the blood left me drunk with joy. As the euphoria wore off, I tried to vomit him back up. I sobbed in my dark kingdom until I could no longer.

"Are you there?"

I knew the voice in an instant, and rage burned inside me.

"You'll never be able to be near your children again," said Raul. "They'll live their whole lives knowing you only as El Cucuy. You can see them, watch them grow up. But they'll never call you 'Daddy' again."

I followed the voice until I came to a tiny opening in the shadow, a doorway too small for even my hand to go through. I crouched and stared through to find Raul in what appeared to be my son's bedroom.

"There you are," he said. "I knew you'd be nearby."

"Give me back my life," I hissed.

"Why? I just took back mine. You took my life from me. So, I took yours. Can you guess what happened when your children dragged me out of that darkness? What happened after your wife shot you? I told her I was a victim of El Cucuy, too. And it wasn't a lie. I really was. But then your children told her that I was the one who saved them. Not you. Me. And your wife let me stay. I get to live my childhood again. Your children are my brother and sister. Your wife is my mommy now. And you? You're just the monster in the closet. Only my closet has lights."

He flipped a switch, and after a moment of blinding light, the doorway closed. I sat in darkness and screamed.

SCOTT A. JOHNSON WRITES horror, dark fantasy, and sci-fi. He is the author of twelve novels, three short story guides, a short story collection, and a chapbook. In addition, he has numerous short stories published. He currently teaches creative writing in Seton Hill's MFA in Writing Popular Fiction program, and in Emerson College's MFA in Writing and Publishing Popular Fiction program. For more information, see his website at www.creepylittlebastard.com

Gore Vellye (The Autumn Tumult)

By Anne C. Lynch

> "Bit luck thee niver noo in Vore, Cin man hear tale o' Teran Rampagan' on da ocean floor, Fur folk ir little carin Hoo tullyas or brullyas. Fowt wi' de great Sea-mither 'swordship gae lordship, Tae ane or else the tither." – Old Orcadian Verse

"Ye'r lookin' a bit peely wally, lass." The innkeeper smiled behind a dazzling beard. "What can I get ye? A pint?"

I lifted my head off my crossed arms to look at him. "God no...water. I need something to get the taste of sick out of my mouth." *And take the edge off this damn hangover.* I handed him my water bottle. "Could you just fill this for me?"

He nodded as he took it. "The ferry found rough water, then?" He filled it and placed it in front of me.

"Just a bit," I raised an eyebrow and tried to smile. "Is it always like that?"

"Nah always, but the autumn tumult is upon us. Some days are fair, more days not. Teran's rampage is a'brewin'. The Sea Mither will be leaving soon."

I took a drink and swished the water between my teeth, swallowing the foul taste of vomit with a shudder. "Isn't it a bit early for Gore Vellye?"

He raised his eyebrows. "Gore Vellye! Not many outsiders know that name."

"Yeah, well," I took another long drink of water, "Orkney folklore is kinda my specialty. Hey, you wouldn't happen to be Magnus Craigie, would you?"

The eyebrows inched higher. "Aye," he said slowly. "Now how'd ye ken that?"

I took a deep breath and pushed past the fear of making a complete ass of myself. Had I made the long trip to this wind-blasted island for nothing? Or had I come because some random, gorgeous stranger in a pub convinced cross-eyed-drunk me that a brilliant oral story for my dissertation waited in this place?

Honestly, by the time I was sobering up, I was already on the ferry to Kirkwall wondering what the hell I was doing. Not that it stopped me from renting a car and boarding a second ferry to take me the rest of the way.

"This is going to sound crazy," I smiled sheepishly, "but I met a man in Aberdeen who knew a man who knew a man on Sanday Island, that saw the Nuckelavee and lived to tell the tale. He told me the name of the man who knew that lucky soul—Magnus Craigie."

I waited for him to howl with laughter. God knows I would've. In retrospect, the previous 48 hours felt like a fever dream.

ALMOST TWO DAYS BEFORE, I woke up in a tangle of sheets with a heavy arm draped across my back. I didn't remember how he and I got to my flat, but there we were. And, if I remembered correctly, it had been good. Very good. I smiled and gently tried to extract myself from the bed and the stranger named James. When I lifted his arm, he said, "Ah, good. Ye'r finally awake. Let's go. There's no time to waste."

He released me, stood up, and started yanking on his jeans. I sat up and my head spun from the drink.

"What are you waiting for?" he asked.

"Where?" I studied him and blinked slowly.

"What?"

"No. Where. You said, 'Let's go.' Let's go where?" I rubbed my eyes, which felt like I'd poured sand into them.

"Out, of course! I dinnae have much time left." He gestured toward the clock on my bedside table. "It's half three. The sun will rise soon, and I'll be back to sea. I want to walk, and I dinnae want to be alone."

"Oh. A sailor," I said lamely. Now it seemed obvious. His hands were tough and calloused. The right one was missing a finger he said was lost in an accident. His brown hair was streaked light from the sun and salt, his arms strong, the fine lines around his eyes from squinting against the sun on the water. At some level, I felt relief that by morning he would be safely out of port and my life. Not that he was a bad guy...I just didn't know. Now I didn't have to find out. I had terrible taste in men.

"C'mon, Mira," he smiled and held out his hand. "C'mon, love, let's go walk the beach."

I took his hand and let him pull me out of bed.

THE REMAINDER OF THE night was a snarl of memories. We walked the beach all the way to Footdee. I remember snippets about his life on the ocean and how when he was on land, he longed for the sea. I talked about my fascination with the folklore and mythologies of Scotland, particularly the Orkneys.

When the sun began to color the sky, he became quiet and somehow melancholy. "It's time for me to go, lass." He turned to hold me and looked deeply into my eyes. "Are you sure, very sure, that ye must gather these tales? Ye'r chasing trouble. There is some danger in it, ye ken."

"What danger? They're just stories! Made up by simple, uneducated people to explain a harsh and unforgiving world."

"Aye, tis true for some of them, aye. Maybe even all of them." His face grew solemn and grim. "Have ye heard of the Nuckelavee, the demon that rises from the sea?"

I grinned "Yes! One of my favorites—and an excellent example of how folklore tries to explain the unexplainable. Crops fail, sheep die, illness spreads: *obviously,* a relentless

monster from the sea is exacting revenge for burning kelp."
I laughed.

"So, ye dinnae believe in them?"

"Um...no." Surely, he wasn't serious.

"What if I told ye that I ken a man who kens a man on Sanday Island who saw the Nuckelavee, felt its breath on his neck, and lived to tell the tale?"

"I'd say, 'Tell me his name and how to find him!' Of course."

He threw his head back and let out a barking laugh. "Alright then, lass. Your fate cannae be outrun. Na amount o' gieving kin change it so I'll tell ye. His name is Magnus Craigie and ye can find him at The Belsair on Kettletoft Harbor. He's the publican. He'll pull ye a pint and weave ye a tale. Ye can let a room, too."

"Slow down! I can't type that fast," I muttered as I keyed the information into my phone. "Thumbs were never meant to type."

He pulled my face up to look at him. His expression was somber. "I know ye'll suss out this tale, my bonnie lass," he said, "and when ye go looking for the monster, ye will find him. And ye will be changed."

I felt a strange twitch in my stomach, and the hair on the back of my neck prickled. "That's not creepy at all, James MacCodron. You're a real charmer." I tried to laugh it off, but even as I did, my arms broke out in gooseflesh. "You're a sailor *and* a psychic?"

He took no notice. His eyes scanned the sky where the rising sun streaked the high clouds with rose and soft yellow.

"My time is done, hen. I must be off." He took my shoulders in his hands and spun me around so that I faced away from him. I felt his breath in my ear as he whispered, "I dinnae like long goodbyes. Ye walk ye'r way, I'll walk mine. Dinnae look back."

What a strange man. I nodded and began the long walk home. But I wasn't alone—a lone seal played in the waves and swam along the beach beside me until I turned west to walk into the city.

MAGNUS COCKED HIS HEAD to one side and wrinkled his brow. "And who was this man in Aberdeen?"

"James MacCodron."

The blood drained from his face. He tensed and stood up straighter as if pulling his body away from the name.

"No, lass. No, no. James MacCodron is dead at the bottom of the sea. Someone was takin' the piss."

I laughed in surprise. "He was pretty lively when I met him. Maybe I misheard his name."

He crossed his arms across his chest. "Aye. Must have. He was lost seven years ago. Almost to the day." He reached up and scratched his beard.

After a second's hesitation, he asked, "What did he look like?"

"He was handsome, charming. Brown hair, tan, clean-shaven, dark eyes…green, I think." I smiled at the thought of James. "Oh, and he was missing a finger."

"What…which hand?" he stammered. "Which finger?"

"Right index." I held up my hand and wiggled my finger. "And the middle finger was all screwed up."

Magnus' whole body went rigid as a bowstring. Tension—no, disbelief—hummed in the air around us. Muttering to himself, he came out from behind the bar and quickly left the room. A few moments later, he returned with a framed photo.

"So," he said as he sat on the stool next to mine, "This." He held out the picture for me to see. "This is James and me about 3 weeks afore his boat sank. Is this the man ye'r talking aboot?"

I took it from him and looked down at the face of the man who had steered my course to this place and the man sitting in front of me.

"That's him," I whispered. "That's the man I met in Aberdeen."

My heart thumped loudly as alarm bells went off in my head. This was impossible. I couldn't get enough air in my lungs, no matter how hard I tried.

IN THAT PHOTO, IN that moment of recognition, my world slipped off its axis. If a man seven years dead could return for a night...*Jesus Christ...I slept with a dead man?* I gagged at the thought. *Not a dead man, a selkie, like that's any better*. But the pieces fit, down to the lone seal that followed along as I walked home, and the strange warning he gave me.

In all the years that I studied the folklore of these islands, I'd never considered that any of it was based in reality. I'd always believed that the monsters spun into being by these seafaring folk were the product of cold stormy winters spent gazing into an abyss. The stories spoke to unanswerable questions of life and death and were no more accurate than those of the Christians who introduced their mythology centuries later.

James' prediction came ringing back. In my hubris, I chose to ignore his warning. He'd told me not to look for trouble, yet here I was, chasing it with open arms. I shook my head to clear my mind. It never failed to amaze me, the hold that legends had on people.

But that night, I dreamed of selkies and the monsters of Orkney.

I WOKE THE NEXT morning with sweaty sheets knotted around me. Even in sleep, I couldn't shake the gut feeling that something very weird and very dangerous was afoot.

However, by the light of day, the feeling of unreality began to fade. The strange events of the evening before were easier to rationalize. Realistically, I didn't know what I saw, or really, *who* I saw. Considering how utterly sozzled I was, that man could've been anyone. I couldn't even be sure if his last name was MacCodron. The pub had been dark and loud.

"The one thing you *do* know, Mira," I said to myself, "is that James Whoever-he-was was certainly not a selkie."

I FOUND MAGNUS AND his wife, Aileen, in the dining room. "G'morning, lass." "G'morning, hen."

"Good morning! Last night I completely forgot to get the name of the man-who-survived and where I can find him."

"Aye!" said Magnus. "His name is Petyr Rendall."

"Oh, he's an odd one, him," chimed in Aileen with a shudder. "I avoid him if I can. Lives out on the point across the bay there," she nodded out of the window, "on Els Ness."

"Ach, there's no harm in him, Aileen," Magnus said. He looked at me and smiled to reassure me. "He's a bit odd, but it's nae like he's dangerous."

His wife raised an eyebrow and frowned at him. "I dinnae trust him. There's odd and then there's doolally. Be canny, Mira."

I looked from one to the other, wondering which I should listen to. "I'll be careful, Aileen. I promise. So, um, he lives where, exactly? Is there an address?"

"It mid be best if Magnus takes ye. That tiny car ye'r driving wilnae be a match for that muddy track."

He rolled his eyes and sighed. "She'll be fine."

"I'll be fine. I grew up on a farm. I've driven on dirt roads and through fields. I got it," I assured them. "All I need is directions."

"Type 'Quoyayre' intae ye'r phone map and download it afore ye go," Magnus said. "Mobile signal here is shite. Mind, if Petyr isn't at home, he'll be down at the Cairn. Take the sea track, it's marked. It's not far, maybe a 20-minute walk."

I plugged in the cottage name and waited for the map to download. After a solid minute, I sighed in frustration. "My phone isn't connecting to the wi-fi."

"No problem, lass. It's easy. Go doon the road. Take the first turn to the right, then go 'til the road ends, just past the Lady Kirk ruins and the Kirkyard cemetery. Turn right and go along the Little Sea. Then the road bends to follow the beach. Quoyayre is the only cottage ye'll see."

"So, up the road, right at the first intersection, past the ruins, turn right, drive until you see the cottage?"

"Exactly."

As I headed to the door, Magnus called behind me, "Be back afore the sun sets. There's no moon tonight, the roads will be dark."

THE COUNTRYSIDE STARTED JUST past the last building. The wind had scattered the early morning clouds to reveal a shockingly blue sky. Lush green pastures lined the narrow road and rolled off to the horizon. Even though it was chilly, I cracked the windows so I could smell the sea. A person could fall in love with this place.

I made the first turn and followed the sign to Lady Village. Stacked stone walls grew up from the grass on the left and the stony beach on the Little Sea lay to the right. A long, narrow ribbon of road stretched ahead, untroubled by another person or car. I slowed at a stone bridge to watch a rock-bottomed stream flow quickly to the bay. After all, I had scheduled time for seeing the sights.

When I came to the ruined kirk and cemetery, I pulled to the side of the road and got out. The night before I had read that up the high outer stairs was something the locals called the "Devil's Claw Marks." As a folklorist, this type of story was irresistible.

In the kirkyard headstones rose from the ground like crooked, rotting teeth. The grave's occupants had not only suffered death, but also the indignity of their names being erased by the power of the wind and sand and salt air.

The kirk itself stood grey and imposing on the landscape. Its roof gone, the interior filled with dying grass and weeds, the structure was another victim of time, weather, and a changing world. As people had abandoned their God, so too they had abandoned His "House." I looked up at the soaring stone walls reaching toward the pewter heavens and saw that the clouds had returned.

I exited the church and walked around to the stairs that had once led the faithful to the north gallery. The most interesting feature of the structure waited at the top. There, on the balustrade, I saw the six wickedly long, deep grooves gouged from the stone. They lay in parallel as if the hand of Old Nick had marked his new territory. I understood how the story came to be. They were creepy. I reached out to place my hand into the depressions, but only hovered over it. My skin crawled with the overwhelming feeling that what was once sacred had been defiled.

I needed to leave this place. "No such thing as demons, Mira," I told myself firmly. "Let's get out of here before you start believing in this nonsense."

I pulled my coat tightly around me and hurried back to the car.

I PARKED NEXT TO the old white cottage. It sat at the edge of a stunning white sand beach where sleek brown seals lounged, unperturbed by my arrival. The noonday sun peeked through the clouds for a moment and danced on the clear, blue water.

I was stalling. I forced myself to get out of the car and walk to the door. I stared at the peeling paint and took a deep breath before knocking. When there was no answer, I tried again. After the third unsuccessful attempt, I found the track leading south and started the seaside hike to Quoyness Cairn.

The wind coming off the ocean blew harder as I walked. Breakers formed on the water. I picked up the pace, my fingers already bright red and numb. The thought of walking back in the rain wasn't particularly appealing. When I saw the ancient cairn appear between the ocean and open fields, I stopped. Standing in the keen wind, awash in the sounds and smells of the sea, I felt deeply alone...and utterly alive. This piece of the island seemed to stand outside of time.

Isolated from the rest of the island on a point of land jutting into the sea, the massive stone mound crowned a green hill rising from the beach. It was built from the same lichen-spotted stone as the headstones in the kirkyard and the hand-stacked walls that enclosed the calves in the surrounding fields.

The approach to the entrance was a V-shaped slice extracted from the earth that exposed the towering, stacked walls. I walked along the stone-covered portion that remained open to the sky and misty rain. Coming up to the original entrance, I shivered reflexively. The passage leading to the inner chambers of the cairn was barely big enough for a substantial modern adult to pass through. It couldn't have been more than 2.5 feet tall by 2 feet wide. The website had said it was 12 feet long and completely unlit.

The metaphor for life and death was tangible—we were first born into the world of the living. Its ancient architects had constructed the cairn almost as a womb for the dead. They carried their departed loved ones through this tunnel away from this world to be reborn into the inky world beyond.

I took a deep breath, got on my hands and knees, and crawled inside. The clay floor was cold and slick under my hands. Loose stones dug into my knees. When I saw a dim light at the end of the tunnel, I picked up the pace.

As I emerged into the central chamber, an older man with a grizzled beard and long hair leaned against the far wall. Long, white hands poked out of the sleeves of an old grey jumper. His eyes were large and pale, staring at me as I unfolded from the cramped confines of the tunnel. The interior smelled of damp and unwashed man.

"Hello," I said with a smile. I looked around. There were six openings along the walls—side chambers where people had been laid to rest 3,000 years ago. "What a fascinating place! I mean, how did they make this? How long must it have taken?"

He grunted and scratched his ear.

Obviously, he wasn't the outgoing type. I kept smiling. There was plenty to look at while he got used to the idea that

I wasn't going anywhere. I ducked in and out of the smaller chambers, using the flashlight on my phone to illuminate the dark spaces. Each was a miniature version of the main chamber, minus the strange hole dug into the floor.

"What is that, a firepit?" I joked. If I just kept talking, I would eventually say something stupid enough to prod him into a response.

Murky light filtered in from the ceiling. I tipped my head back to see where it came from. High above my head, a distinctly non-Neolithic window light was inset next to four huge slabs of stone set longwise to form a roof. I huffed and shook my head.

"Huh! Didn't know they did glass in the Bronze Age." I mused.

The strange man's braying laugh made me jump. I turned back to him and grinned. "Oops! Did I say that out loud?"

"Aye. Aye, ye did." For the first time, he smiled.

"Well, glad I didn't offend." I shrugged. "It seems almost heretical to allow the light into a place where it was never intended."

His eyes lit up. "Exactly right, lass! Ye ken this place. Not many do."

"How so?" Now that I had finally gotten him talking, I needed to keep him talking.

"Like ye said, lass. Light was ne'er intended here." He waved his hand around, indicating the space. "Light is for the living. The dead dinnae need it. The ancients understood that and made a suitable home for them."

I nodded in agreement. "Interesting."

"And that," he pointed to the mystery hole, "is a cist. A coffin for bones and ash."

"Ah! So, I was right...sort of." I chuckled. "A firepit."

I decided now was the best time to get my story, and if I could get him to tell it *in this place*...what a score that would be! I casually sat down across from him and leaned back against the rocks.

"My name's Mira." I paused. "Would you happen to be Petyr Rendall? Magnus said I would find you here."

He lowered his head, letting his white hair fall across half of his face. He remained silent for a moment, but then looked up at me through the tangles. "Aye," he said. "What do ye want with me, then?"

"He says you have an extraordinary story about the Nuckelavee."

Petyr froze for a moment, his eyes drilling into mine. A strange, fierce light burned in them. "You came out all this way to hear an old man's stories?"

"You're not old," I insisted.

"I'm 66, lass. I've been 66 for a very long time." He sighed. "I'm as old as this place, at least."

I shook my head and laughed. "Fine, have it your way. You are prehistoric. But I do want to hear your story. I'd like to record it if you agree."

"How come?" he asked.

Sensing his unease and suspicion, I quickly replied, "I'm a folklorist. I'm writing my dissertation specifically on Orcadian folklore. A firsthand account of a man who survived an encounter with the Nuckelavee would be the crowning glory!"

His face changed—his mouth drooped and his eyes became hooded—he aged in front of me. "Well, I cannae tell ye *that* tale. Because I dinnae survive, ye ken?"

"What do you mean?" The sudden change in his demeanor troubled me.

"I mean what I say," he said forcefully. "The man I was that night died. I'm not the same man today."

I nodded. I thought I understood.

"Why don't we go to the Belsair? You can tell me the whole story over dinner and a pint." Now I wasn't so sure staying in the cairn for story time was the best idea. The chamber suddenly held a whiff of ashes and death. The combination of the confined space and his belligerent suspicion put me on edge.

"I'll not be out in the rain." He crossed his arms over his chest and set his lips in a line.

"It's just a smirr, barely a drizzle," I cajoled, "think how snug it will be–"

"No! I don't go about in the rain." He squinted his eyes and looked me in the face, taking my measure. "So, ye'v come a long way to hear my story and to learn about the beast, and if ye want, I will teach ye. I'll tell ye everything. Is that what ye truly want?"

"It's why I'm here."

"Are ye very sure? Because ye can't un-ring a bell. Once ye'v heard the tale, it's yers forever, like it or not." He looked away from me, staring into the long, dark passage. He didn't look at me again. Not once.

"Tell me what happened, Petyr." I slipped my hand into my pocket and extracted my phone. I quietly opened the recorder and pressed the button.

He began, "It was near to Gore Vellye, when the time of light and the time of night are equal. The Sea Mither was still with us, though. The sun shinin' and the water calm. The winter monster, Teran, hadn't broken free yet. But the dark was creeping closer."

GORE VELLYE (THE AUTUMN TUMULT)   45

I knew the story of the battle between the Sea Mother and Teran, but I held my tongue. I didn't dare interrupt him now that he'd begun to talk.

"So, I walked into town for a pint or two. But I stayed too long. As I walked home, the sun set as I got back to the Little Sea."

"Were you worried?"

"Not of the monster. I dinnae believe such things then. I was worried that there was only a bit of moon to light the way home."

He went silent for a minute. I saw his breath coming quicker as he went on.

"I had just made the turn at the Lady Kirk when I saw something coming out from the fields behind it. Big, it was. I cuid nae make it out, but I thought, 'oh, stupid coo got loose and is wandering the road.' I feared it might be hit, or run afoul of the sea, so I went towards it. Dear God, I e'en called to it, like a fool. Then, I got close enough to see it wasn't any type of coo I'd ever seen afore. It had but one eye, red as blood. 'Twas neither a horse nor a man, but both, all raw flesh. The demon astride bellowed, and the beast leapt forward, the muscles bunching and digging towards me.

I prayed to God to save me from all evil, but the evil came anyway. The huge head of the demon jerked and rolled with every hoofbeat. Its arms, those mingin' tairible arms, almost to the ground they were.

I ran. I ran to the kirk and hid inside. I dinnae know how to escape. I'd ne'er paid attention to my granny when she tellt th' auld stories."

"How did you get away? Did you cross fresh water?"

"There wasn't any, that I know. The truth, lass, is that I dinnae remember it all. I remember hearing the horse whinny. It was inside the walls, then. I jumped through a window and ran. Sat shaking behind a headstone, I did. I heard the hooves on the road, moving away. Then it was quiet. Next I know, the sun is up, and I reek of death.

I thought maybe I'd passed out in the kirkyard. But the next night, the nightmare came again. And the next night, and the next. One morning I woke up right here. This very spot.

There's not a night or a day that I dinnae think about that demon. It's gripped my mind and I cannot exorcise it. I used to lie awake at night and wonder what it wants. Why?"

He pulled both hands through his hair and gripped it at the scalp. "And every day I come and sit inside this cairn. I dinnae know why. I can't help myself." He began to rock back and forth as he spoke. "But when I'm in the chamber, I hear them speak."

"Them?"

"Him—no, no—it. I hear it speak to me. It whispers in my ears. And now I know what it is and why it is."

I shifted uncomfortably. Something had happened to this guy, and it was clear now that he was a little insane. Okay, not a little, full-blown psychotic. The question was, was he dangerous?

I SUDDENLY REALIZED THAT while he'd spun out his story, daylight had retreated unobserved, as if time inside had stood still while the world outside moved on. The cairn was dark. A trickle of dread slid down my back.

"I should be going now. I should get back to the hotel. Magnus must wonder where I am." At least, I hoped he wondered.

"Not in the rain, Mira. It's not safe to walk that path in the dark." When he looked at me, my heart stuttered. Something about him was terribly wrong. My gut kept screaming at me to leave. Leave now. Leave fast.

"Oh, the rain's stopped. I'll be fine."

His shoulders dropped and he smiled as if nothing had happened. "I'll lead ye back then," he said.

I wasn't happy, but what could I have done? Once I was in the open again, I would be safe. Open fields on three sides and a body 40 years younger than his. I could take him.

"I'll go first." I rolled over from my sitting position and ducked my head into the passage. The slippery clay made progress slow. About halfway to the opening, I stopped. Scrabbling sounds raised the hair on my neck. A metallic taste lodged in my mouth. *What the hell was back there? Go, go, go!* Every fiber in my body flooded with adrenaline.

"Petyr?"

A strange snuffle and a grunt came back. I scrambled forward, snagging my jacket, scraping my face. I could feel my breath coming in short gasps. The noises, they kept coming closer, a snorting exhalation...*and dear God, the stench*. It didn't smell like a man. It smelled like a charnel fire.

I saw the exit and lunged to the end. I pulled myself out and gulped the cold night air. Jamming my hands into the ground, I stood. I had taken one step when it clamped onto my ankle. I yelped in pain.

The hand gripped harder. With one tremendous yank, I landed on my stomach. The first blade of terror stabbed through me. The hand became something else. Something strong and jagged dug into my flesh. I kicked back ferociously with my free leg. I landed one hard enough to send an electric current of pain up my leg. I tried to roll over onto my back to use my hands.

My head snapped forward as the unseen captor jerked me back into the tunnel. I grabbed wildly at the crevices in the walls. The skin of my hands and fingers peeled back as I clutched at the rock, pulling, desperate, failing.

"Oh, God, please God, help me! No, no, no, no, no!"

Childhood catechisms flooded my mind as my faith in science fell away like scales from my eyes. I screamed as I disappeared further into the tunnel.

I barely noticed when a fingernail ripped from the bed. What I did notice was the gouged lines in the earth that my fingers made. *Like the Devil's claw marks.*

The remaining journey back to the main chamber was vicious and swift.

As suddenly as it began, it ended. My leg was freed. I knew I was the mouse and Petyr was the cat playing with its prey. I scrambled blindly into a side chamber fumbling for the phone in my jacket. The blackness was impenetrable.

Scooting back, I hunched against the side wall. I swallowed my whimpers and crossed myself. All the years I'd spent studying and collecting these stories, and this is what it came down to? I felt the tears trace down my cheek. Killed by my lack of belief.

He stamped in circles around the main chamber, snorting air through his nose so loudly that it echoed. The fetid smell of his breath filled my nose at his every pass.

Can't be, can't be, can't be

My brain clutched at reality. I felt the weight of the phone in my hand and the decision I must make. I covered the flash and pressed the flashlight button. I would never find the tunnel in the dark. I had to try to get there first and fastest. Surprise was my only chance.

I moved to the threshold of the side chamber and aimed the shaft of light into the center room.

Petyr turned and glared at me with a single, blood-red eye.

WHEN I AWOKE, I was alone. Like Petyr, I had lived to tell the tale. And, like the old man, I can hear The Others whisper to me. (*time to leave.*) The window in the roof of the cairn reveals a sky shifting in color from pitch to grey.

"The rain is gone. The sky is dark." I murmur. "Time to leave."

SHE PUSHES BACK THROUGH the tunnel, born again and changed. (*beware the water*) She picks her way through the fresh puddles that formed in the night.

Out at sea, thunder greets her and lightning splits the skies. The rain is coming again. (*run or swim, run or swim*)

She runs along the shore through the waning night. And as she gallops, she grows. Legs stretch up and multiply, arms dangle closer and closer to the wet grass, swinging loose above pounding hooves. Her head lolls like a drowned man floating on the waves. (*yield*)

She gives herself over and waits for the pain of flaying flesh. She isn't afraid. The change, the transformation, will be over soon. The beast knows the way home.

> "*Whoever fights monsters should see to it that in the process he does not become a monster. And if you gaze long enough into an abyss, the abyss will gaze back into you.*"-Friedrich Nietzsche

A<small>NNE</small> C. L<small>YNCH</small> <small>TEACHES</small> magic—the magic of books and the world of ideas. Words have power. Stories can change the world. So, yeah, she's an English teacher. She is also a writer of historical fiction with degrees from The University of Texas-Austin and an MFA in Writing Popular Fiction from Seton Hill University. She is a closet lover of all things horror; books, short stories, and movies. (Not the bloody stuff. That's gross.) Anne lives in Austin, Texas with her husband and two dogs, Penny-the-slightly-defective beagle and Luna-the-delightfully-derpy ~~house pony~~ Great Dane. Her debut novel is *The Mercenary's Son*. She is currently completing her second novel, *Gold Star Pilgrims*.

PREY ANIMALS

By Sen R.L. Scherb

Our first choice was buying horses. We'd always dreamed of them—trail riding across rivers, weaving through the trees, nothing but laughs, love, and pure, unadulterated life. We needed a big barn to accommodate five horses, but, well, we were rich, so what did we care? The five of us had wanted to take the next step in our relationship for a long time. Buying a house with a barn was an easy decision with the profits from finding oil. It was the find of a lifetime. Instant riches.

The horses stared at us warily whenever we passed their fence or by a window. Nothing unusual. They are prey animals after all—they're always on alert. And there's scarcely anything more dangerous than a prey animal large enough to trample someone to death, so we gave them space to trust us on their own terms.

I leaned against the fence to the paddock, splinters digging into my skin, watching my horse. Originally, I bought a buckskin, but now he was dappled. The black sock markings on his legs had spread into a blotched pattern across his golden back, and a dorsal stripe like watercolor now darkened his spine. Splotches like the oil we found that let me buy him looped around his snout. His mane was long and stringy and the color of ink.

Young horses are supposed to change color when they shed out. Ours seemed a little old for that, but there was a steep learning curve when it came to horse ownership as opposed to the dream of having one.

But we were rich now. Whatever we didn't know could easily be bought.

The house had been blue when we bought it, a color that blended in with the sky at the right angle. It had turned the color of a purple-brown bruise at the same time the horses started shedding out. Houses rot though. There's always something needing to be fixed. Declarations of needing to call a painter or rent a power-washer echoed around the kitchen and bedrooms, though no one ever called. We were rich. We'd always have enough money to worry about it later. We watched and laughed and ignored how both the horses and the houses became iridescent black.

The walls of the house oozed. The paint flaked under the moisture. The horses became sluggish. All of them were black—but, remembering now, we had bought black horses, surely. Their eyes followed us, dark and void, and their coats dripped with liquid even though there had been no rain. A stream ran through their pasture. They must have liked swimming.

My fingernails turned black. But I had painted them. Or they were stained from working outside—surely.

It was morning. Katja was making breakfast. The sunlight outside shone dimmer through the kitchen window as a cloud passed over—maybe a storm was on the way. There were lots of clouds lately. One of the horses neighed, long and lilting.

A pancake flipped through the air. It landed on the pan with a hot sizzle.

"*Deck den tisch, liebes,*" Katja said. She paused from her pancake-flipping to kiss my cheek and smile softly.

Right. My turn to set the table. Was it Wednesday already? I removed the fine china, five plates decorated with intricate dark designs. My favorite was a tree branching out in every direction to the edges like spilled oil.

Astor arrived just as I finished placing silverware. Deep blackish-purple bags lined his eyes. He wore a blanket wrapped around his shoulders and little else.

"You look like death," I said.

"Shut the hell up," he said. "I couldn't sleep."

"Should have taken your meds."

"I *did*—" He squinted his eyes. "No, wait. I ran out. That explains it." He groaned, long and hard, dropping his head on the table. The plates clattered from the impact. "I forgot to write a reminder to get a refill."

"Watch the plate."

"Whatever. We can buy a new one."

"*Denk nicht so,*" Katja said, ruffling her free hand through his spiky auburn hair while the other carried the hot plate of pancakes. He'd dyed the tips brown recently. "Just because we have money doesn't mean we need to waste it."

"I'm pretty sure that's *exactly* what it means."

"I don't think it works like that." I picked at my fingernails, trying to chip off the black nail polish. It was stubborn—maybe it was dirt. I hadn't worked outside lately.

"Good morning, loves. What did I miss?" Solé entered, dragging her chair back and flopping into it. She pointed a finger at Astor—netted gloves spidered around her hands and up her wrists.

I'd never known her as the type to wear stuff like that. Maybe she was trying out a new style.

Solé nodded to Astor. "What's with him?"

"Didn't take his meds and didn't sleep."

Astor groaned again. "You don't have to remind me."

"Sleep with one of us next time then."

With another sympathetic pat to his head, Katja put the plate of pancakes in the center of the table. "Okay, everyone—wait, where's Hannah?"

Hannah. The name sounded familiar. I looked at the empty chair across the table. Blonde hair, brown eyes. A smile that crinkled at the corners. A bright laugh that turned into a snort when it was too forceful. *Hannah.* Right.

"Maybe she's out with the horses," Astor said.

"Ponies," Katja said. "They aren't big enough to be horses."

"Unnecessary."

Katja shrugged. "Just saying. But no one was outside."

I looked out the window over the sink. Underneath the white, cloudy day, four ponies grazed peacefully in the paddock. A dark stream the color of their hair ran through the center of the field. Waves rippled out from the middle of the stream, like something big had just entered it.

One pony glanced up, as though knowing I was watching. It met my eyes through the glass. Even from so far away, its own were bright and clear and endless.

I didn't see anyone. No one walked through the fields.

I turned back to the table, confused why I looked out in the first place. My partners sat in all the chairs around me. Pancakes piled each of the four plates, covered in slow-dripping ochre syrup.

Nothing was different than normal.

"**D**ID YOU DYE YOUR hair again?" I pulled my fingers through the dark strands of Astor's hair. He forgot to shower often, and his hair felt especially greasy. Usually, Astor was the one to run his fingers through mine or one of our other partners' hair, but since he'd been so tired I wanted to return the gesture.

"What?" His eyes opened, meeting mine. We sat on the couch with his head in my lap, the TV quiet in the background, playing a show I didn't know the name of. "I've never dyed my hair."

"Oh," I said.

We fell silent.

I turned the TV off—I wasn't paying attention anyway. I couldn't seem to focus on the subtitles long enough to understand what they were saying.

"... Lif?" Astor said, voice distant as though he'd said my name multiple times.

"Huh?"

"I said, 'What about you?'"

"What about what?"

He stared up at me, unblinking, and brushed a finger over my forehead. "When did you start wearing contacts?"

This morning.

"This morning," I repeated. "Why, do they look cool?"

"Yeah, they're like an oil spill. All iridescent and multicolored. Didn't know you could get those."

"Wanted to try something new. I'm glad you like them."

"You'll have to show Katja and Solé."

"I will."

The silence sat longer. My stomach growled—we hadn't eaten that morning. Katja was the one in charge of breakfast, but Solé, Astor, and I hadn't seen her. Wednesdays I set the table. Fridays and Tuesdays I cleaned the dishes.

It was humid in the house, though the AC blew strong. Curtains waved where they'd been opened to combat the moisture. It didn't help.

"Let's go out to the ponies," I said. "We haven't ridden them in a while."

Astor groaned. "Now? Really? I was just about to get to sleep."

"You know you can't sleep without your meds."

"I can try. You're comfortable."

"Have you gotten your refill yet?"

He covered his eyes with the back of his hand. "No. I don't..." He rubbed his eyes and scrunched the bridge of his nose like he always did when he was thinking. "I'm going soon. The clinic said it'd take a few days for the refill."

I pushed his hand away. "Maybe spending time with the ponies will tire you out enough to sleep without them."

"You're not going to let this go, are you?"

"Come on, I just want you to feel better."

"You know there are plenty of other ways to get me in bed without forcing me outside first."

"Nothing like good old-fashioned fresh air."

He sighed. "Fine, fine." He wiggled his fingers, and I smiled, lifting him up by his shoulders, then pushing him to his feet and following behind. We both wore jeans—there was no need to change.

The sky was overcast again. Dusk came earlier every day. Some of the dark clouds glowed a murky, greenish-purple, almost like the color of the house's peeling paint. "Doesn't that mean a tornado is going to come?"

"We don't get tornados in this area," Astor said.

"I don't think that's how that works." But I ignored it. The colors were a nice change from the white cast of sky.

Three of the ponies stood at the far end of the field. Their necks tilted to the ground like they were grazing, but they stood motionless, lips frozen at their jaws. Their tails streamed into the grass like small black waterfalls. Their manes brushed their knees.

Astor nudged me in the side with his elbow—a feat, since I was already supporting most of his weight. "Look," he mumbled.

Katja stood off to the side of the field, the last pony in front of her. Its neck stretched toward her, nibbling at her hand but not quite making contact.

"Katja!" My voice came out quieter than intended—still loud in the silent field.

She brushed her hair behind her ear, staring into the pony's eyes as if we didn't exist, even though we hadn't seen her since the afternoon before.

"Do you think she spent the night out here?" Astor leaned his head on my shoulder.

I didn't know. "What is she doing?"

"Probably what we were about to. Maybe she can hang out with you instead. I'm tired."

"Wait." I clenched his elbow.

Katja's pony stepped forward to the side of her still body. Made a noise like a whicker.

Katja smiled, a slow stretch of her blushed lips.

Wrong.

Right.

This was normal.

"This is normal," I mumbled to Astor.

He didn't say anything. We couldn't look away from Katja and her pony.

The pony stepped forward again, its shiny pelt glistening like water in the overcast light. It brushed against Katja's hand. She reached with her free hand and caressed the side of the pony. She leaned forward, pressing her cheek into its fur, that smile still on her face.

Black veins crept over her skin like a web, wrapping her into a cocoon. The pony turned its head toward me and Astor. Its void eyes stared at us, unblinking, as the cocoon melded into its body.

Then it collapsed into nothing, a dark stream snaking through the grass to join the river in the center of the field.

"SOMETHING'S WRONG."

Nothing's wrong.

Solé looked up from her book. I couldn't read the cover, even though I could see it. The words slipped away from my grasp when I tried. "What do you mean?"

I paused. "I don't know." Nothing was wrong. Nothing was different. I shifted my legs from her lap, curling them to my chest. "The house seems strange."

"It's the same house as always."

"The paint is gross. It's all peeling and grey and dirty."

"You're crazy. It was like that when we got it." She returned to her book, thumbing a page.

Astor slumped in the nearby armchair. His eyes were closed, head lolled against the back cushion, legs slung over the armrest. I'd laid a knit blanket over him earlier, and he hadn't moved it.

I scratched at my hands. Black flakes drifted to the floor. *Charcoal.*

I'd been drawing that morning. Working with charcoal.

I frowned, hugging my knees tighter. I'd never been good at art. Why would I be working with charcoal? Instead, I asked, "Why would we get a house with peeling paint?"

Solé didn't look up this time. "Because we wanted a fixer-upper, remember? You, Astor, and I said that it would be a fun project. Something for us to do together as partners."

"Oh." I ran my fingers through my hair. The short strands felt wet, almost oily. Wasn't it the moisture that made the paint peel? "We've been here for months."

A pause. "No, we haven't."

"What?"

She stared at me, her dark brows furrowed. "Lif, are you feeling okay? *You* remembered to refill your meds, right?"

"I don't take any."

"What?" She laughed, though didn't look very amused. "Yes, you do."

"I've never taken them. Astor does."

Solé looked at Astor for a long minute. His greasy hair blended in with the color of the armchair. The bags under his eyes had deepened. They looked almost iridescent in the light. "We've only been here a week."

She's right.

No. "No," I said. "It's been months. We found the oil and sold it and bought the house. That was months ago." I set the table on Wednesdays—I'd set the table more than once. Right?

"Maybe you should go out with the ponies," she said. "Some fresh air might do you good."

But her words were slow. Her eyes fixed on me, a question in them. An underlying panic.

Come out.

The ponies. I shouldn't go out with them. "No, I don't think that's a good idea." Something pulled at me. Yanked. I squeezed my eyes shut and saw swirling manes dripping with darkness. It smelled foul, filled my nose and throat.

Solé stood.

Astor remained motionless on the chair. The blanket hardly rose and fell with his breaths.

She shook her head. "Maybe *I'll* go out there then."

"No!" I jerked to my feet and clenched Solé's arm.

Her breathing came quick. "Lif, let go of me."

"You can't go out there."

"You're hurting me."

I let go like I'd been touched by a brand. My heart rose to my throat.

Let her come to us.

Shut up.

"Don't go out there." I could only imagine what I looked like. Astor mentioned my contacts—eyes—were multicolored. How wild they must look. "You can't. That's where the others went."

"What others?"

Their names. What were their names? My mouth went dry. My throat burned with thirst. When was the last time I ate? Someone else made the breakfast. I set the table on Wednesdays.

A bead of sweat dripped down my hand.

It glistened black against the floorboards.

It's only ever been three.

"There were more than three of us."

"There are only three ponies."

The ponies. Outside, all three ponies' heads were raised. They stared through the sink window, past the kitchen doorway, and directly at us.

"We have to get out of here."

"What are you talking about?" Solé wasn't watching me. She fixated on the ponies. Her mouth moved like the words weren't her own. "Everything is fine. You're just tired. Like Astor."

Astor.

He still hadn't stirred. Was the blanket moving?

I walked to him and yanked the blanket off.

Black lines covered him to the neck, a cocoon of webbing spidering across his skin and under his clothing. Little tan showed through.

He breathed—barely.

Solé gasped behind me.

There was no hiding whatever *this* was. I picked him up. He was heavier than I was used to, a waterlogged sack in my arms. The webbing coated my hands, slimy like seaweed. Black liquid dripped down, pooling on the hardwood floors.

"What are you doing?" Solé clutched her hands to her chest. The spider-webbed gloves stretched almost to her bicep. "Where are you going?"

To where the others disappeared. To the only thing that ran for as far as we could see. Nothing in the blank sky moved. The land past the paddock was empty, except for the river that trailed into nothing.

"Lif?" Astor's voice was soft. Hoarse. Muffled—like he was underwater.

I held him close to my chest and walked out the door. Solé trailed close behind, though her steps were reluctant.

She followed me to the field, illuminated by the blank white sky, where the ponies watched our every step. Their manes and tails swirled around them. And their eyes—

Their eyes were *angry*. They buzzed with life I had never seen in them before.

"Shit," I breathed.

Astor slipped in my grasp, falling heavily to the ground. I hooked my hands under his arms and dragged him to the paddock. Fumbled with one hand on the gate's latch until Solé pushed me aside and unhooked it.

The ponies walked closer.

I hip checked the gate. It swung open without a sound. Well-oiled hinges.

"What are they doing?" Solé said. The ponies stared at us, their bellies bloating from their sides. They took a step, legs elongating.

The river is ours.

"Stay away from us!" I snapped.

Astor's eyes closed again. He coughed, violent and hacking. Like he was choking.

The river ran through the center of the paddock, the heart of the ponies' pasture. Dark and murky and black.

Solé grabbed for me. Her hand snagged the back of my shirt.

A horse reared up in front of me, iridescent black hooves flashing like daggers.

I dove into the river.

AND OPENED MY EYES into darkness. It was cold. Ink-black. My throat burned.

Two glowing flames from a narrow, bony skull stared at me, seething with rage. A darker shadow loomed behind them.

I screamed. Bubbles raced up.

I kicked and broke the surface, gasping in a breath of thick air. The creature under the water shrieked. Its knife-sharp teeth closed around my leg, tugging me under again.

Sleep.

I thrashed, my shoe knocking against the creature. It jerked back and the current rushed around me, though I couldn't see it. Hooves like blades flashed in front of my face.

I breached the surface once more. Something floated nearby. I lunged away, water-blinded, until I saw the tanned skin. Auburn hair. Black veins crisscrossing their body.

Astor.

He vanished underwater.

Another splash—then a scream. Solé's scream.

"Solé!" I whirled around.

Another creature surged out of the water, vaguely horse-shaped. It loomed above the water-drenched form of Solé as she struggled to swim away.

It screeched at her, a high-pitched warbling hiss, and stretched its dripping long neck down. Its burning, void eyes met hers. Her foot caught its skeletal chest, then dropped away. Its maw opened, broken and jagged teeth gleaming.

I hit the bank. My feet slipped on the slick surface, scrabbling for purchase.

A creature rose from the river, its water so black and deep that it could have been oil. The horse-like thing dripped with the same essence. Behind it were two more creatures with dark, viscous liquid slavering from their jaws, each leaning over a body.

Hannah and Katja.

Nausea pressed against my throat. I stumbled back, nearly falling into the mud.

The creature hissed.

My leg burned where I'd been bitten.

I turned and ran away from where we had stumbled across the river, leaving my partners behind. A warbling neigh echoed in my footsteps, but the creature didn't follow.

I was a prey animal, after all. I was supposed to run.

Sen R. L. Scherb is a writer and middle school English teacher. They currently live in south Florida with their horse, Caspian, two cats, Salem and Wren, and two pigeons (yes, pigeons), Rosencrantz and Guildenstern. They are set to graduate with their Master's from Seton Hill University and graduated in 2019 from University of Iowa with a Bachelor's in Creative Writing. You can find their frequent haunts at www.linktr.ee/SenRider.

THE DEVIL AND SCOTT

By W. H. Horner

THE WARM AIR HELD the Devil aloft, the feeling of weightlessness pushing up on his wings, stretching the sore muscles of his back. His bones ached, from his powerful horse legs to his short arms and long-taloned fingers. Especially the thin, brittle bones that held together the thick skin that allowed him to fly. The right wing always hurt more, having never healed properly after he broke it fleeing a regiment of redcoats when he was still young, too adventurous, too curious.

He stretched, lengthening his body and pointing his hooves as far back as possible. His wings he held in place, keeping pockets of warm air under them. His head lifted, his neck cracking with equal parts pain and pleasure, the relief of unrestricted movement after being too long cramped in the piney wilderness, hiding, sleeping.

Thick trees gave way to fields and roads and farmhouses and towns, all illuminated by the moon and the human-made lights. The steady illumination encased in tiny glass containers fascinated him, the humans pushing back the darkness of night more than their feeble candles and lanterns ever had. Those lights had pulled him along a similar path years before, and the sheer number of them had called to him from across the water. He'd danced on rooftops, leaving gleeful hoofprints in the snow and terrified people below. Some let out startled cries as he touched down and screams of terror as he bounced about. He'd been forced to hide well, after that, mostly sleeping until the number of hunting parties dwindled.

The ferry lay docked ahead. The Devil blinked against the wind that caressed the tiny hairs covering his face as he pushed with body and wings to climb higher, higher, just into the cover of clouds. And then he was over the river. Hunger rumbled in his belly, and he would, eventually, find shallows and hunt for fish or crabs.

But for now, the stretch. The joy of flight, of freedom, and–

Lights. Brilliant lights in the distance. Flashes through the clouds of an illuminated lawn near the edge of the water. Tiny people moving about.

Sounds. A steady murmur of voices flowing under sharp bursts that coalesced into... music? Nothing like the Devil had ever heard. Nothing like the individual musicians who strummed on their instruments in taverns when he was young, stalking the streets of towns at night. Nothing like the music he'd heard played on the strange rotating plates when he'd last visited the city across the water.

It pumped, sharp noises of air mixing with deep thrumming strings. It bounced in his blood, made him want to dance.

The illumination and noise came from a large home that looked out on the water. He'd flown by and over it before, but he never paid it much attention. Yes, it was large, more ornate than most of the homes in and around the Barrens, but it was just one more fancy building in a line along that side of the water. It had never been alive. Not surrounded by people in fancy clothes, music pouring out of it, and magical eel-ec-trick lights creating day when there should be late-evening darkness.

The Devil banked and drew closer in tighter and tighter circles, lowering, lowering, the music becoming clearer, the sounds of raucous conversations, jubilant cheers, and cries of laughter overwhelming his sensitive hearing. He was accustomed to the quiet, the sounds of crickets and owls and other night creatures, all of whom fell silent when he moved through the brush.

This maddening sound of...joy...felt like...

He didn't know. Didn't have the words or concepts that fit the tingling he felt jittering down his spine and dancing over his hide. His heart beat faster than it should. Maybe it was the long sleep, his body, impossibly old already, having aged further. But he didn't feel that different.

No. His heart was dancing to the music, and his hooves yearned to dance as well.

The Devil aimed for the house. For the tiny room built on top of the main roof. He straightened even more, holding his wings close to his body. He dove. Wind whipped by, howling in his big ears and around the horns that snagged on tree branches.

The house grew larger. Larger. Looming below as he shot toward the little roof-room.

The Devil released his wings and dropped his legs, catching the wind to arrest his fall. Still, his hooves slammed the roof, and he bounced once, twice, skittered across the shingles, stumbled, and rolled off the small roof onto the main one. The jolt reawakened all the old soreness.

No time to feel. Momentum dragged him to the edge—threatened to drop him into the party below. He fought twin desires: He longed to join them. To dance in their laughing company. And he longed to crash to the ground with his horrible screech to see them flee in terror. But his instinct for hiding forced his claws to dig in and his hooves to find purchase, heedless of his wants. He gasped for air at the precipice, and then he crept back up the roof, making sure there were no shouts of alarm.

The music commanded his attention again, and the Devil gave a hopping shake, clearing the cobwebs from his mind and loosening all the joints and connective tissue, a full-body wiggle from head through forked tail.

And then the Devil danced.

He danced his best dances, bouncing on his hooves with wonderful, joyous clatter. Kicking his legs up and flinging his taloned fingers into the air like the fancy people below, who danced unlike any people he'd ever seen. Wild dancing for wild music.

He danced and he danced. Lost himself in the music, only stopping between songs.

It was in one of those brief moments of partial calm when he heard, just barely over the sounds of the party, a child crying out from below. One of his ears flicked up, trying to capture the sound again. Yes, a girl-child calling for her parents, ignored in favor of friends and drink and music.

The next song started up, and so did the Devil, resuming his clomping across the roof. The child didn't seem to warrant her parents' attention, so he need not pay her any mind. They probably wouldn't check on her until after the music was over. Until the fancy people had left. He'd be gone by then, safely in the air, gliding over the water and back to his quiet solitude in the Barrens.

But for the time being, the laughter. The party. The music. Dancing.

When the music finally stopped, the Devil fell to the roof, panting, exhausted in the best way. Exhausted in a joyful way he'd never experienced in his cursed existence. He crept to the edge of the roof and watched as the men in their suits and the women in their tiny shimmering dresses dispersed, some to their motorized carriages and others inside the house, and the Devil felt as if their cries of "Until the next one!" and "Have a good night, egg!" were for him.

But what did that even mean?

The Devil didn't much care.

And he didn't much care about the soft crying he could barely hear from below. What human ever cared for him?

The Devil inched as quietly as possible away from the front of the house, sneaking not out of concern for the girl-child below but from increasing worry over discovery, his self-preservation instincts taking over from euphoria.

He moved to the edge of the roof and peered down to make sure no stragglers remained below before simply letting gravity carry him out into the air. His wings spread. And the Devil flew low for a few heartbeats, barely above the ground, then flapped his wings and climbed into the air, over the river, leaving behind the big house on the riverbank. Leaving behind the lights, the dwindling laughter. And a child quietly weeping herself to sleep.

SCOTT STOOD FROM HIS writing desk, the throbbing pain of a hangover pulsing inside his head. The gin he'd downed wasn't cutting it. He'd wrestled with the words. He'd tried to find some part of himself that he could turn into sentences and paragraphs and pages that could bring him the admiration he craved and the money he needed.

The damned money. Bills to pay. Parties weren't cheap.

He wasn't supposed to still be struggling. Goddamn Gatsby. It was supposed to be his masterpiece. The novel that elevated him to new heights of fame and fortune.

And damn the idiots who didn't understand. Didn't understand what it was about. Didn't see it for anything more than a glitzy crime book that would vanish from cultural memory. It certainly hadn't sold, so maybe they were right about that. It burned. There was so much of himself in that book...a rejection of it was a rejection of him.

The next book just wasn't coming together. If his masterpiece was worthless, what was the point? No. He had to keep going. Had to prove himself. And he had a family to take care of. The stories were keeping them afloat, but he needed a book.

Ever the supportive editor, Max Perkins suggested they move somewhere quiet, that the area around Wilmington, Delaware, would provide both peace and material for his next project. He was supposed to cut back on the jag juice.

To rest so the words would come. Ellerslie Mansion was probably what Max had hoped for them, and he likely grinned under his fedora when he heard the news that Scott's Princeton buddy, John Biggs, had found it. A rental on the site of a recently defunct ironworks plant—they'd built the superstructure of the Brooklyn Bridge there!

They wouldn't stay forever. They were used to moving around.

The calm life had worked for a while, but it was boring. He and Zelda needed excitement. Needed the people and the action, to be the center of it all, to feel something other than the anxiety and the simmering anger and insecurity. Scott began fleeing to New York on the train. To get a taste of life because sitting all day and fighting with words wasn't living.

But that wasn't enough. Max and John probably hadn't expected the parties to resume in little Edgemoor, Delaware, on the outskirts of Wilmington, in the big old house on the Delaware River. Who would come? But they did. The Fitzgeralds left the scene, but the scene followed them to their new home. Lavish parties. Friends and literary luminaries who rode the train to Wilmington to be picked up by the chauffeur and brought to stay the weekend with "the Colonel" and "de old Missus," the old house making them feel like Southern gentry.

And there was enough trouble to be found in town on the weeknights. It was useful to have a local attorney as a friend to take their calls in the middle of the night and get them out of jail. Biggs was a good sport.

They had another successful party to their credit after the previous weekend. But another party meant more debt. And more debt meant more pressure to write.

He needed another gin to quiet the pain and the thoughts that kept racing. As he prepared the drink, he wondered what Scottie was doing. What was all that nonsense about something crashing about on the roof? She was getting old enough to not make up stories.

Scott laughed. Isn't that what he did? And if her head was full of stories, it was his fault, playing imagination games with her, describing magical scenarios behind the actions of everyday people they encountered. He should write down some of those imaginings. There was probably a story there that he could sell.

He had to write. For Scottie.

Scott turned, ready to work, when a huge shadow momentarily darkened the second-story bay window more completely than a cloud could. Some kind of huge bird? Did they have wild turkeys in Delaware?

He headed toward the window for a glance out, wondering if he'd spot the bird over the water, but a strange current passed through him. A surge of adrenaline chased away the hangover. Some primal instinct stopped him, tumbler held loosely. Was the hair on his neck actually standing up?

It was ridiculous. Scottie's fancies about monsters cavorting on rooftops infecting his brain and mixing with too much drink. Ridiculous. He was ridiculous. He needed to relax, raised his hand to take a sip.

The scream jangled the nerves of his arms and shoulders before his brain registered the sound.

"Scottie!"

He tore through the room, tumbler falling to the floor, and he made for the door without knowing exactly where he was headed. Another wordless scream. Outside.

THE DEVIL AND SCOTT   75

"Zelda!"

He ran for the stairs, cursing. What if it was kidnappers? They would assume he was made of money. What would they do to Scottie if he couldn't pay up?

Sunlight blinded him for a moment after he crashed through the front door. He half tumbled, half leaped from the columned portico, his shoes kicking up dirt as he landed.

"Scottie!"

"Daddy!"

She was pointing to the sky, and Scott spared a glance in that direction as he ran to his daughter. Nothing but sky and clouds.

He skidded to a kneeling stop and grabbed Scottie's shoulders. "What is it? What?"

"A monster." She stared up at the clouds, her face gone white.

This again. "There are no monsters." His heart was still pounding. Why wasn't he feeling relief?

"It was flying. Huge wings."

"I saw something pass by." Focus on convincing the child. "Probably a turkey."

She finally looked at him. She was shaking. "I know what a turkey is. It had long legs behind it. A huge head."

Think. "A crane, maybe." He had to convince himself. "They get big, can look scary if one startles you."

She glared.

Scott stood and brushed the dust from his knees. He reached to pat the back of her head, and she dodged him. He put on a smile, fought through the anxiety, tried to sound...normal. "How about a break...from..." Damned if he knew what she was up to. They needed the DuPonts or Wanamakers to bring the children for a visit. Scottie needed companionship. "Let's go inside."

A final glare of defiance before she ran for the door.

Where the hell was Zelda? Dance lessons?

That same old crushing feeling of never being enough gnawed at his gut, taking the edge off the lingering fear. How was he supposed to find the clarity of mind to write when he had to manage every detail of their lives, to be both father and mother?

Nothing else to do but get back to work.

He looked to the sky again, working his clenched jaw loose, wondering what could have flown by. Wondering about the strange sense of danger that was receding, being subsumed by more mundane fear.

Of course there aren't monsters.

As Scott walked back to the big old house, a shadow passed over him, and that feeling crept up his spine again. Stronger even than before. He was out in the open without the protection of the house. The feeling grew. Cold terror replaced blood. He stiffened, kept his eyes on the open door, and tried to walk calmly. Tried not to feel small. Tried not to feel like prey doing its best to avoid attracting attention.

He got inside and slammed the door, resting against it to keep from slumping down on suddenly weak legs.

Of course there aren't monsters.

No sign of Scottie. Probably fled to her room to cry. The shame burned deep. He was always doing the wrong thing, and regretting it later.

Where was Zelda? He needed a drink.

No, he had an apology to make. A little girl's tears to wipe away.

There were no monsters but for himself and the woman he'd married.

THE DEVIL WATCHED THE girl run inside the house. Not so much from the sight of him, even though her scream had alerted him to the fact that he had been spotted. Careless. Foolish. But she had fled the man. From whatever words had passed between them.

All parents were monsters.

No. Not all. Some were loving. Caring. He hated them the most. Why hadn't he deserved that?

What had brought him back to that house? There was no party. No music. Why would there be? In the daylight, no less.

Did he think he could recapture the joy? There was no joy there.

The Devil flew.

HE RETURNED TO THE big house on the river when next he heard the music, and the lights and laughter called to him. Told him that joy was to be found, if only from the rooftop.

He continued to return, sometimes even in the day, despite his better instincts. He was too curious about the man, woman, and child who lived there. Curious about the kind of people who had such parties.

Mostly, he danced on that roof. He embraced the sounds. Fell in love with the antics of the drunken humans. It was all exciting and intoxicating, but it made the longing worse. He wanted to be called an "egg," to be patted on the back by other men and to have pretty women fawning over him the way some of them fawned over the men.

He had been robbed of a life. His mother cursed him to be a devil, but she was the monster.

Each time he returned was a mixture of joy and longing and anger. Exhilaration and frustration. Envy deeper than the Delaware or even the ocean it emptied into. And each time he left, he swore he was done with the fancy people and their fancy clothes and the lights and music that called to him.

He should sleep.

Go gorge on fish and crabs and small woodland creatures and whatever fruits and vegetables he could take from the farms. Raid a few chicken coops for eggs—real eggs, not whatever those fancy idiots called each other—and bird flesh.

Then sleep again. Sleep for as many years as his hunger would allow. And these people would be gone. He would outlive them just as he had outlived the wretched family that had cast him out. Outlived the soldiers and the trappers who had hunted him. Outlived the smugglers and outlaws. Outlived generations.

The stupid, arrogant humans were nothing compared to him. He would outlive that age of excess, outlive those empty fancy people, and watch the big house crumble into dust.

He was already high in the air, soaring above the river. The house and the lights and music and laughter fell away behind him. He didn't know when he had left. He shook his head to clear the disorientation, banked toward the Barrens.

He'd heard tales people told about him to scare one another in the evening hours. How he had killed all those redcoats. How he kidnapped children, took them into the Pine Barrens, and consumed them. He'd thought of murder. Thought of taking out all his anger and frustration on some hapless human who experienced far more joy than they deserved.

The Devil crashed through the trees as he landed, heedless of the noise and the pain as branches splintered against his bulk. His rage burned away all care for such things.

He could picture the big house so clearly. The parties. Could picture the mother and father. How they tormented each other and pursued their passions and interests, sometimes targeting the girl with their anger and frustration, mostly ignoring her. She'd be better off alone in the woods like him. At least they couldn't be mean to her there.

They didn't appreciate what they had. They were a family. They had a big, wonderful house. Uncountable friends. Unlimited food and drink.

Parties. Parties. Parties. Meaningless, stupid parties.

The Devil pictured himself landing in the middle of one of those parties. Crashing through dancing idiot eggs. Knocking over tables of fancy food. Smashing fancy glasses and bottles of alcohol as he brayed and laughed and the people scrambled to escape the monster that had appeared from out of the night.

No. Too risky. Too dangerous, no matter how fun it sounded. He'd be hunted endlessly.

And what would the parents learn? Nothing except that monsters exist.

No. He could teach them a different lesson. Teach them what they should truly value. Make them see what they had.

Scott lay in complete darkness. He'd lost track of time.... Wasn't sure how long he'd been there. Maybe time wasn't important. Maybe there weren't deadlines for greatness.

Sounds were so muffled that he couldn't tell what they were or if he was merely imagining them; mostly, he listened to the rushing of blood in his ears.

His damned nose itched, and the automatic reaction made him slam his hand against the lid. God that hurt. Stupid. Did anyone hear that?

The reality of the situation pressed down. He was so closed in. What if he couldn't get out?

His heart raced, and he gulped air.

There wasn't enough air. Not enough room.

Lightheadedness made his thoughts even swimmier. Why couldn't he breathe? No air...

He couldn't die without proving himself.

Scottie!

He couldn't leave her. He had to escape.

He maneuvered his arms above his chest, pressed against the lid, pushed.

He was breathing hard. Taking up the oxygen too fast.

No. No, no, no.

That was the wrong thing to do.

Just get ahold of yourself. Breathe slowly. Calm down. Just a matter of time.

The clack of latches.

Scott flinched then gulped a breath. It didn't matter now. He tensed, readying to spring like a jack-in-the-box.

Light and air burst in, and Scott lunged up, arms raised high.

"Happy birthday!" The cheer of the crowd filled his chest as much as the cool fresh air did. The lightheadedness faded.

As the cries and applause died down, Scott surveyed the beaming faces, nodding to better acquaintances and smiling wider for friends.

She stood in front of the coffin, having unlatched it as planned. Zelda smiled up at him, radiant. At her best, in her element. All the resentment and insecurity fled. How she consumed him. She was the best drink, his biggest addiction. His Zelda.

He'd been staring.

Scott pulled himself away from the gravity that was his wife, and he gave the "settle down" gesture with his hands. "I hope you've all mourned my passing thoroughly, that there has been sufficient weeping and gnashing of teeth."

Somewhere, a man gave an exaggerated "boo-hoo," and the crowd laughed.

Scott pointed in the general direction of the crier. "That didn't sound nearly sincere enough! Seriously, though, thank you all for coming to help me ring in another decade of this sparkling existence!"

Zelda took hold of his shin, still beaming up at him. "Happy thirtieth birthday to my brilliant husband!"

The crowd cheered.

The Devil didn't dance that night. He watched the stupid fools make themselves look like idiots as he waited for the cheers and the music and laughing to end. For the vain, vapid guests to depart and for the house to fall into silence.

Then he leaped into the air and circled the darkened house three times to make sure there was no one to see him. The Devil descended as gently as possible, flapping his wings to stay even with the large bay window that looked out on the river.

With sharpened claws, he pried and tore. Pulling, yanking, he forced open one of the side windows. He shouldn't have been able to fit through, but he was used to contorting himself to hide in the wilderness.

He grabbed where he could and heaved, his hooves finding little purchase, his wings beating frantically to keep aloft as he wriggled himself inside.

Wood snapped. A pane of glass shattered.

He tumbled to the floor.

THE DEVIL AND SCOTT

Scott jerked awake at the sound of the world collapsing around him. An explosion of glass and wood, and he pictured chandeliers falling from grand ceilings and great towers of champagne flutes collapsing in on themselves as his brain tried to come to terms with being ripped from sleep while still intoxicated.

He fell to the floor from his chair, realizing that he was in his office, remembering that he'd been sitting in the dark, drinking after everyone had gone to bed. He'd put on a good face, but the passing of the decade without achieving his goal.... It had gnawed at him, emptying him of joy.

Glass crunched. Something huge stood backlit by moonlight, part of the bay window behind it a ruin.

The Leeds Devil was real.

He'd asked around and had done the research after Scottie's continued complaints of noises and shadows. He learned of the sightings in 1909 of the Leeds Devil all across the area. Armed gangs had hunted the beast. Just two years before, a taxi driver in Salem, NJ, claimed it had attacked his vehicle.

Some people were calling it "the Jersey Devil."

"What do you want?" Scott said as he rolled from his side to an awkward crouch.

The creature's head followed his motion. It let out a high-pitched yelping noise, its horse head bobbing up and down, its legs quivering. Was it laughing?

The whole world seemed to be buzzing. Scott wanted to run. Some deep part concerned only with his own skin was telling him to flee. But another part said it would attack from behind if he did that. Another part worried for the others in the house. Zelda. Scottie. He made a shooing motion as if it were some highly aggressive chicken. "Go!"

He felt ridiculous.

That braying laughter stopped.

"There's nothing here for you!"

Its jaw worked, lips peeled back from giant horse teeth.

Scott fell back, scooting away as fast as he could.

A sound came from the creature's throat, a choking noise that finally formed a single stuttering word. "Ch-i-ld."

It ate children, according to the old legends.

Ate children.

Scottie.

Scottie!

"No!" Scott pushed himself to his feet, the world wobbling around him, but he had to see her safe. "Not my daughter!" He lurched for the golf club he had taken to leaving at the door to his writing room as the paranoia and worry had grown. His hands found it, but he tumbled into the door jam and turned with a wild blind swing, his eyes clamped shut. The club put a hole in the wall, stuck there.

The creature hadn't moved.

Scott ripped his weapon free, and dust and debris rained down. "You can't take her."

It lunged forward. Impossibly fast! Jaws wide open.

Scott fell to the side, avoiding chomping teeth. He landed awkwardly on one foot and swung. The creature lurched back with a flutter of wings. The club found nothing but air. The momentum carried Scott off balance, and he did a little twirl before landing on the floor in a tangle of his own limbs. The world spun around him, and Scott fought the need to vomit.

Crunching glass.

The creature stood in front of the ruined window again, its head tilting back and forth. There was something canine to the motion. It was an unholy conglomeration of creatures...but it spoke.

Scott pushed himself up on the backs of his arms. He kept one fist around the club, but he didn't heft it. "You...speak."

Dark as it was, Scott couldn't tell, but he thought the thing was studying him. He felt its eyes narrow.

"You watch us."

"Yesssss." A slow exhalation of sound.

"Why?"

A shift, a hoof clacking on the floor. "Curious. Lights...across...river."

Scott felt a pang of an emotion he wasn't even sure he could name. Not pity. Not sympathy. Not for this creature. But he saw Gatsby reaching for the green light.

"Sounds. Music."

"You like parties?"

The horse head bobbed.

The noises Scottie heard. "You dance?" Scott unconsciously motioned above, hefting the club.

The creature tensed, looked ready to spring—upon Scott or out the window? "I like...dancing."

Would it attack again? Try to get past him, out into the house?

"Why Scottie?"

"You...don't..." Its wings twitched. A tiny flap of wings, and the creature just barely hopped. "Don't deserve her!"

Something stabbed Scott square in the heart. He was sure the creature had impaled him with something. He felt around for a wound, but–

It moved faster than before, straight for Scott, its wings wide, horse mouth open with crazy red eyes, its short arms stretched out with talons pointed at his chest.

Scott had never been a great athlete, had seen his football dreams at Princeton die, but he brought the club around and smashed it across the creature's face, deflecting its momentum. The wood snapped, and the head of the club sailed into the wall with a clatter.

The Jersey Devil shrieked that horrendous noise, and Scott dropped to the ground, covering his head and wailing along with it.

Powerful hind legs kicked off with a clomp. Great bat wings flapped, and the Jersey Devil crashed through the remains of the bay window and glided into the night. It banked and climbed, then disappeared.

"STRANGE TO BE OUT here for something other than a noise complaint," one of the cops said as they walked up the stairs to Scott's office.

There was just enough time to come up with a story: an intruder, a burglar or maybe even a crazed fan, had somehow reached the bay window and broken in, but Scott had scared them off after a struggle, and they tumbled through the window as they tried to escape.

Except for bits of the broken window, there was no evidence of an intruder below, no evidence of anyone having fallen or how they would have reached the window in the first place, but there was a splatter of blood on the wall of the office that couldn't be accounted for otherwise.

That's what convinced him that it hadn't been some kind of hallucination or stress dream, and it's the only reason anyone believed that he hadn't simply lost his mind and smashed out the window himself. Zelda still seemed to think that's what happened.

He couldn't tell anyone the truth, though. He'd be locked up. Locked up by fools who don't understand the reality of the world. Maybe there was a story there....

But what if the creature came back? Came back for Scottie, who clung to his hand, her sense of safety shattered like the window in his office. She'd refused to play in the yard by herself, and he considered making some phone calls for company to take her mind off the excitement, but the fancy local families wouldn't want their kids around an actual crime scene.

The part-time nanny finally encouraged Scottie to read with her, and Scott smoothed things over with the guests who had stayed the night after the party and the police, who promised to watch the premises for a while. But what would they do against such a creature?

"IT'S A FINE JOB, Edward." The new window was beautiful, and it was far less drafty than the old one. "I'm sure the Sellers will be pleased."

"Thank you, Mr. Fitzgerald," the craftsman said, looking up from where he was packing the last of his tools.

"So your family is from the area?"

"Yes, sir, Mr. Fitzger–"

"Please. It's 'Scott.'"

"Yes, Mr. Scott—Scott, sir." The man looked away for a moment, shook his head back and forth ever so slightly. "Family in Delaware, Philadelphia, and across the river in Jersey. Branches of the family been here since before the Revolutionary War."

"A Son of the American Revolution."

The man beamed up at him as he continued to pack.

Scott stared out the window a moment, the river and the far bank of New Jersey seeming to stare back. Where was the beast? He couldn't just allow it to take his daughter. "Have you ever heard of the Jersey Devil?"

The man barked. A laugh. "The Jersey Devil? The Leeds Devil?" He snapped shut his toolbox and rose, heading toward the door. "Of course. There's Piney blood in my family. Stories go way back. My grandfather talked about missing chickens, swears he saw the creature one summer evening."

Scott gestured for the man to precede him. "Really? Huh."

The man bobbed his head. "Yes, sir. Lotta stories. 'sposed to have been the thirteenth child of Mother Leeds, who cursed it in a fit of frustration over having another mouth to feed."

"You think it's real?"

The man looked back, searched his face for a moment, maybe checking to see if Scott was making fun of him. Scott tried to smile a genuine encouraging smile.

"I can't say one way or the other—it sounds impossible—but with all the stories, hell—excuse me, Mr. Fitzgerald—"

Scott waved.

"There's got to be somethin' to it. All those accounts twenty-some years ago, and old Pap wasn't a liar."

"What if I were to tell you I'd seen it?"

The man stopped at the bottom of the stairs and looked at Scott from the corner of his eye, a slight grin on his face. "Really? Ha! That's a good one. Had me there."

"I'm serious." Scott kept his face as neutral as possible. How would the man take it? Scott needed help. But to tell someone.... He couldn't be locked up. Couldn't leave Scottie alone.

The man stared, mouth slightly open. "I guess I'd believe you."

"Then I'd like you to take a look at the windows in the cupola. I think I might have some additional work for you and your men."

The man's eyes narrowed, but he shrugged his shoulders and seemed ready to head back upstairs.

Relief. He had found help. Scottie would be safe. Part of the worry slipped off, like a too-heavy blanket on a warm spring day. If they could come up with a plan...capture the beast.... His mind wandered to the hunting parties throughout the decades. He thought about the hoaxes, fake devils paraded around for entertainment. Ticket sales. And what if they managed to do it? Capture the real live Jersey Devil?

What was he thinking? It felt cheap. He believed in hard work. What was this?

But this wasn't a hoax. It was like capturing a deadly wild animal. Protecting civilization. That was honest work, right? Work that deserved compensation.

Showmanship was work. And the Fitzgeralds knew showmanship. He and Zelda were good at staying in the spotlight, and that's what they would do.

"If this works, I don't think any of us will need to worry about money for the rest of our lives."

Scott didn't mind the look he was getting. A humoring look. A "this rich idiot is insane, but if he's going to pay me, I'll go along with it" look.

The man wouldn't look at him the same way if he were Hemingway.

Scott felt an unforced smile. Hemingway had never survived an attack by a legendary monster. A surge of sudden pride, and Scott's back straightened a bit as he led the way to the highest part of the mansion.

HE'D STAYED AWAY FOR a while, but eventually both the fear and the anger faded, and the Devil wondered if the family still lived in the house on the water and if they still had their parties. When he next landed on the roof of the big old house, having followed the music and laughter, the Devil found, sitting just outside one of the windows in the roof-room, a platter of food and a bowl with a bitter-smelling liquid.

What was it? Some gesture of peace? An offering so he wouldn't take the girl? Poison? He stared at the food as if by simply looking hard enough, he would be able to learn the truth.

His stomach growled. Saliva filled his mouth. Those were not scraps. Not a fresh kill covered in mud or dust. Real human food. Clean meat and vegetables with spices and cooked, he assumed, by the best cook who had ever existed.

It was all gone faster than he would have liked, the bitter liquid burning nicely on the way down. He felt content in a way he'd never before felt, a warmth spreading through him.

The Devil patted his belly. He plopped to the roof and grinned down at the partygoers. His hooves tapped to the music.

E D KEPT HIS HANDS clamped over his mouth the entire time, from the moment he heard what sounded like the biggest, clumsiest bird landing on the roof. He pressed his hands there, nearly suffocating himself, as the monster from all those legends stomped into view.

He pressed all the harder as the scream welled up from his belly and into his chest, and he squeezed as far back into the corner of the cupola as he could, praying the creature wouldn't hear him screaming, wouldn't smell his fear.

But it ate, drank, like it had never had food or drink before. And it sat there, tapping its hooves, its giant horse head bobbing, a forked tail dancing in the air behind it.

Ed trembled, screaming that silent scream, the sounds of muffled jazz and laughter stretching on and on.

Goddamned F. Scott Fitzgerald had fought the goddamned Leeds Devil, and now it was sitting on his roof, intoxicated, listening to jazz.

THE WEEKS PASSED, THE Devil crossing the river as often as his irregular sleep and the need to stay hidden allowed. The air cooled and became cold, but even when the parties moved completely inside, the Devil still found food and drink left out on the roof of the big old house.

One cool evening between the long cold nights and the shorter warmer ones, the Devil landed on the roof, already drooling over the food left there for him.

The party was inside, just like all the others since things got cold, but he could still enjoy the music as distant as it sounded. And at least there was the meal, and the drink, which scared away the chill.

The warmth was spreading through him as usual, and his hooves were feeling that extra dancery feeling. He stood, swung his arms, and let his legs loose, tapping his hooves on the roof. He spun, just a little turnabout, nothing fancy for one who did somersaults in the sky, but the world kept going when he stopped, and then the world tilted hard to the side.

The roof slammed his whole body, his head, and everything went fuzzy. The music, already muffled, sounded elongated. Dragged out. Unreal.

THE DEVIL AND SCOTT 93

Noises from someplace far away. Scraping. The tap tap tap of footsteps.

He tried to roll, but nothing wanted to respond. Why wouldn't his arms work? His legs? His eyes were closed. When did he close his eyes?

With enormous effort, his eyes slid open to the sight of human boots clomping toward him. Many of them.

Something heavy fell over him. It felt like burrowing under a deep cover of leaves and branches. Comforting, actually. Was that what it was like to be tucked in at night? Sleep. It was time to sleep.

The world rolled. He closed his eyes so the sight of stars smearing across the sky didn't make him sick. The blanket drew tighter. Something yanked him to the side. His face scraped against the roof. Another yank, and something deep inside the Devil screamed. Danger. Wake up. Wake. Up. Waaaake uuuuuuuuup!

His eyes opened again. His foggy brain registered a man standing a few feet away, pointing at him, his eyes wide, his mouth moving.

Flee.

Get.

Away.

Something surged inside. It wasn't much, but it was enough to allow the Devil to lurch over. He half found his hooves and kicked away.

THUMPING FROM ABOVE.

Scott looked up as if the ceiling in Scottie's room would reveal the outcome of the ambush.

Scottie pulled her blankets close with a gasp, stared with big eyes. "You heard it!"

He reached out. Tussled her hair. His smile probably looked condescending. "Yes."

"I–"

"It's why I'm here. Why there's music playing downstairs but no party."

"What are you talking about?"

More thumps. Scott reached down to scratch at this ankle where the pistol holster was chaffing him. He was wearing a gun. Like some kind of gangster. He needed it, needed to be there, with Scottie, just in case.

"You were right."

Scottie was blank. Staring. Trying to figure him out.

"There was a monster. Is."

She started to smile. Vindication. But the smile fled before it had the chance to take up residence in her entire face—like them in Ellerslie and the rooms in the mansion they left empty and would probably never use before they left. The last bits of happy emotion fled her face, and fear moved in.

Another thump, and Scottie screamed. Jumped in place on the bed. Scott crushed her against himself. He rocked back and forth, stroking her hair and making shushing noises as if she were still a baby.

"It's all right. I've had a plan. Men are—men are capturing it right now."

She wriggled away slightly. "What men?" Confusion fought to evict fear.

He didn't have an explanation.

"Capturing it?" Confusion and maybe a hint of pity. "To do what?"

Ticket sales. A stream of cash.

"I don't know exactly." The guilt. Doubt. It kept him from telling the truth. "To study it? Figure out what it is."

To parade it around the area. People would flock to Philadelphia. When it got boring for the locals, travel the country. Travel the world.

With a creature in a cage. A creature that seemed to be able to reason. To feel human emotion. Envy and longing. He knew those feelings. Knew the feeling of being on the outside. Of seeing what others had. The feeling of reaching for something more, but it's always just out of reach.

No.

The creature came for Scottie, so it deserved the fate it got. And if it could help him hold on...to solve that damned question of money once and for all.... Hemingway wouldn't hesitate. Wouldn't consider the thing's point of view. He'd be up on that roof, elephant gun at the ready. The world is a harsh place, everyone and everything fighting for whatever they can get. It was time for Francis Scott Key Fitzgerald to get to fighting.

THE LEEDS DEVIL. THEY had the Leeds Devil, drugged and netted.

The Leeds Devil.

Nothing in Ed's life could have prepared him for that moment. What would old Pap say if he could have been there?

The boys turned the thing around, and its horse-like head scraped the roof. It was moving, body parts twitching without coordination.

He felt that scream from when he had hidden in the cupola, watching for proof as Mr. Fitzgerald had asked, as he had done a half-dozen times. The scream was distant, buried deeper, but it was there.

The creature stirred as the boys worked to secure the net. Its eyes slowly opened, and Ed felt as if he would fall into the bright red that glowed from them. The scream inside grew louder. He was pointing. He couldn't remember raising his arm. "It's waking up," he whispered.

The Leeds Devil shifted with more direction than before. Slowly, but with enough force that it pulled Donny down as he fought for control of the net.

It stood, one arm hanging free, its hooves planted underneath it, and those horse legs bent.

Hank lunged at the beast from behind, taking a swing with his baseball bat just as the creature pushed off like some deranged suicidal kangaroo, leaping from the edge of the roof.

Its wings were free, though the net still draped its back, one arm still pressed awkwardly against its side. It managed to avoid crashing, its wings beating slowly, almost languidly. Just barely enough to keep it from dragging its hooves against the dirt.

The Leeds Devil rose slowly into the sky, the net trailing behind. Higher. It reached the river. It was getting away, climbing higher with each slow beat of its wings, slowly moving out above deeper water.

And then it canted to the side, plummeted. It flapped its wings almost sleepily three times before splashing far out in the frigid water of the Delaware River.

A BLAST OF COLD jolted the Devil awake. He gasped, filling his mouth and some of his lungs with water. His chest burned. He tried to swim, to find the surface, but one arm was pinned to his body, and something kept tangling his legs. A weight pulled him down, down, down.

His lungs tried to breathe again, and he took in more water, more pain. His whole body thrashed.

The darkness grew thicker. The moon hung above him, but it was harder and harder to see as more and more water came between him and it.

He struggled, desperate to get his other arm moving. Why couldn't he move both arms?

Something held him. He was stuck in a net. People on the roof. A trap. He pushed against ropes, straining his chest and shoulder. Break one rope. Stretch some just enough to move. Just shift something enough to get loose.

Nothing. A howl of frustration. More air escaped. Bubbles worked their way to the surface.

No. He had to be calm. The water was hunting him, and if he stopped thinking, it would have him.

He brought his free arm around and pulled at the rope with his talons. Dug a point between strands, sawed. He kept working, clawing, even as increasing darkness made it harder to see what he was doing.

The darkness was more than just the depth of the water.

He thrashed. Sharp pain on his chest and across his shoulder brought fresh awareness. He'd slashed himself in his blind tearing of the net.

He managed to grab a handful of torn net, and he pulled. It gave. His trapped arm came free. He wiggled, and the weight dropped down, snagged his hooves, but he kicked and was free.

The Devil pressed his wings against his body and angled his head up to the barely visible moon. His arms and legs worked, he was getting closer to the surface and the moonlight grew brighter, but the darkness at the edges of his vision was growing just as rapidly. He thought his arms were still going. Still working to pull him up...but he wasn't sure. Couldn't feel them anymore. Everything was collapsing down to a tiny pinpoint of light above him.

And then he bobbed to the surface. Found air for his lungs.

The Devil floated there, a part of his mind telling him that he needed to swim. Get to shore before someone saw him. Before the men with nets got in boats and fished him from the water. But there wasn't enough energy for that. His old bones were too weary.

He spread his wings across the water like a raft and floated, breathing in the night air through the raw pain in his throat and lungs.

WHEN, EXACTLY, THE FAMILY left the big old house on the bank of the river, the Devil couldn't say.

He'd avoided the place, though he'd seen the lights, heard the music calling him. He craved the excitement, but he'd learned his lesson. He wasn't meant for that world. Wasn't meant for the fancy people and their fancy homes and motorized carriages and all the things fancy people did. He wasn't even people. Just a monster. A devil.

He flew. He hunted. He ate, and he slept, and at some point the house went silent. Eventually, his curiosity grew, and he missed the sound of the music, and maybe if he got close to the building, he'd remember the sound better.

But the house was no longer a home. People came and went, but they didn't live there. Some kind of business the Devil didn't care about. Gone were the parties. The music. More and more houses seemed to appear overnight. The Devil's bones ached more deeply. His world constricted, humanity becoming too numerous, and he flew freely above the river less frequently.

An industrial plant expanded around the house, and though the humans still worked in it, it crumbled with neglect. One night, after another long sleep, he found it gone completely. Something didn't smell right in the air and in the water around the strange buildings, and he didn't come close again.

Sometimes, as he covered himself in a nest of branches and Pine Barrens debris, he thought about those glittering parties and the family in the house. He wondered where they went. If they found happiness. Sometimes, he hummed himself to sleep, the sound of that magical music in his blood, his hooves lightly tapping a beat.

W. H. HORNER (WWW.WHHORNER.COM) is an editor, educator, and publisher, who writes occasionally. An adjunct English instructor and writing tutor at Wilmington University, Will also teaches in Seton Hill University's MFA program in Writing Popular Fiction. He provides editorial services to private clients and has over twenty years' experience working with writers of varying levels, from beginning authors to *New York Times*-bestsellers. His small press, which is currently on hiatus, specializes in illustrated fantasy and horror literature. When he isn't telling other people how to rearrange their words, he can be found playing Jumanji with his daughter, working on home-improvement projects, or messing around in the guts of his PC or with his cinema camera. Will's other interests include mythology, history, martial arts, the occasional video game, tabletop games and miniatures, and dabbling in voice-over. His crowning achievement was a standing ovation for karaoke at a crowded bar in 2007.

A Thing of Hope

By Carrie Gessner

THE CREATURE IS ALONE. He always has been. He has no memory of how he arrived here. But then, he doesn't know a lot of things. He doesn't know his species. He doesn't know his name—if he ever had one. He doesn't know if there is anyone else like him out there.

There are things he *does* know, of course. He's on a planet called Earth, and he has been for almost fifteen years. If one wanted to zoom in more—and he does because facts are good, facts are comfortable, facts keep him safe—on the planet called Earth, he lives on a continent called North America, in a country called the United States of America, in a state called Pennsylvania, in a small town, almost a village really, called Amity.

And he knows how to read. This skill, more than anything, has kept him alive, has turned "surviving" into "living," even if this life of his is strange and unusual to most people. Or it would seem so if he didn't hide himself away for his own safety. He can't trust how humans would react to him, can't trust that they would treat him with anything but fear.

So, as long as he stays out of their way, he has a pretty good life. It's routine, and routine is something he likes. The best part of his night is his walk through the forest where he lives. Now that it's summer, the forest is a vibrant green, even in the moonlight. In the moonlight, everything is softer and sweeter. The tiny white flowers of trailing arbutus, the silky petals of the common violet, the perfect asymmetry of the trillium. Purple deadnettle, buttercups, bluebells, bergamot, phlox, milkweed, aster. All so beautiful. All so aromatic, the scents of honey and earthy green mingling with hints of citrus and vanilla.

And the *animals*. The plants are lovely to look at, but it's the animals that make him feel alive. The birdsong isn't as active at night. That doesn't bother him. He listens to their morning songs as he falls asleep, and at night, when he walks, the owls and the bats provide symphony enough.

And the stars! Don't get him started on the perfect night sky. Truly miraculous. Sometimes, he finds a break in the canopy and stares at that inky firmament, pierced with specks of light, knowing his home is out there somewhere. He has to believe there are beings like himself on a distant planet. Maybe someday, if he keeps wishing and hoping and *wanting*, they'll find him and he'll no longer be alone. In that way, the starlight is a nightly reminder that even if he feels alone, it's statistically unlikely that he's the only one of his kind.

His walk always takes him to the edge of the forest. Beyond that is a wide field of tall grass. He crosses it with a smile on his face because of the way the grass tickles his fingers. And because across the field is a road and across the road is a building called a library. His destination every night, and his favorite place.

There are no streetlights here, only the light of the waning moon. He toddles across the road. The shorter grass here is dotted with dandelions. He likes dandelions, too, although the old man who comes in the early morning always shakes his fist at them and yanks them out. He likes the dandelions *more* because the old man doesn't.

He circles the building. On its east side, there's a window with a loose latch and, unlike the other windows, no screen. Tonight, like every night, he jiggles the window until the latch gives, slides the pane upward, and squeezes through the opening. He plops onto the floor on the other side and takes a moment to savor the air in here. It smells like knowledge.

Well, not literally. It smells like books, some newer than others. It's the old ones that smell better from the process of the paper breaking down. He read that in a book once. He's read a lot of books. With so much time on his hands, he's made his way through a fifth of the biographies and nearly half the mysteries—he likes those best, except when there's lots of violence—and he's carved out a good chunk from each of the science and history sections. His hunger to know about this planet will likely never be sated. The books meant for children, with their rhymes and pictures, are a special treat. He reads at least two each night.

Since they're so short, he doesn't need to take those from the library to read back in the cave he calls his home. When he does need to borrow something, he takes only one at a time and always brings it back. Always. According to the cute little sign featuring a cute little hedgehog that hangs on the front door, that's the number-one rule of the library. He likes rules. They're good for understanding the world.

The real reason he comes here, though, isn't the books, as wonderful as they are. No, it's the room in the back of the building. It's a small, windowless room, made smaller by its being crowded with cabinets. Along the back wall is a desk with a machine that magnifies pictures of things called newspapers so they're big enough to read. The pictures are stored on a roll, and after nights of trial and error, he figured out how to load the roll into the machine and navigate through it.

The cabinets are filled with the rolls, rows and rows and rows of them. Different papers with names like *The New York Times*, *The Washington Post*, *The Pittsburgh Post-Gazette*, and *The Philadelphia Inquirer*. Each time he starts a new one, he finds the city on the map of America that hangs in the children's room. Sometimes, the towns are too small to be on there, so he looks them up in the children's state atlas. He has to know where they are because if he finds the evidence he's looking for in one of these newspapers, he will have to know where to go.

He will have to know where to go to find someone like him.

Tonight, he chooses the thirty-fourth reel of *USA Today*, having done the thirty-third last night. He's nothing if not methodical in his search. It is the only way he knows how to proceed. After so many years of looking, he's well aware of the truth—that this might take him his whole life. Worse, he may never find anything at all. But even if the chance is minuscule, microscopic, he has to take it.

Hope—that he's not alone, that he won't have to endure this lonely existence forever—is the only thing that keeps him going. It's the thing that motivates him to make this trek every single night, to have the patience to scroll through these newspaper images for the tiniest scrap of information.

Half the time, he doesn't even know what he's looking for. Without a name for his species, he doesn't have a keyword to scan for. Even if he had, though, would it help? It's unlikely the humans know what he is, either. With that in mind, words like "creature" and "monster" and "alien" are on his list of words to watch for.

It's long and tedious work, but at least it keeps him occupied.

He's reading through page eleven when four things happen in quick succession.

First, a light shines on him and the screen.

Second, he turns toward the source of the light.

Third, a person gasps.

Fourth, the light in the person's hand drops to the floor, its beam bouncing erratically.

When it settles, he's left in a staring contest with the person in the doorway. It's human, certainly, and, he thinks, female. Taller than he is by at least two feet, she wears jean shorts and a pullover sweatshirt that looks very soft. He's appropriated ones like it to take back to his cave for bedding and blankets. A warm hat is jammed over brown curly hair, and glasses are perched on her freckled nose. Her brown skin shines in the light thrown from his screen.

He stays still. It's what he's seen animals do in the forest. Sometimes, with predators who hunt by sight, their prey not moving confuses them.

But humans are strange hunters, and there's nothing in this room for him to blend in. The only recourse available to him is to hope she's not a threat.

There's that word again. *Hope.*

"Are you... What... Um..." she stammers, lifting a hand to her forehead like she's seeing things. As if she closes her eyes and shakes her head and looks again, the thing in front of her won't be there.

He's never understood the phrase: "seeing things." Because she *is* seeing things. Only what she's seeing is real and not a figment of her imagination. *He's* real.

"What are you?" she breathes. Then, more to herself than to him, she adds, "When I thought someone was breaking into the library, I thought it would be, like, annoying teenagers who were under-stimulated or something. Not..." Her follow-up gesture encompasses all of him.

His brow furrows as he considers his next move. She's not running away, she's not screaming anymore, and she's not trying to hurt him. Perhaps she could be...safe. Perhaps she could help him.

"You don't want to hurt me, do you?"

Oh. Just as he was afraid of being hurt by her, she was afraid of being hurt by him. But neither of them wants to hurt anyone. Surely, they can build a truce on that common, solid ground.

Without a mouth, though, he can't communicate in the way humans do. Hopefully, the way he *can* communicate won't terrify her.

He touches his temple and says telepathically, *No, I have no wish to harm you. And you have no wish to harm me, I think?*

She stumbles back a step, her eyes wide. To her credit, though, she recovers from hearing his voice in her head surprisingly quickly.

"You...you can talk to me?"

Yes.

She lets out a low, long whistle. "Wow. Whoa. This is...wild. Okay, I need to sit down for a sec."

She pulls a stool on wheels from the corner and sits, her hands in front of her mouth as she stares at him. What is she looking for, and why doesn't she just ask him?

After a long moment, she straightens on the stool. "My name's Teresa. What's your name?"

I don't have a name.

"You don't have... Well, do you want one?"

A name means he's less a mysterious creature of unknown origin and a more unique individual. A name means you are no longer content with surviving; it means you want to thrive instead. A name is a thing of hope.

Yes. Yes, I want a name, but I don't have one.

She shrugs like this is no obstacle at all. "You can give yourself a name."

You can? What a notion. He brightens at the idea. What should he choose? Should he call himself after one of the things he loves about his home? Honeybee or Sunlight or Azure Sky or Birdsong? Something like that?

"What about Carl?" Teresa suggests.

He shakes his head vigorously. Carl? What kind of human name is that? If he had a nose, he would wrinkle it.

Teresa chuckles, but she's not laughing at him. "Not Carl, then! Never mind! You can think about what you want to be called. We'll come back to that."

He nods absently, still running over name ideas in his mind. He thinks about the books he's read, the authors and characters he's admired.

"You like microfilm, huh?" she asks.

It's a new word for him, and he doesn't answer. He tilts his head in a question.

She points to the rolls. "The newspapers. You like newspapers?"

Oh. Yes. Nodding, he says, *They're informative.*

"Informative? What kind of information are you looking for?"

What your world is like. The types of people who live here. If there are other planets with life out there. And...

"And?"

He looks over at the screen, down at his feet, and finally back to her. She's the first person he'd ever come into contact with, and so far, she seems like someone he can trust. Why not trust her all the way?

And if there's any of my kind here on Earth.

"Your kind?" she asks. "You're alone?"

He nods again. For much of his day, he can keep it at bay, but now, his sadness threatens to overwhelm him.

"I'm so sorry," she says. "I know it's not the same, but I'm kind of alone, too. Ever since I aged out of foster care a couple of years ago, it's been me against the world. Is that what you feel like?"

Yes.

Scooting her chair forward, she places her hand over his. They're so different. His fingers are longer and thinner, and he has fewer of them. But the similarities are heartening, too. More than that, it's the first time anyone has touched him with purpose and tenderness. This is what humans must feel like when they need to cry.

"I think... Let me go find something." She stands, looks through the cabinets for the newspaper she's after, and opens a drawer. A second later, she's back with a roll for *The Nashua Telegraph* from 1977.

After winding up the roll he was looking at, she unloads it and loads the new one she brought. She scrolls quickly to April, then slows as she skims the articles. He has no idea what she's looking for, but his eyes are glued to the screen as he tries to help.

Eventually, she stops on a May 16th issue, on an article with the headline, "'Creatures Are Sighted in the Dover, Mass. Area." The article details how three different teens had seen a strange creature over the course of a night.

It reads, "The teenagers said the creature had no ears, no mouth, and no nose. It is described as 3 ½ feet tall with a white, melon-like head, rough skin, and glowing eyes,"

Below that is what catches his eye. The sketch, drawn by one of the kids in the article, shows a creature that matches that description. *His* description. It's too rough a sketch for the sensation to be like looking into a mirror, but it's unmistakable that it's of a creature just like him.

He gasps. Pointing at the screen, he jumps up and down. *That's me! He looks like me!*

Teresa beams. "That's what I was hoping! I thought you looked familiar."

He rests a palm over his heart. If his new friend hadn't found him, how long would it have taken him to find this information? 1977 was so long ago, and *The Nashua Telegraph* was a small newspaper that was far down on his list.

He feels like he might burst with joy. He's *not* alone.

I need to go, he says. *I need to find him.*

"I thought you might say that," she says. "I can't promise you'll find them. It's been forty-five years. They weren't seen again after that night."

I understand, but I have to try.

If he doesn't, he'll never forgive himself.

"I know," she says. "I know you do."

Dover, Massachusetts. From his study of the national map, he knows that Pennsylvania and Massachusetts aren't too close, but they aren't that far apart, either. First, he'll figure out the distance in miles, and that will help him figure out how long it will take him to walk there. However long it takes, it'll be worth it.

Maybe this creature has a cave like his, where they collect the things they need to live, things like sweatshirts and blankets and flashlights and batteries and books. The things they need to live, but the things that make life worth living, too.

Teresa bites her lip.

What is it? he asks.

"I just bought myself a used car."

That's nice, he says, without understanding why she's telling him this.

"I'd have to look it up, but I bet we could get there in a day."

His heart beats double-time. *We?*

"I'd like to come with you, if that's okay," she says.

If he could smile, he'd do that right now. Going on this adventure with a friend at his side sounds so much better than going it alone. He reaches out and takes her hand, and she squeezes it.

He's not alone anymore.

He squeezes her hand back and says, *Call me Starlight.*

Carrie Gessner specializes in fantasy and science fiction but loves reading and writing all genres. She's written three novels, and her short stories have appeared in various online magazines and anthologies. Outside of writing, she cohosts the *Positively Pop Culture* podcast, enjoys hiking and disc golfing, and is always up for playing Dungeons & Dragons or trying a new TTRPG. You can find her online at www.carriegessner.com or on Twitter @carriegessner.

Two

MYTHS

GNOMIES

By Kevin Plybon

THE BEAST TOOK GLADYS at midday, in plain sight, right in the middle of our name game. I saw it from the corner of my eye: paws landing lightly, a purr, the clink of teeth on Gladys's porcelain robes, tail swishing between the rest of us.

Then the cat was off, leaping the backyard fence and down the hill, into the next yard with Gladys in its mouth.

The funny thing was that Gladys kept playing the name game even as it took her. *Kevin Bacon!* she cried, her thoughts fading as she went farther away.

The game was simple, but it passed the time. Use the first letter of the previous last name to say a famous person. Double up to send it back to the previous player.

Barry Bonds, I stammered. A double, hoping I could keep Gladys talking.

Her faint reply: *Bill Burr—*

It cut off.

Beside me, Johnny gulped. He was short and chubby, with sad, pea-colored robes. *Is she?*, he said.

Seems like it, I said.

Can you see her, Linda?

A little.

I was a half-foot taller than him. Grace, the Overlord, had placed the four of us beside the backyard pool this morning on a glass tabletop, and I was closest to the edge.

The back door of the neighbor's brick house at the bottom of the hill stood open. The cat trotted inside, and I caught a flash of Gladys's pointy red hat.

Is she all right? Wendell said with a whimper. Wendell was the oldest, his own hat faded from the sun. His body listed, as if the heat had melted him over time.

It took her inside, I said. *She might be back. Someone just moved in down there.*

A moment of silence, then Wendell said, *I was so scared just now that I could have sworn I flinched.*

Give it a rest, I scoffed.

I swear I scooted a millimeter.

You have no muscles, *old-timer.*

The morning sun emerged from a cloud and beat on my porcelain front, everything pleasantly warm. The back of me was cool, damp with dew. None of us knew what to say.

Then the rear door to our house opened and I saw the shadow of the Overlord. She watched us for a moment before retreating inside.

She must have seen that Gladys was missing, Johnny whispered.

The screen door at the front of the house slammed, then footsteps crunched down the hill on the gravel path toward the neighbor's house. As the Overlord came into view, I saw her in black jeans, sandals, and an oversized T-shirt.

She's going down there, I hissed.

Thank the Overlord, Wendell said.

A faint knock echoed up the hill, then the creak of hinges. Muffled voices. Beside us, a breeze rippled the green-gunk surface of the pool, a good little gust that rocked me.

What do you suppose they're talking about? Wendell said.

Johnny's voice was pitched high, terrified. *Gladys has to be okay.*

After an eternity, I heard footsteps crunching back. The Overlord came out to the pool and clinked Gladys down in her proper spot: the fourth corner of our square arrangement.

She rotated us inward, so we all faced each other. Showing off our colorful robes, white beards, rosy cheeks. Nobody could compete with my polished boots, of course, the tips curled perfectly.

"The four gnomies reunite," the Overlord said. "I'll figure out a fix for you, Gladys." She patted my head and went back inside.

We all noticed at the same time that the tip of Gladys's red hat was cracked right off.

Wendell gasped. *Oh, Gladys!*

It's kind of chic, I offered.

Gladys said something very quiet.

What was that? Johnny said.

She cleared her throat. *I'm. I'm all right.* Her voice was faint.

Does it hurt?

A little.

What happened? Wendell whispered. He must have been thinking of his own brittleness if those teeth had snatched him, instead.

...dropped me on the kitchen floor, Gladys said.

The Overlord will fix it, I said. *They need to lock that animal up.*

She was angry when she came in. Yelling at that woman. But after a few minutes, they were laughing in the kitchen.

Johnny gasped. *She can't be* friends *with her.*

I don't know. Bad form.

She'll fix your hat, I said. *She said she would.*

BUT THE DAMN CAT returned that evening.

The Overlord had rearranged us into a straight line, so I couldn't even see when Wendell was taken. All I know is that Gladys shrieked, and then it was Wendell crying hysterically for help, fading down the hill.

The Overlord reacted fast this time—she must have been watching out the window—and dashed after the cat. Nearly caught him. I saw her bang on the back door of the neighbor's house.

Still, I felt sick. Wendell was old and mossy, no way he'd survive.

We aren't safe, Johnny cried out.

I wish I could kick it in its rear, I muttered. But I couldn't help the fear that bubbled up. Sooner or later, one of us was going to get smashed or knocked into the dark, slimy pool.

Gladys was a blubbering mess. She hadn't been herself since her hat broke, her thoughts soft and getting softer. Johnny had whispered to me that Gladys might just fade away.

But thank the Overlord, it was only a few minutes before she came back up the hill. And another woman walked with her.

Tall, with long, brown hair, wearing a neon tank top. She sauntered beside the Overlord like an equal.

They came out to the pool deck. The Overlord settled Wendell beside us. The old-timer was still hyperventilating.

You're safe, I said, *you're back. Look around.*

Thank the Overlord you're safe, Johnny said.

Wendell let out a few long breaths. His hat wasn't damaged, and his robes had only the usual scratches and scuffs. His limp brown shoes were whole.

The Overlord gestured at us, and the tall woman from the house down the hill folded her arms, glancing at the murky pool. She squatted to get eye-level with us.

"You collect these things?" she said.

The Overlord smiled. "Just the four, for now. Two boys, two girls."

"I'm so sorry about Jammers. She doesn't usually act like this." The woman leaned over Wendell. "It was this guy, right? Nothing broken?"

"He's fine. I appreciate it."

I felt it again, Wendell muttered, *I almost moved, I swear. Could have got away.*

I nearly snapped back that he was a fool, but Gladys was staring at me. Her hat was still broken.

"I'm Eleanor, by the way," the woman said, holding out her hand to the Overlord. "I didn't get your name, earlier."

The Overlord took it. "Grace."

ELEANOR LEFT, AND THE Overlord set about cleaning us. Wiped each of us down with a wet rag, even peeled the old price tag off Johnny's boot. Not that it did much to help his outfit, poor fellow. Lottery of birth. She scraped at some dirt in Gladys's broken cap.

"I'm sorry, I've been lazy," she muttered. "I shouldn't let you all go like this."

It *did* feel nice to be clean. She kissed each of our foreheads and tickled our bellies.

You look great, Linda, Johnny said to me, clearing his throat.

I stood proudly. The tallest of the four, in robes of brightest green.

The Overlord arranged us in a square and set a candle in the precise center. Then she sat and folded her legs, then closed her eyes.

"Goddamned cat had better watch herself," she muttered. She gestured sharply in the air, once, twice, and said, "Wendell Walker."

Wendell gave a deep sigh and quieted.

She turned to me, gestured once, twice. "Linda Letty."

The pool went dark, and I fell asleep.

THE NEXT DAY, THE Overlord wrapped each of us carefully in tissue paper and bubble wrap, placed us in a cardboard box, and shut the lid.

The box rose. We clinked against each other.

She's selling us, Gladys wailed. It was the loudest she'd been since her injury.

She needs us, I said. *She wouldn't.*

The box had holes punched in the sides, and I saw that we were passing through the Overlord's house. Jars of dried, green leaves, bundles of sticks wrapped in twine, candles in a star shape.

Then we were out the front door. The facade that faced the lane outside was stately brick, a view I'd only seen once before when the Overlord brought me home.

Gravel crunched. We were going down the hill.

She's giving us to the cat! yelled Johnny.

Cold terror suffused me. I wished that I could flex my arms, tear the tissue wrappings from my body.

After a moment, the crunching stopped. The rap of knuckles on wood. Squeaky hinges.

"Hi!" Eleanor's voice.

"Thanks for having me," the Overlord said.

"Come on in."

Hard footsteps, the rustle of carpet. The box rocked, the Overlord setting us down.

"It's a mess, sorry," Eleanor said.

"I didn't even notice."

There was a song playing in the house. A woman's voice, pure and slow.

IIIIII'm sticking with you. 'Cause IIIIII'm made out of glue.

"I love this song," the Overlord said.

Light flooded the box and I rose, the Overlord undoing my wrappings and clinking me down.

Linda, Johnny cried.

I stood on a coffee table in a modest living room. Cardboard boxes were stacked against the walls. Above a bare mantle hung a single painting of Jammers the cat in spotted glory, precisely rendered in oil.

In fact, Eleanor seemed to have focused only on unpacking for Jammers. Fuzzy cat climbers stood around the room with ropes strung between them. I could smell the faint musk of a litter box.

Wendell shouted after me. *What's happening?*

There was no sugar-coating it. *She's giving us to the cat,* I whispered.

Overlord, please! Gladys wailed.

The Overlord set the others beside me, arranging us in a half-circle pattern that usually meant she was pleased. Their eyes were wide with fear.

Eleanor tapped her lip, looking down at us. She wore jean shorts and a Radiohead T-shirt today. "I found that little piece of her, hang on."

She disappeared into the next room. I heard ripping cardboard.

The Overlord glanced at the cat climbers, a small smile on her face. I couldn't tell what she was thinking. Not that I ever can.

Eleanor returned with something in her hand.

It's a gun! Wendell screamed.

It's a glue gun, idiot, I said.

Eleanor plugged in the blue plastic tool and waited for it to heat up. She gestured at Gladys's broken hat. "May I?"

"Please," the Overlord said.

Eleanor gently squeezed a dollop of hot glue on the jagged white porcelain. Then she carefully rotated the small, broken piece of the hat until it fit.

"There."

The Overlord smiled. "Almost like new."

Gladys? I said.

It...doesn't hurt anymore, she said. *It feels fixed.*

"Let's try Jammers," Eleanor said. She walked to a closed door. "If you still want to?"

The Overlord nodded. "It's worth a try."

The door cracked open and something brown flashed through.

Cat, cried Johnny.

No, Gladys shouted.

Jammers streaked to her owner first, curling her body around Eleanor's ankles. She made two full rotations and then she saw us.

She landed softly on the coffee table. Her tail swished across the polished wood. Her golden eyes pierced my soul.

We are dead, dead, dead, Wendell moaned.

"Hey!" Eleanor said.

The cat's head snapped toward her.

"Play nice with the gnomies."

Those demon eyes locked onto me, and she purred, crouched.

"Hey!" Eleanor said again. "Play nice!"

She repeated the process a few times until Jammers flinched whenever she looked at us. Finally, Eleanor allowed her forward and she passed right through our formation. I giggled as her tail brushed across my back.

Miraculously, Jammers reached the other side without even glancing at us. She leaped back to Eleanor and curled around her ankles twice.

"Fantastic," the Overlord said. She even clapped, which I'd never seen her do.

Eleanor shrugged. "Easy with such cute gnomies."

"You know the way to a girl's heart."

"If we do it a few more days, I think I'll be able to let him out."

The Overlord rose and brushed off her jeans. "Could I get a tour of the house?"

"Let me put Jammers up."

The cat was scooped away, shut behind the door in what Eleanor described as "the seedy-hotel bathroom." The two women piled through another door, into the primary bedroom, and I heard them giggling.

Never in all my years, whispered Wendell. *She's never let anything touch us like that.*

Johnny grunted. His portly cheeks shone in the lamplight. *Burn that cat with fire.*

I don't trust her, I agreed. *She'll steal us again as soon as we're alone, we'll end up like—*

I stopped myself from saying Gladys. Beside me, she sniffled, her thoughts still far too quiet.

We need a plan, I said.

There's nothing to plan, Wendell said, *it's hopeless—*

I have to tell you something.

T HE OVERLORD BROUGHT US back to the pool-side glass table, arranged us in a perfect square. "Farmer's market day," she said in a sing-song tone and left.

And once she was gone, I told them: I could move.

Not a lot. No more than a half-inch scoot, and even that was exhausting. But I hadn't told anyone. I certainly hadn't shown the Overlord. I made sure to always scoot back into formation so that when she came out in the morning, I was right where I needed to be.

I would have preferred to keep it to myself. It was my special thing. But these were desperate times.

The others were dumbfounded.

Are you joking? Wendell asked.

That isn't right, Johnny said. *You made such fun of him. Anyhow, I don't believe you.*

I could almost imagine his chubby cheeks crinkling with disapproval if they weren't made of porcelain.

It was harsh, I said. *I'm sorry about that.*

Johnny huffed. *It isn't right.*

Wendell himself was curious, though.

Show me, he insisted. *I'll bet I can do it.*

I waited a moment, letting them take me in, tall and gorgeous in green. Until I knew that Wendell was itching to speak.

It's the name game, I said. *But only use the double letters. You just need one of those and you can do it.*

How do you mean? Johnny said.

Concentrating, I let my awareness meander from the point of my hat to the end of my beard, to the tips of my shoes. I flexed...something...and said, *Tina Turner!* and then—

Scoot.

My unpainted bottom scraped on scalloped glass.

Wendell and Johnny gasped.

We can use it if Jammers comes back, I said proudly. *It isn't difficult.*

I had noticed the new awareness a few weeks ago, while we played the name game to pass the time. I didn't know why the double letter triggered it.

Gladys sat quietly. I wondered whether the hairline crack in her hat was still having some effect. Her polished face betrayed nothing.

I can do it, too, she said. Her voice was barely audible. *I thought it was just me.*

I stared, shocked.

Wendell sighed. *No respect.*

For how long? I said, a bit deflated.

A month or two. I woke up one morning and accidentally... Tiny Tim!

She jerked forward a half-inch, her face glinting in the sun.

I was impressed. Of all people, I didn't expect Gladys to keep such a secret.

You aren't the only one, Johnny said to me.

Next, we'll find out that you can leap tall buildings, I grumbled.

He ignored me. *Teach me. Somebody!*

We spent the afternoon practicing mindfulness, feeling the sun spread along our porcelain trousers, up our robes, along our shiny skin. There were a lot of curses, but eventually, Johnny and Wendell both scooted. Little impossible scrapes.

Peter Parker!

Farrah Fawcett!

Kevin Kline!

For my part, I think I could go a whole inch by the end of the day. Strafing sideways, then back into formation. I scooted all the way to the edge of the table and watched the green pool, dark moss in its depths.

Behind me, Johnny was getting frustrated.

How is this going to save us from the cat? he whined. *I suppose I'll scoot to the other side of the table and hope for the best.*

It might scare him, Gladys said. *He won't expect it.*

A surprised cat, that's all we need.

I summoned my calmest mind and said, *Charlie Chaplin!*, rotating this time. Facing them. *We can't just sit here and wait. At least now we can act.*

It's not enough, Wendell said. *J is right.*

The front door creaked. The Overlord was home from the market.

Inside, I heard her fiddling with something, then a record scratching. And then a woman's voice.

IIIII'm sticking with you. 'Cause IIIIII'm made out of glue.

Footsteps, coming toward the back door.

Move! I hissed. *Move!*

We scooted back into a square formation as quickly as we could. Johnny was lagging, huffing and puffing, and only got himself on his mark with seconds to spare.

The Overlord came out. Walked to us, smiling faintly. She carried a bowl of soup—chicken and wild rice—it looked like.

I held my breath. I wasn't sure what she would do if she knew we'd been moving.

"It's trapezoid night," she said, grabbing Wendell and Gladys gently by the caps and sliding them into position. Then she lit a candle and set it in the center of us.

She sat down, folding her legs beneath her. She kissed each of us on the hat, taking special care with Gladys. Then she raised a hand and gestured sharply once, twice, and said, "Johnny James." Johnny had been breathing heavily but fell silent.

The candle flared and the bowl of soup steamed. The Overlord lifted a spoonful to her lips and blew. She ate slowly, watching us.

When she was finished, she said, "Sleep well, friends." She gestured sharply once, twice, said, "Linda Letty," and I slept.

THE NEXT MORNING, JAMMERS returned.

Eleanor must have let him out. Johnny was the first one up and shrieked, *Cat!*

In an instant, we were all awake and shouting at once. Jammers sat on the chain link fence, the sun rising behind her, watching. Her tail swished, her golden eyes pierced.

What do we do? Wendell whispered.

She isn't moving, Johnny said. *Maybe she's afraid.*

Jammers' head rotated left, then right, and I understood: she was testing us.

I let my awareness flow to the tip of my cap and back to my toes. Felt the cool morning dew on my shoulders. And then I yelled, *Mickey Mantle!* and scooted forward.

Jammers twitched.

It's the training, I said, *she thinks somebody's going to yell at her. Everybody move!*

One by one we jerked forward, scraping across the glass table. With each movement, Jammers hissed and pawed at the air.

That's it, Gladys cried, *forward!*

She scooted faster than any of us until she was nearly at the edge—and tipped.

Her pink nose described a slow-motion arc toward the table, her entire body rotating down, and then the point of Gladys's cap smacked the glass and snapped off for a second time.

She screamed. Startled by the sound of tinkling porcelain, Jammers hissed one last time and leaped off the fence, headed back down the hill.

Gladys, I shouted.

Gladys whimpered. Desperately I yelled double names, scooting forward, and I heard Johnny and Wendell scraping along behind me.

But then we heard that song start up, playing from the record player inside.

IIIIII'm sticking with you.

The Overlord must be awake. She'd be coming.

I nudged Gladys, trying to find any leverage, but of course it was useless. *Help me!* I called to the others.

They were too far.

I can't think of a double, Gladys whispered. I couldn't see her face—her back was to me.

Mike Meyers, try it!

You have to leave me.

I will not, I growled, scooting.

It was the dew, I think, that I slipped on. It made the glass slick beneath my bottom. And then I was tipping like Gladys had.

Falling over the side, off the table, the concrete deck rushing up at me, the murky water.

I splashed into the pool and sank.

It was quiet at the bottom. Scummy green light. A frog kicked by on its way to the drain.

I cursed myself. I supposed this was what I deserved.

Maybe I should have shown the Overlord what I could do. Maybe she would have loved it, polished me up, watched me.

Maybe I shouldn't have been such a tool to Wendell.

Something splashed. I was rising through the muck, the dark bottom receding. I broke the surface and heard the Overlord cry out.

"Linda!"

She reeled in her pool basket and lifted me carefully out, inspecting me. "No cracks," she muttered. She toweled me off and set me back on the table beside the others.

You're alive! Wendell said.

What about Gladys, is she all right? I asked.

Then I saw her. Her entire cap snapped off and a jagged, hollow shell was where most of her face used to be. She stood in the sunlight like a broken monument.

Wendell gasped, horrified.

Gladys? I whispered.

I...can't see, she said.

Thank the Overlord you can speak, Johnny said.

The Overlord stood over us, arms folded. She tsked. "You all saw that I warned her about that cat."

You're damn right, Wendell said.

"I'll fix this. Don't you worry."

THE OVERLORD DISAPPEARED DOWN the hill again, presumably to speak with Eleanor.

Me, Johnny, and Wendell crowded around Gladys, trying to comfort her.

Are you in pain? Johnny asked.

I feel...thin, she said.

Can you scoot?

I don't think I could move an inch.

The sun was fully risen now, and it poured through the hole in her head. It illuminated her hollow guts: unpainted porcelain, the dark cavity that was the inside of her arm.

I couldn't look away. There was no getting around it; this was my fault. My stupid plan.

Gladys murmured something.

What's that? I said.

I think I'll go to sleep, she whispered.

I scooted forward and nudged her. *I'll start the game. Jason Bourne.*

Billy Bush, she said.

Barbara Bush.

You can't use the same...last name. Bad form.

We continued, and for a time it almost seemed like she was getting stronger. But her voice was fading. It took her longer and longer to speak, and eventually she stopped talking altogether.

The rest of us went quiet. Wendell wept softly.

The Overlord's footsteps crunched up the hill. Then, a little later, another set of feet arrived, and she and Eleanor both came out onto the pool deck.

Eleanor was biting her lip as if she couldn't wait to get out of there. She carried a brown paper bag with something heavy in it. When she set it down beside our table, it clinked.

"Oh, God," she said. "I'm so sorry."

The Overlord didn't say anything, just reached into the bag. She pulled out something blue, about my height, and set it on the table, beside Gladys.

Another gnome.

"Is she about what you wanted?" Eleanor said.

It was a female with starry robes of deep blue. Her boots were thick and sturdy, her cap a full inch taller than mine. Her cheeks puffed beneath eyes of pleasant green.

I felt a twinge of jealousy. She was maybe as beautiful as me.

Hello? I asked.

The new gnome said nothing.

"It can't replace the one that Jammers broke," Eleanor said, touching the Overlord's arm. "But she's just a gnome. This one's beautiful, right?"

"Just a gnome," the Overlord said. "Your last name is Edwards, right?"

Eleanor frowned. "What about it?"

"Eleanor Edwards. It's hard to find a double. Powerful, though."

The Overlord bent over the table and began to rearrange us in a new pattern. A straight line, with the new gnome at the head. She held Gladys in one hand upside-down, by her bottom.

"Why do you put them in these formations?" Eleanor asked, watching.

A breeze rippled the surface of the pool. The Overlord took Eleanor's hand and drew her toward the edge.

"So I know if they're getting antsy," she said. She glanced at me, and I nearly jumped.

Eleanor examined the pool. "What do you mean?"

The Overlord took her by the hips. Looked back at the four of us in a row—well, three and the newbie—and moved Eleanor slightly to the right. The real tip of the line.

"You never know," the Overlord said. "Gladys Gable was so bright, I swear she might have just walked away one day."

Eleanor tsked, drawing the Overlord's arm around her waist. "Gladys Gable. There was somebody on the news with that name. I can't remember."

"Yes."

"It was that woman at the farmer's market. The one who vanished."

"I'll never get her back. You broke her. I have to have four, it's always four."

Eleanor tried to turn around. "What—"

With calculated force, the Overlord raised Gladys's lifeless body and brought it down on Eleanor's head. Gladys broke into three large pieces of porcelain that fell to the concrete and smashed to bits.

Eleanor cried out once, then toppled into the pool. The Overlord jumped in after her, and in two minutes it was over.

THE OVERLORD DRAGGED ELEANOR'S body up the green-stained pool stairs and across the deck. She went back inside for a moment, and I heard that glue song start up. It echoed out the kitchen window. She came back with a shovel, then pulled Eleanor behind the hedge row beside the pool.

IT WAS EVENING, AN orange sliver of sun showing just above the Overlord's house. The four of us stood in a perfect square formation on the glass table. Me, Wendell, Johnny, and the blue female. At each corner and in the exact center of the square sat a flickering candle.

Ungh, Johnny said.

Wendell was waking up, too. *What happened?*

The new gnome spoke.

Where am I? Her voice was soft, like she was far away.

She speaks! Johnny said.

You're by the pool, I said. *Are you all right?*

I had a memory then of doing this same thing. Only it was me waking up. Wendell and Johnny with their shiny faces pointed right at me. And someone else, whose name I couldn't remember.

I'm...all right. Her voice was getting louder, I thought.

I wished that I could get closer, provide some comfort. But gnomes couldn't move, everybody knew that.

Welcome to the party, Wendell said.

Johnny grunted. *We should introduce her to the name game.*

What's that? she asked.

I knew her voice from somewhere, but I couldn't place it.

From inside the house, I heard the Overlord moving in the kitchen. Plates clinking. And then a song, floating over the pool.

IIIIII'm sticking with you. 'Cause IIIII'm made out of glue.

I love that song, the newbie murmured.

I've never heard it, I said, *it's nice.*

Is that a cat? Wendell said.

It was. A spotted cat perched on the fence, watching us with golden eyes.

It's cute, Johnny said.

The cat leaped onto the table and came between us. It curled around the newbie's body and circled her twice.

The back door banged open, and the Overlord appeared, shooing the cat away. "I'll have to set a ward," she muttered. She set down a bowl of soup.

Do you have a name? I asked as the Overlord arranged her meal.

The newbie watched shadows play on the green surface of the pool. The cat was back, eyeing us from the fence.

Eleanor, she said.

KEVIN PLYBON IS A technical writer and author based in the Bronx. He lives with his wife, her preposterous collection of sewing machines, and their two-year-old monster (er, daughter). He's the author of three novels—one fantasy, one speculative fiction, one murder mystery—and is dreaming up a fourth. You can find him on Twitter @kevilknc and find other published work at kevinplybon.com

DON'T FEED THE TROLL

by Katharine Dow

Humans are blowing up my bridge. *Humans are blowing up my bridge!*

"Get up, troll, humans are blowing up your bridge. We have to run. Now!"

The hydra who lives down the river is crouched over me, and all nine of her heads are screaming in my face.

I'm flat on my back. The air is so thick with dust it's choking me. The loot I'd been counting is scattered everywhere.

I think I've lost my club.

The hydra smacks me across the face with one of her paws. She hits me so hard her sharp claws nearly puncture my thick skin. I gingerly wrap my arms around one of her necks and she yanks me to my feet. We stagger down the bank of the river in a clumsy run.

For weeks, I follow the hydra who saved me. I don't know what to do, but I hope at least one of her heads does.

I eventually run across a banshee lurking on the outskirts of some mostly human city who tells me that if I venture inside, I'll discover a farm for trolls.

Like a fool, I weep with relief, forgetting that banshees never speak to you unless it's about death.

"Hey new guy, if someone wants to impress a siren, where would you take her on a date?"

I look up to see Jayson, my human manager, peeking over the top of my cubicle. I have no idea why he thinks a troll would have any idea what to do on a date with a siren, but I answer anyway.

"Don't take her to the beach. Or a river. Or a pool. Do you have running water at your place?"

"Umm. Yeah..."

"Don't take her to your apartment, then." I think about it for a while, ignoring the messages popping up on my screen. "Has she tried to kill you yet?"

"Only once or twice. Is that a good or bad sign?"

"That means it's going really well so far," I guess. Jayson blinks at me. Out of advice, I turn back to my computer. He tosses a bag of donuts at my back and backs away so quickly he almost knocks one of the "don't feed the troll" signs off the wall.

My chair wobbles ominously when I shift to look for the food he threw at me. I go through a couple of new chairs a month. My manager doesn't understand that human chairs are never going to work for me and refuses to invest in a standing desk.

I pick up the bag and chew it slowly. He clears his throat, and I realize that I'm supposed to eat the donuts outside of the bag, like humans do.

"Take her to a karaoke bar," I suggest. "Sirens like to sing."

His eyes grow wide with excitement. I've done well.

"Thanks, that's perfect. I owe you!"

"So, am I getting the raise we talked about?"

He laughs the way he always does. He knows I don't have anywhere else to go.

Before I found my way to the nondescript building that would become both my workplace and occasional crash pad, and before I discovered what a human troll farm actually was, I was just a simple troll who lived alone under a bridge, following the path of my ancestors. Humans were just creatures I chased around and took money from. It never occurred to me to wonder what humans thought I was. I was a fool.

But, if I'm honest, before I turned into some corporate loser with a Wi-Fi connection pushing conspiracy theories for whoever wanted to pay us, I hadn't actually pulled off a proper shakedown in at least a hundred years. I'd barely even scared anyone for decades. Instead, my life had gradually shrunk into a mundane daily routine consisting of hiding under my bridge from the sun during the day and listening to the roar of traffic above at night, wondering why everyone was in such a hurry. It was lovely down there. The rocks I sat among were covered with verdant green moss in the summer and slick icy crowns in the winter. The spiders, my friends, wove their tough, sticky webs in every shadow.

I occasionally had a visitor, usually some *thing* on vacation from haunting a house or in-between possessions. Once in a while, another troll stopped by to fill me in on what was happening in the world, which I liked the most. But most of the time, I simply shivered alone, wrapped in the darkness under my old stone bridge, thinking.

There had been a time when I could just demand whatever I wanted from whoever was dumb enough to walk past. I used to love watching humans tiptoe across my bridge. I knew they hoped I'd be taking a nap and wouldn't feel the vibration. I loved the way they screamed when I suddenly appeared, howling at the top of my lungs, waving my muscular arms in the air, the odor from my unwashed armpits knocking them straight to their knees, choking for breath. It was wonderful. It was simple. It was a little predictable, but it worked for me.

The minute the car was invented, my luck started to change. Sure, at first, cars were slow and clumsy and didn't cause me too many problems. I could catch up to them pretty quickly. Frankly, the chases were fun—lots of chaos for very little effort. I would swat at those little cars until they spun around on their metal backs like overturned beetles. But eventually, the cars got bigger and sturdier, the drivers more confident, and just like all of my kind, I started to feel more like roadkill than monster.

If that wasn't bad enough, at some point, people stopped carrying coins around with them. First it was cash, which got wet and moldy no matter what hole I buried it in. Then the humans started carrying plastic cards around, claiming they were the same as gold and silver when they clearly were not anything of the sort.

I should have realized it was all over the day I caught a human, and he begged me to let him send me invisible money, through the air, from some small metal box called a "cell phone." As if I would fall for that rotten lie. I held that fool upside down and shook him, expecting money to fall out. The only thing that fell out of his pocket was his buzzing phone. The one he claimed was magic.

"WHAT ONLINE IDENTITY DID I assign you?" My manager is back. He's brought me a pizza this time. I notice that the sign about not feeding me is still on the wall.

"I'm a nineteen-year-old college student in Chicago. I'm in a band. I have controversial food opinions, and I love astrology."

"Why can't your student spell?"

I look down at my hands, embarrassed by his question. Technically, I have fingers like humans do, but mine are so thick and so clumsy, they operate more like clubs. I tried to hold hands with another troll once, tried to tenderly tuck a clump of matted hair behind a pointed ear, but my attempt ended with an accidental poke to an eye, followed by a hard kick to my tender places in return.

When I use my computer at work, I have to type on a specially designed keyboard, each key as big and clumsy as a baby's fist. It barely works. Because typing is difficult for me, none of my fake personas can spell. He's just never noticed before.

My manager is leaning over my shoulder, peering at my screen. "Is this true?" he asks. "Is St. Louis style pizza really better than Chicago style?"

"That's not the point. People are very sensitive about pizza. Which is exactly why he's pushing it so hard. Next, he's going to pick a fight with New Yorkers."

"He's going to insult their pizza? He'll be murdered."

"He's not real. He'll be fine."

He laughs at my comment with unnecessary zest. I hear a high-pitched giggle from a nearby cubicle and watch as he straightens his shirt, a grin spreading slowly across his face. He winks at me and walks off in search of the giggle.

I like to get him back when he annoys me by stealing his car and leaving it in different places around town. He always finds it eventually, but even with my lingering scent on the seats to alert him, he's never figured out that it's me.

A<small>FTER A YEAR OF</small> pretending online to be everything from a yoga enthusiast in California to a fashion designer in Dakar, I finally go viral. I panic when my manager first brings it up, as I assume he's figured out that I'm the cause of the illness that has spread rapidly through the humans in the office.

To my relief, it turns out that "going viral" has nothing to do with the complexities of troll digestion and everything to do with the success of one of my online identities. He tells me that because of my hard work, within a week, over a million parents had pulled their children out of school, and someone tried to drive a golf cart through a library window.

My manager plans to take me out for drinks to celebrate, until he realizes that with me along as company, the only places in which he's likely to get served would be the sort where he is also likely to end the evening as dinner.

He runs out for some cans of troll beer instead. I had been under the impression that humans had banned it, but he makes some calls and claims to know a guy who knows a guy who has some. For hours, I wait patiently for him to return. When he finally comes back, without beer, he is covered in blood, and he seems to have forgotten about celebrating. I feel a bit bad for him, but humans never seem to know when you can trust someone with your life, and when it's time to run.

"IT DOESN'T MATTER IF what you're promoting makes sense, or if it completely contradicts with other things the same identity is promoting, it just has to be simple. It should speak to some kind of fear about the future, and it needs to provide someone with at least the illusion of community. It's lonely out there. People want to feel like they belong."

My manager is giving us one of his occasional refresher trainings. Things have gotten a bit weird with him since the night he went out to buy us beer and came back injured.

We've started an office pool to try to figure out what's wrong with him. Given his brand-new sun allergy and craving for fresh blood, vampire is the most obvious choice, and has generated the most excitement so far—especially among the ladies. But someone from the second floor claimed she walked in on him hiding a bloody axe under his desk the other night, so there is an active rumor that he could have turned into something more locally menacing, like a Pope Lick monster or a real estate investor. Then again, the bloody axe would also make sense if he was transforming into something exotic and old, like a minotaur. But no one is sure if a human can transform into a minotaur, so that option isn't popular either.

I've been in a slump since my big moment. Sure, it spiraled into a movement to somehow ban both the treatment for Parkinson's disease and the *Real Florists of Tennessee* show, but if anyone even remembered what—or who—started it all, I would have been shocked. My manager is so preoccupied with his new issues, whatever they are, that he hasn't threatened my job in a week. I'm taking advantage of the break in daily harassment to ignore my assignments and order a couple of plastic sporks to send anonymously to my coworkers. To my delight, I've recently discovered that receiving a spork in the mail for no reason at all is absolutely terrifying.

I roll my shoulders. *Nothing exists until we say it exists.* I close my eyes and take a deep breath. *The truth changes when we change it.*

Memories of ruined bridges intrude. The horror of stepping in a puddle of blood and squeezing my eyes shut, hoping I wouldn't see what it belonged to. *As long as what we tell them allows people to feel powerful, they'll believe anything. More important, they'll do anything.* I take another deep breath and crack my knuckles. The sound is as sharp as a slap. *There is nothing stronger in humans than that desire—not family, not friends, not gods, nothing.*

MY MANAGER IS SLUMPED in the corner behind me eating something he insists is a tomato. The bright juices run down his chin and stain the collar of his shirt. His story would be more believable if our security guard had not just gone missing.

"WE HAVE A NEW account. I want you to work on it." My manager is staring at my neck while he talks. It would take him hours to gnaw through my skin, so I'm not really worried about it, but his intense interest is still unsettling.

"More health stuff?"

"No, we've been hired to work on a local election in a town so small and broke that the mayor is basically a voluntary position. The incumbent is some older lady. Owns the local diner as her day job or something like that. Our job is to make sure she loses."

"To whom?"

"Someone from the town next door, some guy who moved just in time to qualify as a resident. Our job is not only to get the newcomer elected, but also to dismantle the current mayor's life. Just burn it to the ground. The account is massive so I'm putting like five or six of you on this job."

His shirt is torn. He's wearing all black—better to hide bloodstains, I suppose. He's also sniffing the air. I suspect he's already forgotten our conversation.

"Who do you want me to be?" I ask him.

"Your pick," he answers, after an uncomfortably long pause. "You can choose a concerned mom account or a husband/pastor/father account, and of course we need a variety of fake activists from various other places with a range of very strong opinions both for and against the incumbent—you have creative freedom for one of those."

"Jayson, why would anyone pay a bunch of money to swing a local election?"

"Not your problem, troll."

My manager has started to pull himself together, but every couple of days another team member goes missing, so no one is really watching me too closely. They're mostly just watching him. I'm curious about the weirdness of this assignment, so I decide to dig.

I LIVE IN A room above an abandoned garage. It's the only thing I love in my new life. No one else is around to complain that I use ash to bathe instead of water, or that I don't wear pants. I don't mind that the windows are cracked or that the electricity is out. It's exactly the kind of dark, moldy space that suits me just fine.

On nights I'm not working, I like to sit on the roof and stare at the bridge the city is building across the river nearby. It was apparently blown up the same year as my bridge, and construction has been progressing ever since at a sluggish pace. Better to drive the costs up, I assume.

I often wonder where the troll who used to live there went, and if they found something better to do with their life than I did.

THE CHIEF OPERATING OFFICER and her assistant work during the day, so by the time I arrive for the night shift, they're usually long gone. They have access to all kinds of confidential information, so they're supposed to keep their office locked.

To my delight, not only is the door half open, but the filing cabinet is also on its side and folders are scattered everywhere. A smear of blood is on the carpet right next to the cabinet.

I squat down to search the piles, cursing the ridiculously fine texture of human paper. It doesn't take me long to find what I'm looking for. It's a copy of an invoice sent to my new project's mystery funder. It's a construction company, Thump Construction, Inc. I flip through the folder and find invoices going back a decade. All billed to the same company for ridiculous amounts of money.

My manager floats past down the hall. He appears to be sharpening his teeth against a whetstone. He doesn't see me hiding my bulky body behind the cabinet.

G<small>IVEN THE NUMBER OF</small> employees who have disappeared, I figure it's going to be a while before anyone notices a pack of missing invoices, so I find an empty room to hide out in and start looking up Thump Construction and the geographic locations listed in the invoices. It doesn't take long for a pattern to emerge. Each location is the site of a bridge blown up during the height of the persecution of trolls. The era when most of us lost our bridges, and some of us, our lives.

And then I see it in the stack of invoices. The name of the small town near *my* former bridge. For a full minute, I can't breathe.

The amount of money on the invoice is pathetic. This was clearly treated as a part-time job, assigned to someone new and inexperienced. They destroyed my life for the price of a nice bottle of whisky.

Hands shaking, I do a quick search to see if Thump Construction won the contract to rebuild my bridge. Unsurprisingly, they did, exactly two years after they hired my 'fellow farmers' to ruin my life.

For the first time, I look up the human news to see what happened to my old bridge and me from their perspective.

Turns out that, while I had never had a lot of fans, things had changed for the worse after voters threw out the long-time mayor, and an ambitious new mayor had come into power with funding from Thump Construction and the online assistance of our troll farm.

The new mayor understood that you don't have to solve anything to get elected, you just have to give people someone or something to hate and they'll give you whatever you want.

All it took was one of my colleagues to go online and blame trolls for everything. Some human I probably work with now convinced the voters to throw the old mayor out of power. My company convinced people to blow up the troll bridges. And when they ran out of bridges to destroy, the new mayor made sure Thump Construction won the bids to rebuild.

I force myself to my feet and squeeze out the door, barely able to process what I've learned.

My company and Thump Construction ran the same stupid con across the entire country. Now, it seems, I work for Thump Construction, running stupid cons too.

THE ENTIRE OFFICE BUILDING is nothing but overturned chairs and blood splatters. I find my manager hiding under his desk, sobbing. He and I are the only ones around.

"Everyone still alive just quit on me," he wails. "What am I supposed to do now?"

I couldn't be less interested in his problems right now. Part of being a monster is figuring out how to manage your own chaos, and he's frankly doing a terrible job of it. I pick him up and set him on top of a filing cabinet. He stops crying and sits quietly for once. He stares at me without blinking, his eyes enormous in his face.

"When you hired me, did you know Thump Construction was behind the destruction of my bridge? Did you know they were behind a campaign of terror against trolls?"

He nods, too full of self-pity to be afraid that an enormous troll, with skin as thick and difficult to pierce as wood, is looming over him.

His indifference to my suffering is so astonishing it takes me a moment to catch my breath. When I can finally process my feelings, my entire body begins to tremble. I've never felt this level of pure, unadulterated rage before. Not when I lost my bridge. Not even the night I realized I would never have a home again.

We trolls believe that there is no such thing as justice in the afterlife. We believe that once death comes, all feuds end too, as the afterlife is a place of eternal peace. Therefore, if something unpleasant is going to happen to our enemies, it must happen while we're still alive, or it will never happen at all. We call it *dómr*.

"You know the abandoned window factory by the river?"

He shrugs, confused by the change of topic.

"Trolls like me like to hang out there. You should go, Jayson. Make some friends. Feel normal again. They know me there. Tell them I sent you, for *dómr*. They'll let you right in."

"For *dómr*?"

"It's a troll thing. They'll know what it means."

He looks at me with something resembling hope, and floats out the nearest window, bumping it with his shoulder on the way out. I'll probably see him again, in the afterlife. But not again at the office.

I TAKE A DEEP breath. The building's empty and I'm unobserved. I suspect I could be alone for quite some time.

I turn on my computer and get to work. I have a mayor to save and a construction company to destroy.

KATHARINE DOW IS THE author of "The Funeral Company," in *Working Futures: 14 Speculative Stories About the Future of Work* and "The Brooklyn Dragon Racing Club" in *Dragons of a Different Tail: 17 Unusual Dragon Tales*. Dow is a graduate of Seton Hill University's MFA in Writing Popular Fiction program. Raised in Kenya by U.S. born parents, and a subsequent resident of six other countries, Dow currently lives in New York state. You can find her on instagram and twitter as @suggestionize

DON'T LOSE YOUR HEAD

by Victoria L. Scott

WASHINGTON IRVING WAS A son of a bitch.
Harsh, you say? Hardly. His gothic tale of Ichabod Crane in Sleepy Hollow sent my family into hiding for 200 years.

But, I'm getting ahead of myself.

Here's a pro tip—do not get on the wrong side of a powerful Iron Age Gallic witch. The family story of how we ended up with our...how shall we say...unique cranial situation, claims one of my ancient forebears left a rotting deer head on a witch's doorstep as a joke. She didn't find it funny and cursed him and his family with detachable heads. The descendants of that idiot, realizing to their horror that the curse was permanent, became adept at hiding their head-losing tendencies to avoid freaked-out neighbors.

Saint Denis of Paris was one of us, in fact, though his flock believed God made Denis special. His preaching a sermon while he held his head in his hands was a normal Sunday morning for him. He was a lot more extroverted than the rest of his family, which he parlayed into a lucrative career. I hear the church they built in his honor is pretty nice.

Unlike Denis, most cephalophore are shy. The American branch of my family, centered at Sleepy Hollow, managed to keep a lid on their secret. Until that bastard Irving.

Here are the facts. When he encountered Ichabod, my multiple-great-grandfather, Paul Lagarde, wasn't a Hessian soldier menacing the countryside looking for his lost head. He was walking home minding his own business. In fact, a drunken Crane made an unprovoked attack on my unlucky grandpa, whose head fell off. Crane freaked out and told a version of the story that Irving never fact-checked. It became famous, and in Sleepy Hollow, life for us became awkward. People associated the Lagardes with the menacing Headless Horseman. The shopkeepers shut their doors on my ancestors, the village clergyman shouted that we were 'Devil's Spawn' every time he saw a Lagarde, and the Lagarde children were mercilessly bullied at school. When a group of men approached the house with torches and pitchforks, the Lagardes left Sleepy Hollow once and for all.

My family retreated as far into obscurity as possible, finding a rural area in the Finger Lakes region of Upstate New York to hide. As time passed, life with normal people became harder to navigate. We couldn't give birth in hospitals, since obstetricians ended up with the infant's disembodied, silently screaming head in their hands. Even though the rest of the body followed, the initial shock of a headless baby was hard for the doctors to overcome. School yard antics could result in head loss, scarring everyone involved for life. Everywhere we looked, there was a risk of exposure.

Safe from prying eyes in our own homes, the family attitude about our curse was more relaxed. Head loss was often the punchline of a joke. Everyone laughed, Cousin Fred picked his cranium out of the salad bowl, and dinner continued. Half the time, Uncle Eugene had his head on the fireplace mantel so he could see the TV better.

Therefore, it was easier to stay on the family compound than it was to build lives elsewhere. Over time, marrying cousins became...well...not frequent, really...but I thought it happened more often than was chromosomally healthy.

My father, George Lagarde, a quiet, thoughtful man, went in search of someone from outside the family to wed, thank God. My mother, Annie Tawas-Legarde, PhD. was a ruthlessly pragmatic sort. And, while my life wasn't normal compared to the lives of other American families, it was a happy home.

I loved my family, but I wanted more. With my parents' encouragement, I moved into a small apartment in Geneseo. I started taking night classes in accounting at the local community college. After I passed the civil service exam, the postal service hired me as a letter carrier. I spent the first week terrified, certain the other employees would suss out that I was different. They paid more attention to their phones on breaks than they did to me, which was a relief.

When I wasn't working at the post office sorting mail, I was out in my mail truck. Driving my route, I saw people with their partners, happy. I envied them and their normal lives as I sat in my apartment alone, puzzling over asset depreciation.

Soooo...tired of my solitary life, and not liking the goo-goo eyes my cousin Lucretia was making at me, I decided to try online dating.

I pulled up the HarmoniousMatch website and started my profile. I quickly realized how boring I was. I didn't have hobbies, or a favorite band, or a desire to travel, nor did I 'enjoy hiking.' My talents included tractor-driving, pig-slaughtering, and sausage-making, but it seemed creepy to put those down. I couldn't come up with witty responses to the questions the website asked to help potential dates 'get to know me.' Having spent my life so afraid that people would find out what I really was, I had done nothing intriguing or exciting. Even my job was boring.

At a loss of what else to do, I made use of the 'free response' area. There, I wrote about my extended family, what I'd loved about living on the farm, my desire to run my own business, and how I wanted to be with someone who could be more than a girlfriend. I sought a true companion who would take me, warts and all...and that person could expect me to accept them in the same way.

It took me three hours to take a selfie that didn't make me look like a complete idiot. Though to be fair, I spent more of that time figuring out how to take a selfie then fretting about what the best background for it would be. Looking at the pitiful product I posted after four hours of effort, I knew no one would contact me for a date. Hell, I wouldn't have contacted me for a date. I sounded like a boring, foolish romantic.

I got an email a few days later. Maressa, a woman about my age, wanted to meet me. I freaked. I popped my head off and put it between my knees so I wouldn't faint. Once I calmed down, I looked up her profile.

Maressa was new to the area, having recently moved to Geneseo from Washington State. Her hobbies included baseball (she was a big fan of the Seattle Mariners), swimming, and weaving. She worked as a paralegal at the Ricardi Law Office, and she had no pets. Her profile picture showed a beautiful, dark-haired woman with a warm smile. She'd done a better job than I had of coming up with witty responses to the website's questions, which I envied. She tantalized her potential dates with quips like "There's more to me than you can possibly imagine," and "I'm better under water."

I was intrigued. She sounded more interesting than me, which was heartening, even if that standard was easily surpassed. Maybe this dating thing wouldn't be so bad.

Over the next two hours I crafted my response. I put Maressa off, suggesting we get to know each other over email first. I went to bed hopeful and nervous.

THE FOLLOWING MORNING, I discovered Maressa had emailed me back, telling me a bit more about herself and asking some questions about me. I laughed out loud at some of what she wrote, glad that she had a robust sense of humor. I answered her questions, and soon we were emailing each other every day. She liked her job at the law office and was getting used to Upstate New York. I asked her questions about the West Coast, and she told me what growing up was like living in a fishing family a stone's throw from the Pacific Ocean. She came from a big, insular family just like I did, and was one of the few to leave her hometown, much less the state.

I answered her questions about my upbringing and hometown as honestly as I could. Our experiences with big families and living secluded from the rest of the world gave us something in common, so long as I didn't reveal too much.

Our first 'in-person date' was at Cricket's Coffee on Main Street for Sunday Brunch, a lively place with a bright blue façade. I got there first, sitting in the back, facing the door so I could see everyone come in. I wiped my sweaty hands on my jeans, glad that I'd ironed my job interview shirt for our first meeting.

What if she didn't come?

Then the door opened. A tall woman in a blue short-sleeved tee and capri khakis stepped into Cricket's. She had on what my mother called 'sensible tan flats.'. Maressa's dark hair hung in a long braid draped over her left shoulder, with the bottom three inches dyed a vibrant, nearly neon green. Her face was heart shaped, with dark eyes and a pert nose. She scanned the room, saw me, and smiled. My heart flipped over.

I smiled back.

"When I read your profile before I saw your picture, I didn't think you'd be blond," she said, swirling the dregs of coffee in her cup.

Her French toast was half-eaten on her plate, slathered with butter and syrup. I'd gone with bacon and eggs. She was vivacious and fascinating. Why the hell had she wanted to go out with me?

"But, you've got that 'intellectual farmhand vibe' thing going on, which I quite like. Not what I expected in an accounting student."

I chuckled. "Thanks, I think?"

Setting down her cup, she said, "I remember reading Charlotte's Web and thinking how fun it would be to live on a farm. The talking pig left quite an impression on me. I was very pro-Wilbur."

I'd killed a fair share of Wilburs but decided not to bring that up. "It was more like busy and crowded. I was surrounded by uncles and cousins, with few opportunities to be alone or meet new people."

"Same for me in many ways. I spent a lot of time on boats, hauling in lines and nets, my dad and brothers discussing the Angels and hating on the Mariners, that sort of thing."

I thought about the stuff my brothers and I talked about. "Yeah. Brothers are good at that."

"The only alone time I had was when I went swimming at night. The stars overhead were so beautiful, and the sea so welcoming."

I couldn't imagine swimming alone in the Pacific at night. "Wow. You weren't afraid of drowning?"

She smiled, and there was a glint of mischief in her eyes. "I swim exceptionally well. Almost like a fish. Do you have any special talents you'd like to share?"

I cleared my throat. "Uh...not really. Would you like some more coffee?"

After that, we met for lunch a few days a week, since her law office was within easy walking distance of the post office. We traded off deciding what we did on our weekly evening date. It was hard to decide if she was pragmatic or eccentric, since she had moments of both, but whenever I was with her, I felt alive and hopeful. She was full of joy. I relished our time together.

On Saturdays, we went to Little League baseball games, since baseball was her great love, and she cheered louder than some of the parents. As she yelled at the umpire over a foul ball, her braid bouncing on her back, I thought of our pick-up games at home by the barn, the sun setting as I stepped up to home plate.

We talked a lot, with me self-editing out the head-losing family trait as needed. I grew increasingly fond of her. The feeling was mutual—she told me she loved me in early September.

But, I held back. I thought I loved her, but I'd never been in love before. I'd also not disclosed my cephalophoric nature to her. While it was true that romantic partners kept some information to themselves, this seemed too big an issue not to mention it. Problem was, I didn't know how to bring it up.

"WE NEED TO GO to the batting cages," Maressa said one warm September afternoon following lunch at Mama Mia's. "Isn't there a place in Lakeville, up Lakeville Road?"

It was a brief window of Indian Summer, warm enough to go without a jacket, but with the bite of autumn still in the air. Since we'd gone to a cider mill at my request the previous week, it was her call.

"Yeah..." I checked my phone. "Minnehan's. They have go-karts, mini-golf, and batting cages. We could have dinner there, play golf, do some laps in the go-karts, and hit the batting cages before they close."

"You ever been to a batting cage before?"

"I have three brothers. We traded off hitting and pitching balls behind the barn. Didn't need to go into town. We had Seth, who threw a blistering curve ball."

She beamed. "Great! You can teach me."

I stopped walking. "Wait a minute. You, the massive Mariners fan, have never gone to a batting cage? Didn't you play softball in high school?"

She turned to face me. "Nope. I was on the swim team."

"Huh."

"Yup," she said, looping her arm in mine, "I am a woman of mysterious contradictions."

That Saturday we went to Minnehan's and made a night of it. By the time we got to the batting cages, it was nearly closing time. Standing in the 'beginner's' cage, surrounded by tarp-covered chain link, I noted the sunlight was fading fast. It was quiet. We were essentially alone. I showed her the basics of a decent swing. She watched and asked questions, vibrating with excitement.

Then it was her turn to hit a ball. I stood behind and around her, placing my hands over hers to help her get the hang of the swing. As I surrounded her body with mine, the scents of sandalwood and the sea filled my nostrils. It was exotic and intoxicating. After a few swings together, I backed out of the way so she could try on her own.

The baseball shot out of the machine like a cannonball. She swung at it, missed, and carried the movement through high and behind her, smacking me in the face.

The world went out like a light.

When I awoke, I looked up into Maressa's tear-streaked face. My face hurt. Blood pulsed in my brain. I was going to have one hell of a headache.

We sat in a corner of the batting cage. The machine continued to spit out balls, which hit the fence and rattled the chain link. My head, and only my head, sat in her lap. I sensed my body to my left, starting to stir as more of my mental faculties came back online.

Oh, God.

She knew.

"I am so sorry," she said, placing a palm on my cheek and snuffling. She wiped her nose with the back of her other hand. Words came out in a rush. "I didn't mean to hit you. Then your head came off, and I wasn't sure if I should put it back on, or if that would make things worse, or..."

I blinked. She was more concerned about hurting me than she was about my being headless. I'd never been so glad to be clobbered by a baseball bat in my life.

I rolled my eyes to indicate my body, now on its hands and knees, moving toward us. She looked from my body to my head.

"You want me to get you over there?"

I mouthed, "yes."

Maressa nodded, took a deep breath and, with great gentleness, managed to hold my head and stand up. My body sat and held out its hands, and in a moment, I was in one piece again.

"I'm sorry I-" I began.

Her kiss was warm and gentle on my lips. I put my arms out and gathered her into my lap, kissing her back with enthusiasm. The balls slammed into the fence next to us, but I didn't care.

"Uh, folks?"

We stopped kissing. An embarrassed teenager in the Minnehan's employee uniform scratched the back of his head, eyes fixed firmly on his feet. "We're closing. You'll...ah...have to go now."

"We're done hitting balls anyway," she told him as she slipped out of my embrace and stood.

I joined her but was a bit wobbly on my feet. Maressa noticed and took me by the arm.

"Looks like I'm driving you home. You have ice in your freezer, or shall we pick some up?"

I HAD ICE. As I applied a plastic bag full of it to the side of my face, I answered Maressa's questions about my headless abilities. For her, I simply possessed a singular trait, like being double-jointed.

We talked into the night.

By sunrise, I proposed.

She accepted.

Everything happened pretty quickly after that. She met my family, whose antics left her unfazed. She got along great with my mother, who thought we made a lovely couple.

We took some vacation time to drive to Maressa's home in La Push, Oregon so I could meet her family. Once we hit the coast, she took us to a secluded beach so I could see the Pacific, or so I thought. We left our socks and shoes in the car and rolled up our pant legs.

When we got to the cold water and the waves lapped over our feet, Maressa took my hands. Shimmering turquoise scales started to run up her arms.

"You aren't the only one with a secret," she said.

F IVE WORDS DESCRIBE **VICTORIA Scott**'s knowledge base: "How hard can it be?" This can-do attitude inspired her to learn to speak Latin, to quilt, and to operate a blueprint machine. Sometimes what she tries can be damn hard, like learning Ancient Greek, studying karate, and taking Calculus. Those...were not as successful.

Victoria writes Contemporary Fantasy and Science Fiction usually while hanging out with her dog Red the Wonder Husky. She teaches Social Studies and Latin by day and earned her MFA at Seton Hill University. Her bucket list is simple: drive a Zamboni, cruise down the Nile River, and get a book published. How hard can it be?

EYES LIKE BURNING COAL

By Jeremiah Dylan Cook

I clutched my trench coat tighter around my slinky, blue dress when I realized my exit from the dark alley was blocked by a tall man with eyes like burning coal. His ensemble, a black top hat and suit, looked like it'd come straight from the Victorian era. Behind him, Bleeker Street offered the dim light of closed businesses, but no pedestrians due to the late hour. The stranger took one tentative step closer, but we remained separated by the length of a subway car.

He leapt into the air and closed the distance between us in a single bound.

Startled, I fell backward onto the hard concrete. Up close, the man smelled of oil. Light glimmered off the tips of his fingers, where metallic claws jutted from his nailbeds. As I tried to squirm away, I got my first look at his face. His skin was a deep crimson, his mustache curled on both sides, and he had a pointed goatee. In any other setting, I would've laughed at his cartoonish attempt to resemble the devil.

He took another step forward. Instead of normal shoes, his toes were covered by a clog-like front, and a fleshy spring-like appendage protruded from where his heel should've been. He was in position, and it was time to stop acting.

I reached into my coat and removed my revolver from its hiding place. "Spring-Heeled Jack, you're under arrest by the Department of Cryptid Collection. Don't move."

Jack lashed out with his metallic claws. He tore deep gouges in my right hand and sent my gun clattering to the concrete. I pulled my injured hand close to my chest. The thought of dying with my hair and makeup presenting me as a high-class call girl made me want to puke.

Helicopter rotors whooshed overhead. Lights burst to life above and behind us. Tires screeched to a halt as boots pounded across pavement.

A dozen soldiers aimed automatic rifles at Jack from the alley's only exit. Each trooper wore a visored helmet and body armor that covered their chest, thighs, shins, forearms, and shoulders. I prayed they wouldn't have to open fire. My chances of surviving their barrage were about as good as surviving Jack's onslaught.

The cryptid in front of me did as his name implied, he sprang. Jack jumped toward the nearest wall and used it to bound toward the opposite wall. It was an inhuman parkour performance. His pace increased as he scaled toward the alley's roofs. A moment later he lit up like a Christmas tree as he collided with the electrified net the department had installed earlier in the day. Jack plummeted back to earth and landed with a thud in front of me.

Soldiers funneled into the alley to surround him. Dr. Zarka, a man with greying hair and wrinkles across his face, followed in his white lab coat and directed his team of scientists to apply the restraints they'd developed specifically for Jack. In a matter of moments, the cryptid's metallic claws were contained in what looked like a mix between futuristic handcuffs and boxing gloves. Next, his spring-heels were wrapped in a specialized carbon fiber fabric. Lastly, a mouthguard was applied to block his undemonstrated, but well documented, ability to breathe fire.

Dr. Zarka let out a sigh of relief. "After all these years. Our work is complete."

A medical technician saw to my hand as I remained where I was. I didn't think Dr. Zarka's comment was meant for me. I'd only been with the department for the last five years. This was my first field operation. I'd been volunteered for it because I fit the profile of Jack's victims, not because of my countless hours of training. The medical technician finished cleaning my wound with antiseptic, wrapped it in a bandage, and went to check on our capture.

I got to my feet and collected my revolver. "I'm aware my clearance level might not be high enough for an answer, but I'm curious why we left Jack for last?"

Dr. Zarka stared at the restrained cryptid. "A simple cost-to-benefit calculation. All this one does is hunt women in urban populations, London in the 1800s and here in New York City since about 1920. Sometimes he doesn't even kill the women. Compared to some of our other captures, he's practically a puppy."

Frustration at the department's disregard for female protection flooded through me, and I had to take a deep breath to avoid an angry retort. Repeated beeping announced the arrival of the transport truck, which backed up to the mouth of the alley. The soldiers worked with the scientists to move Jack into the trailer. The interior was reinforced by the strongest known materials to ensure physical escape was impossible, and occult symbols had been added to trap the more mystical types of cryptids.

The electronic cargo door slammed shut, and the vehicle pulled away with its prize. The soldiers and scientists flooded back to their various vehicles, which rolled out to follow the truck. Dr. Zarka left the alley and Gary Hadley, my supervising agent, entered. He was dressed in his typical khaki pants, white button down, and red tie. His hair was fading fast, and he wore black horn-rimmed glasses.

"Excellent work tonight, Jill." Gary led me out of the alley back into the light of Bleeker Street. Opposite us was a closed tattoo shop, record store, and a bodega. Despite being in Manhattan, I couldn't see any famous landmarks from within the confines of Greenwich Village.

"Do you think any locals saw our operation?" I asked.

"Not a chance. We cordoned off the block and introduced a sleeping agent into the surrounding buildings at precisely 9 PM. If any questions are asked, the incident will be blamed on a harmless gas leak." Gary turned right and walked.

I followed. "Sir, what now?"

"Jill, I've told you a dozen times. You don't need to address me as sir. This isn't the military. And right now, I think we've earned breakfast. There's a twenty-four-hour bagel shop just ahead. After that, we report back to the department, and we get you assigned to whatever security detail you want. I can even get you added to the Secret Service if you so desire."

"Thank you. I don't know if I've earned that kind of reward after one mission."

"Jill, we've lost dozens of field agents trying to capture cryptids. You've read the records just like me, but you still chose to participate in this operation knowing it could mean your life."

"But I was only selected because—"

"Yes, I know Dr. Zarka picked you because you fit the profile for Jack's victims, but you could've decided to leave the department and you didn't. You stayed and did your duty. In my book, that earns you whatever reward you'd like." Gary stopped and sniffed the air. "There's nothing more heavenly than the scent of bagels in the morning."

The aroma of freshly baked bread wafted from the nearby bagel store. I followed my supervisor as he closed the distance to the shop and opened the door. A bell hung in the doorway rang out. Normally, I was a plain bagel kind of girl, but after a confrontation with Spring-Heeled Jack, I thought I deserved something a bit more luxurious. Looking at the display window in the store, my mouth watered as I laid eyes on a bagel coated in cheese, onion, and jalapenos.

AFTER A FIVE-HOUR DRIVE south, Gary and I arrived at the Department of Cryptid Collection. A large razor wire-lined fence surrounded the plain, glass office building. A sign by the gate announced the location was the headquarters for the Society of Cryptozoological Study.

"Do you think any of the Bigfoot hunters who visit the office ever suspect he's locked up in the basement?" I asked.

Gary put his window down and reached out to scan his badge on the card reader. "Unlikely. On the other hand, we've gotten a few hot tips from the Society over the years. Dr. Zarka debated long and hard about how best to hide the department when it started. I suggested something modest to cover our operations. Paper company was my idea." The gates opened, and Gary drove us into the parking lot. "Dr. Zarka came up with the idea to invite the Society and build an office for them above our HQ. He argued that it would give us access to their information, and, if there ever was a breach, no one would believe them because people were programmed to dismiss cryptozoologists as quacks."

Overhead, the sun shined down from a clear sky. In the distance, behind the office, the Potomac River flowed by on its way to the Chesapeake Bay. Outside the fence, trees surrounded the building at a distance. Regular landscaping kept the flora from growing near enough to the fence for anyone to hop over. The parking lot was moderately full, but most of the cars belonged to the department's agents.

"End of the road." Gary parked in a spot reserved for the Head of Maintenance, his fake role that the Society thought he performed.

I stepped out of the car, relieved to be back to my usual attire. I had rubbed the makeup off my face at a rest stop in Maryland and changed into gray slacks, black flats, and a white button up blouse. My revolver now resided in my purse. I clipped my badge to the belt loop on my slacks and followed Gary to the side entrance. My fake title was Maintenance Procurement Secretary, but a computer algorithm handled all the work associated with my contrived position.

A concrete hallway led to the maintenance elevator. After scanning our badges, we rode down to B1. When the doors opened, I followed Gary through a sterile, white hallway. We passed several closed doors, which housed offices for various researchers. The breakroom door was open, and six scientists hovered around a small table sharing a bottle of champagne. Bags of chips and a small cake were set out on the counter next to the fridge.

After passing a few more conference and research rooms, we reached Dr. Zarka's office. Gary knocked twice before opening. Inside Dr. Zarka sat at his desk with a bottle of whiskey and a single, half-filled glass.

"I take it everything went well with transferring Jack to his new home on B4?" Gary asked.

Dr. Zarka downed his drink and poured another. "No problems. Now that our country is freed from the chaos of the supernatural, order will reign." Dr. Zarka laughed. "Once we've learned the secrets of the cryptid's powers, we can finally figure out how to dispose of them for good."

Gary chuckled in response. "Well, I don't want to hold up your celebration. I just need your approval to get Jill reassigned."

"Who?"

Gary nodded in my direction.

"Oh, my apologies. The bait. Yes, I—"

Alarms blared as the lights flashed a bright orange.

Dr. Zarka picked up his tablet, which displayed a large message. "Containment breach on B4."

Gary sighed. "I'll check it out. Probably just another system malfunction."

I set my purse down and pulled out my revolver. The gun was heavy in my injured hand, but I'd wielded a weapon with worse injuries in the past. "I'm coming too."

Gary shook his head. "You already risked your life once today."

"I'll leave right after this. Like you said, probably just a system malfunction."

"The elevator will be shut down. Use the stairs and get word back to me as soon as you figure out what's going on down there. I'll initiate lockdown protocols up here." Dr. Zarka started poking and swiping at his tablet.

Gary and I left the office and headed to the nearby stairwell door. We made our way down the four flights of metal steps and paused at the entrance to B4. A message above the door read: WARNING: Cryptid Collection Level. Specimens are EXTREMELY Dangerous. Maximum Clearnce Level Required. Next to the door was a keypad, a retinal scanner, and a badge reader. In addition, the door required an antiquated key, of which Gary and Dr. Zarka held the only two in existence. My supervisor swiped his badge, bent forward for the eye scan, input the necessary code, and pulled out his key, an ornately detailed item that reminded me of something out of a gothic novel.

He slid the key into the lock. "Ready?"

I nodded and raised my revolver to put me in an adequate shooting stance.

Gary took a breath, turned the key, and pushed the door open.

Unlike upstairs, where the alarms blared, this level was quiet. Orange lights flashed above, illuminating the two huge pipes that ran along the ceiling to deliver power and water. The hallway was little more than a mining tunnel.

Some great machine had bored out the path, and the department hadn't bothered to dress the area up. Blinking lights ran along the floor grating to direct followers to this exit. Unfortunately, no one was here.

Gary stepped forward. "There's a phone at the T-junction ahead. We can update Dr. Zarka there."

I pushed my supervisor behind me. "Let the one with the gun go first."

With my weapon raised, I jogged down the tunnel toward the junction ahead. With every step forward, I expected to see Jack's fiery eyes appear. My heart pounded. Something splashed onto me, and I whipped my gun to aim above. A drip came from a leaky pipe. I continued to the junction, and Gary followed close behind.

At the intersection of tunnel paths, a desk with a phone, tablet, and spilled coffee stood unmanned. The phone was an old-fashioned landline. Due to the facility's depth, cellphones didn't work, and a closed communication circuit had been installed.

"There should be someone here." Gary grabbed the phone.

"There *was* someone here." With my gun, I gestured to a trail of blood leading into the tunnel on our left.

"Christ." Gary dialed and put the phone to his ear. "Dr. Zarka, we've got blood down here. Something definitely got out." He scowled before speaking again. "Dr. Zarka?"

"What is it?" I asked.

Gary hung up the phone. "Line went dead."

"Orders?"

My supervisor reached under the desk and pulled out a high-powered stun rod. Blue sparks danced at the end of the weapon. "Well, we can evacuate and wait for backup. Or we can see where that blood leads."

I started down the path smeared with crimson. A sign hanging from above read: Containment Block A. The orange lights continued to flash overhead, and the lights lining the floor continued to direct us back to the exit. The tunnel curved inward, and my muscles tensed as I waited to see what appeared around the bend. Again, I expected to see Jack's eyes flare to life ahead of me. Sweat trickled from my forehead, and each step forward clanged off the metal grating.

The tunnel ended abruptly and opened into a cavernous space. Large fluorescent bulbs buzzed from high above. On each side of me, six cryptid containment cells had been carved into the rocky earth. Stairs in the center of the chamber led up to scaffolding walkways that provided access to the other twelve cells on the second level. Blast doors, some human sized and others bus sized, kept their residents contained. Each was made of the same kind of metal as the transport truck. White lettering across the doors identified the imprisoned cryptids. The largest cell belonged to Champ, an amphibious serpent the department had fished out of Lake Champlain. I passed smaller cells for the Headless Horseman, Mothman, the Jersey Devil, and the Chupacabra. The blood trail we'd been following turned toward the last cell in the row. The door had been forced open enough for a person to crawl in or out. The cell belonged to Spring-Heeled Jack.

I aimed at the dark gap between the floor and the door, waiting for Jack's burning eyes to find me. I could feel my blood coursing through my veins, and I wanted to turn and run. The bottom of the blast door had been marred by thousands of tiny cuts. I hoped my bullets would be enough to at least stun the cryptid. My research and preparation for his capture clearly illustrated that there was no known way to kill him.

Gary held his hand up, indicating for me to wait. He lowered to the floor slowly and crawled forward with his stun rod ready. He raised his index finger to indicate one person was in the cell. Gary prepared to plunge the stun rod into the space.

I tried to calm my rapid breathing as I kept my finger ready to squeeze my gun's trigger.

My supervisor shoved his arm forward and sparks shot from the cell as a buzz of electricity echoed through the area.

"Damn." Gary got to his feet. "It's just the guard in there. I recognized the uniform in the flash."

"Then where's Jack?"

Thunder reverberated in the distance, and we turned back toward the tunnel.

"It appears our scientists underestimated Jack's powers," I said.

"Jill, I believe that's the understatement of the year."

The thunder grew closer, and I aimed my gun at the mouth of the dark tunnel we'd entered from. "It's been an honor serving with you, sir."

Gary put his hand on my arms and forced my weapon down. "I recognize the sound."

Fifty soldiers filed into the room. They were outfitted with the same weapons and body armor as the soldiers I'd seen hours earlier. They fanned out and aimed their automatic rifles at the surrounding cells.

One of the soldiers stepped forward and lifted his helmet's visor. "Dr. Zarka dispatched us when you didn't report in. What's the issue?"

Gary shook his head in frustration. "Spring-Heeled Jack managed to spring himself."

I chuckled at my supervisor's quip despite the intensity of the moment.

The soldier looked annoyed. "Where is he now?"

The sound of heavy machinery coming to life resonated through the space.

Gary's eyes widened. "My god. Jack's gotten to the cell controls."

"Aren't they with Dr. Zarka?" The soldier asked.

Before Gary could reply, the nearest door shot open.

The group tensed and trained its weapons on the threshold.

I tried to figure out what cryptid we were dealing with by process of elimination, but I couldn't think clearly as my pulse pounded. A shadowy figure with glowing eyes the color of suns flew out and passed through the soldiers like a mist. It was gone before anyone could fire a shot.

I sighed with relief. "Only Mothman. He generally just brings omens."

"Yes, but he brings omens of tragedies. Everyone, run!" Gary shouted.

More heavy machinery came to life, and doors opened all around us. Champ's plesiosaur-like jaws shot forth from their cell and snatched a soldier away. The Headless Horseman ran out, dressed in his American Revolution era army uniform, and decapitated the nearest person. Sasquatch dropped into the fray from above and sent a dozen men flying in different directions as his claws, teeth, and fur flashed through the crowd. Gunfire erupted all over as cryptids attacked from every direction.

The Chupacabra ran at me on all fours with its fangs bared and its serpentine tongue seeking blood. I fired all six chambers of my revolver into its scaled body. The creature was dissuaded from its attack. Before I could take a breath, the Jersey Devil landed next to me with its goat feet clopping on the metal floor. It whipped its tail at me, and I fell to the ground. It leaned in with its deer-like visage and tried to bite me.

My supervisor zapped the Jersey Devil with his stun rod. The scent of burning hair overwhelmed my nostrils as Gary's weapon turned the creature's hide black. The cryptid spread its wings and leapt off to find easier prey.

Gary offered me his hand to help me up. "If we don't get out of here, we're done for."

The Dover Demon, a small gray humanoid with large red eyes, dropped from above and landed on Gary's shoulders. Before I knew what had happened, Gary fell limply to the ground. The glassy gaze in his eyes told me he was dead. In a panic, I turned and ran for Jack's partially open cell door. I plunged inside and closed my eyes.

WHEN I RETURNED TO consciousness, I didn't know how much time had passed. Shock had forced my body to sleep while I hid. I checked myself over and found no wounds. The same could not be said for my deceased cell companion, who Gary had accidentally prodded earlier.

Jack's claw marks were all over him, and his blue guard's uniform was torn to shreds along with the cryptid's former restraints. I was thankful that only a little light penetrated the chamber from under the door, which remained open just enough for a person to squeeze through. The sounds of battle in the containment block had been replaced by silence. I crawled forward as quietly as possible to get a look outside.

Carnage. That was the only word to describe the scene in the cavernous space. I'd never been to war, but the scene reminded me of historic pictures from World War One. I did my best not to focus on the deceased soldiers littering the ground. Instead, I surveyed for any cryptids. None seemed to have remained.

Satisfied it was safe to leave, I crawled out from under Jack's cell door. Before progressing further, I picked up the nearest soldier's rifle and checked to ensure it still contained some ammunition. Pulling out the magazine, I verified there were several rounds remaining. I jammed it back into the gun and proceeded through the dozens of downed men, collecting more spare ammo as I found it. Of the dead, none were monsters.

I re-entered the tunnel. Some orange lights continued to flash overhead, but several were broken. Water now gushed out of one of the damaged pipes and the other was covered in dozens of scratch marks from all manner of beasts. Rocks had been scraped off the walls from the various sized creatures who'd recently come through the passageway. All the white lights on the floor were out from being trampled. I proceeded down the tunnel cautiously, with my gun raised. Each step forward felt like it would be my last.

When I reached the desk at the T-Junction, I identified more bodies leading down the way Gary and I hadn't investigated. The elevator was accessed there, and Jack had obviously released that wing of cryptids as well. I turned back toward the exit. The door at the end was smashed open and lay on the floor by the stairs. I took a deep breath as I continued.

Once I was in the stairwell, I aimed up through the various metal stairs and grated landings to verify no cryptids remained. Even with no visible threats, getting to B3, B2, and B1 took an agonizingly long time as I practically crawled up the stairs to avoid any surprises. The doors for B3 and B2 remained shut and locked, but the door for B1 was destroyed.

I stepped back into the sterile hallway I'd left from with Gary. My last pass through this area felt like days ago, and the changes were numerous. Like below, the walls, floors, and ceilings were damaged by the passing cryptids. I spotted three downed scientists in their white lab coats near the break room ahead. The doors to the elevator were forced open, and I assumed most, if not all, of the cryptids had managed to climb or jump back to the surface. Stunned by the magnitude of the department's failure, I turned around, intending to check whether Dr. Zarka had survived, and spotted eyes like burning coal.

Spring-Heeled Jack stood within spitting distance outside Dr. Zarka's bloody office door.

As I raised my weapon, Jack sent a plume of flame in my direction. I fell backward and narrowly missed having my face melted. Before I could put the cryptid back in my sights, he leaped toward me and sliced my gun in two with his metal claws.

My heart raced, my adrenaline pumped, and I knew death was coming. I waited for Jack to end my life with his vicious claws. I would not give him the satisfaction of cowering.

Jack smiled. "Enough blood has been spilled this day. Jack will go on his merry way. But a word of warning for those who bear a heart, coming after cryptids is not very smart." The creature sprang over me, once more down the hall, and lastly, up the elevator shaft.

I lay on the floor shaking in terror. Jack's words rang in my skull. It was clear that all the department had done was manage to make cryptids angry. Now they were free to pursue whatever strange ends they desired. Contrary to Dr. Zarka's earlier statement, the chaos of the supernatural would continue to reign.

JEREMIAH DYLAN COOK IS a horror writer whose work has been published by The NoSleep Podcast, Castle Bridge Media, Ghost Orchid Press, The Lovecraft eZine, Hippocampus Press, Necronomicon Press, and Eye Contact. He won Purple Wall Stories February 2021 Writing Competition, and the Ligonier Valley Writers 2018 Flash Fiction Contest. While pursuing his bachelor's degree at St. John's University, Jeremiah received the Mario Mezzacappa Memorial Award for Outstanding Achievement in Poetry and Prose. He completed his Master of Fine Arts in Writing Popular Fiction at Seton Hill University. Jeremiah is an affiliate member of the Horror

Writers Association, and the Managing Editor of New Pulp Tales. You can follow him on twitter @JeremiahCook1, where he loves to discuss David Bowie, Resident Evil, Comic Books, Board Games, and the works of H.P. Lovecraft.

Magicland Mischief

By J.C. Mastro

Ah, Magicland. The Merriest Place on Earth... Unless you're a corporate-level Crew Member just trying to get home after a fourteen-hour day. Laura John's morning had begun with project oversight of a new character installation at one of the park's most beloved attractions, Pirates of the High Seas. The afternoon found her scrolling through endless hotel budget reports. Her greatest desire at the end of the night was to get home and slip into her soft pajamas and sleep like the dead.

After-hours in the deserted Magicland was an eerie time of day—but cutting through the park was by far the fastest route to the parking structure. The guests were gone, the pathways swept, the attractions powered down, and not a soul to bother her as she listened to her favorite metal band, DragonFraggen, over the tinny-sounding speaker in her phone.

As "Spirit of the Dragon" played its opening heavy-chugging chords, Laura couldn't help but wonder at the outrageous events that occurred at the band's concert several months prior. She still didn't believe it despite all the social media hype and evidence. Animatronic creatures don't come to life. It must have been a well-engineered effect, one she was fairly familiar with in her position with the company. Lifelike attraction characters are what Magicland did best.

Laura's heavy-metal-fueled daydream was broken when—near the Trollheim Mountain Bobsled ride at the edge of the Fantasticland region of the park—a dazzling, green-hued light spectacle danced and burst in the air. She silenced the music, noting a whirling, tinkling sound backed by a deep and ominous groan.

Always the curious sort, and aware that whatever this mystery event was should not be occurring, Laura made her way over to the ride. There, near the entrance, she found an intriguing man dressed in a flowing, black robe tied at the waist with rope, and a billowing hood raised over his head. He stood on a rock before the water flume where the bobsled splashed down during the ride, waving his arms and seemingly manipulating the greenish tendrils of energy pouring into the mountain. The air seemed to buzz with static.

Heart and mind racing, but duty-bound to inquire, Laura called out to the robed man's back, "Excuse me! What's going on here?"

He gave no reply, simply continued his light-weaving.

I bet I know what this is, she thought. "Hello? Are you with the Imaginator team?"

"Apologies, dear woman," the man spoke without turning around, "now is not an appropriate time for idle pleasantries." Even through his almost mumbling, somewhere from the UK accent, his tone seemed strained, urgent.

"It's not exactly an 'appropriate time' for whatever you're doing, either," she said, rolling her eyes. "The park is closed, and no project work was scheduled for Trollheim."

The strange man's light show, obviously some new effect the Imaginator team was testing, intensified and swirled wildly. Green orbs popped like tiny fireworks, reflecting in the murky water below. The ground under Laura's feet trembled as though the ride were in operation, yet it was most definitely powered down.

"Please do not interrupt the spell," the man glanced over his shoulder. Only his chin was visible in a flash of light, and... green glowing eyes? "The consequences would be quite undesirable, I assure you."

Spell? Man, he's really selling this thing, she mused. "It's kind of my job to know what you're working on," she said. "Here, why don't you show me." Laura pushed through the turnstile and began to climb up on the rock next to the man.

"No! That is not a wise course of—" she fumbled on the slick stone and grabbed the thick hem of his robe. The man lost his balance and tumbled backward off his rock. His arms flailed, sending waves of light darting in every direction. As he caught himself on the railing, a brilliant, blinding flash erupted from the mountain like a shockwave that encompassed the entire park with a deafening whoosh.

Magicland was once again dark and quiet save for the glowing streetlamps and occasional chirp of a cricket. The man turned his fading, green glare upon Laura.

"Oops... Sorry," she said sheepishly.

"You're sorry? Confound it, woman, do you have any idea what you may have done?"

"What have *you* done? You never answered my question. And what are you supposed to be, anyway? Some druid guy?"

A wide grin wrinkled the man's cheeks. "I have been many things, my dear. Perhaps a druid, perhaps not. Most recently I spent time as a boatman who assisted bungling musicians in summoning an old dragon friend from the abyss. Yet, I suppose... Druid Guy will suffice."

Laura hopped down and laughed. She found Druid Guy's lilting pattern of speech humorous, not to mention the unintentional name. But his talk of a dragon and musicians triggered her memory of a certain event she'd recalled minutes before.

"Wait... Are you talking about DragonFraggen? That was so cool! I didn't know the company Imaginators were involved in the animatronic dragon effect."

"Yes, one and the same. However, I know nothing of this 'Imaginator' or 'effect' you continue to mention." Trollheim Mountain grumbled deep and low. He turned to face it. "My purpose is to summon the mystical spirits of olde back to this magicless world. To usher in a new age of myth and legend. A purpose you so clumsily interrupted."

Impressed, confused, and achingly tired, Laura decided that this enigmatic weirdo, whatever his so-called purpose, needed to go. "I'm sorry I interrupted you. But, the park is closed. You're not supposed to be here, so you'll have to leave. And I just wanna go home."

An angry, guttural roar echoed from the cave entrance of Trollheim, followed by heavy, rhythmic thuds. It sent a cold shiver down her back. "Umm... What was that?"

Druid Guy stepped forward. "Perhaps your intrusion of the spell-weaving was not as ill-timed as I feared."

A hulking, monstrously proportioned shadow ducked out from within the ride. Its overlarge feet splashed through the water with each plodding step. The giant crossed through a pool of ambient light from a nearby lamp, revealing mottled, leathery skin stretched over taut, bulging muscles. Bulbous, malformed facial features leered in her direction. A club like the gnarled stump of a tree rested over its broad shoulder.

Laura's eyes grew wide, and she back peddled into the line queue railing. "Har... Harry the Troll?" The nickname, of course, for the animatronic creature that frightened guests as they'd zip by on the bobsled coaster. Apparently no longer in his grotto home. And no longer made of foam latex and metal mechanisms.

Druid Guy laughed. "Harry the Troll, you say? An amusing name, yet surprisingly accurate! Some might call their species trolls, others the ettin, jotuun, giant. It matters not. This particular spirit beast is named Hereweald. He's been lost to time for many centuries. But Harry is very apropos."

Harry flipped the club from his shoulder and smashed it down in the water. The violent spray splattered at Laura's feet. She instinctively hurdled over the railing to create some distance but was too transfixed to run.

"How the hell...?" she said in a voice strained with paralyzing dread.

Druid Guy's mischievous grin returned, and his eyes flashed green once again. "I already explained my purpose to you, Laura," he pointed at her name badge, "not that you cared to listen. Hereweald has been returned to have a bit of fun. To spread his special bombastic magic, starting in this park of amusement... Much to my own."

"This isn't happening," Laura said, shaking her head. "I'm just exhausted... I'm seeing things."

"Oh no, my dear. It is very much happening." The troll stomped forward and hunched down. "Say hello, Harry!"

Harry opened its massive maw and bellowed a spine-chilling roar. The putrid breath turned her stomach.

And, having quite enough of that, Laura bolted out of the ride entrance without looking back.

"Hang on to your hats and glasses!" Druid Guy called as Harry smashed his club through one of the bobsled cars. "And enjoy the ride!"

Laura didn't consider which way she should run—as is often the case when fleeing from horrors—but happened to choose the most expeditious route to the main entrance through Futureland. Harry's hollers and crashing mayhem followed behind. She didn't dare slow down or risk a look. There was only escape, survival, and...

A pair of droids? Rounding the corner of a UFO-shaped concessions booth, she nearly plowed right into a copper-colored humanoid robot and his rolling trashcan-looking companion.

"Oh my!" it said, "I'm terribly sorry."

She skidded to a halt and stared incredulously at them. "Aren't you supposed to be in..."

The smaller droid warbled a series of excited beeps and chirps.

Something curiouser and curiouser was definitely going on in Magicland. But, she'd have no time to ponder it as an entire yellow submarine from the nearby lagoon flew through the air and crashed into the overhead track of the monorail with a screech of buckling metal and cracking of fiberglass.

"Ahh!" the copper droid cried. "It's a nightmare!"

"You should probably run," Laura said, and took off again through Futureland.

This can't be happening, she thought, *this must be a dream!* She pressed on. If that reanimated troll had the strength to throw a submarine ride through the air, what chance could she possibly have?

Her escape was once again cut off as up ahead, streams of laser bolts blasted across the pathway. A pack of murmuring, tiny aliens fled from a very large, dark metal armored character with evil, glowing red eyes.

"Overlord Zorg," she whispered. Laser bolts dinged off its armor. "Does that mean...?"

A man with an oversized chin and bubble-like spacesuit lept from within the nearby building. "The Space Marshals will save you, aliens!" he said.

"Yeah, nope!" Laura spun on her heels to head in the opposite direction. In that moment, all became clear. Druid Guy really wasn't an Imaginator, and that spell he'd mentioned did indeed have undesirable paranormal consequences.

It had brought the characters of Magicland to life. Like what had happened to DragonFraggen. Like what *should not* happen based on the laws of nature as she understood them. A horrifying realization gripped her. She was in incredible danger. Many people would be when the park reopened. Or worse, if these monsters got out.

She had to escape and find help. Call emergency services once she'd gotten clear of the chaos. But how? Would anyone believe her?

Off to her right, she spotted Harry tearing through the entrance of a rocket ship-shaped pizza restaurant. He ripped the glass doors off their hinges and smashed them on the ground.

"Hungry, big fella?" she said to herself. "You just stay right there, okay?" She had her opening, but it was a long way around the park in that direction to the main gate. If what she'd experienced so far was this widespread, she'd do well to avoid as much of the park as possible. There had to be a shortcut to First Street...

The train! she thought. *The tracks go right to the gate!* With Harry occupied, she could probably make it. Laura bolted for the station at the back of Futureland.

The tracks were empty, and no reanimated characters seemed to be nearby. Hopes running high, she climbed over the railing and down onto the tracks. Dark pressed in on her like a heavy blanket in that lightless area of the park. She jogged as carefully as she could between the tracks toward the pitch-black tunnel ahead that separated Futureland from the First Street station.

Inside the tunnel, she took her phone from her pocket. No reception.

"Damn!" her curse echoed down the brick walls. A rustling and faint animal-like growl echoed back. "Um, hello?" She switched on the nearly useless flashlight app and waved it around. Nothing. Her pace quickened, the faint lights of the station at the exit beckoned her to safety.

A space opened up on her right side. Tree limbs and rock formations flashed in the short beam of the light. The growling noise echoed again from deeper down the tunnel.

"What is this?" She was anxiously talking to herself, trying to calm her heart threatening to beat from her chest. It nearly did as the light caught a scaly, lizard-like face peeking out through the foliage.

She screamed and jumped back. But the lizard—no, a dinosaur—didn't move. She stared at it, attempting to catch her breath. It was definitely a dinosaur. A lifeless, rubber dinosaur scaled down to roughly the size of a cow. Part of an original exhibit often missed in the park.

"I forgot this place existed." The rustling sounds ahead returned. While interesting, she suspected that—given the strange magic she'd already witnessed tonight—the train tunnel with its artificial dinosaurs was not the wisest place to be.

She jogged as fast as she dared in the low light over the uneven tracks. The glow from the tunnel exit lay a couple hundred feet away, and beyond it, the First Street station and freedom from this bad dream.

Laura had nearly made it when a gravely, growling sound from behind prickled goosebumps down her arms. She turned, and in the fear-stricken shaking of her phone's light, the scaly, brown face of a triceratops opened its beak and screamed.

Laura ran for the exit. The dinosaur bounded after. She tried to slide her phone into her pocket but missed. It tumbled to the ground. No stopping to retrieve it. The dinosaur's footfalls and heavy breaths continued to pursue, joined by more screeching cries of other creatures.

She burst from the tunnel mouth. The station was just ahead, and down its stairs was the arch to the park exit. The triceratops almost had her, she could feel it at her back. She climbed up and tumbled over the station's safety railing, the creature nearly taking a bite out of her swinging foot. Her side hit the concrete hard, but she recovered and rolled to her feet. Two friends with very sharp teeth had joined the triceratops. She ran for the stairs without looking back.

Laura rounded the bottom of the stairway toward the park's exit arch. She heard the dinosaurs tear through the safety rails in the station above, then pulled up short at the arch. A horse-drawn trolley car had been mangled and wedged into it, cutting off the exit.

"Dammit!" There wasn't time to dwell on how—or what—had done that to the trolley with the dinosaurs barreling down the stairs. She did an about face and bolted across the square toward the firehouse. It was the first place she thought of as a possible location to hide.

Laura crept through the open door into the darkness and worked her way around to the front of the antique fire wagon on display within. She crouched down and tried to slow her ragged breathing and the pulse pounding in her ears. The overgrown lizards wreaked havoc in the square.

"Begging your pardon, miss..." She screamed and nearly jumped out of her skin at the voice. "Oh, I apologize! Didn't mean to give you a fright."

She crawled away from the previously unseen figure, then stopped. Her mouth fell open in recognition. Wide eyes adjusted in the dark, and the unmistakable features of a tall, lanky man with a rugged jawline covered in a beard with no mustache grew clear.

"President Lincoln?"

Laura couldn't believe her eyes. Abraham Lincoln crouched in the corner of the Magicland firehouse. It wasn't the fact that he was there, she'd already deduced the effect of Druid Guy's spell. It was that it was freaking Abraham Lincoln, her favorite president from history, thanks in part to the A Conversation with President Lincoln attraction at the park.

"No need to stand on formalities, given our present situation," he said. "Call me Abe. You seem to be in a right state of distress. Forgive me for startling you."

"It's... It's okay, Abe. Please tell me you aren't going to try and eat me."

"Eat you?" he snorted a laugh. "Great heavens above, why would I do that? May I inquire as to your name, miss?"

A cautious relief washed over her, and she relaxed slightly. But only slightly. This was always the part in horror movies where an assumed ally twisted the narrative and attacked. "I'm Laura. I work for Magicland."

"A pleasure to make your acquaintance, Miss Laura. If I were a betting man, I'd wager you're running from the calamity ensuing this night?"

"Yes! This Druid Guy cast some crazy spell that brought characters to life—which, I'm sorry, seems to include you—and Harry the Troll is destroying everything, there's robots, dinosaurs are chasing me, and—"

"Whoa, slow down and breathe! I am well aware of what is occurring here. Twisted, evil magic, if you ask me. You should have seen the beast that blocked the entrance." The dinosaurs screeched in the square. "Seems you brought a few more with you," he chuckled.

"I've gotta get out of here and find help or stop this guy. But we're trapped and I lost my way to call anyone."

"An astute observation. Well..." Abe stood with a groan, his lean, six-foot-four frame towering over her, and offered a hand. "Looks to me like solving this predicament is our burden to bear." Laura took it, noting it was cool to the touch, not warm like real flesh.

I guess they aren't really alive, then, she thought. *Good to know.*

"For reasons beyond my comprehension," he rubbed his chin as he mused, "I seem to recall that there's some person or creature in this park who may be able to undo all this. Though an actual name escapes me."

"If that's true, I have to find them. Will you help me?"

"The honor would be mine. Though, we shall have to get past the creatures outside this door." Abe walked over to a wall where vintage fireman's equipment was displayed and took down an axe. He hefted it in his large hands, giving it a few test swings. "This will do nicely."

Laura couldn't help herself and giggled. "Abraham Lincoln, Dinosaur Hunter. Get those bitches, Abe."

He raised an eyebrow. "Bitches? As in..."

She felt suddenly sheepish for having cursed in front of the great man. "Sorry, it's just an expression. Like... Oh, nevermind."

Abe looked confused at first, then shrugged. "Dinosaur, you say? I've heard of those. Hunter, however, is a fine stretch of the imagination. But I was known to swing an axe a time or two during my youth in Indiana." A sly smile wrinkled his cheeks.

Laura giggled again. "You have no idea how awesome this is."

"Much obliged, Miss Laura. Now, what say we divest ourselves of this hiding spot, and stop those monsters so you can find the help you need?" He laid the axe over his shoulder, and Laura followed his long strides out of the firehouse.

As luck would have it—or rather bad luck—the animatronic dinosaurs were tearing into a store front at the only route down First Street headed deeper into the park. Abe and Laura crept closer, keeping distance between them and the creatures.

"Can we sneak past them?" she asked quietly.

"Not likely." Abe rubbed his chin again. "Miss Laura, it has been a pleasure, but I believe I must take my leave of you and create a distraction so you might fulfill your destiny."

"Wait, what? No! We're going together. I can't do this alone. I need your help."

"Now, now, it will not do to waste time in debate. I am helping by clearing your path. I shall draw them off, and you run toward the river... Something tells me that's where you will find who you need."

Not one to argue with an axe-wielding former President, Laura nodded in resignation and readied herself to make a run for it. "Thank you, Abe."

He dipped his head in a stately gesture, then gripped the axe in both hands before strolling casually toward the ravenous beasts.

"Well now," Abe called out. The dinosaurs whipped their heads around and leered at him. "Aren't you a trio of terrible lizards. Time you went back to whatever hell you came from."

They charged him. Abe dropped into a defensive stance, axe at the ready. "Laura, run!"

She did, shooting straight down First Street.

"For liberty, bitches!" Abe bellowed over the shrieks of the creatures and sickening crunch of what she could only assume was his axe blow into latex and gears. But she didn't look back. She couldn't bear to. Abe had sacrificed himself for her, and whether he was truly alive or not, she was eternally grateful to him.

MOMENTS LATER, LAURA REACHED the center pavilion of the park. Every manner of debris littered the walkways. Trees broken off mid-trunk, fencing lying in mangled heaps. And a deep, banging ruckus coming from the castle not far ahead.

As she crept through the shadows along the perimeter heading toward the entrance to Wild West Land and the river beyond, she saw the source of the commotion. Harry the Troll was beating on the massive castle gate with the bronze statue of the park's founder normally displayed in a place of honor in the pavilion's center. Druid Guy stood behind him laughing.

"Hereweald, you are ever the persistent creature!" he said.

"Princess..." Harry yelled in a thunderous, inhuman growl of a voice.

"I'm afraid your dear princess is long gone, my friend. Let us find you another! Perhaps that meddling young woman Laura we met earlier? I'm certain she's still here. In fact..." Druid Guy turned and glared with those eerie, green-glowing eyes directly at her hiding spot. "She's here now."

Laura's breath caught in her chest. *How does he know I'm here? Run!* She backed out of the dark toward the Land entrance.

"So kind of you to join us again, Laura." Druid Guy said. Harry stopped beating the gate and whipped his grotesque head around. "Harry wishes to properly introduce himself!"

The freakish troll chucked the statue aside and roared before stomping his bulk across the bridge. Druid Guy burst into laughter.

All pretense of hiding no longer necessary, Laura ran through the wooden beam arch into Wild West Land, past the vintage shooting arcade and the saloon-themed restaurant. Harry's heavy, pounding footfalls grew louder behind her. Wood cracked and splintered as he smashed through the arch. The river was just ahead, its iconic riverboat docked for the night. If she could just make it down the bank to Southern Town Square where there were plenty of places to hide...

She took a hard left at the shore, the masts of the pirate ship ahead silhouetted by the moon. Harry was gaining on her. Full panic raced her heart. Leg muscles flushed with adrenaline gave all that they had. The monster's chugging, grunting breaths filled her ears. A gust of air displaced by its swinging club blew across her back. She wasn't going to make it. Harry had her.

A loud snap rang out in the dark followed by a stretching-back twang of taut rope and whirring friction through pulleys. A war cry wailed in the air above, and the near miss of a flying figure skewed her balance and sent her to the ground. A powerful collision thudded into the charging beast behind her.

She rolled and looked back to see the airborne figure flip off the troll's thick skull to land gracefully while Harry stumbled backward to crash hard on its bulbous backside. The person straightened a pointed hat then sauntered over.

He reached out a hand to help her up. "Might I suggest we make our hasty escape before that ugly beastie gains his wits, eh?"

Laura recognized the beloved character instantly. "John Arrow? No freaking way…"

"Captain. *Captain* John Arrow. You've heard of me?"

"You could say that."

"May I inquire as to what has a dashing lass such as yourself gallivanting past my ship in the middle of the night—aside from big ugly over there?"

"This druid-looking wizard, or whatever, cast a spell bringing you and the troll and a bunch of other characters to life, and I'm trying to fix it. Abe Lincoln said I'd find someone near the river to help me."

Arrow put a finger to the side of his mouth and cocked his head. "Abe Lincoln? Tall fellow, funny beard, big hat?"

"Yes, that's him."

"Never heard of him." Harry moaned and rolled over on his side. "Ah, time to go! Talk on the way!"

Arrow grabbed Laura's hand and took off in the direction of Southern Town Square.

"Way to where?" Laura said. "Are you the one I'm looking for? I mean, you *are* helping, obviously, but you don't do magic or anything to reverse all this."

"Nay, mystical mumbo jumbo isn't my specialty, as it were. If memory serves, I know someone whose is."

They rounded the end of the river, passing by the ride where Captain John Arrow hailed from, into the area of the park where buildings turned to fleur de lis-embellished balcony railings and colonial-style columns. Up ahead along the brick-walled row, its gables peeking through the thick tree canopy, sat the stateliest of them all.

"Ghost Manor, Captain? You really think that's a good idea?" On a normal day, the whimsical homage to the ghoulish and ghastly was one of her favorite attractions. Given all she'd experienced so far... Well, let's just say dread didn't quite cover it.

"Aye. There's a witch. Goes by the name Mistress Leona."

Harry's angry yell carried over the water followed by the bashing noise of troll club on wood. Arrow slowed their pace and let go of her hand, meandering to the riverbank to gaze in that direction.

"Oy! Stop smashing holes in my ship!"

"Don't bring him over here! He's after me. Thinks I'm his princess." She shuddered in disgust.

Arrow flashed a sly grin. "Can't say as I blame him. Fine, upstanding lass such as you... What say you and Captain John procure a bottle of rum and have ourselves a frolic 'round Pirate Island, eh?"

Laura laughed at the cheeky pirate's advance. In the moment of contemplating her response—not that there were really options in this situation despite the character's charm and roguish sex appeal—a chorus of singing warbled up the pathway. As it drew near, the unmistakable, waddling form of a gaggle of oversized, anthropomorphic geese became clear in the lamplight.

"That's interesting," Arrow said.

"Don't trust them," Laura said. "Those Log Ride Mountain characters always freaked me the hell out."

"How d'ya do?" one of the geese said. Its southern-drawled greeting was friendly enough, but Laura couldn't shake the feeling this wouldn't end well. "Mighty fine evening for a stroll, wouldn't you say?"

"If you say so," Laura said. "We'll let you get back to it." Harry's roar and bashing club echoed off the masonry louder than before. He was headed their way. "We have to stop him and send all you monsters back where you came from."

"Why I do declare," another goose said, "that's our old pal Harry over there!"

"Who you callin' monsters, missy? And what d'ya mean send us back?" said another.

"Sounds a might bit rude, don't y'all think?" said the last.

Laura hated being right and nudged Arrow in the arm.

"Right! We bid you lovely geeses good day." He tipped his hat and moved to leave.

"Oh, y'all ain't going anywhere!" The first goose spread its wings and snarled its bill. The other three did the same. Their eyes glowed red.

And Captain Arrow shot the lead goose right in the face.

"Rude, indeed," it said, voice electronically crackling and distorted through the musket ball hole in its beak.

"I hate geese," Arrow said and whipped out his cutlass as the freakish fowls lunged.

Laura kicked the closest hard in its breast, knocking it back into its fellow. Arrow fenced and parried flapping wings and clapping bills, lopping off tufts of feathers and goofy hats.

"Go find Leona!" he said. "I'll handle the birds!" He cut clean through the neck of one, the head tumbling to the ground.

"That's a fine how do ya do," the head said.

Laura kicked her way past another and turned back. "Will you be ok?"

Arrow slashed through a wing. "You're forgetting one thing, love."

"What's that?"

He struck a wide-armed pose and devilish grin. "I'm Captain John Arrow."

She couldn't help but laugh at the famous character's persona as she ran for Ghost Manor.

THE FRONT OF THE colonial-style mansion was dark, but warm, flickering light glowed through the windows. *It shouldn't be powered on,* she thought. *I better be careful in there.*

The front entrance was closed, though she knew that wasn't the easiest way in due to the spooky elevator portion at the beginning of the ride. Harry hollered somewhere from the direction she'd come—or was it something else—and she worried about Arrow.

Like Abe, he'd covered her escape and she was genuinely grateful. She hoped the clever pirate continued to live up to his cunning and nigh impossible to kill namesake. She'd likely need more help before this was all over.

Laura made her way around the building to a recently created "secret" entrance that bypassed the elevator. The door to the stairway was locked, as it should be. But, being a Magicland employee had its advantages. She waved her name badge over the hidden sensor, and the door clicked open.

The Manor was eerily quiet as she traversed the stairs and entered the onboarding area of the ride where passengers climbed onto the rounded, black carriages. They sat still in their track. The musty air felt heavy, the gloom seemed to press in on her. The dim illumination of artificial candles cast strange shadows across the floor.

A shriek drifted out of the carriage tunnel, and she nearly jumped out of her skin. "Get it together, girl," she whispered to herself trying to calm her frazzling nerves. That was the way she needed to go to get to Mistress Leona, an early fixture of the ride. She edged around the first carriage before the entrance to the black tunnel.

"I wouldn't go in there if I were you," a ghostly female voice said to her left and she tumbled backward into the carriage in fright.

"Holy shit!" Laura yelled. Standing in a hidden alcove was a blueish-hued bride in a tattered wedding dress. A red glowing heart thumped audibly in her chest.

"Be warned," the bride said. "He's near."

"I have to get Mistress Leona," Laura found her feet and climbed out of the carriage. "She's the only one who can stop this."

"He won't let you stop him."

"*He* doesn't have a choice." Laura ducked into the tunnel.

"Good luck... For better or worse."

Laura crept through the ride, weaving between the carriages, and constantly scanning for more spooky surprises. Leona wasn't far. She rounded a corner, and there she was. Mistress Leona, just the head of a spectral woman floating in a blue crystal ball that hovered over an ornate pillow. During the ride, she'd chant rhyming calls to the spirit world. But her eyes were closed, silently resting.

Laura hoped Arrow wasn't wrong about Leona. Was she even "alive" like so many other characters had become? So far, the human-based characters had been kind and helpful to her. The creatures had been quite the opposite. Where did Leona fall in the otherworldly trend of the night? *Only one way to find out*, she thought, and tapped gently on the crystal ball.

Leona's eyes shot open, and her head whirled in Laura's direction. "What in the hell did you do that for? Do you have any idea how loud that is in here?"

Laura recoiled. "I'm sorry! I didn't mean to scare you."

"You didn't scare me, you woke me up." Leona did not sound like her usual mystical self. Instead, her voice had an American East Coast manner to it, and she certainly wasn't rhyming incantations.

"I'm sorry," Laura repeated, "but I need your help. It's been a wild night..."

"Oh yeah, I know why you're here, dearie." Something clanged and shrieked somewhere within the Manor. Leona's eyes narrowed as she gazed off into the dark. "Kinda obvious."

"Are you able to reverse the Druid Guy's spell and stop all this craziness?"

"I can, yes. But not from here. I need to be in the center of the park. And I'm pretty sure I know who you're talking about."

"You do? How? Aren't you just a character brought to life?"

Leona laughed. "Some of these oddballs are just reanimated characters. Me, I was once a real practitioner of the magic arts long ago. And I've tangled with that fellow a time or two. His magic has a way of bringing spirits back from the void to possess objects similar to their true forms." Leona's eyes darted around. "Though I seem to be missing a few of my bits and pieces."

Laura thought over the implications of Leona's statement. Druid Guy had said that Harry was the spirit of a troll. Leona claimed to be similar. Did that mean Abe was the real Abraham Lincoln? But Captain John was his movie character... It made her head hurt trying to understand it.

"We need to stop this," she said. "What do I have to do?"

"Simple, dearie. Take me to the center of the park, and I'll reverse the spell."

"That's it?"

"That's it." Leona winked at her.

Excitement and hope rushed through Laura. "Then let's go!" She grabbed Leona's crystal ball with both hands and made toward the exit.

"Careful with me!" Leona said. "I ain't made of rubber, you know."

Laura tucked the crystal mystic securely into the crook of her arm and weaved through the ride carriages back into the boarding area.

"Ah, well played. I see you retrieved the witch," said a familiar, lilting voice from the shadows. Laura jumped and turned to the hooded silhouette of Druid Guy.

"I warned you..." the unseen bride's voice floated in the dusty air.

"Back to your old mischief, are you?" Leona said. Laura shifted her grip to hold the ball facing him. "Did you really think you'd get away with this?"

"I admit, the spell had some unforeseen complications, thanks to our mutual friend here."

"This isn't my fault!" Laura said. "You caused all this."

"Regardless, my mischief—as you call it, witch—has brought back so many more spirits than anticipated. Wonderful!" He clapped his hands together. "To my chagrin, that seems to include you. I cannot allow you to disrupt what I've done here." His eyes glowed their menacing green.

"Sorry to tell you this, pal," Leona said. Laura felt warmth radiating from the ball. "But that's not how this is gonna work."

Light flared from within Leona and a burst of magical energy shot forth striking Druid Guy square in the chest. He flew back and smacked into a far wall. Blue, electrical-like magic arced across and through his body.

"Run!" Leona said. "That'll only slow him down."

Laura did as commanded and bolted back to the stairway. Her breaths came quick and panting. A stitch in her side flared as she bounded up the steps and back into the night. But she ignored it all. She had to end this.

Down the pathway through Southern Town Square, she raced past the hacked corpses and piles of feathers of the demon geese from earlier. There was no sign of Arrow, much to her relief. She pressed on.

"Where do we need to go?" she asked.

"The middle pavilion near the castle should do!"

She looked across the river in the direction of the castle. It's illuminated towers and spires visible in the sky above Magicland. And audible over her footfalls and heavy breathing was a cacophony of bangs, crashes, roars, and yells.

"That doesn't sound good," she said.

"Hell's broken loose," Leona said. "This won't be easy."

"All I wanted to do was go home for the night. But no... I had to confront the Druid Guy..."

Around the curve of the river, past the pirate ship with troll club holes in its side, and back through the splintered remnants of the Wild West Land entrance, Laura raced toward unknown dangers and Leona's promised magical end to a night of mayhem. Her body ached, muscles protested, and fear squeezed her heart in its unyielding grip. But she pressed on, committed to save the park and countless people should the unnatural creatures get loose on the world.

She skidded to an abrupt halt at the scene playing out before her in the pavilion.

"Oh, shit..." Her mouth hung open and eyes grew wide.

It was an absolute melee. Every character and creature imaginable from throughout the park clashed with each other. Debris from various rides and smashed animatronics littered the ground. Pirates from the High Seas ride swashbuckled droids and aliens from Futureland. Doll-like children toddled and bit the ankles of human-like bears and foxes. Talking parrots and macaws divebombed and pecked at a fedora-wearing adventurer. Harry the Troll was there, growling and wildly swinging his club at grayscale specters. Elephants, hippos, a tiger—

Tiger! Laura's brain realized a split second before the bounding beast lunged. She dived away, losing her grip on Mistress Leona's crystal ball which went rolling down the path. Glass tinkled and the witch within screamed in distress.

Laura flipped to her back and crab-crawled away from the snarling, hunched tiger, ready to pounce again. That was it. She was done for.

"Like hell you will!" A lean, axe-wielding man lept through the air and delivered a massive, overhand blow that nearly took the tiger's head off.

"Abe!" The relief she felt at seeing her presidential friend, beaten and tattered as he was, couldn't have been measured. He wrenched the axe free of the unmoving beast and let out a huge sigh.

"Miss Laura, aren't you a sight for sore eyes." He reached down and helped her up. "Did you find who you needed?"

"Oh shit! Yes! Where'd she go?" She quickly scanned the area and spotted Leona resting against a curb some distance away. "Get her! She can reverse the spell." She dashed toward the ball.

As Laura was about to scoop up Leona, a flying boy with pointy ears wearing green tights swooped down from the sky and snatched her first. He laughed mischievously as he soared away over the heads of the battling creatures.

"Dammit!" Laura yelled and shook her fist. "Curse you, Pe—"

An elephant trumpeted behind them and thundered past. "Confounded elf-boy! I'll get him!" Balancing atop the pounding pachyderm was none other than Captain John Arrow.

"I believe I have seen just about everything," Abe said.

Laura could only laugh at his serious understatement.

Arrow steered the elephant with a rope around its neck like a bridle after the flying boy through the circle of the pavilion, gaining ground. "This is the day you'll long remember..." He whipped the rope off the elephant and twirled it over his head like a lasso, then released it. It tangled up the boy, sending him careening to the ground, and the screeching Leona up into the air. Arrow deftly reached out and caught her, then flipped off the animal's back and landed wobbly on his feet. "That you almost got away from Captain John Arrow."

"No, Abe... *Now* I think we've seen everything," Laura said.

Arrow strode over to them, casually stepping over flotsam and wearing a lopsided grin. He handed Mistress Leona to Laura. "What say we conclude these dastardly proceedings and keelhaul that wicked robed fellow, savvy?"

"Ah!" Leona let out a cry of relief, "Yes, before I get smashed!"

"Thank you all," Laura said. "I wish I didn't have to send you away."

"T'was no trouble, miss," Abe said. "Stop those bitches."

"It would've never worked out between us, love." Arrow said.

They walked into the middle of the pavilion. The two men stood guard at her side.

"Pay it no mind, dearie," Leona said. "I was comfortable in the afterlife. At least I had a body!" she laughed heartily. "Now, hold me up and I'll begin the spell." Laura held her high above her head.

"Stop!" A voice bellowed over the carnage. Druid Guy stood at the front of the castle bridge. "You mustn't undo what I've accomplished here!"

"No freaking way!" Laura yelled back. "You've caused enough trouble and destruction!"

"What she said!" Arrow added.

"I only need a moment to cast the reversal spell," Leona said. "Just don't let him interrupt me."

"You will not succeed, witch!" Druid Guy said. "Hereweald, get them!"

With a blood-curdling roar, Harry the Troll charged from across the way. Abe and Arrow took defensive postures. Every muscle in Laura's body tensed. Her heart raced. "Now, Leona!"

The crystal ball grew hot in her hands, but she didn't dare let go. A magical glow welled up from within its center, spreading outward in all directions and bathing the trio in brilliant light. Harry was nearly to them. Abe and Arrow threw themselves at the troll, axe and cutlass whirling.

"Incantamentum rescindi!" Leona yelled.

"No!" Druid Guy reached forward as if to cast his own counter spell.

But he was too late. The powerful, magical essence of Mistress Leona's spell erupted in all directions in a blinding flash, as though the heavens themselves had opened up in a thundering storm of all storms. Laura dropped to her knees, nearly overcome by energy. The wave of power dispersed through the park in a shockwave that reverberated through the air in a deafening whoosh.

The lifeless hulk of Harry the Troll, impaled by the equally lifeless Abe and Arrow, skidded across the ground to rest mere inches from Laura's utterly exhausted self. She expelled her held breath all at once and shakily rose to her feet.

Druid Guy walked menacingly toward her. "You think you've won the day, do you?" His hands were outstretched, green arcs flicking between his fingertips. A contemptuous smile spread across the lower half of his face just visible under the hood. "Alas, you'd be gravely mistaken. Your friends are gone, your body weakened. I'll simply recast the spell as-"

"Oh, shut up you mumbling asshole." Laura reared back and chucked Leona's now dark and empty crystal ball straight at his head.

It beaned Druid Guy between his glowing eyes, knocking him back with a grunt before he suddenly disappeared in a burst of greenish haze. Laura collapsed on the pavement, completely spent, and not bothering to care where the enigmatic man had gone.

She wasn't sure how long she lay there before the thumping rotors of a helicopter and chirping of police sirens broke the stillness. She was sure of one thing, however.

"No one is ever going to believe this."

J.C. MASTRO GREW UP in California in the 1980's. As a child, he enjoyed science fiction and fantasy, spending sunny days outside battling invisible aliens and flying through space in oversized, cardboard ships. Evenings and lazy afternoons were spent consuming 1980's TV and movie favorites like reruns of *Star Trek*, and *Star Wars* on worn-down VHS tapes. In his teens, J.C. discovered a love of reading sci-fi and fantasy novels by authors such as Frank Herbert, Michael Crichton, and Timothy Zahn. Nowadays, he's a huge fan of authors like Brandon Sanderson, John Scalzi, and Andy Weir.

J.C. is a graduate of the Master of Fine Arts in Writing Popular Fiction program at Seton Hill University and a visually impaired author. His debut young adult science fiction novel, *Academy Bound*, released in 2022, and his short story "Spirit of the Dragon" appears in the Outstanding Creator Award winning anthology, *Dragons of a Different Tail*, where he also served as an editor. He lives in sunny southern California with a bunch of kids and dogs—and wouldn't want it any other way.

Website: www.jcmastroauthor.com   Instagram: @jcmastroauthor   Twitter: @JCMastroAuthor

GHOULY GIRL

By Sophia DeSensi

Grady's song by David Fowler

I KNOW THIS IS a terrible, embarrassing idea. I could toss the frosting and cake batter box into the bushes and be done with this whole thing. Still, my traitorous legs wobble up the porch of the salt-box framed house. As soon as these residents find out who—er—what I am, they'll kick me out just the same as all the others.

But I refuse. I simply refuse to 'haunt' another house just for a free place to stay. After I drove that Poe guy mad just because I wanted to see what it felt like to dress up as an elderly man. Call it a mid-centennial crisis or boredom, but apparently it really freaked Poe out. I suppose I never could pull off cataracts. Only ever in one eye.

And then there was that time back in 1692—or was it 1693—when I was living with the mayor of Salem. He wasn't home. Or, I thought he wasn't when I shook out of the black feline into my typical human skin. And, oh boy, the repercussions of that one have lived even into this century.

So, this time, for the first time, I'm going to move in the human way. I'm going to walk up to their house, roommate ad saved on my phone, and pay rent.

I'm sick of being called demon, evil eyes thrust in my direction, or swat with a broom. I mean, seriously, residents don't have any respect for the warmth it takes to summon shiny, frizz-less waves like this every day. Without the tether of four walls, I won't even have the warmth to summon the appearance of a skeleton. And I've realized, without the skin part, humans freak.

Today, without a home to tether, I'm dull and gaunt from wallowing through the streets last night without a tether. My hair can't even be considered blonde anymore. It's basically sallow. And worst of all, I don't even have enough warmth to summon fingernail polish.

"Okay, be honest." I set Juniper on the porch beside a wilted pumpkin carved to resemble Baby Yoda. The gourd greets me with an uneasy, almost nauseated smile. I feel you, buddy. "On a scale of crazy ex-girlfriend to middle-aged cat hoarder, how pathetic do I look?" I raise the Publix bags and duffle.

"Hmm." Juniper lifts a vine in contemplation. "I'd say middle-aged vir—"

"Scratch that. I don't want to know."

"What?" Juniper whacks my groceries with a vine, peering inside. "Confetti cake and buttercream frosting?" She snaps her berries.

"I know. I know, okay? It's stupid. No amount of baked goods will convince them I'm human. But who wouldn't welcome a wholesome baker into their home?"

"What do you think is going to happen? One of those human guys are going to bite into the cake, ditch his spoon full of frosting to spoon you instead?" Juniper's leaves ruffle in that somewhat spooky chuckle of hers.

"No. Obviously, no. And can you prune the sarcasm, please?" I stand, my knees cracking. I'm nervous enough without Juniper trying to make this something it's not. I have no interest in humans besides the shelter and warmth they can provide. Is a ghoulish life lonesome? Yes. Do I think a human could fill that void? No.

"Let's aim for a good impression," I say in my most cheerful, optimist tone. "Or at least, a normal one this time."

"Maybe we'd make a better first impression if you conditioned me. You spend enough time taming your own rat's nest."

"Oh, you're so right, Juniper. The fact that my talking plant's leaves aren't conditioned is the reason no one will let the ghoul into their home."

She nods, caressing her vines.

"Now," I say. "Can you be quiet so we don't scare away our potential human roommates? Otherwise, with me vaporous and unable to sustain a physical form, no one else will bother to water my bratty houseplant."

"Whoopie." Juniper twirls a mocking vine, spritzing the little white ghosts on my pumpkin-colored dress in fertilizer. "What a happy haunt this will be."

She folds her vines across her stem and turns her blossom toward the front door.

I summon my last bit of warmth into a fist and knock. The duffle strap slips over sheer skin. I jostle it so it conceals the white of bone.

"It's open," a guy calls from inside.

I balance my things in my arms and use my free hand to twist the knob and bump it ajar. The scent of cologne and dirty dish water sloshes through the foyer. Or what I suppose attempts to be a foyer. Rumpled graphic tees, basketball shorts, and loose socks litter the hardwood. I step over the threshold and onto a musky, oriental rug that's so stiff and lined in dust, I'd guess it hadn't been cleaned since the historic home was first built.

"Oh, hey, new roomie." The guy lies upside down on the couch. His beanie slips over his brunette bangs as he sits upright.

"Survive on human flesh," blares the TV. A truly offensive anime flashes on the screen. An animated girl with red eyes and teeth dripping in blood seethes.

"Ha—hi—" A potato chip cracks beneath my pumps.

"Oh, ah, I got you." He shifts the lollipop between his teeth, tosses his Switch, and grabs my bags.

"You just threw your Switch," I say.

"Oh, yeah, it's batteriezed. Doesn't matter." He shrugs. "You can set your duffle over there. And, uh, your plant."

I set both down beside a blow-up llama with a mustache that holds a plastic bowl filled with Reese's peanut butter cups.

"Don't ask." He drops the groceries on a laminate counter in the kitchenette.

The door adjacent to the kitchen slams against the wall and stirs a dancing skeleton on the countertop.

"Hey—whoa," the second roommate says. I recognize his aquiline nose and gelled hair from the ad. "What's all that? Grady, did you tell her she could move right in?" He waves a razor, fluffed in shaving cream. Foam splatters on his overly muscled bare chest. He looks like a total frat-bro. To my relief, frat-bro wears joggers, so he's not completely naked when meeting with his potential roommate. "Of course, you would. Seriously? We haven't even done the interview." Which, apparently, he's not even prepared for in the first place.

"Dude, where's your shirt? There's a lady present." Sloppy-nerdy guy flattens a guitar pick on a leather cord around his neck.

"Not moving in." I sit on the couch and move a snickerdoodle cookie onto the glass coffee table. "Just had nowhere else to put my stuff, so I thought I'd bring it all with me." I smooth my pleated skirt. "Anyway, ask away."

Frat-bro wipes his face on a dish towel and folds it neatly back on the counter, then sits on an ottoman across from me. He crosses his legs like he's about to pose for a Roman sculptor or something.

"What's your profession? Rent is high and we don't need any free loaders," frat-bro says. "We're barely making ends meet as is."

"Dude, manners," sloppy-nerdy guy says. "He doesn't mean to be offensive, I promise."

"No, no, it's direct. I like it. I have a job." I twist a curl around my freckled finger. I knew this was coming. Hence the groceries. "I'm a baker."

Frat-bro raises his manicured brow.

"Ignore him." Grady shakes his head. "Doesn't matter what your job is as long as you can pay rent. Anyway, this is the place. Kind of an open concept layout."

Yellow stains suffuse the corners of the low-ceiling. Dingy and historic doesn't bother me. I tend to take comfort in cobwebs, linoleum, and the acrylic scent of silver polish. All I need to tuck my spirit into the home are sharp angles to bind my tether and keep myself intact in this physical world. Though a crackling fireplace never hurt a ghoul, but it doesn't look like I'll be getting that in my Florida reprieve.

"Jerk-face's bedroom is there. Mine and the spare are down the hall." Grady points to the chalk-board walls, covered in sketches and powdered baseboards. This place could seriously use garnish and flounce, but I'm happy to take on the project.

"There wasn't an application online," I say.

"Pshh." Frat-boy stands, flicking his wrist. "None of those formalities are necessary here. Six hundred is due on the first of each month. You can make it out to Lyle Properties. Pay that and you're good to go."

"Okay. Easy peasy." I've gathered enough cash for that—a perk of an immortal life.

"I'm Grady, by the way." Sloppy-nerdy guy offers his hand. "And the guy pretending he's a developer is Lyle."

"Nice to meet you." I shake Grady's hand. "Everleigh. Ever for short."

"Cute. Ever." A blush tinges his cheeks as he shakes my hand, hopefully not feeling the lack of density in my fingertips that's growing fainter and fainter with each squeeze of his own solid limb. "Not that you're cute, but your name is—I mean, you are too, but I didn't—" He breaks off, releasing my hand all at once and shifts his beanie over the edge of his brow.

"Smooth." Lyle laughs.

"So, I don't mean to impose," I stand, reaching for Juniper, "but I kind of don't have anywhere else to go at the moment. Any chance you'd let me move in now?"

Lyle opens his mouth.

"Of course," Grady says, slinging his arm over Lyle's broad shoulders. "We're glad to have you. Make yourself at home." He chomps down on the lollipop, cracking the center of the tootsie pop.

Lyle sighs. "Just don't be trying to scoop any of my body butter in the shower room and we'll get along just great. I'm a monster when my skin's dry."

That makes two of us.

I pick up my belongings, ready to warm myself in the privacy of my new room.

"Just so you know," Grady says and I pause. "We're having a Halloween party tonight. I hope that won't bother you."

"Grady, here, thinks he's famous." Lyle squeezes Grady's shoulder. "Lynyrd Skynyrd for the Gen-Zs."

"Hey, I am famous. At least between the blocks of Flamingo Park."

I balance Juniper in the crook of my arm. "Then you're in luck, Samhain's my favorite. And I already brought supplies to whip up some tasty treats." I drop the grocery bags. A container of black and orange bat sprinkles rolls across the counter.

"See. I told you a girl roommate would come with benefits," Grady says.

"Benefits?" Lyle raises an eyebrow.

"No. What? I didn't mean—I mean she's a snack—no. She makes snacks. The food. Her cooking." He shouts the last part.

And with that wave of embarrassment, I carry my things into the empty bedroom. Sunlight fills the space with warmth as it pours from the hopper window, illuminating motes caught in the traps of the pecky cypress banisters. It's just about perfect with the angled glass and pitched roof. I just need… I unzip my duffle and pull out a fluffy heated blanket and toss it across the twin-sized bed. The iron frame creaks a cozy welcome home.

I plug in the space heater from my duffle. And once the room is nice and toasty, I tuck myself beneath the heated blanket just as I tuck my spirit into the ninety-degree angles of the roof. My freckles grow more and more visible along my forearms as warmth energizes my specter. I pull the heated blanket to my chin and wiggle my solid, human toes. "As toasty and roasty as a marshmallow."

"Roasty." Juniper snorts, twirling her vines with Balanchine leaves in the speckled rays of the marbleized glass panes. "That's what I'll be when they find out what you are, salt you out, and toss me into some decayed garden to writhe in the sun."

"That won't happen." I scoot with my back against the iron frame.

"It's the truth."

"Is not. There's no reason for them to find out, and after tonight, I'll be tethered here for good. Our pastoral life will be over."

"Ha," Juniper barks out. "What-Ever, we'll see."

A decayed oak leaf flickers in from the open window, landing right atop my toe. The heart-shaped leaf crumbles.

I toss my legs to the side of the bed. "You'll see. I'll make this work." I just need to do some nesting. Make this bachelor-pad my home.

After a quick redecoration, I pre-heat the oven and peruse their cabinets for spices. Thankfully, I find red pepper flakes, ground cayenne, and a jar of jalapenos in their kitchen for my go-to move in recipe. I smear a rack of ribs, a whole filet, and a chicken with a nice, thick layer of the ground seasoning.

"Smells amazing," Grady says, tapping a ballpoint against his jeans where song lyrics and music notes are scribbled across the worn fabric. He sits on the bottle-cap barstool across from me and pulls a plastic bowl of popcorn over the counter. He tosses a handful in his mouth and wipes pink crumbs from his chin with a lopsided smile. "What is this—strawberry frosting?" He inspects a piece.

"Yep. Dipped them myself."

He tosses more popcorn into his mouth in this kind of cute, kind of awkward way.

"It's my specialty." I dry my hands on the frayed threads of butterflies and dandelions of my linen apron. I used to make them for my ex-ghoulfriend, but he never appreciated it. He'd prefer chocolate, or it wasn't warm enough, or it tasted stale. He always had a reason my cooking wasn't good enough.

"What's wrong? You've got this sad look on your face."

"Nothing."

"We're friends now. You can talk to me. I'm a good listener." Grady smiles another one of those dopey grins that just makes you want to hug him and tell him everything.

"Well," I trace a crack in the counter, stained with coffee and dehydrated Jell-o. "To be honest," I bend down beneath the sink and grab a bottle of Windex so old the label is yellow and crumbling. "I just went through a breakup. Kind of the reason I needed a new place to live."

"Ah, you've got the heart stinger." Grady nods. "That's why I refuse to date. But Lyle basically goes through a breakup a week. I'm sure he'll underst—"

Lyle tosses open his bedroom door. "Not cool. Spilling my secrets? My heartbreaks? Bro-code." He places a hand to his now, thankfully, clothed chest. A simple white t-shirt with three unbuttoned buttons at the top and the sleeves scrunched up over his elbows.

"Bro-code? That's not a thing." Grady laughs. "Never has been. Never will be."

"What's this?" Lyle strips a throw blanket from the couch. "It's all pink and—" He stretches the fabric. "Knitted."

"And totally cozy," I say. "Made by yours truly."

He swaddles it against his cheek with a look of genuine pleasure and then scoffs, discarding it on the hardwood. "And this? 'Hey, Boo'?" He smushes the pillow like an accordion. "You've—you've defaced, mangled our pillows with girly sewing." He sniffs. "And what is that? Pumpkin spice? This is a bachelor pad. Not the Bath and Body Works."

"Please." I open the oven. Steam pours over the roast chicken. Butter sizzles atop crispy, spiced skin. A chef kiss moment. "Like I'd ever shop at Bath and Body Works. Those are Nest."

"Whoa. What are you feeding, the entire neighborhood?" Grady leans over the counter. I set down the filet to rest, soaking in all the juices beneath tin foil. "No.I made you guys the chicken." I swivel the roast in a white ceramic dish, tucked with pears, apples, and spiced yams.

"I can get on board with the cooking," Lyle says, padding over to us in ankle-high socks "But the girly décor has got to go. We're men. We bask in the scent of musk." He all but beats his chest to assert his masculinity.

"Speak for yourself. I kind of like the place cleaned up," Grady says, grabbing an oversized fork from the utensil holder. "A professional chef just cooked your dinner. How about be grateful for once?"

"I cleaned up that rotted pumpkin you had on the porch too." I slice the roast and drop a piece on Grady's plate. He practically drools, inhaling in the spiced steam.

"You didn't—baby Grogu? Grady, fix this." He drags his hands down his clean-shaven face.

Grady shakes his head. "You've gone too far, Ever. One thing you should know about Lyle is that he's got all the makings of a dad, besides the bod, beneath his stone-cold appearance. And surprisingly enough, has a soft spot for miniature Star Wars characters."

"It's Yoda. In tiny, baby form." Lyle slumps on the stool, looking rigid and statuesque and in serious need of a cupcake.

"For the hangry, manly man," I say in a mock Vin Diesel voice and hand him a mummy cookie wrapped in frosting with chocolate chip eyes. "I'm sorry for tossing out the melted gourd. How about a cookie to make up for it?"

He swats it away. "I don't eat high fructose corn syrup."

"Maybe you should. It'd make you sweeter." Grady pops the cookie in his mouth and tares off a piece of chicken and eats that too in one gulp.

"Gross." I laugh and fork the filet onto my plate, dousing it in hot sauce..

"You're eating all that?" Grady asks.

"Yeah." I shrug, setting my plate on a pumpkin-shaped mat. I may have found a pair of scissors and made a slight improvement to the previous ones. Really, it was just to trim off the ketchup stains.

"See. She fits right in." Grady smacks Lyle on the shoulder and dips a carving knife into the roast chicken.

I bite into the meat, hot sauce dripping down my lips. Each mouthful feels like a stolen ounce of humanity, and I cherish every single gulp.

"Holy—" Grady drops his fork, mouth hung open, and fanning his tongue. "What the hell?" He tears open the fridge door and yanks out a gallon of milk, gulping it down. His face brightens a shade of eggplant.

"What? What happened?" I crinkle a paper towel between my saucy hands. "Is it burnt?"

With wide eyes, he downs half the milk gallon, slams it and wipes his swollen lips. "Did you stuff the chicken—" Grady rips open the freezer. "Ice. I need ice." He pops cubes into his mouth. "—with ghost peppers?" He leans against the counter. "I've never tasted anything so hot in my entire life, and I once won a hot wing contest senior year of high school."

"Oh, don't be a tender-tongue." Lyle bites into his own chicken breast, then spits it out. He practically kicks over his stool as he scrambles across the hardwood and snatches the jug from Grady. Milk spills down his chin, but he doesn't seem to mind as he continues to drink and drink.

"Guys, come on. It's fine." I pluck a piece from Grady's abandoned plate. Perfectly seasoned and moist.

"How can you eat that?" Grady garbles with a mouth full of ice.

"How can you not?"

"Ly—" Grady points at him.

"Pizza. On it. Ordering now." Lyle pulls his phone from his pocket.

"You're crazy." Grady shakes his head and smiles. "Hell, that was spicy."

"Hell's not that spicy."

Grady huffs a laugh, wiping his lips with the back of his hand. "Speaking of hell—that's the theme for tonight's show."

Lyle slides his phone back into his pocket. "Here's hoping your ballads bring in enough guests to call an electrician for those flaky wires."

After I finished off the filet and the boys' pizza arrived, I'm filled with fizzy, anxious energy for tonight's party. Sure. I'vve been to parties before. The best of them being in New Orleans on All Hallows Eve. Though. I'm not going to lie, I may have wafted onto the Myrtle's Plantation a few years ago, hyped up on all the drunken body warmth in the streets, only to find that ghosts scare the bejeezus out of me. The ghost of Chloe really got her linen in a twist when a pair of teenagers tried to summon her with one of those plastic, store-bought Ouiji boards. And that's when I decided parties in New Orleans were not my thing. Dead residents can be awfully angry. I shiver just thinking about the ghost governess.

"I guess I don't have much time to find another costume," I say as I sit on the edge of my bed and pull white fishnets over my knees. "This old one will have to do."

"Uhm, excuse me." Juniper taps a leaf against my knee. "Where's my costume?" She flattens a leaf to her stem and drags it across her forehead. "Don't tell me. Can it be? Dare I even speak the betrayal? I'm not invited."

"You're a plant." I walk over to the mirror hung on the back of the door that must have been left by the previous tenant. Who apparently had a crush on Lyle, as hard to believe as that is, since his name is scrawled in market inside red hearts all over the edge."

"And? I could be part of your costume." Juniper hops her pot across the hardwood.

I smooth my hair, running my fingers through the blonde and summoning streaks of turquoise.

"I'm not going to carry a plant around all night."

"Why? Just because I'm coniferious? I bet if I was of the gourd variety you would. I see all those girls posing with pumpkins on Insta."

"Oh, please. Do you want to be carved? No? I didn't think so." I shift one eye to Tiffany blue and the other an Elizabeth Taylor violet. I press my energy into rhinestones across my eyelids and cascade bubblegum glitter across my cheeks.

"No one would carve me. I'd be the prettiest pumpkin of the patch." She takes a ginormous gulp of air and swells her foliage and barriers into an awkwardly shaped gourd with ombre blue-orange knobs. "See."

"You look ridiculous." I poke a berry and she deflates back into her typical form.

"And you don't with mix-matched eyes? Humans don't look like that."

"They could be contacts." I press the spaghetti straps of my sequined dress over my shoulders.

The ceiling fan's light suddenly shuts off.

"Damn electric company and their incessant bills," Grady says in the hall. He knocks. "Ready?"

I twist the knob and pause, fingers gripping the glass knob. Juniper droops her blades, skimming the floor in a completely pathetic manner. "Behave and I'll bring you sugar water at the end of the night, okay?"

Her vines brighten. "Promise? Like last Halloween? You'll melt some candy corn?"

"Promise. Be back in a few hours."

She makes a zip motion with her leaves.

"Whoa," Grady says as I open the door.

"Too much?" I tuck my hair behind both ears, stepping into the hall and shutting the door behind me. Just as I hear a small sneeze. That's not what I call quiet, but thankfully Grady doesn't seem to notice.

"I like it. Punk vibes," he says, smiling a smile that makes my stomach feel all dissolve-y and floaty.

"I was going for a punky-mermaid kind of look." I trace my coral ballet flats across a loose floorboard.

"Then, I'd say you nailed it." He raises to his tiptoes. "Wait, right here." He turns on his Converses and rushes into his room opposite mine. When he returns, he holds out a pooka shell necklace. "I know they've been out of style since the early 2000's, but it might make a nice hair accessory."

"I never cared much about trends."

He tucks the necklace into the back of my half-up-half-down hairdo. "There." He turns me around and tiny tendrils of emerald swirl around his brown iris. Three freckles dot the bridge of his nose, and a single dot marks just above his brow.

"I swear, if one of those adolescents you DM'd the invites to spills a single drink on me, I'm mailing you the dry-cleaning bill." Lyle folds the collar of a crisp, black button-down. I'm not surprised.

Grady clears his throat, tugging the side of his Hufflepuff cape. "No one will spill a drink on you. It only gets rowdy here on Friday nights." He taps Lyle's shoulder with the tip of a wooden wand.

"It *is* a Friday night," Lyle says.

"Oh, damn. Is it?" Grady grins crookedly at me, and I swear, I feel my cheeks disappear.

"Tell your friends this is linen," Lyle says. "And I don't appreciate them acting as if I'm a terry cloth."

"Maybe if you wore a costume for once, you wouldn't have to worry about staining your clothes." Grady presses his wand to his temple. "Ever think of that?"

"One of us has to look presentable," Lyle says. "I attract the crowd." He flicks his collar. "You entertain them. And hopefully well enough that I can raise this year's cover charge to ten a head." "What about the headless?" Grady asks.

"Funny. Really funny."

I hook my arm around Lyle's. "Hey, no grumbling." I sizzle a bit of warmth through the lamps as we walk into the living room. I need a little more confidence tonight if I'm going to be with residents all night.

When the rest of Grady's bandmates arrive, the music hops from bass to bass in the living room. Not Elvis hopping, but an electric beat that makes everyone need to dance. Grady tunes his guitar just outside the porch doors, so at peace with his eyes shut and air pods blocking the chatter of his guests as they arrive.

Lyle hands me a red solo cup. Even after two-hundred years of various trendy cocktails, I have to say, jungle juice has got to be the worst. With pursed lips and tearing eyes, I gulp down the contents that taste like Cholera.

Before long, I'm smushed between bodies that stink of Jäger, candy corn, and vanilla perfume. Pendant lights blink blue and red and green across the living room. Illuminating a neon splatter portrait of a pug into a pink suit, holding a lime balloon. .

Grady walks around the couch to where he's shoved the TV against the wall to make room for the make-shift stage.

He taps against his thigh with this casual nonchalance that seems so juxtaposed with the chaos of the rest of the party. Like he's not sure if he's even supposed to be here, but that's just where the season took him. He tosses a stick to the drummer and grips the mic, guitar hung against his chest. The music pauses and he taps his foot to a new beat.

Someone bumps me, liquid drips down my shoulder, and I stumble forward, hands out to brace myself against the couch when my fingers fade right through the fabric. I knew I should have warmed longer. I'm fading. A bit of knee bone shows beneath my fishnet tights.

I can't let Grady see me—or see through me. Strands of blue hair tumble to the floor.

"I'm sorry," I say to Lyle. An iridescent nail peels from my finger. "I've got to go to bed." I tuck my fingers into a fist.

"What? Grady's just about to start. You can't sleep *now*."

"Sorry." I don't know what I'll say to Grady, but I'm sure I can come up with some excuse. Food poisoning or Cholera. Some human illness.

"You're beautiful," Grady sings. His voice carries over the speakers. "You're everything I ever need."

I pause.

"You're beautiful."

The drummer picks up tempo. He plucks the cords of his guitar. One chord by one chord. Purple, blue, orange lights pulse.

"When I close my eyes." Grady dips his chin, lashes fluttering. His smile reaches his chocolate eyes. "It's you I see." He grips the mic to his lips, stretching out the syllables. "It's you."

Like a spell, goosebumps rise.

The drummer rolls his sticks to the rhythm.

Grady grins. Right. At. Me. I have to be hallucinating. I'm cooling and evaporating and completely hallucinating. There's no way Grady's singing to me.

He hugs his chest, mimicking the lyrics, and sways his hips. And I—I'm all shocked thoughts twisted in the current of his liquid voice.

"I realize how much I need to say," he sings.

"He's singing to you." A girl in a Morticia Adams costume flicks her frayed sleeve. Gossamer scrubs my bone and I slap a hand to my shoulder.

"No." But I feel the smile on my lips as I meet Grady's eyes. "No?" I mouth.

He shrugs as if in answer or just the next lyric, I'm not sure. "I realize how much I need to say…"

"Whoa. You okay?" Faux Morticia asks. "You look pale."

I need warmth. I weave through the crowd toward the hall.

"But as you walk away," Grady sings, voice wavering. The drummer stumbles over the beat. The mic squeals. "I realize how much—"

My pumps all but disappeared. Hardwood visible through my feet.

"I like you?" Grady sings, a question on his voice. "Yes, I do." I can't stay. I can't let him see me like this. I'm a ghoul. He likes the figment of a girl he thinks he knows. Not me. Not this phantom curse of a foam.

"As sure as the sky is blue—" He strums the strings. "I like you."

A scream erupts. I push my way through, ignoring their shrieks. The drummer skitters to a stop. There's a knock and a clattering crash.

"I like you," Grady says, barely more than a whisper. "I think." He slings the strap of his guitar over his head. "I might." He sets it down. "Just go tell you." The microphone squeals as it drops to the floor.

In the safety of the hall, I reach for the knob to my bedroom. Finger bones evaporate to the knuckle. I can't—

I use the base of my palms to try to grip, twist. I slip. And slip, vaporizing and cooling by the second. This can't be the way I finish my two-hundred years in the world of the living. I'm not ready for the endless warmth of the underworld. I want to stay here a little longer. Among the residents. Maybe among Grady and even Lyle.

"Hey."

I lean against the door. Grady stands behind me.

"What are you doing? You're supposed to be performing." My legs give out and I tumble to a heap of bone, too frozen to cling to my painstakingly crafted human form.

"I couldn't. Not when—" He glances across my smoke plumes of skeletal legs.

"Warm. Get warmth," I say out of breath.

He must see right through me, but still, he stays.

"Then let's get you warmed," he says. "What do you need?"

"My room," I say, my voice perforates into the humid night air like the rustles of a branch. "I can't...turn...the knob." The last of my breath comes out in a huff. I'm no ghost; I can't waft through walls.

Grady shoves open the door with his shoulder and cradles me inside. He rests me beside the space heater.

"Damn—" I rest my head against the metal frame, feeling the tiniest fragments of warmth. It cools beneath my fading hand. I breathe it in. I feel my spirit tethered to every windowsill, every corner, every crevice of this house, and feed on the warmth of every body. Every racing heart, every trickle of sweat, every adrenaline rush of fear.

I don't want to, but I want to.

Grady cups my hand. Skin solidifying over bone. Still, he sits beside me.

For the first time in two-hundred years, I feel—I don't know what it is, really. That rush of belonging and comfort all wrapped up in one touch. A wholly human feeling, even though I'm not.

"I've ruined your show." I pull away and rest my hand on my tights. Seafoam sequins emerge along the crisscross threads.

"That's what you're worried about?" Grady shifts his weight and tugs his beanie. "When you just, uh. I don't know how to put this, but, Ever, are you, er, dead?" He scratches his cheek. "I mean, no offence. All respect for ghosts. If that's what you are."

I huff a laugh. "Not a ghost."

"Then, care to explain? Because that was really... I don't know what it was, really."

"You wouldn't believe me if I tried."

"I'd like to try." His chin dips low and he skims a calloused thumb over my wrist.

"Oh, the dramatics of you two," Juniper says from her pot beneath the window. "She's a ghoul. And one whose completely neglected me since she moved in with you two bags of flesh. Would I like a baked good? You wouldn't know." She flicks a berry at me. "You never offered."

"Juniper," I sigh. "You don't eat pastries."

"I'd still like the consideration of an offer."

"I'm a ghoul." I tuck my knees to my chest. "Not dead. Not a ghost. Born an apparition."

"A ghoul and a talking plant." Grady raises to his feet. I brace my legs against my chest, ready for whatever comes next. Salt or evil eyes or fainting.

He pauses and glances between Juniper and me.

"Do you want me to leave?" I dare to ask.

"That depends. Are you the soul sucking kind?" A smile plays on his lips.

"Hmm." I tap my finger. "Well, I wouldn't need a space heater with a soul to absorb." I laugh.

"You wouldn't." He slaps a hand to his chest.

"Eh, you never know. You're a human living with a ghoul. Better be on your best behavior."

"Nah, Ever, I believe you're a friendly ghoul," Grady says, wrapping an arm around my shoulders and pulling me close.

"Then you'd be right."

"Both of you," Lyle says, tossing open the door with a candle in hand. "I don't know what kind of trick that was, Ever, but the crowd loved it." He shakes a jar filled with cash. "You terrified everyone into emptying their pockets into our tip jar."

"See, you didn't ruin anything," Grady says, sitting beside me and pulling me against him.

"There's talk of an encore tomorrow night," Lyle says.

I slump on my bed and pull the heated blanket over me. "I, uhm..." I stretch out my legs. "I don't—I mean—"

Grady blinks long lashes, just barely skimming a freckle below his brow. I will him to understand. For me not to speak what I am.

"Tell them the house is haunted," Grady says, shifting to turn toward Lyle. "Every Friday night, I'll perform, for a fee of course, and the guests can listen to the ballads as our phantom roams the manor."

"Good, because if the two of you can perform like that then we're going to be rich." He shakes his head, smiling and clinging to the plastic jar of cash and walks out of the room, mumbling to himself.

"Truly, it doesn't freak you out to live with a ghoul?" I ask once Lyle's footsteps fade.

"A little, but I've always wanted to live in a haunted house." He sits beside me. "You're basically a dream come true."

"It's going to be insufferable living with you two," Juniper says, rolling her fronds.

"I don't know. It feels pretty sufferable to me." Grady slips his fingers between mine. If I wasn't already warm, I am now.

"Yeah, pretty sufferable." I interlace my fingers with his. Soft drizzles of rain trill against the windowpanes, and I rest my head against Grady's.

Juniper was right. What a happy haunt this will be.

Sophia DeSensi earned her Bachelor's in creative writing with a minor degree in medical anthropology from the University of Central Florida, and a Master of Fine Arts in Writing Popular Fiction from Seton Hill University. She furthered her education with developmental editing courses at the Editorial Freelancers Association. She's the award-winning author of "Tiny Hearts" in the anthology *Dragons of a Different Tail*, and "Bone Kindling" in the anthology *A Very Ghostly Christmas*. She previously worked as an editor at The Parliament House Press. Her clients went on to become an Amazon #1 New Release in Teen & YA Magical Realism, featured as one of the 'Most Anticipated YA Books of Fall 2021' by YA.Buzz, appear in Fae Crate's September 2021 book of the month subscription box, receive glowing reviews by Tor.com and Kirkus Reviews, and translated internationally.

Worst Vacation Ever: A Frederick Moody Story

By Jeannie Rivera

Siguijor, Philippines
The Summer before High School

Fred was supposed to be on vacation. No strange goings-on. No missing people. No weird mythical entities rising from the mountains. And absolutely no dodging a blood-sucking bat lady. But he should've known better. No matter where he went, the monster world intruded upon his plans.

Forty-eight hours after Fred and Cindy flew from Albany International with his aunt, they were crouched behind an ancient Balete tree, spying the legs of a flying half-woman.

"I can't believe we traveled forty-one hours. Five flights and a flipping ferry to wind up in a Filipino forest fighting a fiend!"

Cindy's lips were pressed together and her face pinched, making the freckles across her nose scrunch together.

Fred laughed. "That's a lot of f-words."

"I'm working on my language skills. We could be singing karaoke at the pool right now."

Cindy had been Fred's best friend since they were in kindergarten. Except for the summer before sixth grade when she wouldn't speak to him because he'd been a dumb head.

That was the same year Fred learned about his family's monster-hunting traditions. The year he and Cindy found Bigfoot and saved a classmate from certain death. The year Fred's parents didn't return from their trip to South America.

Since then, he'd lived with his Aunt Faye full time. She trained him and Cindy in all the ways to kill a monster, just as she'd trained Fred's father when they were still living in the Philippines.

Aunt Faye was an eccentric old woman who lived in a large house on a corner lot in a tiny town in the Adirondacks with stereotypically too many cats. She seemed harmless, but underestimating her would be a huge mistake. She knew more about folklore and legends than most library books, and that was nothing compared to her knowledge of monster-hunting.

She and his dad grew up on the remote island of Siquijor in the Philippines, famed for being a hot spot for the Aswangs—shapeshifting demon monsters. Most people thought folklore was just stories to scare children. But on Siquijor, the stories were true.

In the past two years, Fred dealt with all sorts of beings. Some he relocated, or even befriended, but others like were-beasts and cannibalistic giants were beyond saving. He was ready for a vacation, but a summer on the beach was too good to be true.

On day one of their vacation, Cindy was the first to wake, and by the time Fred rolled out of bed, she was at the door in her bathing suit ready for a day in the sun. A few hours later, they were lounging at the pool on a gorgeous beach sipping virgin, frozen drinks while crystal blue waves lapped the shores.

A bright smile crossed Cindy's face. "Best vacation ever."

He'd been completely happy that day, save for Cindy acting all girly smiling at the DJ running the karaoke. He wasn't jealous or anything. It was... just... he didn't like it.

Aunt Faye was sitting in the shade wearing her big hat and sunglasses, reading a romance novel when an older lady with long silver-white hair, and a very pregnant girl, approached. The girl was beautiful, with dark brown hair flowing nearly to her waist. Something about the scene struck Fred as odd.

"Sara!" Aunt Faye set her book aside and stood to embrace the older woman.

"Faye, thank the heavens, you came!"

"Of course, I did. When you called, I booked the next flight out."

Fred and Cindy looked at each other.

"Who's that?" Cindy whispered.

"I don't know."

"You must meet my nephew," Aunt Faye said, waving them over. "Fred, this is my oldest friend, Sara. And..." She turned to the pregnant girl. "This must be your granddaughter?"

"Yes, this is Mona."

Mona smiled. "It's nice to meet you."

Faye pushed her sunglasses on top of her head. "Are you due soon?"

"Another week," Mona said.

"Do you know what you're having?"

Mona's eyes shone. "A girl."

"Congratulations, my dear." Aunt Faye motioned for them to sit, and Fred pulled over a few chairs. "Now, tell me what's happened."

Mona looked at Fred and Cindy, then at her grandmother. "Lola, do you think it's wise to...they're just children."

"They're well-trained," Faye said with pride.

Mona glanced at Fred and Cindy and pulled her bottom lip between her teeth, but continued. "It's a manananggal." She crossed her arms over her round belly as if giving her child a reassuring hug.

Aunt Faye's eyes widened, and she clenched the side of her chair. "Are you certain?"

Sara nodded. "Quite, it's after my granddaughter."

Faye turned to Mona. "You've seen it?"

"Yes," Mona said, gravely. "It's followed us all over the island. We went to Manila to escape, but it was there, too."

"You've *seen* it?" Faye asked. "And you're alive."

The girl nodded.

"We have to do something," Sara said. "Will you help? Please?"

"This is worse than I feared," Faye said. "Of course, we'll help."

Fred couldn't contain himself any longer. "What's a manana—whatever it is?"

"Manananggal," Sara said. "It's an Aswang." As if that helped at all.

Cindy already had her phone out and was tapping away. "Oh, that's not good." She turned the screen to show Fred a woman with no legs and entrails hanging from her torso flying around with giant bat wings. Her hair was long and scraggly, and her eyes bright red. Talons where fingers should be. "It says it's a vampiric creature that separates from the lower half of its body at nighttime and flies around to hunt its prey."

"Why would it be after Mona?" Fred took the phone from Cindy and scrolled. "Seriously? It feeds on pregnant women and their babies. Gross."

"That's awful," Cindy pointed to the text further down the screen. "It says the manananggal makes its home on *this* island." She read further. "Well, that explains why so many people smell like garlic. Why don't you just wear a garlic necklace? Wouldn't that keep you safe from this thing?"

Sara shook her head. "It's not that simple. Garlic and herbs can help, but if it's determined... destroying it is the only way."

Faye reached over and took her friend's hand. "We'll do everything we can. Why is it focused on Mona? I've not heard of one leaving the forest and following someone to a new location. Usually, they prey on what's easiest. Certainly, there are other pregnant women in the village."

"I can't explain it either."

Fred continued reading as the women talked.

"According to the text, if the manananggal cannot reattach to its lower half, and transform back into human form, like a vampire, the sunlight will destroy it. It can't live past sunrise."

Cindy crinkled her nose. "How do we stop it?"

"We can either move its legs so it can't find them, or pour salt and garlic on them."

"Exactly," Sara said.

"One problem," Aunt Faye said. "Several actually. First, we'd have to find it, and seeing a manananggal is often deadly. Second, we've no way of predicting where it'll leave its legs."

"I know where she leaves her legs," Sara said. "We must destroy it—tonight."

"If you know where," Fred said, "why haven't you destroyed it?"

Sara took a deep breath. "That's the difficult part. It's high in the forest on a cliff, and I would go after it myself, but I can't climb the rocks at my age."

Faye pressed her lips into a fine line. "Nor I."

Sara patted her granddaughter's belly. "And clearly, neither can Mona."

"Then you're in luck," Fred said. "Rock climbing is Cindy's specialty."

ABANDONING THEIR POOL DAY, Fred and Cindy spent the afternoon studying lore and gathering supplies.

Garlic, salt, and paint guns with pellets filled with holy water. Just the regular stuff Fred traveled with.

They visited a local "magic" shop that sold stingray whips. The owner also gifted them a special herbal oil that smelled like garlic-infused salad dressing with a hint of something bitter Fred could not identify. The man said it was "to keep them safe."

After Sara described the location of the high outcropping where she was certain the manananggal would go to transform, she and Mona went back to their small village on the other side of the forest while Aunt Faye, Fred, and Cindy worked out a plan.

His aunt would travel to the village and prepare Mona's house with herbs, salt, and rice pots to deter the creature from entering the home. She'd stay there to protect the villagers while Fred and Cindy went to the outcropping to wait for the creature.

"The forest is treacherous and the climb steep. You'll need to take extra care," Aunt Faye warned. "And use a compass. Sara said to enter at the old, enchanted tree and head west for about half a mile until you reach the rope bridge over the ravine. Try to get there before nightfall. Do *not* approach the manananggal. Wait until it leaves."

Fred fake yawned, indicating he'd heard it all before and would be fine.

"I'm serious, Frederick. This creature is dangerous."

CINDY HAD SMILED AT Fred's confidence in her climbing abilities that morning, but as they moved quickly past the 400-year-old "enchanted tree" on their way to kill the monster, she wasn't as thrilled.

In the daylight, the old Balete was weird looking with its thick core and tentacles. But as the sun nestled into the horizon in a blaze of orange and purple, its creepy extended branches and hanging aerial roots made it look more like a swamp creature.

They moved deeper into the Visayan Forest.

Cindy squashed a mosquito the size of her thumb, then smashed another insect nipping the back of her neck. She dragged her wrist across her eyebrow.

The lei of garlic cloves and white Sampaguita blossoms thumped against Fred's chest like a tribal drum. Thyme and basil mixed with sweet floral and sticky air. He'd hoped the manananggal repellent neckwear would deter insects too. Clearly, it didn't.

Fred double-checked their gear, ensuring the climbing equipment was in working order. He tried not to gloat since Cindy had insisted before they'd left that he didn't need to pack his hunting or climbing equipment. She was likely glad he did now. Slinging the paintball gun over his shoulder, he led the way through the forest, weaving between trees and shrubs.

Fred stopped, looking at the purpling sky. "It's getting dark."

He rummaged around in his backpack and pulled out night vision binoculars, two red LED flashlights, and two sets of goggles. He smiled. Fred was proud of the spectacles. He handed Cindy a set and a light, and then adjusted the homemade infrared headlamp strapped to his forehead. "Shouldn't be too much farther."

By the time they reached the rope bridge, the sky had turned an inky shade of indigo with pinpoint sparkles. The bridge crossed a small ravine—short in distance, but a long drop.

He pointed across the expanse at the cliff jutting out over the water. A twisted old tree stood on the outcropping, its roots and branches reaching down the sides of the rock, making it resemble a melting candle. "There it is."

He looked through his binoculars, scanning the area for a hiding place.

"Anything?" Cindy asked.

"Not yet." His skin prickled, and he had the sudden feeling of being watched.

Perhaps he was just getting anxious to be done with the whole vampire half-woman business and get back to his vacay. "Let's stay and wait it out here. I don't want to be on that bridge when the creature shows up."

"Me neither."

Fred and Cindy sat side-by-side, backs against a huge rock, their knees pulled to their chests for what felt like forever.

Cindy slathered the stingray whip with oil. She rubbed some on her face and handed it to Fred. "Put some of this on." Then she used a combination of rope and a belt to fasten the whip to her back. When she was done, Cindy settled back against the rock. "We could be singing karaoke right now."

Fred gritted his teeth. *Again with the karaoke. I'd like to see Mr. DJ Skinny Jeans scale those rocks.*

"I see something." Cindy cupped her hand above her eyes. "Is that her?"

Fred examined the cliff through the binoculars. What he assumed was a woman hobbled across the outcropping and stepped close to the edge. He scrambled to his feet, then snapped the goggles down over his eyes and flipped on the red lights.

The hunched figure straightened, and its body lengthened. Dark hair burst out of a high bun and flowed down to her waist. The woman's clothes dropped to the ground. She held out her arms to the side and they grew longer. Fingers stretched into sharp claws. Its inhuman scream echoed through the forest, ping-ponging from tree to tree.

If ever a monster resembled the cartoon character of the devil, it was the manananggal. Its upper body turned blood red. Giant bat-like leathery wings ripped through its shoulder blades. Something darted out its mouth, looking like a snake, thrashing from side to side. Fred shuddered thinking about that tongue stabbing Mona's belly and sucking out her unborn daughter.

Cindy grabbed Fred's arm. Her hands were shaking. And when she spoke, her voice trembled. "It's terrible."

The vampiric monster batted its wings twice and drew up into the air with an ear-piercing scream. A tearing sound like ripping cloth, only a gazillion times louder, cut across the forest. Then the upper part of the manananggal's lady-body rose into the air, but her human legs stood straight, disconnected and frozen in place. The creature's top half screeched and shrieked and flapped into the night sky. Hanging entrails shimmered in the moonlight like blood-slicked, jellyfish tentacles.

Fred stared into the sky listening to the TICK, TICK, TICK of its wingbeats.

THE AIR IN THE forest was thick with humidity, and the sun setting did little to cool the temperature. They moved slowly and carefully across the rope bridge. It took longer than Fred had anticipated. Cindy was much quieter than usual. "You okay?"

"Just thinking about Mona and her baby."

Fred shrugged. "Whatever it is, if we succeed tonight, problem solved." He had to admit, it was strange for a monster to set its sights on a specific human. And embarrassingly, he didn't know much about the manananggal—or Siguiror legends, for that matter. Now that he thought about it, that was weird too. Aunt Faye hardly mentioned the island, or the mystical beings that roamed the forest. But he knew plenty about monster nature to know this particular creature was not behaving *normally*.

A memory tickled the back of Fred's mind. Something about a story his grandmother told his mother... with a chicken, an armpit, and a murder... He shook his head. He couldn't be remembering that right.

By the time they crossed the bridge, reached the top of the cliff, and set down their gear, the moon had traveled halfway across the sky. There, standing just as the manananggal had left them, were a set of legs, looking how he'd imagined a torn in half human would.

Cindy wretched. "That's nasty."

Fred glanced at her sideways, making sure she wasn't yacking all over her boots. Wouldn't be the first time. But, she seemed to have recovered and pulled bags of herbs from her backpack.

Moving as quickly as he could, Fred retrieved the mashed garlic spread they'd prepped earlier. He dumped it over the open wounds in the manananggal's ripped intestines. Cindy dumped bags of basil and rosemary and then doused the extremities with vinegar for good measure. "Are you sure this will work?" she asked.

"Yup," he said as confidently as he could. "She'll be a dead bat-lady by morning."

"I hope you're right. It feels too easy."

"Let's head back."

The two friends moved toward the edge, preparing to rappel down the rock. But Fred stopped, thinking about what Cindy had said. Was it too easy? Then he turned back toward the slathered lower torso. "Maybe we should burn it."

"I didn't read anything about burning the legs in the legends," Cindy said.

"No, it makes sense," Fred continued. "With regular vampires, if you cut off their heads, and dismember their bodies, and burn them, you can kill it. The manananggal is like a vampire. And it's already sort of... dismembered."

Cindy put her hands on her hips and seemed to think for a moment. "I guess it couldn't hurt."

Fred took a fire starter from his sack and inched toward the legs.

"Hurry," Cindy said.

Fred touched the flame to the garlic and oil-covered flesh. A scream shot through the night. Fire launched into the sky, and he gagged on the sickening smell of burning flesh and herbs. Then a booming, TICK, TICK, TICK.

"What did you do?" Cindy turned in a circle.

TICK TICK TICK, tick tick tick...

The sound softened.

"Go, go, go!" Fred yelled.

Cindy dashed toward the cliff. The rolled whip slapped against her legs. She clipped the harness around her waist and pulled on the latches to her climbing gear. But Fred stopped mid-run and raced back toward the fire.

"Freddie!"

He slid across the ground kicking up dust and gravel and skinning the side of his leg. He snatched his backpack, tugged on his safety line, and bounded toward the edge.

The *tick, tick, tick,* was barely audible. Another angry roar came from above, and the manananggal nosedived Kamikaze-style. Fred and Cindy rappelled down the side of the cliff.

From summit to base, Fred estimated the drop to be fifty feet, a manageable distance, but the mossy growth proved slippery underfoot. He eased up on the descender lever to allow the rope to run smoothly. But the cord raced through the mechanism, sending Fred plummeting the first twenty feet in a free fall.

Cindy's feet bounced off the rock face.

Fred yanked hard on the descender, halting him at once, dangling and spinning in midair. He loosened his grip and moved again, the cable running steadily through the tackle and harness as he attempted to control his descent.

Cindy screamed below. Fred released his descender, falling the rest of the way. The creature was on him in a breath's time, trying to lick his head. Cindy lashed it with her stingray whip. The creature recoiled.

Fred released the paintball pistol from the holder strapped around his thigh. As the creature dove toward Cindy, Fred nailed it with two holy water pellets.

The manananggal howled and backed away before diving again, but two more pellets to the midsection and another lashing from Cindy's whip sent it soaring into the sky. Only a loud TICK, TICK, TICK in its wake.

Fred disengaged from his rappelling equipment. "Thanks."

"Is it gone?"

"For now," he said.

"We need to get back to civilization. And let Faye know it's done. They'll be worried."

Clouds moved in front of the moon and plunged the forest into darkness. Thankfully, the infrared headlamps and goggles allowed them to see where they were going. Otherwise, who knew what cliff they'd fall from, or what monster they'd not see coming.

As they walked in silence, Fred's mind worked reviewing everything that had happened and what he knew about the creature. He returned to the same question. Why was it after Mona? There had to be something. Some connection. And then it came rushing back. The chicks, the armpits, the murder, all of it. It was about the Aswang called tik tik. Why hadn't Fred put the two together?

His mother had said, "Once, there was a woman who was a tik tik. A tik tik was another name for the manananggal. She was young and beautiful and had many suitors. Though she shouldn't have, the woman fell in love and married. But he didn't know what she was. One becomes a tik tik when a black chick is passed down from woman to woman in a family. When the old tik tik passes away, the chick passes to her female child. The chick is put in the girl's armpit and is absorbed into her body where it lives in her belly. If the girl is already a woman, she becomes the awful monster who hunts baby's blood. And if she's still a young girl, she'll turn into the tik tik on her 18th birthday.

After the married tik tik gave birth to a baby girl, she told her husband what she was and begged him to kill her so that she wouldn't pass on the curse. And with many tears of sadness, the man did as his wife pleaded. He was left alone to raise the baby girl by himself.

Only neither of them knew it was already too late. The chick had passed from mother to child upon her death, because what her husband did wasn't the proper way to destroy a tik tik.

When the little girl turned 18, she too transformed. And like her mother, she too fell in love, and had a daughter. As long as she lived, the baby was safe from the curse. Only in her death would it be passed on unless she was destroyed in her tik tik form.

Her daughter grew into a beautiful young woman with no knowledge of their family's curse. She became pregnant, but much to the older woman's heartache, her daughter died giving birth to her granddaughter. The old woman raised the girl, never telling her the horrible secret and always worrying that the curse would be passed along. The old woman reasoned there was only one solution. She found a way—with the help of a witch and black magic—to never die. And so, the tik tik lives in the forests of Visayan to this day, cursed to feed on baby's blood and to live forever."

Fred thought it was another weird vampire story, but now he knew better. The tik tik, the manananggal, was real. Oh, crapweasels! The story. The grandmother and the granddaughter... and now the granddaughter having a daughter. No way. If what he suspected was true, could his aunt's friend Sara be the manananggal? It sounded ridiculous even in his head, and so he kept the thought to himself.

FRED HEARD THE SCREAMS long before he saw the carnage.

The village was nestled between the forest and the ocean. He knew they were getting close because the tropical breeze carried the odor of garlic and timber smoke. But it was the screams and the flapping of wings and crying that had him and Cindy barreling through the edge of the forest. They burst onto a narrow dirt road.

Villagers scurried in circles, trying to ward off the manananggal. It beat the air and collided with the closed window of a small, bamboo-and-heap structure in the middle of town with a sickening *thwarp*.

Shadows from Malunggay trees dappled the house's nip-leap roof. The scent of white Sampaguita blossoms by the door was so strong he almost couldn't smell death in the air. The glass barrier infuriated the half bat-lady. She screamed and rammed it again. The hit caused a spiderwebbed crack in the glass.

"I don't understand," Cindy said. "I thought the manananggal fed quietly while the pregnant women were sleeping? This thing is attacking loudly and in plain sight."

"I think we pissed it off," Fred shouted. "It's got nothing to lose. It knows it's already dead."

They hauled butt through the narrow winding village streets rimmed with small pots of uncooked rice, ash, and salt.

In the square, a man threw rocks at the creature. The manananggal swooped down like a giant bird of prey and sunk its teeth into his neck. It hoisted him into the air, shook violently like a cat with a mouse in its mouth, and dropped him to the ground. The man landed on the road, his limbs bent at impossible angles.

An old woman stepped into the street and held up a machete, ready to fend off the attack, but the manananggal flew off screeching through the air. More people came out of their houses, each carrying a weapon—a garden rake, a large piece of wood, stones the size of fists—and made their way to the square.

"We need to lure that thing out of the village, or they'll all die." Fred ducked and dodged the crowd and skid to a stop in front of a house at the end of the street. The manananggal was perched on top, trying to pierce the roof with its snake tongue.

Fred quickly removed his whip from the backpack and snapped it on the ground. "Hey, Monster Face!"

Monster Face didn't hear him, or at least it pretended not to, and continued trying to stab the roof. Fred examined it for a moment, realizing its entrails were tangled in the thorny vines looped around the window. He wasn't sure if she was stuck or holding on.

A brawny man rushed past wielding a bolo.

"No, no, no!" Fred ran to stop him.

Too late.

The man hacked at the window, shattering glass, and slicing the half woman's tentacles. She struck out with the bloody entrails like a whip. It sliced the man in half. His body fell into the dirt in two heavy, distinct thumps. Fred froze. In all his monster-hunting, his fighting, his training, he'd never seen anything like this. Sure, he'd seen a giant break the neck of a deer in one twist and then suck out its blood. But this—these were people. Humans. He was supposed to protect them, and he failed.

The manananggal's screams brought him back to the moment. It circled the house like a vulture. Fred spun, looking for something to climb on to get to the roof. He scanned the streets. The crowd stared at the ground, at the two halves of what was a man and the blood seeping across the dirt. Cindy. Where was Cindy?

Fred whirled again trying to find her. He yelled obscenities at the bat-woman to keep its eyes on him. If he convinced it to follow him into the forest, the remaining holy water pellets might be enough to hold her off until morning. But he knew he was lying to himself.

Just then, Cindy burst from inside the house with Mona in tow.

"Lola!" Mona cried.

"We have to go," Cindy yelled, tugging Mona's arm with one hand, paintball gun at the ready in the other.

"I can't leave," Mona said. "I need to find Lola."

Fred eyed the manananggal flying overhead. "What are you doing?"

"I'm getting Mona to the Pink Church. It has a steel ceiling. She'll be safer inside. And we can restock our supply of holy water."

Mona sobbed and looked back at the doorway, but she moved forward, her slippers shuffling along the dusty path. "Oh no!" she cried when she saw the man on the ground. "Oh, no, Pedro."

Fred was next to her then, trying to get Mona to look away. He grabbed her face. "Look at me. Look at me! Where is your grandmother?"

"She's not in the house. I checked." Cindy said.

"Mona, where is she?" Fred pressed.

"She went hunting for the manananggal. Now, I fear... she's... what if?" Mona shook her head frantically. "I couldn't bear it if that thing got her."

The manananggal chose that moment to snarl and rush toward them. Cindy shot her weapon several times, and the thing retreated further into the sky. But it would be back.

"Nice shot," Fred said, and then turned back to Mona. "Why would your grandmother go after it?" The horrible story was raging through his mind, and he started to get a sick feeling in his stomach.

"To protect me. She goes every night and keeps watch until dawn. Until she knows it's safe."

Cindy pulled on Mona's arm. "I wouldn't worry then. I'm sure she's fine, but we've got to go."

Fred pointed to the sky. "It's coming back. How far is the church?"

"Two blocks," Mona said, regaining some of her composure.

"We need to trick it into chasing us back into the forest," Fred said. "Away from the village. The church is too far."

Cindy shook her head. "It's two hours until dawn. We can't run that long."

There was a gust of air and a giant flapping of wings. Villagers screamed. The three of them ran down a small alley.

"Not too much farther." Mona stumbled and grabbed her huge belly.

"Are you alright?" Cindy asked.

"Just a cramp." Mona led Cindy and Fred down the alley, emerging into another square. They ran past a Balete, and through the monastery's grounds. Acacia trees lined the road separating the convent from the church. Five bells rang from the crumbling tower atop the coral stones. *Less than two hours.*

As they approached the church, a priest held open the arched double doors. Mona ran inside, but Cindy stopped on the portico waiting for Fred, who had turned to face the manananggal.

"Go inside," he yelled. "Bar the door."

Cindy didn't budge. The creature descended.

"Freddie!" Cindy cried. She depressed the trigger of her paintball pistol. Nothing happened. She was out of pellets. She ran toward Fred, the manananggal, and certain death.

Bat-lady dug her claws into Fred's forearm, and her tongue raced toward his face.

"Frederick!" Aunt Faye burst from the church doorway. "Get away from my nephew, you abomination!" She hurled something round at the creature. A popping *splat* sound, and it released Fred. Holy Water balloons! More balloons flew.

Tiny hands grabbed Fred's arms. Children dragged him across the lawn, up the concrete steps, and over the threshold into the sanctuary. The odor of burning incense filled his nose. He heard screaming and screeching outside. All he could think of was Cindy. He had to get back out there and help her and his aunt. He couldn't let them face the manananggal alone. But before he could make it to the door, Aunt Faye and Cindy barreled through the opening.

A wooden board slid in place barring the entrance. They were safe, if they could survive until daybreak.

INSIDE THE NARROW CHURCH, two rows of polished wooden pews stretched to a single altar. The rose-colored walls responsible for its namesake were engraved with intricate designs. Children filled water balloons from a fountain at the front of the room as the Padre hastily blessed the stream. Other villagers strung garlic, warded windows and doorways with salt, and filled paintball pellets. Aunt Faye was barking orders at men to board the entrances. It reminded Fred of the time they got stuck on Long Island during a hurricane. But he wasn't sure it would keep out the tornado that was the manananggal.

Cindy scrambled to Fred's side.

"Let me see your arm," she said.

"It's only a scratch."

Cindy yanked bandages out of Fred's discarded sack on the floor. "Stay still." She wrapped the gauze around his arms. They were a pair, bruised and bleeding.

At the front of the church, there were two windows with bamboo shutters. Fred peeked between the slats and watched the monster go crazy.

The manananggal, mangled and marred, crashed into the church entry. It flapped torn, useless wings and flew in haphazard zigzags.

Children hunkered down in the aisles with water balloons, their anxious eyes darting back and forth from the ceiling to the windows. Mona sat on the floor with her back propped against a pew, looking miserable. Her hair was a mess, and her eyes were red and swollen. "Lola where are you?" she whispered.

Fred thought about the story he'd remembered earlier. He couldn't think of any other reason the she-monster would be after Mona. Nothing else made sense, but still, he wasn't going to put words to his thoughts. Not unless he was certain, which he was far from.

The manananggal crashed into the door, then into the windows. It bounced off only to rush the building again.

"Devil-lady is bat-shit crazy." Fred laughed at his own joke. The manananggal gave new meaning to the phrase.

"Will the building hold?" Cindy asked.

"The salt barriers are working," Aunt Faye yelled over the noise. "Almost dawn. Only a short while more."

Men with stingray whips moved to stand sentry around the children. The slamming and wacking and screaming and screeching went on for what felt like an eternity.

Finally, the night was quiet. Fred thought it gave up until claws scratched across the metal roof. Cold dread washed over him. He checked his watch. 6:36 a.m. "Sunrise in four minutes." Four minutes sounded like a short time, unless you're fighting a monster with only four minutes to live.

"Here she comes." Faye tossed a paintball pistol to Fred.

The window exploded at the front of the church sending the shutters flying overhead. The manananggal plowed through the broken frame. Red and black leathery wings thrashed, shaking the remaining shards lose. Jagged pieces of glass ripped through its cartilage. One talon gripped the sill. It growled.

Children ran toward the back of the church and hid behind the altar. The men followed and made a human wall of arms and legs and whips to protect them.

Mona stayed on the floor, staring at the monster. It opened its mouth, its snake tongue searching the church like antennae. It drew near a group of children crying and cowering in a pew in front of Mona. The eldest tossed a water balloon and missed, but it splattered on the floor and splashed on the manananggal's entrails. It hissed and backed away, but only for a moment before advancing again.

Cindy ran toward it and slapped it with her whip. Sucking the tongue back into its head with slurping sounds, the beast retreated, rising to perch on the rafters. Then its tongue descended again, quick as lightening this time, and stabbed itself into Mona's belly button. She screamed and fell over onto the floor. The tongue pulsed and Fred could see something moving through it. It looked like a nasty black umbilical cord, and it was sucking blood from Mona's baby. He had to do something, but Cindy was already diving for the tongue.

Fred rammed Cindy out of the way like he was on the football field to get her clear of the bloodsucker. Then he shot a paintball at the gross tongue thing.

The manananggal yowled and raged but didn't let go of Mona.

Aunt Faye ran up the aisle toward the girl with a bolo held over her head. She swung it down and sliced through where the monster was sucking the blood-life out of both mother and child. Red splashed on the floor, her clothing, and across her face. The manananggal plunged from the rafter, landing in front of Aunt Faye.

Fred dove and came up in a crouch between his aunt and the bloodsucker. He glimpsed the slight bit of daylight coming through the door behind the monster and glanced at his watch, which he'd set to countdown. He had to get the bat-lady into the sunlight. Out on the lawn. "59 seconds!"

"Cindy, get Mona out of here, she needs help!"

Mona was just regaining consciousness, and Cindy dragged her toward the altar. "Help me!"

Several men lifted Mona and hurried to the back of the church.

Fred emptied his paintball magazine.

"Loose!" Faye yelled from behind him.

Time seemed to stand still as complete pandemonium erupted around him. The children let the holy water balloons fly. The creature groaned, its skin hissing. Chunks of gloppy pieces of flesh hit the floor with sickening splats. It wasn't enough. The mananaggal twisted.

The kids were out of ammunition and Fred was out of pellets. Only the men with whips were still armed with anything that could fend off the hellish half-woman, and they looked exhausted.

How would he get this thing out into the sunlight? Faye already had some of the women pulling down the wood they'd used to block the windows. Sunshine would reach the monster eventually, but not in time. They wouldn't survive much longer.

He glanced over his shoulder at the children, Cindy, Mona, and his aunt—all busy and doing what they could. But the manananggal focused on him, and he took advantage. "Let's do this, Monster Face."

He grabbed the slimy, nasty piece of the severed tongue that lay on the floor next to his feet and wiggled it in the manananggal's face. "Hey! Missing something?" Its eyes burned red like hot coals. "Want it? Come and get it!"

Fred ran for the door. He set his shoulders to tackle it down if he had to. Wings came down to skewer him, but luckily, he made it past them.

"Missed me," he yelled as he pulled on the plank to unbarricade the door. Then tossed the wood at the monster. It didn't slow her.

Fred flung open the door and sprinted onto the lawn.

The she-devil surged into the pale glow of dawn's first ray of sunlight. A sound of excruciating pain that Fred never wanted to hear again knifed through his skull. Then it was quiet.

In the dew-covered grass laid the upper half of a human woman, gray hair splayed around her head like a silver halo. Unseeing eyes stared heavenward. The ends of her wrinkled lips turned up as if in a smile.

"Lola," Mona screamed. She pushed through the crowd, limping and holding her stomach, still bleeding from her belly button. She flung herself over her grandmother's body. "No, Lola! What have you done?"

Faye raced from the church and kneeled in the grass. "Oh, Sara."

"I don't understand..." Cindy's voice caught in her throat as she stifled a sob. "Why would she..."

"Hire us to destroy her?" Aunt Faye wiped a tear from her eye. "For Mona. And her great-grandchild."

Faye took Mona's tear-smeared cheeks in her hands. "Your Lola loved you very much. But, we need to go. That little girl of yours is coming into the world now."

Fred and Cindy sat on the porch of the medicine woman's cottage, exhausted, sweaty, and in need of baths. They'd listened to Mona's screams and cries for the last three hours, and Fred wondered if it was worse than all the screams and screeches they'd heard that night. Cindy wiped the back of her hand across her cheek, scrubbing at an escaped tear.

"You alright?" Fred asked.

"It's just... Lola totally sacrificed herself. Do you think she knew she was the manananggal?"

Fred nodded, not trusting his voice.

"That's so sad, but brave too. And horrible. You know, this is the worst vacation ever."

Fred laughed. It was a pretty bad vacay.

Suddenly, Mona's wails ended in the most wondrous sound—a baby crying. Fred never thought a baby's cry sounded so good. And a few moments later, Aunt Faye came outside, carrying the tiniest bundle all wrapped in a colorful blanket.

"Hey guys, meet Sara."

Fred stood slowly, every muscle in his body aching, but Cindy practically jumped up. "Oh my gosh," she said. "She's so cute. Look at that black hair! She's got so much of it."

"That she does," Faye said, running her hand over the babe's head. "I'd better get her back to her mother. Thought you'd like to see what you've saved. I'm very proud of the two of you."

Aunt Faye smiled and walked through the door with the baby in her arms.

Floating in the air where they'd just stood was a tiny black feather. It drifted this way and that in the gentle breeze and landed just inside the threshold of the tiny cottage.

J EANNIE DAVIDE-RIVERA IS AN award-winning author who splits her time between NY and Florida when she's not traveling the world homeschooling her boys. She has a B.A. in English and Creative Writing, an M.F.A. in Writing Popular Fiction from Seton Hill University, and is a member of the Society of Children's Book Writers and Illustrators (SCBWI).

Her first book, a memoir, *Twirling Naked in the Streets and No One Noticed: Growing Up with Undiagnosed Autism*, won the 2013 International Reader's Favorites Silver Book Award. It's a #ownvoices story about girls struggling with autism.

Her other published non-fiction work appears in "Autism Parenting Magazine," and "The Thinking Person's Guide to Autism." Her debut MG novel, *Frederick Moody and the Secrets of Six Summit Lake*, is set to release late 2022.

Three
Miscreants

THE BRAZEN SKULL: A GOOD NECROMANCER STORY

By Michael La Ronn

Y OU HAVEN'T LIVED UNTIL you've stood at the edge of a river on a starry night, holding a talking skull who's yelling the secrets of life at you in Latin.

You especially haven't lived if the skull isn't covered in pure, reflective brass. Get yourself one of these babies and you'll be the envy of warlocks all over the world. You'll be so envied, that strange people will come to your house in the middle of the night and blow you apart just so they can get their hands on this skull. You'll be the most hated, admired, and dangerous person in the world.

Seriously, you need this skull. Tell you what: I'll give it to you for free.

Don't want it? Me neither.

I'm not a warlock, I don't care to know the secrets of life, and I don't plan on learning Latin anytime soon.

I'm a necromancer. The only reason I had this skull was that I was doing somebody a favor, one that I was seriously rethinking.

The cold river wind off the Mississippi whipped into my face as the skull shouted louder. The St. Louis skyline winked over the ink-dark water like a string of out-of-focus Christmas lights. A faint odor of rotten eggs bubbled off the banks.

The skull was starting to get on my nerves. I couldn't even look the thing in the eye; its hollow eye sockets were smooth and showed my reflection. The mandible rose up and down, its gleaming teeth throwing the city lights behind me into a brassy, milky swirl.

"Will you shut up already?" I asked.

Ironically, my insult shut the skull up.

"I can't take this anymore," I said.

The skull said something quietly in Latin.

I held the skull over the fast-flowing waters. It trembled in my hands.

"Very well, necromancer," the skull said in a reedy voice.

I almost dropped the damn thing upon hearing English for a change.

"Actually, I take that back," I said. "Don't say anything."

All I had to do was drop this skull in the water. If I was lucky, I'd be home just in time for my nighttime tea and a game of cards.

"You would throw me in the river without hearing a prophecy first, Lester Broussard?" it asked.

"Yes," I said, winding back my arms.

"That's what they all say until I start talking," the skull said. "You too will listen to my words, and together, we will conquer this city."

Then the skull said the names of everyone I had ever known, dates that only I could have known, and secrets about myself that no one else knew.

I slowly lowered the skull, enthralled.

As if commanded, I brought the brazen skull up to my face as it whispered its secrets to me.

WHEN YOU HEAR THE term "necromancy," you probably think of skulls, whispering spirits, and evil men in shadowed alleys conjuring the dead. You probably don't think about teddy bears, that's for sure.

I hate to tell you this, but everything you imagined is true. The dark art is every bit as dark as they say.

Trust me, I would know. I'm a necromancer, remember.

Before you grab your rosary beads and pray for my soul, I'll have you know that I use my powers for good. The dead give their secrets to me, and I use those to help the living.

If you saw me on the street, you'd confuse me for a behind-the-times dad. I favor thrift store sweaters, jeans, and a good gabardine. With my salt and pepper beard, I've got the seasoned black man thing going for me too. No one would ever peg me for a necromancer.

I'm just a humble guy who lives in the hood. I use my skills to keep people safe from the things that go bump in the night. That list includes, but is not limited to, giant insect demons who would love to rip you apart, grim reapers, liches, vampires, lions-and-tigers-and-bears-oh-my shifters, and other supernaturals so unspeakable that not even the dead dare to say their names.

I could teach a college class on evil. Seven years ago, I made a deal with a scorpion demon to cure my wife of cancer. When I made the deal, I should've brought my lawyer; the demon used a loophole in semantics. He cured her, but then he killed her *and* my son. Nothing in the deal said he couldn't.

That's the dark art for you—it will give you anything your heart desires, then it will break your heart.

Those necromancers you thought of—they don't have hearts anymore. Somehow, I kept mine.

So, you know what? I turned the dark art against itself. If I die tomorrow, I'll die knowing that I used some darkness to create light.

Speaking of light, let's go back to how this crazy story began.

A dazzle of flame bloomed in my kitchen, drawing my attention from the newspaper I was reading. On the stove, my steak was on fire.

"This damn oven don't cook even, man!" my undead servant Bo cried, running over to the stove. He tossed the newspaper obituaries he was reading, and the paper fluttered down like a sad bird.

"Either it don't cook even, or you can't cook," I said, sipping some cinnamon tea.

Bo flipped on the fan and a gush of warm air circled the kitchen.

THE BRAZEN SKULL: A GOOD NECROMANCER... 271

"This steak is about to be extra crispy, boss man," Bo said, scooting the skillet off the hot eye.

Bo is six foot five and 250 pounds. He's bald and has a penchant for tracksuits, big sunglasses, and white basketball shoes. He makes the perfect bodyguard—he's got the angry, intimidating black man look that stops most fights before they start. That comes in real handy in a profession like mine.

But Bo is a gentle giant. If you get too close to him, you'll get a whiff of Polo cologne and rotting flesh. That's because I recruited him from the spirit world and bound his soul to a funeral home cadaver. We've been bickering like a married couple ever since.

And, if you're wondering, the dead can't eat. Bo does all the cooking and cleaning in my house. It wasn't my idea. It was his. Dead man's gotta do something.

Bo had managed the steak down to a quiet sizzle now.

"It's a good thing you won't be eating this steak," Bo said.

The smell of burning beef intensified and I agreed. "Amen to that," I said, turning the page of my newspaper.

"Of all things, why did that warlock make us fry a steak for this job?" Bo asked. "The guy is bad news."

"I don't like him either, but we owe him."

Necromancy is a game of favors. You talk to the dead and make deals with them in exchange for information that will help you with whatever problem you're trying to solve. Oftentimes, the problem is a life-or-death issue for the person coming to you.

I like to refer to the dark art as a game of tallies. You glean a piece of information from the other side, and you owe that dead person a favor. The dead person who you got the information from had to get that information from somebody else, and they owe that person a favor. At some point, things go sideways and somebody dies, usually—wait for it—the necromancer. That's of course, if you play the game to win.

I play the game carefully. The way I see it, as long as I'm not trying to realize some dastardly plan or get supervillain on somebody, I can keep a cool head. And cool heads tend to stay alive in this game.

No matter how you play, one of the unfortunate downsides to this job is that you owe people favors.

I owed a warlock a favor, and it was time for him to cash in his tally. I know enough about this life to know that you don't cross warlocks. They might turn you into a nematode, shrink your brain to Neanderthal size, or worse, hit you with a curse that makes you bleed out like a chicken.

It didn't help that the warlock I was working with was a certified organic asshole, bold capital letters, size 72 font. I couldn't stand the guy, and Bo couldn't either. But it doesn't matter whether you like someone or not – a favor is a favor is a favor, and this warlock told me to buy a steak, fry it, and meet him in my back alley. I'm normally a questioning man, but now wasn't the time.

Oh, and he told me to read the story in the business section of the paper.

Bo whistled a gangster rap chorus as he tended to the steak. I settled back in my chair and found the story. It was about one of the richest men in the city, a biopic about all his success in building a consultancy empire. There was even a photo of the guy—a Mr. Clancy Burgess. He was a seventy-something billionaire. White guy, green sweater, Coke-bottle glasses, arms folded, and smiling at the camera like he owned it. The headline over his wispy gray hair read "Prophet of Business?"

I scanned the article. It made me sick. According to the so-called journalist, Mr. Burgess was the guy business leaders came to with their questions. He had a 100 percent client success rate, had no faults whatsoever, was responsible for creating 50,000 jobs, a city monument, and a stable of advertising-ready Clydesdale horses, a St. Louis favorite. And don't get me started on the guy's philanthropic work in Africa. Mr. Burgess might as well have been an incarnation of the Good Lord himself.

"Your forehead looks like a hamburger," Bo said. "Is the article as bad as Hank said?"

Bo had made an observation about me. He said my forehead wrinkled up like the lines on a raw hamburger when I was thinking hard about something. The first time he said it, I wanted to throw something at him. But the description was surprisingly accurate.

"It's every bit as bad," I said, crumpling the newspaper and setting it on the table distastefully.

"Steak's ready," Bo said. With a spatula, he slipped the steak into a gallon sandwich bag. Blood ran down the sides.

I grabbed my gabardine off the back of my chair and slid it on.

"Let's ride," I said.

"WHEN I TOLD YOU to buy a steak, I didn't tell you nimrods to cook it."

The stars blinked on and dribbled like sequins in the navy sky over my back alley as Hank Garbo leaned against his red pickup truck. He stared at the bag of steak incredulously.

Hank is what you would think of when you imagine a warlock: long, wet, black hair down to his shoulders that looked like he had just taken a shower, piercing black eyes that stared through you, an untucked button-up shirt, ripped jeans, and leather shoes that look like melted candy bars. He would have been right at home at a grunge concert.

Somewhere, a siren blared. Through the crisscrossing telephone wires, the clouds were underlit with the last remaining gold tints of day.

A necromancer, an undead servant, and a warlock standing in a back alley in the hood. We were a sight.

"You asked for a steak, and you got it," I said.

"Why else would you want a steak if you weren't gonna eat it?" Bo asked.

Hank gave another lingering look to the bag. "I have my reasons. Besides, if there's one thing I ought to especially be suspicious about with you two, it's the dead man's tastebuds."

"Isn't that the truth," I said, ambling over the truck. "Let's get this over with."

Bo held up the bag. "Whatchu need this for anyway, man?"

Hank puffed and walked around to the driver's side of the truck. "I'll keep you two in suspense. Let's go."

Hank had a Native American blanket draped over the bench seat in his pickup. The inside was fireplace-warm.

We rode all the way to the west side of town—rush-hour and highways and twisty suburban roads trailing through tree-lined corridors—and the guy didn't say a word. His truck needed shocks—every pothole jostled us around.

It was better that things stayed quiet. Knowing Hank, he might have said something that set Bo off, and then Bo and I would have both been turned into nematodes. No thanks.

Soon, we were in some ritzy suburb of St. Louis, an old-money part of town where even the smallest home still met the textbook definition of a mansion. All the homes were lit up with landscape lighting as if the homeowners were trying to outdo each other. The lawns were like fairways, full of stripes that you could see even at night. I lost count of the number of swimming pools, carriage houses, and circular driveways.

"Well?" I asked.

Hank parked on the side of a quiet residential drive and cut off the headlights. We sat in silence and darkness for a moment before he angled his head over the steering wheel. He pointed between the branches of a very full sycamore tree.

"Time to get to work," he said.

"You still ain't told us why we need a steak," Bo said.

Hank glanced down at the sandwich bag again. "We don't need it yet."

"If you're wanting us to break and enter," I said, "you might want to think again. In case you haven't noticed, we're both black. Folks aren't gonna take too kindly to me and Bo sneaking around here."

Hank let out a long, condescending laugh. "If I needed someone to rob a house, I wouldn't have hired you two goons."

He got out of the car, and Bo and I followed. The sycamore swayed in the breeze. Its foliage shrouded the truck somewhat.

Hank opened up the tailgate and climbed on.

"I need you to talk to the dead," he said.

Normally, the back of a pickup truck has ridges in it. Hank's was as smooth as plastic. The only thing on it was a sandbag couched against the cab.

"Temporary texture," he said. "Can you make your circle here?"

I arched an eyebrow. "I'm happy to do whatever you want, but I'd like a summary first."

Hank puffed again. "Look through those trees."

I squinted through dark green leaves. A sumptuous, half-timber mansion lay on the other side. Every window in the home was lit up and the place looked like a Thomas Kincade painting if Kincade woke up one morning and decided to paint mansions. I couldn't see anyone inside.

"That's Clancy Burgess's home," Hank said. "We're going to pay him a visit, but to make sure this doesn't get ugly, I need some information first."

To CALL THE DEAD, one must create a magic circle. The circle contains an inner circle and an outer circle. The necromancer sits in the outer circle; whoever the necromancer calls sits in the inner circle. The inner circle is infused with magic and intent so that whatever is inside can't escape. This is for the protection of both parties.

Sometimes, demons show up in magic circles and you most definitely don't want them escaping into the world of the living.

Spirits aren't allowed out of the spirit world either—there's no such thing as fugitives. If you ever let the spirit loose, a reaper would find you and slash your head off.

Sheeeeet...

I wasn't planning on breaking any paranormal rules anytime soon, so I made the safest magic circle I knew how.

I carry around a leather grooming kit with me, but instead of nail clippers, a razor, or dental floss, I carry the tools of the necromancer's trade: birthday candles, string, and chalk. I can make a magic circle anywhere. I've called the dead in vacant homes, public restrooms, and other godforsaken places I don't want to tell you about.

As I drew a circle on Hank's pickup bed, I realized I could add a suburban street to my list.

Bo folded his arms and stood watch like a sentinel next to the bed. With his sunglasses and scowl, no one was going to stop and hassle him. Hank stood next to him, watching Clancy's house through the sycamore leaves.

"You sure no one is going to drive by here?" I asked. "I don't normally do this out in the open."

"No one is going to bother us," Hank said.

Headlights swept across my face and my heart stopped. A black sedan rolled past.

Inside, a middle-aged woman and a brown Labrador looked straight ahead as they passed, like they never saw us. A few yards ahead, the air rippled like a heat mirage as the car passed through it.

Bo tipped his sunglasses after the car. "Yo, how'd you do that?"

Hank laughed. "Do you think I'd let you summon a spirit in the middle of a freaking street for everyone to see you?" he asked.

"Not even the dog sensed us," I said.

Warlock magic. I'd only heard about the supernatural sleight of hand. Boy, was Hank bringing it tonight.

Hank leaped into the pickup bed with a one-handed hop. The truck rocked and I damn near lost my balance.

"This magic circle is algebra teacher-approved," he said. "Wow. You drew two heavenly spheres here, teech."

I resisted the urge to snap back at him. Instead, I flicked my lighter. The ridges in the handle dug into my skin as a flame danced into the night air. I sat down in the outer circle and lit six birthday candles at the edge.

Hank took in a long breath of fresh air. "Nothing like talking to a dead warlock at twilight, eh, gentlemen? Remember, I need a dead warlock—not somebody's dead grandma."

"With your magic at work, attracting one shouldn't be too hard," I said.

I took a deep breath. Hank was the kind of guy they put you up against after an anger management class to see if you learned anything.

Instead, I closed my eyes, rested my hands on my lap, and uttered the saying that I always say when I want to attract spirits.

"Wandering warlock spirits, I send out a beacon of light to you to ask for your help. Please stop and offer your assistance."

A gentle wind blew, rustling the leaves. I became at one with the distant rushing of cars passing by, a dog barking somewhere, water rippling in a pool across the street, and the cold breeze.

I suddenly became aware of the window cracked open in the back of Hank's pickup. His keys dangled in the ignition, jingling together, their sound intensified like wind chimes. Then, rock music on the stereo, like someone turned the dial up, followed by the heater in the car blowing at full blast.

I opened my eyes. A translucent blob hovered in the inner circle, thin as gossamer. A golden core inside the spirit pulsed quietly, throwing shades of gold across the pickup. It didn't have a face.

"You call upon a dead warlock," the spirit said. The voice sounded old and creaky. When you spoke to the dead, you never knew how old they had been when they died or what century they lived in. I could have been talking to a recently deceased or someone from ancient Egypt. They all sounded the same to me.

"I salute you, warlock," Hank said. "My friend here called you because I couldn't do it myself. Necromancy never took to me."

"I sensed your magical energy," the dead warlock said. "How may I be of assistance, fellow?"

"Clancy Burgess's time is up, and he knows it," Hank said.

THE REST OF OUR conversation with the dead warlock churned in and out of my thoughts as we began our mission.

"He sits on his throne in his secluded palace," the dead warlock said. "He will know you are coming."

"Even if we've never met him?" Hank asked.

Hank drove his pickup truck like a rocket down the suburban street. The trees whizzed by, and I couldn't believe what the dead warlock had told us.

We turned onto a private drive. Hank stopped at a curved wrought-iron gate.

"He will let you right in," the dead warlock said. "And then he will kill you quickly, just as he did with the others."

"Others?" I asked.

We could see the half-timber mansion in all its sumptuous glory now. Despite being fully furnished and brightly lit, the place looked empty and cold.

"How do people live in a place like that?" Bo asked. "Seems more like a prison than a home."

"I prefer not to die tonight," Hank said.

"Then you must hit him with a decomposition curse," the dead warlock said.

"Jesus," Hank said. "That's going to take far too much of my energy."

Hank rolled his window down and stuck his head out at the intercom next to the gate.

"Clancy, it's Hank Garbo," he said. "You know why I'm here."

The gates unlatched and opened slowly. Bo and I looked at each other and gulped.

"*He cared more about knowledge and revenge,*" the dead warlock said. "*He has committed a travesty to our kind. A warlock* may use his skills to further his interests privately, but he must never flaunt them publicly."

"Clancy is about as public as you can get," Hank said. "That's how he came to my attention, and that's why I'm taking this into my own hands."

"Wait—Clancy is a warlock?" I asked.

Hank parked in the circular driveway in front of the house next to a stone fountain that shot water six feet into the air.

We stood for a moment looking up at the enormous house with the soundtrack of the burbling fountain.

The front door was made of hardwood and painted red with black iron castle hinges. The door creaked all the way open, beckoning us inside. Rays of orange light leaked out into the night.

"Aww hell naw," Bo said. "This is some Hotel California stuff, man."

"What's the worst that could happen?" Hank asked. "It's not like you're going to die, dead man." He strolled toward the front door, laughing to himself.

"What about me, asshole?" I called after him. My knees were weak.

"Clancy is a warlock, all right," Hank said. "And you're looking at him."

I almost fell out of the magic circle.

"Say what?" Bo asked.

"I am indeed Clancy Burgess," the dead warlock said. "I was murdered fifty years ago."

Clancy Burgess's house was as magazine-ready as I expected. Tall ceilings with wood beam rafters, and swirling marble floors. A family crest hung from the ceiling—a dragon and knight on a yellow tapestry with silver fringes.

The living room was covered in tacky, upholstered couches, divans, and settees that looked as if they were imported from Europe. I'd be shocked if anyone had actually sat on them. Generous floor-to-ceiling windows with diamond grids overlooked the driveway.

A distant voice called us from the depths of the house, echoing on the stone. "I'm in the cellar," he said.

Clancy. Or whoever the hell was pretending to be him.

Hank stepped into the hallway, past the kitchen that was the size of a regular house, replete with hanging pots and pans, multiple sinks, and a refrigerator bigger than my car. He crept quietly across the floor, pointing his wand at everything.

Bo and I trailed behind the warlock.

"Looks like Hank's got this covered," Bo whispered. "It's not too late to bounce."

I shook my head. "If we leave now, I'll forever be wondering whose house this is."

We crept down a dimly-lit stairwell into a cellar. Bo pushed ahead of me; dark steel glinted as he pulled a pistol out of his tracksuit. I found it hard to breathe.

The cellar door was brown and circular, and looked like it belonged in the Shire from *Lord of the Rings*. It was slightly ajar, and candlelight flickered along the edges.

"I want my favor cashed and I want it cashed good, guys," Hank said.

Suddenly, he dashed toward the door and ripped it open, shouting in Latin.

A nuclear flash ripped through the cellar.

I threw myself on the cold marble floor. Bo landed on top of me. The frigid floor's coldness exploded across my cheek.

Two voices yelled and shouted over each other in Latin. Then, the air grew warm, still, and quiet.

Hank stood in the doorway, the tip of his cedar wand still sparking.

"All clear, guys," he said, slipping his wand into his pocket.

Bo and I stood slowly, looking at each other again.

The vaulted cellar was filled wall-to-wall with barrels and old books. There was a long workbench with a battery of candles on it and a very large book in the middle. Its thick spine, wide trim, and yellowed pages gave it away as a spellbook. On the floor, an elderly man lay with his hands over his face like some histrionic Greek character. A broken wand smoldered next to him.

Hank half-turned to us, then fell to his knees. "It's...up to you." He was suddenly pale and drenched in sweat. Whatever spell he cast took everything out of him. "Your time is up," Hank said to the old man.

An arm dropped from the old man's face and he stared at us, alternating between crying and laughing.

"I knew you would come," the old man said. His eyes locked on me. "And that you would bring the famous necromancer."

The old man crawled toward me, but Bo aimed his gun at him.

"All right, old man, give us the thing Hank is looking for, and we'll be out of here," he said.

"The slang-slinging undead servant," the old man said, grinning. He took a crawling step toward us, but his knee gave out and he crashed to the floor.

The old man screamed and reached for me. Bo unloaded his gun into him. Each bullet ripped through him and he fell onto his back, his body twisting like a sick contortionist's.

The gun smoke cleared, and Bo kept it aimed at the old man.

"Boss man, you all right?" he asked.

"Good," I said.

The old man continued to laugh. A normal person would have been in the spirit world right about now.

"What was the point of all this?" Hank asked in a strained voice. "You violated the warlock code."

The old man convulsed in sidesplitting laughter. "You are like the others." He reached up and grabbed the lid of a barrel on a nearby shelf.

Bones poured out of the barrel like spillikins. It didn't take me long to recognize them as human bones.

The old man laughed, but a ravenous black swirl started at his feet and tore across his body like a tornado.

"If you really want to know," the old man said as the shadows ravaged his neck, "it's because I wanted to see humanity suffer for banishing me to the fringe so many centuries ago. First, I would have conquered the world with my money. Then, I would have choked it off. One day, you will understand my bitterness, warlock—"

"You should've told me sooner," Hank said, smirking. "I would've referred you to a therapist. We could have prevented all of this."

The shadows covered the old man's face and he yelled in fright.

"The curse is working," Hank said. "Lester, when the shadows fade, pick up what you see."

Bo helped Hank up and the warlock leaned on him.

"You came in handy," Hank said. "The only reason I wanted you along was so you could carry me to the truck. You're also on driving duty."

"Come on, man," Bo said, wrinkling his brow.

"Trust me," Hank said. "Lester won't be in any condition to drive."

The old man's screams grew louder and louder as the shadows destroyed him. Slowly, they disappeared, leaving a blinding circle on the floor.

I had to look away for a moment. When my eyes adjusted, I glanced down at a shiny brass skull. It lay on a heap of the old man's clothes.

The skull was speaking Latin in a soft whisper.

I bent over it.

"Go on," Hank said. "Pick it up."

I grabbed the skull with both hands. It was cool to the touch.

Its voice was magnetic. I couldn't stop staring at it.

I tucked it into the crook of my arm, feeling the jaws move as it kept speaking in Latin.

"Whatever you do, don't ask it any questions," Hank said.

Like war-torn soldiers, we staggered out of the mansion.

That's the story of how I ended up with this brass skull. What happened next was a blur.

Hank's spell hurt him something awful. The warlock needed a hospital, and fast. Bo offered to take him, but he said, "We have to finish this job."

And the skull. It sat on the dashboard of the truck, whispering in Latin. Even though it didn't have eyes, I got the sinking feeling that it wouldn't stop staring at me.

Bo peeled Hank's pickup out of the rich neighborhood, steering the truck through the winding suburban boulevards. A few times, I repositioned the skull. But no matter how I adjusted it, it kept looking at me. It would rotate as if on a pedestal to keep staring at me. And I didn't know Latin, so that made the gesture even more creepy.

I couldn't shake that it was trying to tell me something, that it wanted to get inside my head.

I didn't buy for a second that a supernatural skull like this would be up to any good. I took Hank's Native American blanket and threw it over the skull.

It didn't stop chanting, and I didn't stop thinking about it.

As Bo turned onto the highway and Hank gave him directions, the skull's voice rang in my ears like bad tinnitus. It was always there.

I came to appreciate the voice. It soothed me on this autumn night.

I came to *need* the damn skull. I didn't want the ringing to stop.

THE BRAZEN SKULL: A GOOD NECROMANCER... 287

Hank guided us to the St. Louis Riverfront. The interstate took us past the Gateway Arch, that treasured monument of my city. As the skull whispered to me, I marveled at the river's reflections on the Arch's silver exterior.

The highway cut over the Mississippi River into darkness. The only shapes on the other side of the river for a few miles were factories and strip clubs whose blue and pink spotlights lit the sky and made it look like a demonic scrim.

Soon, Bo turned off the highway and parked near a dock set off by a row of fading white bollards. The headlights of the truck slashed the water at a diagonal angle.

Hank opened the door and stumbled out. He fell face-first on the gravel. I climbed out and helped him up.

"It had to be done this way," he said weakly, leaning on me.

"Seeing as I'm not dead yet, I'll trust you," I said.

Hank knelt in the gravel and pointed at the river. "The skull," he said. "Throw it."

I knew what Hank wanted me to do, but something nagged at me. If I threw away this skull, I would never know the inner depths of these urges I was feeling. A deep sadness welled within me, like something was dying.

"I can't," I said. The words came out before I realized I had said them.

"You're the only one who can," Hank said. His face took on a serious, soft look of concern. "If I had touched that thing, I wouldn't have been strong enough, Lester."

The sadness spread across my body like ink in water. I didn't want to let it go. "And you think I'm strong enough?"

"Lester, you have to trust me," Hank said, gasping.

Bo wandered to the back of the pickup and lugged the sandbag out, groaning.

"Can we get this over already?" he asked. "I'm not exactly Hercules, y'all."

I walked over to the edge of the river and held the skull up. It knew what was coming. It began shouting in Latin. Then it switched to English, and I leaned in to hear its secrets.

"You would throw me in the river without hearing a prophecy first, Lester Broussard?" it asked. Then, it said the names of everyone I had ever known, dates that only I could have known, and secrets about myself that no one else knew. I couldn't help but lower the skull, listening like a cobra swaying to a flute.

"When you die, you will die alone," the skull said. "With me, you can live forever and alter your fate."

I shook my head, trying to slough off the skull's hold on me. I knew damn well it wasn't going to work. His words were hypnotic, soothing, wrapping around me like a womb. All I could see was the skull and all that mattered was the skull and all that I cared about was the skull.

"Step away from the river, Lester Broussard. Oh, the things we can do together! I will help you hunt down every supernatural in the city who deserves their comeuppance, and I will guide you to victory swiftly. I will lead you to world peace, Lester. You will be the necromancer who saves the world from itself. If not, you will die alone in your game of tallies, and you will be betrayed by the one you trusted."

I remembered Hank's advice, but I couldn't resist...

"Who?" I asked softly. "Who will kill me?"

I wanted to know. I needed to know. Every muscle in my body tensed up as I waited for the answer.

Someone tapped me on the shoulder. I looked over just as Hank punched me in the face.

The skull went flying. I reached out my hands and cried for it, but it was too late.

Exasperated, Hank slipped out his wand and waved it.

The sandbag flew from Bo's hands and attached itself to the skull. A silver chain wove itself out of nothing, securing the dead warlock's jaws to the sandbag.

The skull opened its mouth to scream, but it splashed into the water. The river swallowed it soundlessly.

I fell to my knees, watching as bubbles formed on the surface and rolled away. I felt as if I had woken up from a fever dream. A hand touched my shoulder gently. Hank.

"It wasn't your fault," he said. "No one could have resisted it. All those bodies in the cellar—they were people just like us." He grinned. "The only difference is that the dead ones were warlocks. You're a necromancer. The magic took longer to work on you. That was my advantage."

Hank handed me the bag with the steak. "You're going to need that for your eye, champ."

I put the steak on my face. The sandwich bag molded around the contours of my cheek. It sure felt good...except for the extra crispy parts where Bo had burned it. The crispy bits dug into my skin.

Hank shambled back to the truck and said, "Now you know why I told you to bring a steak."

I stood in the headlights of the truck, regarding his words. Then it all made sense.

"Asshole," I said.

Hank gave a weak laugh as he climbed into the pickup. "Gentlemen, we just saved the world from disaster," he said.

"Now no one will be able to find him at the bottom of the Mississippi except for a few catfish."

"Sure hope so," Bo said.

Hank scoffed. "Take me home and we'll be even."

Bo stood next to me as we stared across the muddy banks of the river.

"Welp, I'd say it's time for a little gin rummy, wouldn't you, boss man?" he asked, heading for the truck.

That's the life of a necromancer. You never know how the game of tallies is going to tally up, but any night things don't go sideways is a good night. I'd live to see another conjuring, and that was a beautiful thing.

On the way home, Bo drove the truck stone-faced, not saying a word. Hank looked like he was going to pass out. I leaned against the window, head propped on my fist, thinking about just what the hell that skull might have told me if Hank hadn't punched me in the face.

We all have an ending. It's an inevitable part of life. After all the souls I've summoned, you'd think maybe, just maybe I would have tried to find out about mine. I had never considered it.

Call me naive, but I just prefer to live, come what may. I don't want to see my sticky end coming. At least that was what I told myself, but that brazen skull sure knew me better than that.

I tried to push the prophecy out of my mind as Bo curved out of the river shadows and plunged back into the blinding, bejeweled heart of the city.

MICHAEL LA RONN IS the author of over 80 science fiction & fantasy books, including *The Good Necromancer* series. He writes from the great plains of Iowa and has managed to write while raising a family, working a full-time job, and even attending law school classes in the evenings. You can find his fiction at www.michaellaronn.com and his videos and books for writers at www.authorlevelup.com

REBEL WITH A CAUSE: AN OBSIDIAN ARCHIVES STORY

By Marx Pyle

THE MARK, IRONICALLY NAMED Mark, never expected to see his long-dead *abuelo* beckoning him into the dirty alley. Once he did, though, how could he *not* follow him into the shadows?

Just as I had hoped.

Speaking of names, I might as well tell you mine: Antonio Santiago, but most people call me Rebel. Neither is my real name, of course. True names have power and must therefore be wielded—and guarded—accordingly. I chose Antonio because Antonio Banderas (my totem papá) is a bad-ass. Anyone who disagrees will have a fight on their hands. And Santiago...well, I liked the sound of it. Plus, it's the title of one of my favorite science fiction novels from my formative years. Oh, and the city is cool, too.

My nickname, Rebel, reflects my lovely attitude toward authority.

"Grandpa Roscoe?" Mark whispered hesitantly as he inched cautiously toward me.

"M... M... Mark?" My voice wavered and my eyes watered. *Damn, I'm good.* "Come here and give your grandpa a big hug."

Mark's reluctance gave way to joy as he rushed in for a hearty embrace.

It was a touching moment. If this had been a TV show, there would have been a swelling musical score to elicit tears from the audience. But in reality, I pulled a syringe from my pocket and injected Mark in the neck.

He dropped unceremoniously to the pavement.

Duh, duh, duh-mmm! Plot twist.

Did I mention I'm not human and most assuredly not Mark's grandpa?

I dragged the poor bastard behind the dumpster and quickly removed his clothes, which I needed to pull this next part off. I shifted to look just like Mr. Sleepytime Mark and quickly got dressed.

There are a handful of shapeshifter species out there, but I'm proud to say, few are as talented as a púca. The only downside is that one part of my body doesn't fit what I shape into, and what that is changes each time. It's my one tell, but at least the fuzzy orange cat tail I was currently sporting disappeared easily down one leg of Mark's baggy suit pants. Worst case scenario, someone would think I'm very "gifted" down there.

"Step one, check," I said to the hidden mic I stuck inside Mark's shirt.

"*That was slick, Rebel,*" Oz replied in my earpiece. "*When he hit the concrete, I was like, 'Flying shit monkeys, that had to hurt!' Being tall's a bitch when gravity slaps you down. That twit human should have known better, considering the kind of fae he hangs out with.*"

Oz (not even close to his real name) is a technomancer, hacker, occasional asshole, and a goblin who hates tall people. But I've always found him bearable. Most of the time. At least he's one of the best at what he does, and he won't stab you in the back. Can't expect more when you work with hired criminals. We've only worked together a handful of times, but when Crick said I could choose the technomancer for my team, I didn't hesitate to recruit Oz. I trusted him about 80%. The rest of the team, not at all.

"Wait. How did you see us?" I asked, suddenly feeling exposed. I quickly scanned the alley.

A huge brown rat scampered from under the dumpster, rose up on its hind legs, and waved.

"*Pay no attention to the goblin behind the curtain,*" Oz chuckled, obviously very proud of himself. "*My little rats see all.*"

I stared hard at the rat. All fae have some talent with glamours. Púcas don't use illusions to bend light or minds, because we can physically shapeshift into almost any humanoid or animal. So, my talents extend only into seeing through others' glamours. Concentrating hard, I managed to push past the rat illusion to see what really stood before me: an odd little rat robot-looking thing that appeared pieced together from garbage parts.

"I hope you got those everywhere inside," I said. "We could use the extra eyes."

"Of course," Oz said. I swear, I could actually *hear* the smug bastard beaming with pride. I smiled.

And that's why he's on my team.

The shadows at the end of the alley retreated unnaturally, and suddenly revealed the rest of the team. The man in a black business suit, with long silver hair and pointy ears, went by the name Mr. Dye. He was an elf and seemed like a pro, but I could tell when I'd met him pre-job that he was dangerous. Must have been those soulless eyes.

Behind him stood two large orc mercenaries. We hadn't been introduced, but I gathered they were related.

"Very smooth." Mr. Dye nodded his approval. "And you look just like him."

I bowed slightly. "Thank you. I'll be here all night. I didn't realize you were watching."

"Of course. I wanted to see you in action."

"And..." I pointed to the hulking orcs packing enormous guns. "I didn't catch their names."

"Just call these gentlemen Peanut Butter and Jelly," he actually said with a straight face.

"Yeah," said one of the orcs. "I'm Jelly."

"Hey," said the other orc. "I thought *I* was going to be Jelly."

I tuned out the rest of their argument. *Yup, definitely brothers.*

Mr. Dye presented me with a pistol. "Gun?"

"Naw." I waved it off. "Don't want to draw suspicion. I'll figure something out once I'm inside."

"Very well. The wards on this building will keep humans from paying any attention. So once inside, we won't have to worry about any police response, just the hostiles within. Now, if you are ready, begin step two."

With a grin, I walked out of the alley to the next part of the job. Things were about to get fun.

I MADE IT PAST the guards easy enough with Mark's face. While I couldn't tell if they were fae or human, their gun bulges showed they were heavily armed. Once inside, I walked past a sketchy-looking group of men and women playing cards, their guns propped up within arms' reach. A grenade sitting on the table completed the tableau. They looked ready for a fight, but no way were they prepared for what we had planned.

I continued slowly down the hallways, pulling memories from Mark's unconscious mind to guide me through the path he took every day, and located the one that should take me to his lab.

The tired-looking building must have housed apartments at one point, but had long ago been overtaken by the gang.

I encountered more members of the Ice Vipers gang. This far in, they weren't bothering to glamour themselves a human facade. I counted a number of orcs, hobgoblins, ogres, and at least one troll. All heavily armed.

By the time I made it to the lab, I had seen where they stored fae-enchanted drugs, stolen property, and illegal guns. I even saw hints of where the human trafficking branch held their prisoner prostitutes. I'd be the first to admit that I'm no saint, but I draw the line *way* before slavery. The Ice Vipers were just scum. It made the job easier. I didn't care if I had to kill a few of them.

"In the lab," I whispered into the mic. Zeroing in on Mark's computer, I hovered my fingers over the keyboard until the password slipped into my mind, then logged in.

"I'm in," I said triumphantly. "Step three."

A fat rat ran up my leg and jumped onto the desk, nearly eliciting a yelp of surprise. I grinned, knowing Oz was probably disappointed. The bastard did that on purpose.

The rat sniffed the USB port, turned around, and stuck its tail into the slot. The screen blinked, then started flashing code.

"*Ha, this firewall is shit,*" Oz said. "*I'm already in. Getting access to security cameras. Unlocking all electronic locks. And for funsies, I'm downloading all of their records.*"

"Where do I go from here?" I asked. "Do you have eyes on the target?"

The moment stretched on as I waited for a reply. "Oz?"

"*Got him,*" Oz finally replied. "*But no camera in the room. You need to go up one floor and two doors west from the elevator. The target should be in there.*"

"Good." This was almost too easy.

"*I think they've saved this whole floor for the target. I see maybe five guards. Want to wait for back-up?*"

"No, let's stick with the plan," I replied. "Start the next step once I get out of the elevators."

"*Your call...and possible funeral.*"

"Oh, ye of little faith."

D^{ING}

The shaky elevator's door creaked open. Guards greeted me as soon as I strutted out.

"What the fuck you doing on this floor?" demanded the seven-foot-tall ogre as he closed in on me.

"Wrong turn?"

BOOM

Did I mention Oz is also good at explosives?

The lights shut off, only to be immediately replaced by red emergency lights.

I shifted into Urkel from the TV show *Family Matters*, shrugged, and in a perfect imitation of the character's annoyingly high-pitched voice, declared, "Oops, did I do that?"

"Son-of-a-bitch! We've got a shapeshifter!" The ogre bellowed as he charged and brandished a pistol, larger than usual, but still dwarfed by his giant hands.

I quickly shifted into a satyr. Not just any satyr, someone I once knew who was a hell of a martial artist.

I rushed the ogre, flipped forward, and kicked him with both hooves right in the middle of his chest, causing a few loud pops from his body as he fell back on his ass. He accidentally discharged a few rounds into the ceiling as he went down.

"Hey, that's my mamá you are talking about!" I responded to his insult as I bounced backwards and rolled to my feet. I pulled out the two pistols I snagged on my way through the building and shifted into my favorite elf shape. With her eagle eyes, she was always my top pick for gunfighting. And while her sharpshooting skills far surpassed mine, I've managed to pick up a few tricks.

I took out three hobgoblins with headshots before they could even aim at me. As they crumpled to the ground, I dashed past the ogre, firing two rounds into his head before he could react.

My elven ears detected major gunfire downstairs. The rest of my team, as planned. They would clear our exit.

The other two orc guards tried to enter the target's room. I managed to shoot one in the back a couple of times, but his buddy made it inside and slammed the door in his face.

I ran to the downed orc. He rolled over and tried to spray me with rounds from his submachine gun. Quickly I shifted back into the satyr and dodged, bounced off the wall, flipped, and smashed his gun arm under my hooves. Orcs are tough, but not indestructible. I inwardly grimaced as his roar failed to drown out the twig-like snapping sound of his shattered arm. Without hesitation, I shifted back to elf and ended his misery with a quick headshot. Knowing these bastards deserved that and worse (hello, human trafficking!) eased my conscience.

My elven ears pricked up at the sound of a shotgun pumping on the other side of the door, giving me just enough time to duck. Buckshot rained down on me, and a stinging pain erupted on my side. Bastard nicked me.

"Oz, do you have eyes in that room?" I yelled through clenched teeth.

"*Remember, no cameras,*" Oz replied. "*But lucky for you, my rats are good at crawling through walls. They're getting there. Exchange some fire so he doesn't hear my rat chewing through the wall.*"

Gladly. Firing through the door at the shotgun-wielding hobgoblin felt oddly cathartic.

"*I've got eyes*," said Oz after what felt like far too many minutes.

Finally.

"Good." I snagged the submachine gun from the dead orc, still mindful of my playmate on the other side of that door. I fired a burst of bullets. "Tell me when he reloads."

I paused to let him fire back.

"*Now!*"

On command, I shifted into a Sasquatch. Now, the Sasquatch Nation are a peaceful species, but boy, you make them angry enough, and they will rip you in half, making this the shape I return to whenever I need extra muscle. As I shifted, I could feel my clothes rip, unable to contain the much larger frame. Hairy Bigfoot-me shattered the door as I charged straight through, slammed into the hobgoblin, and easily pinned him down with my hulking eight-foot-two-inch frame. With a roar, I grabbed his head and slammed it into the floor with a resounding crack. He was out. Dead or not, he wasn't a threat anymore.

I shifted back into my natural long-haired human Latino shape. My shredded Mark clothes clung precariously to my body. Shame. I liked that outfit. At least I bought those Sollypomp Spider Silk boxers a couple of years back. The magical silver fiber shifted with me for most shapes, so my little *púca* doesn't get stuck waving around for all the world to see. It cost a small fortune, but after a few embarrassing jobs, I decided it was well worth the money.

I grabbed the pistols from my waistband and scanned the dark room for the target, coming up empty. When Crick hired me, he didn't know the target's identity, and Mr. Dye would only say it was a 'he.' Now usually, I'm not a fan of being kept in the dark, but the money for this job was too good to pass up.

"Hello, I'm here to help you," I practically cooed into the darkness. That was *mostly* true. After all, the target was kidnapped by the Ice Vipers for a ransom, and we were hired to rescue him. He didn't (need to) know it was so our mystery boss could ask for their own ransom.

"Oz, can I get some light in here?"

"*Piece of cake. My rats are in all of the wires. I should be able to just turn on this floor.*"

The lights clicked on. The room was a wreck with all but one of the lamps shot up. A shape moved in the shadows.

Keeping my guns ready, but pointing down, I continued in a calming voice. "Don't worry. I'm here to save you." *Sort of.*

The form crept toward me, revealing—to my surprise—a human-looking child.

"Are you some kind of superhero?" The kid, eyes wide, lips parted, regarded me hopefully.

"Um, Oz? I need confirmation. Is this *him*?"

"*Checking on the other frequency,*" Oz answered, then I heard him talking on another line with the rest of the team.

"*He* is *the target,*" confirmed Mr. Dye, having switched to my frequency. "*I'll be there in a minute.*"

"No need." We were wasting time. "I'll take him downstairs. Just clear a path."

"Negative," barked Mr. Dye. "*Secure the target and wait for me.*"

Well, this was an annoying turn. The boy continued to stare at me in awe. Somehow, I needed to buy time and not scare the kid.

"Are you a superhero?" The wide-eyed kid repeated his question, slightly louder this time.

"I mean, sorta. I've got superpowers."

Sure, why not?

I shifted into my elf gunfighter, then into the satyr, which won me a chuckle. After a moment, I shifted back to my human shape.

"Oh, my God!" The kid slapped his hands over this mouth and mumbled, "Sorry, didn't mean to take the Lord's name in vain."

Lowering myself to one knee, I reassured him. "No worries, kid. Your mom tell you not to say that?"

He nodded, hands still covering his mouth. I smiled.

"What's your name?"

That got him excited. With lots of hand waving and body movement, he breathlessly relayed the long and interesting tale that was him.

"My parents named me Liam, because...because...uh...after Liam Neeee...uh...Neenson. Yeah, I think that's his name. He's an actor, and he does this cool action stuff." Liam launched into his action-hero impersonation, complete with sound effects as he punched and kicked in the air. "Mom said he's cute, and Dad said he's one of his favorite actors...and, and...well, they won't let me see most of his movies because I'm too young. Buuuuuutttt, they did let me see him in *Star Wars*, where he was a Jedi and that was soooooo cool..." Liam's story was then interrupted by a demonstration of his lightsaber fighting skills, complete with the typical sound effects.

That gave me an idea to buy me more time.

I shifted into Liam *Neenson*, which I knew I could do because I had to pretend to be him once to steal... Never mind, not important.

"Little Liam," I said in a pitch perfect imitation of the actor's voice. "We need to get out of here. Lucky for you, I have a particular set of skills."

Liam laughed, an infectious giggly, hiccuppy laugh, that made it impossible not to join in.

"You're silly," he said when he could talk once again. "You're nicer than these monster people."

"Of course, I'm nicer," I said. "I'm a superhero. They're *supervillians*. Do you have any special powers?"

Since I was going to have to buy time, I figured I might as well get a better idea on why this kid was so important.

"No," Liam said and scrunched his forehead in concentration. "One of them called me a word I didn't know."

"A what?"

"A... 'f' word." Liam slapped his hands over his mouth again, certain he'd said something else he wasn't supposed to.

"Assuming he wasn't just calling you a bad name, did he happen to say 'fae'?"

"Yes!" Liam jumped up and down. "What is that?"

"A very special species. You know, like a fairy."

Liam giggled. "You mean like the tooth fairy? That's silly."

"Not exactly. Like elves and trolls. That is what these monster men are."

"But, you're not a monster... Are you?" Liam suddenly stood very still, all childish glee gone.

"No, no," I quickly reassured him. "These people are just *mean* fae. I'm a *nice* fae."

Liam nodded slowly, processing this new information.

"Do your parents have any special powers or look different than other people? Pointy ears? Or can they make things disappear?"

Liam thought a moment, then slowly shook his head.

Something wasn't adding up. Why would a fae gang kidnap a human kid? Only one thing came to mind.

"Are your parents rich?"

Liam shook his head. "No, they've been having a hard time with money. They think I don't know, but I hear mommy cry sometimes at night about the bad bank people."

Maybe his parents borrowed some money from fae, not knowing what they were getting into? Liam said his kidnappers used the word 'fae.'

"Did they call *you* a fae?"

Liam nodded quickly.

"There are lots and lots of different kinds of fae, Liam. Did they say what kind you are?"

The kid looked like he was going to pop a vein trying to remember. "Yes!" he finally said. "A change something... A *changer*...or something?"

My heart jumped a couple of beats. "A changeling?"

Liam jumped up and down like he had won a prize. "That's it! Can I change into things? Like, like... Can I change into a car?" He then treated me to his impression of a little boy turning into a car, complete with robotic, mechanical noises.

I figured I better set him straight before he has a chance to get too disappointed.

"Sorry, you can't shapeshift into a car."

Changelings, which are technically illegal nowadays, were when a fae would swap out one of their fae babies with a human baby. Reasons varied, but the fae child would be locked into a human form until they were either "unlocked" by a fae or hit puberty, whichever came first.

Of course, 'illegal' didn't mean it didn't happen. Few people knew I was actually a changeling.

I was adopted by human parents, a mixed-race couple. My mom was half-Columbian/half-Filipino and my dad Caucasian. They were told I was a Latino child abandoned on the American side of the border. That shit was all sorts of complicated for a young boy to process growing up, especially when unexpected shapeshifting powers kicked in with puberty and its toxic, chaotic mix of hormones. I still don't know who my fae parents are, and I'm not sure if I care anymore, anyway.

Changelings usually only happen nowadays when a fae needs to hide their offspring from a political enemy.

Yes, that would explain this situation: a royal fae tried to hide a kid and an enemy found them. Damn, I hate political shit.

Gunfire in the hallway pulled me from my thoughts.

"Stay here, Liam." I walked out into the hallway, guns ready.

Mr. Dye strode purposefully toward us as Peanut Butter and Jelly remained a bit behind, firing down the stairwell.

"Oz," ordered Mr. Dye. "Begin the final step."

"*Understood*," Oz sounded...odd. "*Eight minutes, starting.... Now.*"

"Whoa." My spidey senses tingled. This was not the plan. "What happens in eight minutes?"

"The building blows up," Mr. Dye explained calmly. "Oz's rats are also bombs."

"But the innocent people down there–" We certainly didn't discuss that.

"Relax, Rebel. We let anyone who wanted to run out of here. We also freed the women held captive on the third floor, if that's what you're worried about. I even gave one of them a gun in case they felt like killing any of the gang on the way out. I only kill people I'm hired to kill... Or who get in my way," he said pointedly. A raised eyebrow emphasized the importance of that last statement.

Great.

Mr. Dye continued toward me as he checked his clip. Finding it empty, he holstered his pistol and rolled up his sleeves, revealing two very impressively detailed tattoos of black and purple katanas on his surprisingly muscled forearms.

"Nice tats." I whistled, once again feeling jealous of people with tattoos. Any attempts at tattoos in my youth failed. They always faded away after I shifted a few times.

Mr. Dye palmed one of his tattoos and *pulled* out a very solid, very sharp, very *real* black and purple sword, whose edges rippled like slightly shifting ink. He did the same with the other sword tattoo.

"*Very* nice tats!" Without meaning to, I stepped back. "Ink magic isn't cheap."

Mr. Dye nodded slightly, as the corner of his mouth slyly curled. "They weren't, but they paid for themselves after their first kill. Now, where is the boy?"

My púca sixth sense buzzed through me. "We're just kidnapping him, right?"

Mr. Dye stopped and stared at me like he was calculating a solution to a math problem. "No, job changed right after we started." His words were measured and his voice dropped to a menacing pitch. "We terminate the target and get paid double."

Dammit. Of course this had to get complicated. It never just goes smooth.

I shifted into my elf shape and pointed my pistols at him. "No, that was not the agreement. I am not an assassin."

Mr. Dye looked pointedly at the dead bodies on the floor. "Really? You do a very impressive impression of one."

"Killing these asshats in a fight is different than offing some little kid."

Mr. Dye smoothly spun his rippling ink swords with such grace that it would have been beautiful if it wasn't intended as a death threat.

"I would prefer to not kill a child," he explained, as if it absolved him. "But we don't get to choose the target."

"He's an innocent changeling," I argued. "He doesn't even know what he is."

"Then he is already dead. No powers. No idea what is out there. No chance of surviving the people who want him dead. At least I'll make it quick. I doubt the next person would be so generous."

How very gallant of him.

"Who wants him dead?" I asked.

"Someone very powerful. Someone you don't want to piss off. Now get out of my way, *púca*." He practically snarled the last word.

"No, I–"

The elf bastard didn't even let me finish. With one spin and a slash, my guns were in pieces.

Thinking quickly, I shifted into the satyr and managed to evade his blades' continued assault as he forced me back into the room with Liam.

"Liam! Hide!" I hollered before engaging in full martial arts mode, using my hooved legs to kick lamps, chairs, whatever I could at Mr. Dye who, with the ferocity of a tiger, spun and slashed in a deadly ballet. All I managed to do was slow him down mere seconds as he swung his katanas around with impunity. Finally, I ran at a wall and used my momentum as I kicked off it to launch myself behind the couch. I crouched down and shifted into Sasquatch mode (complete with mismatched large, floppy bunny ears) and howled as I threw the couch and charged him.

His wide eyes registered surprise, but he still got a few slices in on the couch before we collided and tumbled across the floor. One of his ink blades slid across the ground, but he used the other to slice my chest. Not deep, but I was bleeding like a stuck... Sasquatch. I was losing this fight unless I did something quick.

Realizing what that 'something' was, I shifted into Mr. Dye, rolled, and grabbed the blade he'd lost. We both simultaneously snapped to our feet, swords poised, postures mirroring each other. Quickly regrouping, he attacked with a flourish, but I countered every move. As we sliced, diced, and blocked in unison, we must have looked like a mirror-image whirlwind.

"Sneaky," Mr. Dye conceded as he paused to catch his breath. "Shift into me and read my surface thoughts."

"It works well *mano a mano*."

"But we have only minutes left. Holding me off will just get us all killed."

"Oz, my goblin friend, who owes me a favor," I spoke into my mic. "Don't forget Vancouver. Can you stop these bombs?"

"*Wish I could,*" Oz said. "*I can't help, Rebel. Mr. Dye had me make the rats impossible to hack for at least 10 minutes, as a precaution in case the gang had their own technomancer.*"

"There is no shame, Rebel." Mr. Dye tried to reason with me. "You tried. We can still survive, and just to show there's no hard feelings, I'll even let you have your money."

I spun the ink sword in the air and struck a pose. "Nope, ask anyone who knows me, I'm stubborn. Stupid stubborn. If we die, then we die."

I attacked and he countered, continuing our fighting whirlwind. He was right about one thing–we were losing time. I needed a way to end this, but truthfully, the elf was just a better fighter.

Then, I got my opening.

Mid-slash, Mr. Dye tripped and tumbled on top of me. As I fell, I caught a glimpse of Liam holding up a TV power cord from the other side of the room. Kid had guts.

I raised my hand to the elf's surprised face. Remember how I said I always have one body part that doesn't match the rest of the shape? With a little focus, I can control what that is. And this time, I was glad I chose something useful, as my mismatched tiger claws slashed Mr. Dye's shocked face. He rolled to his feet and, through the bloody mangled mess, glared at me with his right eye, the only one he had left. Without skipping a beat, I shifted into my satyr form and, after executing a capoeira spin, landed on one of his knees, shattering it.

The ink swords melted with Mr. Dye's guttural roar.

"You're dead! I am going to kill you!" He spat furiously as he yelled at me.

"Yeah, I don't think so."

I ran to the barred window, my focus now on escape.

"Oz, tell me something good."

"*You probably won't feel much pain from the bomb blast?*"

"We can jump," I suggested, ignoring his sarcastic reassurance.

"*Sure, in the right shape, you might not die, but the kid might, and you need to clear the area quick.*"

"Liam, get over here fast!" I had an idea.

THE BLAST NEARLY DISINTEGRATED the building. No surprise there, Oz is very good with explosives. At least he kept the blast radius down.

Oz saw the explosion from the driver's seat of the van parked a couple of blocks away. Staring as the building collapsed, he kept repeating, "*Rebel, Rebel?*"

With a slam, I landed on the hood of the van, as an orangutan with large batwings, and the kid clutched tightly to my back.

"Flying shit monkeys!" Was all Oz could get out.

"That was epic!" Liam added gleefully.

I gently set Liam down on the ground, shifted, and ordered him, "Quick, get in the back of the van."

He jumped in without question.

I slid off the van hood and into the passenger side next to Oz.

"Let's get out of here! I'm going to need a stiff drink after this. A freffrisa...who am I kidding? I need something stronger, a freffrisa-x might do."

But Oz didn't hit the gas. Instead, he fiddled with some controls and started giggling, which turned into full blown laughter.

"What the hell, Oz? Get us out of here!"

"You sure...you aren't missing something?" He managed to get out between laughs.

I glanced down and realized I was naked. Covering myself, I looked out the window for my Sollypomp Spider Silk boxers. While they shrink and grow with my shapes, they do have their limits.

"You could have said something sooner," I pouted.

"And miss that look...on your face? Naw!"

Suddenly, my door popped open and revealed a rat holding my boxers in its mouth. I snatched them up and put them on in a flash.

"Now, can we go?" I sighed and looked at Oz, but he didn't return my gaze.

I followed the gaze of his widened eyes and saw Peanut Butter and Jelly running our way.

"Yeah, I'm good," he agreed as he hit the gas. Finally, we were off.

"WHERE ARE WE GOING?" Liam yelled from the back of the van and tried to get a good look at Oz. "He has big ears and is a funny color," he finally declared.

"He better not ask 'Are we there yet?' every five minutes or I'm throwing him out," Oz warned. "Here, kid, watch some cartoons. The adults need to talk."

Oz pressed a button, and a TV screen popped out of the side of the van, playing what sounded like a cartoon. Liam was mesmerized. "Cool," he declared.

A shaded screen slid between us and Liam.

"So, Rebel, what the hell?"

"He is an innocent kid, a changeling," I told him. "I wasn't going to murder a kid."

"I mean, I like kids because, for one, they're usually shorter than me. But if he is a changeling, he's probably some royal's spawn."

"Yeah, probably," I conceded.

"Which means they are going to want him," Oz explained like I was an idiot. "You don't even know if they are Seelie or Unseelie. You just know that *someone* wants him dead and probably someone else wants to use him."

"Yeah, since when do you care about what royals want?"

"Since I may become their target," he sighed. "Could take him to Obsidian."

"No, then he just becomes a political pawn and I have a feeling it wouldn't turn out good for him."

"Well, good luck, Rebel. I'll drop you two off somewhere, and we can write off Vancouver, since I lost some good money today."

"Actually," I replied with a grin, "I've got some money saved up. I'll pay you the difference, plus more to help me with the kid."

Oz's gaze never left the road as his teeth clinked. His ears perked up as he said, "You're going to get me killed, Rebel."

He sighed dejectedly. "Fine, I'll help, but if it gets too hot, I'm out. Fair warning."

"Good enough," I smiled, suspecting he wouldn't bail, no matter what he said. "Now I just have to figure out what to do with him."

Oz groaned and shook his head. "Great, a Rebel *with* a cause. What could go wrong?"

MARX PYLE IS AN author, screenwriter, filmmaker, podcaster, adjunct professor, and martial artist whose journey has been as complex as his characters and the worlds in which they live. His first degree was to save the world (Psychology), and the next to pay the bills (Computer Information Systems). His third degree (Film Production) helped him follow his storytelling dreams, but his final (Master of Fine Arts in Writing Popular Fiction) allowed him to do so without budget constraints. In addition to urban fantasy, he dabbles in science fiction, fantasy, and horror because he can't filter that "what if" voice in his head. Marx's urban fantasy/thriller, *Obsidian Monsters* was recently released. He enjoys relaxing at home with his supportive wife, their two cats (Veronica & Teddy Bear). He can be found online at https://marxpyle.com and on Twitter as @MrMarx.

An Old Favor

By Marisa Wolf

Sun streamed through the nodding trees, a breeze wove through the air, people laughed and picnicked, and Ochia sat on her bench and hated the lot of it.

A note fluttered on her lap. She would have preferred a live viper.

Her hair rustled in the breeze, muttering imprecations, and she smiled despite the infuriatingly short message she'd been reading.

"No snacks," she said. A susurrus of reluctant agreement answered her.

"I'm sure a dryad will let them have some berries." The statue of a satyr, permanently crouched on the bench next to her, spoke without moving, directly into her mind.

Ochia ran her tongue along the sharp edges of her teeth and tapped the stone knee next to her. The statue did not frown or shrug, but the inflection of his sigh made the expression clear.

"Right. Only meat. Well, Thuja had a slug infestation the last time her tree bloomed, I'm sure she'd be happy to share."

The problem with statues, Ochia thought, even as her hair lifted in interest, was that once they relearned to speak, they hardly ever shut up.

"We're not here for food," she murmured, adjusting her dark glasses. "Tell me again about the note."

"It was left by a normal man, utterly human." The stone satyr grunted. *"He wore glasses like yours—not for the same reason, sure—coat too heavy for the weather—it's still cool out, right?"*

"Yes."

"I figured. The quetzals aren't back yet, days are still a little short. Sun's not as warm on my horns as late spring gets."

"You're discerning variations in temperature quite well, Ode to a Homeland Glen."

"Oh very funny, Ochia. Haha. Ha. Ha-very-ha."

"I would apologize, but you made my hair drool."

"I did, didn't I?" The satyr's pride beamed through his tone, if not his unchanging face.

"He didn't say anything to you? This human delivery person?"

"You know very well you're the only one who talks to me."

Ochia touched the tip of her ear, and a snake wound around her hand, tongue flicking toward the statue next to them.

"There are at least three petramagos in Bard City." She tilted her head back toward the perfectly fluffed clouds speckling the sky and wondered if that was still what stone magicians called themselves. Or had ever called themselves. Ochia avoided them—and all the more mortal sort of magic users—as a general rule.

"And each of them came to me once, tried to un-stone me, failed, and never came to this park again."

"Not very chatty, stone-mages." She rubbed her free hand through the curled mass of her hair, the motion soothing both her and the snakes. "At least that hasn't changed."

"*Have* you *made any progress?*"

"I told you twenty years ago, Glen. It's a one way process, far as I know. My sister never did anything by halves."

The statue of a satyr—whom had once been a non-statued satyr, over a hundred years and an unfortunate encounter with a Gorgon ago—sighed and complained about missing out on all the new craft beers on display across the park.

She made appropriate sounds in mostly appropriate moments, and smoothed over the paper with its brief message on her lap.

I'm calling in the favor. You know where to find me.

Ochia sighed and glared at the cheer and relaxation filling the park. She could question the satyr all day, but it wouldn't change anything.

"May the pit take me whole," she muttered, her snakes laying close to her neck in response. She only owed one favor, and she knew exactly where to go.

"I'VE AVOIDED MORGUES SINCE they were invented." Ochia pushed through double metal doors into a wide, stainless-steel room with four empty tables and a single living human in the painfully clean space. She wrinkled her nose against the antiseptic tang, shoved her hands in her pockets, and stood clear of the doors' swing.

The human—male and wide-eyed—was presumably the delivery person, but not who she was here to see.

Motion to her left roused her snakes, and she turned as a woman shoved a large screen against the wall. Tall, dark-haired, permanent glare—woman was not the right term.

Medical examiner. Battle death goddess. Keres Nikotonos.

"Ochia," she said, with a quirk of her lips that approached a smile. "You still don't have a phone."

"Yet you got a hold of me," Ochia tucked a wandering snake back under her hat. The human on the other side of the morgue retreated to a separate room, which showed that Keres employed staff with sense.

"It took longer than I would have liked. You know how many statues are in this city."

"Did you leave notes on all of them?" Snakes rustled under her hat, and their amusement eased a small measure of tension across her shoulders.

"Enough of them." Keres blew out her breath in a sound that was nearly a laugh. "Phones *are* useful, you know."

"It will be something else the moment I get used to it. A body gets tired, Keres." It wasn't her only complaint about the world she'd been unwillingly dragged into, but it hovered around the top of her list. Usually alongside flying creatures who inevitably chose to defecate on statues and people who tried to peer behind her glasses.

"I'll save the argument for another time." Keres strode to the wall of drawers at the far end of the big square room.

Given they'd last seen each other a century ago, Ochia forbore to worry about the potential argument that would change exactly no part of her mind, and chose to concern herself with the drawer's contents.

"Before you do that." Ochia paused two steps in. "Which part of me are you calling on?" Her snakes coiled close to her scalp, the chill in the air and the comfort of her hat combining to keep them calm even close to so much death. She ran her tongue over her teeth and touched her glasses.

"You're an investigator still, yes?" Keres lifted a brow. "I hear you maintain an office, even if there's no way for potential clients to know when you will appear within it, given they can't call and there are no hours posted."

"No one needs me urgently." She folded her arms and did not point out how purposefully she'd made that a reality. "And yes, I even have my PI certification from the city."

"Very official," Keres murmured.

Ochia dipped her chin to indicate she was looking at the ID card on Keres's lapel—Dr. Keres Nikotonos, Medical Examiner, Bard City—and raised her own eyebrows in turn. Some measure of expression was lost behind her dark sunglasses, but Ochia had plenty of years behind her to compensate for that.

"I'm not the one who—no." Keres held up a hand, then dropped it to a drawer handle and pulled. "Focus on the favor."

The contraption moved smoothly, with a minimum of metallic complaint, and Ochia regarded the sheet-covered body. It was roughly her and Keres's size, and so gave no immediate clue what sort of being had the misfortune of drawer residency.

"I don't do murders," she said reflexively, glaring.

"That's sort of the point, you know." Keres's smile was slow and promising, much in the way of a long knife cutting across burned flesh.

"Not..." Snakes slid against each other across her scalp. "Of course I don't go around murdering people. I also don't *investigate* murders. There are police for that."

"Not for this."

"Keres." Ochia uncrossed her arms and shoved her hands back in the deep pockets of her long coat. "I focus on minor inconveniences. Missing property, lost connections, the occasional beneficiary of a once-lonely, now-dead relative. Minor blackmail or petty theft. Nothing major."

"And yet you owe me a favor." Her eyes, dark to begin with, grew larger and darker, the pupils bleeding black into the surrounding sclera. "Or should we argue that as well?"

"That was a long time ago."

"I see. Is there a statute of limitations on favors?"

"Flayed god," Ochia spat, one hand lifting for her glasses before she shoved it back into her pocket. A small tongue flickered over the tip of her ear and she bit back additional curses. "You know very well there isn't."

"You've avoided me a long time, Ochia—"

"Whyever could that be?" Ochia muttered.

The entirety of Keres's eyes shone eerily even as she continued smiling that coldly perfect smile. "And I know you don't want to be needed, but here we are."

Ochia clenched her jaw tightly, unsure what she'd say otherwise, then bit her own tongue for good measure. Iron and wine flooded her mouth, and a chorus of hisses attempted to soothe her from under the hat.

After another handful of silent moments, Keres twitched back the sheet, and the hissing stopped abruptly.

"Is that..."

"Sterape Poulic," Keres said, her expression neutral. "The only siren to try living on the mainland, recently the headline act at the Venenosa. A friend, once, from the days when I had those."

"It looks..." Ochia had no proper words for what it looked like, so she rubbed her bleeding tongue across her teeth and kept her eyes on Keres to avoid looking at the mess of a body between them. Sirens did not die easily, and Sterape had been no exception. The bulk of her midsection was tattered, and gouges marked every limb.

Stone would have been kinder, she thought, and a larger snake drooped under her hat to curl around the back of her neck.

"Best I can tell, something thin and sharp pierced her eye. It's the only entry wound in her head, and something wiped her brain clean out of her skull." Keres' voice was clipped and professional.

Bile rose in Ochia's throat, overpowering the sweeter tang of blood in her mouth. She swallowed, brushed her fingers against the snake on her neck, and swallowed again for good measure.

"That's not violent enough for you to see more of what happened?"

"Ochia Berus, you are old enough to know better. I don't 'see' anything."

"What's the point in being a death goddess if you can't—" Ochia knew better than to poke at Keres. But if she were getting dragged into this, she'd dig her fangs into any convenient soft surface along the way.

"You of all people know perfectly well it doesn't work that way anymore." Keres's cool tone slipped, the medical examiner mask sliding off the edge of the ancient daughter of night.

"Why me, of all people?" Ochia had no mask to hide her Gorgon's face, only sunglasses and a hat. Keres had held on to the favor a long time; why call it in now?

"Ochia. Ochia, Ochia, Ochia." Keres's eyes stared through her. "You can't frustrate me until I forgive your favor. You have a debt, and you're paying it."

"And you want me to..."

"I assumed that would be obvious. Find out who killed her, look them in the eye, and bring me their stone head to use as a paperweight."

NOTHING SWAYED KERES IN a temper, and Ochia didn't linger in the morgue to see if that had changed over the decades. People like Keres and her... they didn't change. She collected what information Keres had and grumbled her way across town to the Venenosa.

She hadn't been near the place since the new management took over, forty years ago. Skine was an old acquaintance, and not a friendly one. He was an ogre, her sister's ex, and immune to her stare, which made for an uncomfortable combination. Maybe he stayed away from the bar in daylight hours, given how busy the place must get at night.

On a beautiful spring day—a rare one in Bard City, with clear skies and no hint of rain—many denizens took advantage of the weather and went frolicking outside. Still, there was no shortage of people who preferred indoor amusements, and more than a few patrons were scattered across the delicately crafted tables and glowingly golden bar that filled the wide semi-circle of the Venenosa.

"What can I get you?" The tentacle-bearded bartender, with a nametag that said 'Bethann' smiled as she approached, though it didn't reach her eyes.

"Whatever you have on special." Ochia enjoyed the sort of wine that flirted with vinegar, and she didn't need to distract herself with the delicious burning bite of good swill. The bartender assembled far too many small beakers and mixers to promise a good drink, and she tilted her head to get a better view of the people around her.

The three at the bar looked more or less human, each sitting on their own and hunched over various beverages. More than half of the tables were occupied, and a waitress all in black and white—down to the streaks in her hair—fast-walked by with a tray full of various sized bowls.

"Seems a little busy." Starting with small talk was safest—she only took jobs that *didn't* require charming people, dammit all to the endless hells, and she was sorely out of practice at trying to get information without looming at her targets.

She might be crap at charm, but a bartender who worked for an ogre probably wouldn't be much moved by her loom, anyway.

"More than some days, less than others. We're a little short-staffed though, so it feels busy."

"Oh?" Sterape had been the headline, not a server.

"Been a hard couple of weeks." Bethann shrugged and leaned over to pull up another three bottles. Ochia's hopes for the drink—already low—became non-existent. Her snakes whispered in disappointment, and one wound over her forehead to get a better look at the drink-making process.

"I like your hair," Bethann said, and her smile seemed more genuine.

"I like your beard," she responded. The woman's tentacles curled in pleasure.

"Afternoon's a good time to check out the place," she said, pouring her growing concoction into yet another container and shaking it. "Not sure if it'll be busy or a ghost town tonight."

"Actual ghosts?" she asked, because one could never tell. "Or lack of customers?"

"Either." She poured the drink through a strainer that did something besides the obvious, as the liquid changed shades entirely as it hit the new glass. "Both. We usually have a few acts—fire-singers, the swampmaids—but our headliner..." Bethann's tentacles undulated softly. "Please, enjoy your drink."

"Your headliner?" She chose not to look directly at the glowingly blue drink the bartender slid toward her, delaying the moment she'd have to taste it. "I heard the Venenosa had a siren, I was hoping to hear her from the safety of land. Is that... is that who you mean?"

"It is. Sterape is exactly as good as you'd imagine. Was, I should say. We've been bleeding staff for weeks, and now..." Bethann spun a small key hanging from one of her bracelets—an amulet for some sort of protection, Ochia guessed—and glanced to the side, toward the stage. "The police came by this morning. Sterape... she was murdered last night. On her walk home from work."

"Who could possibly murder a siren?" Ochia asked, reaching for her drink as though it were an idle question. The bartender shook her head, but it seemed she was considering rather than closing out the question, so Ochia took a sip to hold the silence longer.

Sweetness bloomed on her tongue, followed by a bite so strong the snakes on her head curled in pleasure. She coughed in surprise and regarded the glass, and the bartender blinked and shook himself again.

"You like it?" Bethann asked, with a hesitant smile.

"It's... not what I expected. What is it?"

"Boss calls it the freffrisa. Meant to be sharp and refreshing, but it tastes a little different to each palate. Gets enchanted berries for it."

"Some special," she said, and the air she breathed in to speak burned its way down into her chest.

"Come to a monster bar, get monster drinks," a new voice interjected, and snakes slipped from under her hat to twine around and get a view behind her.

"Long time, Skine. How's things?" Ochia swiveled on her stool, taking another sip of her drink.

"Been better, been worse. What brings you to my bar?"

"Trying something new."

"You haven't tried something new in going on a hundred years, Ochia." He made a point of giving her a long once-over and waved a hand at the bartender to leave them. "I take it back. The hat's... new." His laugh was guttural, from the depths of his massive chest. "Don't want to let your hair down anymore?"

"Glad you found some personality to balance out that face, Skine." Ochia knocked back half the freffrisa. "Can't see how my sister ever got over you."

"Whoever said she did? You seen Xanthina lately?" Skine snorted, because he knew the answer. Ochia and her sister had fallen out long before Xanthina had ditched the ogre and gone walkabout for the bulk of a century.

"Why, you thinking she'll give your staff pointers on how to avoid Bard City?" She finished her drink and considered throwing the empty glass at his face. It would do about as much damage to Skine as the full weight of her gaze, which was disappointingly none, so she reached behind her and thunked it down on the bar. "Heard they've been disappearing on you like Xan did."

"Ah." He rocked back on his heels and loomed better than she ever had. Of course, he was half again as tall as she, and coated in a pebbled magic-resistant hide that might as well be stone. "You're on the job."

She wished she had another freffrisa to chug, but chances were good that'd set her mouth on literal fire—and worse, dull her wits. He'd already rumbled her—while he looked big and dumb, he was anything but—and she had been trying to be subtle, in case he'd had anything to do with Sterape's murder. When it came to murder, bosses and lovers were top of the suspect list.

It had been awhile, but she was fairly certain that was the rule.

"We all have jobs to do." She shrugged, like it didn't matter he'd figured her out.

"You here about the waiters or Sterape?" He cocked his head and twisted his fingers as if to beckon someone over.

She didn't deign to look for whom—if he were going to have her removed from the Venenosa, so be it. Her snakes would warn her if it were about to go sideways. "Seems like you got a problem on your hand either way."

"Did you know any of them?" He frowned, his small eyes almost disappearing into the craggy edges of his cheeks.

"Nah. Who's paying you to look into it?"

"What's it matter?"

"It's not good for business." He grunted and glared around his bar, then settled his gaze on her. "Losing so many staff. Losing my headline. Kinda feels personal, and anyone who can take out a siren might be a handful even for someone like me or you."

Ochia frowned and couldn't hide it. Sirens were near-indestructible—from the damage done to Sterape's body, whatever had killed her had put a great deal of effort into it.

"So you want to add to my pay?"

"Sure. Drink's on me, and I'll give you what I gave the BCPD. Who's missing, their addresses, the usual." His jaw flexed. "There wasn't much for them, either. Probably for the best, if it's Sterape you're looking into. Cops aren't worth a damn against someone playing at this level."

"You're a generous boss, Skine. Looking out for your people."

"Yeah, yeah. Bethann, give her another, on the house. Put it in a to-go mug." Skine lifted his chin, motioned behind her, and she rolled her eyes behind her sunglasses as she turned.

A folder lay on the bar behind her. The ogre hadn't been gesturing for someone to come over, she realized, he'd been working some kind of spell. She opened her mouth to say something to him about learning magic, but a whisper against her ear told her Skine was already gone. She scratched one of the snakes under its chin in thanks and stood.

"Take that second drink for yourself." Ochia slid the folder from the bar and attempted a smile for Bethann and her tentacles. "Seems like you could use it."

"You work with the cops?" she asked, leaning forward, voice pitched low.

"Not if I can help it." When Bethann blinked at her in confusion, Ochia tsked to herself and added, "I'm a private investigator."

Comprehension brightened across her face, and her beard writhed in bright reds and oranges. "If you *are* going to Sterape's... can you look in on Ty? He's...he's one of the waiters that stopped coming in, and none of us have heard from him in a while. It's not...it's not like him, but he was going through some relationship drama. He lives just down the corner from her. I'll—I'll give you some extra drink vouchers—just hand them to any bartender here, we'll make you all the freffrisa you can handle."

Several immediate responses crowded her throat—*That's not how this works, I already have a job, no thanks, give him a call, I hear phones are all the rage these days*—but the bartender's openly worried expression twisted at her stomach.

This is why I don't do jobs like this. She swallowed back everything she wanted to say. "Write it on the folder, and I'll swing by."

Bethann's effusive thanks burned more than the drink.

THE FOXLIKE STATUE AT the intersection near Sterape's apartment had been mounted to a tall pedestal, but her voice rang as clear in Ochia's mind as if she were at her shoulder.

"You haven't visited in ages. No one loses anything in this neighborhood anymore?"

Ochia leaned against the dark stone square at the base of what had once been a living, breathing kitsune, and smiled as two of her snakes stretched upward to brush against the statue's outreaching paw. "Come now, Katherine—I saw you last month when that kelpie was trying to find who was taking the change from his fountains."

"I'm sure I don't know what you mean," the kitsune replied, her voice giving every impression of nine tails twitching dismissively. *"Time carries less weight than it once did. And you said you'd visit."*

"Here I am."

"What's gone missing now?"

"Some waiters, it seems, but I'm here about the siren. She was murdered."

"Murder!" Katherine's surprise sent Ochia's snakes curling back down under her hat. *"I thought she just wasn't coming home again. She does that sometimes. More lately."*

Like Ochia herself, Sterape had been the only one of her kind in Bard City. Ochia had hoped that would make her stand out to a statue on her street, and was gratified to find it true. "Seems like she was attacked in an alley between the Venenosa and her home, but no witnesses."

Ochia kept her voice low, and paused whenever a pedestrian crossed the street and passed close by. People were used to all kinds of things in Bard City, but she had zero desire to speak with citizens interested in the inner lives of some of their city's statues-that-had-once-been-fellow-citizens. That led far too easily to the topic of how they'd become statues, and where the person who had done it had gone. And why she'd been allowed to go.

She passed on the description of the waiter Bethann the bartender had shared, but the kitsune wasn't sure she recognized him. After a few more minutes of talking—Katherine didn't have much to add, but even Ochia wasn't heartless enough to leave after only a few lines of conversation—Ochia straightened away from the statue. Late afternoon was edging closer to evening, and before long there would be more pedestrians to avoid.

Sterape's apartment—easy enough to get into after slipping a few Venenosa vouchers into the right hands—revealed little. The siren had decorated lavishly, with mosaics on every wall to reflect the sea, deep blue glass flawed enough to make the sunlight reflect on the gleaming floors like water, silk cushions stacked around rough stone furniture. Salt and copper tinged the air—the smell of siren, or her magic.

Ochia breathed deep and remembered a cave by the ocean where she'd lived with her sister, so many years ago it might have been a dream. She slid back out without talking to any of the bored watchmen on duty and was halfway to Ty's apartment before she'd consciously made the decision.

We don't have many better options, she thought as her snakes murmured at her direction. *Murder site was clean enough that people are walking through it already. Sterape's list of friends is like mine—outdated and little used, and her enemies don't have the firepower to take out a siren.*

Ty's apartment was a block from Sterape's, in a row of buildings smaller, slightly newer, and less moss-strewn than the siren's. There was no police tape or onlookers, so after a few minutes of knocking, listening, and ultimately lock-picking, Ochia slipped inside.

She'd finished a single scan of the open room when her hat flew off her head. The snakes formed a defensive halo around her, and it took a full breath before she registered what they'd responded to.

A pigeon-sized griffin flapped angrily in the air in front of her. It darted once, twice more, and fell back as one snake and then another snapped at it.

"Down!" she said, meaning all of them, and the griffin squawked in outrage. Ochia pushed two snakes clear of her line of vision and held out a hand, palm up.

"I'm sorry there, bud. This is your home, and I barged in." She pitched her voice low, trying for soothing, but neither snakes nor griffin were particularly inclined to listen. "I'm here looking for Ty. Do you know where he is?"

At the sound of his person's name, the griffin made a sad whistling noise and swooped around her rather than feinting attacks. Her snakes subsided, smug in their success, though she knew there'd be no getting the hat back on them with a potential threat in motion.

The griffin landed on her palm, its furred tail twining around her wrist, and chirruped, cocking its head as it stared up at her.

"I don't know where he is either, bud." She took in a deep breath, but the apartment smelled stale despite the cracked window over the small kitchen. A big enough opening for the griffin to fly through, but not for human use. Griffins weren't known for tracking skills—hunting, yes, with exceptional vision, but their eagle beaks couldn't catch much in the way of scents.

"What about you all?" she asked, and her snakes stirred again, pointedly ignoring the warm-blooded creature in their space. Twenty-four tongues flickered through the air, but all the smells were old and dry and...

One was familiar. Something they'd smelled recently.

Salt and iron.

"Sterape was *here*?"

The griffin dug his talons into her palm, the feather along his neck ruffling.

"Ok, you know that name too. Ty wasn't listed as one of her close..."

Of course he wasn't. An ogre with missing staff and a dead singer had no reason to connect those dots for his ex's sister. No one had seen Ty in a week though, according to Bethann, and Sterape had been murdered last night. Had Ty gone into hiding before taking out the siren?

It didn't make any sense. By all appearances, Ty was fully human. The odds of him successfully taking on Sterape without a ruckus that brought the entire neighborhood out to watch were infinitesimal.

Ochia took another deep breath, sifting the faint scents and letting her eyes unfocus as she considered. In the old days, when the world was still unsettled and far more violent, she would have made different assumptions. A bunch of missing humans mixed up with a siren? She'd have been looking at the siren as the culprit. The current balance of their reality—creatures of all kinds living together—meant compromises had been made. While once upon an ancient time a siren might have fed on the humans until they were withered husks, now Sterape performed on stage and sated herself with their resulting emotions. Everybody won.

But Ochia knew first hand that compromises weren't always truly satisfying, didn't she?

"Keres," Ochia said in the tone of voice usually reserved for cursing. "What in the endless hells did you get me into?" The snakes drooped, braiding around each other in frustration.

Why had Sterape been in Ty's apartment, but no one had mentioned they'd known each other? Why *had* so many of the Venenosa's waitstaff gone missing?

"All right, bud." She turned slowly with the griffin to take in the apartment. "Let's look for clues."

*M*EET ME AT THE *bridge.* The note was signed with a kiss—literally—no name, someone wearing purple lipstick had pressed their lips to it. The faint scent of Sterape's magic lingered over it, and that was Ochia's best clue.

She backtracked along the likeliest route Sterape had taken home from work that involved a bridge. It was a leap, but given there'd been no witnesses to the murder, it was what she had. The griffin alternately flew ahead and landed on Ochia's hand—he'd aimed for her shoulder once, been warned off by the snakes, and was smart enough not to try again.

For the first time since they'd been invented, Ochia wished she had a phone. *Just long enough to call Keres and tell her I've done all I can do, it's a bad job, I tried, and I'm out.*

She imagined the conversation—and how frustratingly stubborn Keres would be in it—so well she riled up her snakes. She considered going home and calling it a night, but their energy fed hers, and she decided to trace the blocks to either end of the bridge. Sometimes walking calmed them all down.

Third street over was quieter than the rest, fewer pedestrians and only dark, closed shops. The streetlights flickered on, alternating green and gold, and Ochia decided Keres at the least owed her dinner if she was going to keep working at this frustratingly opaque case.

Something pinged off the edge of her perception, and she slowed her steps.

Her snakes curled close to her scalp and stilled, listening with her.

An awareness, not of a person speaking to her, but of something... something holding its breath? Trying *not* to be heard. Prey going quiet in a hidey-hole, hoping the predator would pass it by even as its thundering heart betrayed it.

Somewhere around her was stone that had once been alive. None of the statues she knew. She'd been so sure she'd found all of her sister's targets...

The griffin shrieked, its piercing cry her only indication of its direction, and she craned her head back, looking up, scanning for the *some*thing...

There.

A small gargoyle, perched over an ornate drain spout, at the corner of the building in front of her.

"Hello there," she said, and the feeling of a presence desperately attempting not to be present intensified. "You're not new...I'm sorry I haven't found you before."

"*Very fine, it's ok, I was stone a long time before I was stoned.*" Nervous laughter followed the words, and Ochia sighed. Had the small statue gone mad? She visited them as much as she could to give them some external anchor, but she couldn't possibly be enough to tether them all to sanity.

It had never occurred to her that a Gorgon's stare could transmute such a creature. Ogres were immune, she would have assumed gargoyles would be too.

"Why were you trying to hide from me?" she asked as gently as she knew how. The griffin landed on the gargoyle's horned head and pecked ineffectively at its eyes.

"*Hide? Not hiding! No, just... just quiet. Minding business. Being my mind.*"

"Mad," she murmured, but her snakes muttered amongst themselves, unconvinced. One, and then another, and then three more, pivoted their heads and stretched out, tongues flicking through the air.

"What have you seen that frightened you so?"

The gargoyle garbled nonsense until Ochia's head pounded. The griffin shrieked again, a hunting cry, and dove from the gargoyle's head into the bushes across the street.

The snakes oriented in the same direction, and Ochia shrugged and walked across the deserted road. The griffin stalked out of the bushes, dragging something sleek and furred.

That wasn't food the griffin had, she realized belatedly. It was... hair? She crouched down, letting her snakes taste the air. The griffin flapped its feathered wings angrily and ducked back under the bushes. She ducked her head further to see what he was up to—surely he wasn't going to eat a wig?

The griffin stalked over broken branches and rocks, some...no, not rocks. Stone, yes, but not rocks. Smoothed by an expert sculptor, a perfect hand, part of a leg. She moved the branches and trusted the snakes to keep themselves from tangling against the undergrowth—she really should have shoved them back under a hat.

A few minutes later she sat back into a squat, staring at six pieces of what must have been a beautiful statue. Who would have destroyed such a thing, and hid the pieces under a—

Her snakes hid under each other, twisted so tightly her scalp ached, and she knew.

"What do you smell?" she asked, and it didn't matter that they didn't answer. The scent was faint, but the wig and the stone together carried the barest trace, a hint of something she would only ever need a whiff of to remember.

The smell was lodged in her snakes, in her.

Her sister had come home.

IT TOOK THREE MORE days to find her. Ochia should have gone to Keres, but she told herself it was a coincidence. Her sister's return had nothing to do with Sterape's murder. Maybe the disappearance of Skine's waitstaff—Xanthina and Skine had always had a warped way of courting each other—but that was less likely. Ochia had found enough circumstantial links between Sterape and various waitstaff that it seemed Sterape had, in fact, turned to feeding on humans in her off hours. Either way, none of that was Keres's concern.

So Ochia told the medical examiner she was working on it and stalked her sister through their city. She left notes in all her sister's old hiding places, taking a page out of Keres's book, and forgot about Sterape and the waiters entirely.

The spring weather was perfect and clear, and the people of Bard City wandered around her unknowing, marveling over the clear skies and secure in the impossibility of an old monster coming home to roost. The griffin dogged her footsteps until she was forced to acknowledge that she'd named him Bud, and she'd never take off her sunglasses again to keep him safe. It was all so wholesome and lovely, her skin felt as though it would slough off her back to be free of her.

In the end, she sat on a park bench, not far from Glen the satyr, and waited.

"I got your note." The voice, so familiar the nerves in her neck sparked with pain, came from behind her before a figure moved around the bench.

"Took your time," Ochia said, tipping back her newly purchased hat.

"You came by my warehouse when I was out. I'm glad you wanted to see me. Is that... griffin I smell?"

Ochia had left Bud at the morgue, in the hands of Keres's hapless human assistant. She rather hoped she lived to hear Keres's reaction upon returning to her pristine, sterile workplace to find a tiny shedding griffin with as much rage in it as the medical examiner herself.

"No." She swallowed back the scream of frustration that crowded up her throat after the word and fixed her gaze at the midpoint of the park. Toward Glen, and the helpless, ignorant picnickers. "To be clear, I *didn't* want to see you here in my city. Why are you back?" Her snakes curved around her head, settling on the shoulder further from Xanthina.

"Things to do, little sister. I've been staying busy." Xanthina's snakes, longer and wider than Ochia's own, stretched toward her, and Ochia bit a hole in her tongue to keep from lashing out or, worse, flinching away.

"And what is it you have to do here? Pick off Skine's waitstaff?"

"*What?*" A laugh burbled through Xanthina's exclamation, and despite her best efforts, Ochia turned to look directly at her sister for the first time in nearly a hundred years.

"I'm not the one who's been eating Skine's snacky little servers. Chi, how little you think of me." She laughed again, and her snakes weaved in the air between them as though laughing along. "No, no, that was Sterape."

Ochia blinked. It had seemed likely, but she'd stopped looking into it. For Xanthina to confirm it so blithely—to be so *sure*... Her mind blanked, unable to connect how her sister could be so well informed.

"Oh my little viper, how I missed that face of yours." Xanthina smiled, her fangs brilliant in the sun. "I thought this was your job now. I thought you figured it all out."

"Sterape..." Shock faded into an understanding so complete, Ochia only held herself steady because of the blood in her mouth. She'd reasoned it out, before she dropped the matter in favor of finding her sister. Sirens feed on emotions—the stronger, the better. The bits of soul they eat make their music better, stronger, which gives them more emotions to feed on...

Sterape's scent in Ty's apartment. Relationship troubles. A steady uptick in waitstaff going missing...

Ochia knew damn well how heady it could be, power flooding, the thrill of that reservoir growing inside, taking up all the air and coloring it in shades of iron and wine.

Not all of Bard City's statues had been made by Xanthina, after all. Just the ones that were left.

But that was a long time ago, and Ochia wasn't that person anymore.

"How did *you* know?" Dread twisted low in her gut—she knew the answer. Knew her sister was involved with Sterape, one way or another.

"You told me I disgusted you. That I was a monster and you never wanted to see me again." There was no venom in her voice or her smile, but Ochia felt the sting all the same. "I went hunting for worse monsters, to show you how wrong you were about me." She shrugged, the motion as sinuous as her snakes, and her smile grew broader. "Killing them..." Her snakes shivered and twisted around each other.

"Turning prey to stone, that's fun. But taking up a sword, digging a snake into skulls...oh Chi, it's marvelous." Xanthina kept speaking, though Ochia desperately wanted her to stop. "But I wanted you to be proud of me, little sister. I wanted you to want me back. So, I found the worst of the worst, the ones preying on the weak—you know, like we used to, when the worlds were young—and I took them off the board. It's fun!"

"Fun," Ochia whispered, her eyes fixed on her sister's. Her sister's eyes, she realized, which were perfectly visible through her barely tinted glasses. Yet no one who passed by turned to stone.

"I heard about a siren singing songs a little too well, if you know what I mean, and thought, hm, maybe I should come home, see the sights. Make sure my sister was still on her high and mighty pedestal." Xanthina leaned closer, and one of her larger snakes flicked its tongue over Ochia's nose.

"You didn't turn her to stone."

"I tried, but Sterape had been feeding far too well. Besides, a little variety is nice, you know. It got...messy." Xanthina shrugged, flicking her fingers. "Took me awhile to wear her down and get close enough to put a snake through her eye."

"But you did make a statue...?"

"She had a little late night morsel along with her. I wasn't going to stone him, but he went wild when she died." She sighed and draped her arms over the back of the bench. "I didn't want you to see, so I broke him down into pieces and tried to hide it, but I'm guessing that's what brought you knocking on my warehouse door."

"What do you mean you weren't going to stone him—your eyes weren't covered, if you tried to turn Sterape. How could you have kept him from turning?" Half a dozen questions crowded in her throat, but that was the one that burst out.

"We're all monsters, Ochia. I just found a better way to live with it than making myself small. You should try it." Her snakes sh-sh-sh'd a chorus of laughter. "And now you're all caught up."

"Xan..." Ochia lifted a hand to her glasses, and her sister laughed.

"Now, now. I'm going to leave the park, and Bard City, and you're going to let me. Again." Xanthina stood and blew her sister a kiss, each of her snakes flicking their tongues in perfect synchronicity. A chill froze Ochia in place.

"Or you'll turn everyone in this park into stone?"

"There's my clever sister. Give me a call when you figure it out for yourself, won't you?"

OCHIA RETURNED TO THE morgue, her snakes drooping, her shoulders heavy. She'd left those days behind—heady days, imposing her will on the world no matter who was hurt. Flexing her power, competing with her sister. But not anymore.

She was small, and made small moves. Small cases—blackmail, missing persons. She kept the statues company; she didn't make them. Not anymore. She wasn't a monster.

At least, she wasn't *that* monster.

Keres stroked the back of Bud's head and listened to the tale without interruption.

"You still owe me a favor." After the long silence, her tone was cold enough to stiffen Ochia's spine.

"At least we know who—"

"No." Keres lifted a hand, and Bud poked it with his curved beak. "The deal was a stone head on my desk. I have few friends in this world, Ochia, and I wouldn't have called this in for less than that. Do you want to protect your sister?"

"No!"

"Do you truly believe she's out there taking out only the 'worst of the worst?'"

"No... she was too comfortable with collateral damage." Ochia said the words before she was sure she believed them, then nodded sharply.

"Monsters hunting monsters, is it?" Keres asked, her eyes entirely black. "What do you say we give it a try?"

MARISA WOLF WAS BORN in New England and raised on Boston sports teams, Star Wars, Star Trek, and the longest books in the library (usually fantasy). Over the years she majored in English, in part to get credits for reading (this...only partly worked), taught middle school, was headbutted by an alligator, built a career in education, earned a black belt in Tae Kwon Do, and finally decided to finish all those half-started stories in her head.

She's currently based in Texas, but has moved into an RV with her husband and their two ridiculous rescue dogs, and it's anyone's guess where in the country she is at any given moment. Learn more at www.marisawolf.net

THE ADVENTURES OF ELENA AND NED, GARGOYLE P.I.

By Jeff Burns

THE DOOR CRASHED OPEN, jolting me awake.

"No one's sleeping!" I announced sleepily, lifting my head from the desk. A piece of paper was stuck to my face, covered in drool.

A huge creature squeezed through the entrance, spreading its wings once it got inside. It was seven and a half feet tall, had dark gray skin, and eerie-looking violet eyes.

"You drooled all over yourself again."

"I did not!" I unglued the paper from my face and used it to wipe up the spittle.

"I hope that document isn't important."

"Of course, it's not." I crumpled it up and tossed it into the wastebasket. It was an annoying bill we had to pay.

Definitely not important. "Now stop being all judgy and fork over the food."

He sighed but complied, setting out a bevy of Chinese food cartons.

I dug in immediately, stuffing noodles in my mouth. "You're the best, Ned!"

Oh right, I should do some introductions. Hi, I'm Elena Awiakta, the most amazing private eye in Greater Gradena. According to whom, you might ask? Well, me. What other reference do you need?

My cool last name is Cherokee, in case you're wondering. I'm fifty percent Native American, fifty percent Brazilian. And one hundred percent foxy!

Ned is my detective partner. He's a gargoyle. I thought Ned was a pretty weird name for a gargoyle, but that's what he was going with. I generally made it a practice not to argue with five-hundred-pound creatures. Unless they were keeping delicious food from me.

Ned delicately popped chicken into his huge mouth. I had no idea how he was able to use chopsticks so well with those hot dog-sized fingers.

I not-so-delicately tore open the containers and shoved sweet and sour chicken between my lips, sauce dribbling down my chin.

Ned scrutinized my messy face. "How are you able to get so many dates?"

I wiped the sauce off with my arm, chewing noisily. "Hey, Ibn ery aractiv."

"What?"

I swallowed, the sweet and soury goodness coating my throat. "I said, I'm very attractive."

"You certainly are," a sweet-sounding voice called from the doorway.

A petite woman bounded into our office, brightening the dim lighting with her smile. She was light and airy, seeming to float across the room like something out of a dream.

I gaped at her, noodles hanging from my mouth. I slurped them up. "Oh, um, thank you. I, uh, usually don't have food dripping from my mouth."

"Yes she does," Ned supplied.

I elbowed him as I walked around the desk, which probably hurt my arm more than his stomach. Stupid thick-skinned gargoyle.

I swatted a bunch of papers and leftover food containers off a chair and cleaned it with the bottom of my T-shirt.

"There you go, Miss..."

"Kalypise. But please, call me Kaly." Her voice was like a sweet melody carried on a gentle breeze across a beautiful meadow.

I stared at her for way too long. She wore a bright, aqua dress that seemed to move perfectly to show off her shapely legs. My gaze trailed to a brilliant anklet, filled with stones of swirling blue. A similar one encircled her tiny wrist.

"Sooo pretty... I mean your name, it's, uh, really pretty."

She clasped her hands together adorably. "Oh, my goodness, thank you!"

I hopped onto the desk, swinging my legs and trying to keep my gaze locked on her vibrant green orbs and not the larger orbs slightly south of there. "We don't get many naiads in here."

Her eyes expanded. "How did you know?"

Yes! I got to show off my amazing detective skills. I loved this part of the job.

"Well, I knew you were a nymph with the bright colors, airy clothing, and the ethereal way you move. Your jewelry is water-themed but doesn't contain specific ocean iconography. So, you're likely a fresh-water nymph, which makes sense with all the lakes around here. Naiad was a likely choice."

"You're amazing!"

"Well, you know, I don't like to brag."

"Yes you do," Ned snorted.

"I think I detect a whiff of Lucent Lake," I said, ignoring him.

"I'm surprised you can smell anything with all the leftover food containers," my gargoyle buddy remarked.

I tossed said container at him. He flicked his wing, whacking it into the garbage pail. Show-off.

"Yes!" Kaly replied, not perturbed by our bickering. "Lucent is my lake."

I smiled. "I'll have to go there more often."

"Since my irreverent partner is too busy analyzing your body, let me take over," Ned interjected. Though more like inter-jerk-ted. "What can we do for you Naiad Kaly?"

I folded my arms and pouted. Why did he have to ruin my fun? Like solving cases was more important than my love life.

Kaly jumped up and down like a teenager on a sugar rush. "I'm competing in the annual Monster Mash Dance Competition!"

I smiled at her bubbly exuberance. "That sounds fun." I wondered if she needed a dance partner.

"Yes, it's a most enjoyable event," Ned added.

I gaped at him. "You can dance?"

"Of course."

"You never told me that. As your amazing partner, you're supposed to tell me everything."

He harrumphed. He liked doing that when he disagreed with me.

"C'mon, I tell you all my secrets."

"I don't want to know all your secrets."

"I do!" Kaly exclaimed.

"Thank you!" This was a girl after my own heart. "I always knew naiads were really smart. Besides being beautiful, of course."

She gave me that radiant smile again, and I almost fell off the desk. Yes! I was so getting laid.

Ned harrumphed louder. Geez, how was a girl supposed to hook up with a hot naiad with a grumpy gargoyle in the room?

"How do you need our assistance with the Monster Mash?" he asked.

I leaped off the desk. "You need an amazing partner to help you win it. I'm your girl!"

"Oh, that's so nice of you to offer. But I already have a partner and, um..."

She bit her lip like she was nervous to tell me something.

"Humans aren't allowed in the competition," Ned finished for her.

"What?! That's an outrage. I'm sending a strongly-worded e-mail. After I finish eating."

"You realize humans have tons of competitions, and this is one of the few for supernatural beings?"

I plopped on the desk, pouting again. I hated it when he was right. "I know. That's really cool you guys have that. But I like hanging out with supernats way better than boring old humans."

"Please stop calling us supernats."

"It's short for supernatural," I explained to Kaly before turning back to Ned. "It's totally going to catch on."

"It makes us sound like super-powered bugs."

"Some of you *are* super-powered bugs."

Another harrumph before turning his attention back to the lovely naiad. "I believe you were about to tell us how we can help."

"Yes! Someone is trying to rig the competition and be a big meanie!"

I stifled a giggle. Naiads were adorable.

Ned's eyes narrowed. "No one has ever tried to cheat during the Monster Mash."

"I know. It's where we all come together in friendly competition and hardly anyone ever dies."

I wrinkled my nose. That was reassuring.

"This is one of our most time-honored events that has helped keep the peace between species. But now everyone is accusing each other of trying to cheat, and it's a big, poopy mess. Oops, please excuse my language."

I knelt in front of Kaly and took her hand. "Don't worry. We'll ferret out the sneaky supernat and stop them from ruining your fun."

"Thank you so much!" She toppled off the chair, falling into a wonderfully warm embrace. Fuck, nymphs really knew how to hug. "Whatever your expenses, money is no problem."

She floated over to the door. "I'm sorry humans can't attend, but maybe you can watch me some other time."

"I'll watch you do anything," I blurted out like a creepy stalker. "I mean, I'd love to watch you dance. I bet you're amazing."

She smiled and disappeared out the door like flowing water.

Ned smirked.

"Oh, shut up."

"Is it possible for you not to have sexual intercourse with one of our clients?"

"Hey, I didn't have sex with that mummy. Mainly because it was taking forever to unwrap him and find his—"

"Let's focus on the case."

"Okay, geez, you brought it up. I know the perfect place to get some leads."

"Oh no."

"Oh yes! Let's go."

I walked into The Temptress, a club that managed to look both swanky and casual. It was full of supernats. But unlike the stupid dance competition, humans were allowed. This club had taste!

Ned had decided to wait outside. Clubs weren't his scene. I guess he expected every informant to be an opera lover.

I sauntered up to the bar and was greeted by a breathtaking sight.

Cassia.

The proprietress of the bar befitted her namesake: a Malaysian goddess whose long black hair framed her exquisite face and flowed toward curves that should be criminal.

She was the kind of girl who made you soak your shorts just being in her vicinity.

She was also a vampire.

"Hey, sexy," she greeted me with a warm smile, rubbing my hand gently.

"Uhh," I replied eloquently. I was always momentarily stunned into silence whenever I saw her. "Hi Cass, how's business?"

"Much better now that you're here." She set a sparkling blue drink in front of me with one of those cute umbrellas sticking out of it.

"Ooh, freffrisa! Thanks!" I slurped it up, the tropical delight coating my throat and sending a pleasurable shiver through me.

Her hand was now on my forearm, making my hairs stand on end. "On an exciting case?"

"Yes! We have to foil a fiendish dance delinquent."

She smiled knowingly. "Oh, the Monster Mash. I've heard the rumors."

Cass knew everything that happened in the city. That's why she was my favorite informant. It definitely had nothing to do with me staring dreamily into her mesmerizing jade eyes. "You're amazing. Spill."

"Information doesn't come free, love."

I stopped slurping on the straw and shuddered. Cassia always charged a very specific price.

"Um, okay, but could you bite me somewhere more discreet this time?"

"Sure." She leaned in and whispered in my ear.

I spit out my drink. "Cass!"

"You didn't protest much last time."

Her hair tickled my cheek, and my body turned to putty. I caught myself just before my knees buckled.

"I'm, uh, on a bit of a time crunch. Can I take a rain check on the payment?"

"Sure. But I'm going to charge extra."

I gulped. Oh boy.

I REJOINED NED, WHO was standing under a flickering lamp post.

"You told her she could suck your blood again, didn't you?"

"What? Of course not!" How did he always know this stuff? Oh right, he was a detective.

"I hope you don't let her chomp on your posterior."

"I am not letting her bite me on the ass!"

I was totally letting her bite me on the ass. But for some reason, he didn't like hearing about my kinky escapades. What a weirdo.

"Oh c'mon," I continued. "You know you're hard for her too."

"Of course I'm hard. I'm a gargoyle."

I groaned. "Well, I got the information we needed, so you should be singing my praises as the most amazing partner in the universe."

He grunted, apparently not wanting to acknowledge my amazingness. But I wasn't letting that dampen my enthusiasm.

"Let's go track down this lead before the sun comes up!"

I STOOD ON TOP of a roof, dangling our quarry upside down over the pavement far below. Every good detective knows that's how you get information out of suspects.

Ned stood next to me, sighing and shaking his head. If he had his way, we'd sit down and have a nice chat with the fellow. Boring!

"Ahhh!" the green-clad gentleman screamed. "Pull me up. Please!"

"Not feeling so lucky now, are you?" I gloated.

"That's a gross stereotype. Leprechauns aren't any luckier than any other creature."

I glanced down at him. Hmm, there weren't any gold coins dropping from his pockets. But c'mon, he was totally ruining my cool line.

"We know you're one of the judges for the Monster Mash," Ned informed him in his gravelly voice.

"And we know you owe lots of money," I added in my super-sultry voice. "Who's blackmailing you?"

"I... I don't owe anyone any money. If you don't pull me up this instant, I'm making an official complaint to..."

I dropped him. Hey, we didn't need any more bad ratings for our detective agency. People should keep their stupid negative reviews to themselves.

My hair whipped across my face as Ned swooped off the roof.

Four seconds later, he deposited the trembling leprechaun next to me. Who proceeded to collapse to his knees and vomit. Delightful.

Ned crossed his arms. "What did we say about dropping people off buildings?"

"That it's a very effective way to get them to confess?"

He gave me a frowny face. Well, an even deeper frowny face than usual.

"Oh c'mon. You haven't missed one yet. Wanna do it again?" I hauled our green friend to his feet.

"No! Please, no. I'll tell you what you want to know. I... I owe thousands of dollars to the Goblin King."

Ned and I glanced at each other. Shit, the Goblin King. And not the David Bowie version.

"For what?" Ned inquired. "Gambling? Drugs?"

The leprechaun glanced around, making sure no one was listening. Like people just hung around rooftops eavesdropping.

He motioned us closer. "I... I have an addiction... to... Chibibibis."

I blinked. Okay, that was definitely not what I was expecting. But it was so much better!

"Chibibibis!" I exclaimed, shaking him. "I love them! I have a huge collection."

Ned let out one of his long sighs. But don't listen to him. Chibibibis were the cutest collectibles ever: anime-style girls and critters with oversized heads and adorable outfits. Ned had even scored me the super-rare Pookyooky character. See? He was a big softie under his gargoyle grumpiness.

My fellow collectible comrade relaxed after finding a kindred spirit. "Aren't they the most adorable things on the planet? Would you like to see my collection?"

"Would I?" I squealed.

Ned cleared his throat. "May I remind you we're on a case?"

"No, you may not. Nothing's more important than Chibibibis!"

The not-so-lucky leprechaun and I walked arm-in-arm, chatting non-stop, as we made our way toward the stairs.

Ned stomped along behind us, probably wondering why he ever agreed to have a super-weird human as his partner.

After bonding over our collectible crushes, Larry spilled the beans. Oh, that was my Chibibibi buddy's name. Yup, Larry the Leprechaun. Just go with it.

The Goblin King agreed to wipe Larry's debts clean if he voted for Gobby's choice in the Monster Mash. But Larry didn't know who he was supposed to vote for. That information would apparently come right before the competition.

We told Larry we'd keep him safe while we figured out the Goblin King's sneaky plans. Our new leprechaun friend was hesitant, but when I told him he could play with my entire Chibibibi collection, he instantly agreed. I knew my cute obsession would come in handy someday.

Ned flew off with Larry to stash him in my apartment, while I went to pay off my own debt.

And man, did I pay for it. I walked out of The Temptress rubbing my sore tush. Did Cass really have to bite me that hard? Well, her information had totally paid off. And I always honored my agreements. Especially when a gorgeous vampire was involved.

The starry blackness above me was almost ready to give way to the dawn. Being a private eye meant sleeping at very strange hours.

I stretched, craving some shuteye. And that's when I realized I was being followed.

Crap. Can't a girl geek out over Chibibibis, let a hot vampire chomp her cute butt, and go home without dealing with scummy criminals?

I crossed the street, stepping over puddles from yesterday's storm. I caught the reflection of my pursuers in the window of a parked car. There were two of them, both wearing trench coats and fedoras. Real original guys.

I fished around in the pockets of my jean jacket. I knew I had put it somewhere.

That was a bad move. They must have thought I was going for a gun because they pulled out two pistols and shot at me.

Goddammit. I'd gone a whole week without getting shot at. Almost a new record.

I dove over a car, the bullets shattering glass and making Swiss cheese out of the body.

I stayed low, using other cars as shields. Which meant a lot of property damage. That seemed to happen all too often on our cases.

I reached the end of the block, about to run out of protection.

Two clicks told me the goons were releasing their clips and were about to reload. Now was my chance.

I bolted from my hiding spot across the street, my ass muscles burning.

I zipped into an alley, bullets taking out chunks of the wall and spitting bits of stone into my face.

I skidded to a halt. Dead end. Of course. I had broken Rule #1 of fleeing from bad guys. Never run into alleys. Ned was going to scold me something fierce. If I got out of here alive.

Before I could come up with an ingenious plan, the two dull-dressed individuals strolled into the alley.

Shit.

"Hi guys, you don't happen to be Chibibibi fans, do you? I can score you some super-rare ones."

They glanced at each other. Then raised their guns. Dammit, why couldn't I get chased by bad guys with good taste in collectibles?

A roar reverberated through the alley, and a large shape blotted out the moon.

A mammoth creature landed in front of me, wings spread wide.

"Ned!" I had never been happier to see him.

He pulled me into his muscular body, wrapping his wings around me.

Bullets tore into his back. He grimaced, trying not to show how much it hurt. Gargoyles were a lot tougher than humans, but they weren't invulnerable.

"Cover your ears," he ordered.

He turned and let out an ear-piercing roar. The mooks dropped their weapons, clutching their orifices.

"Yeah, Ned. Ear-fuck those baddies!"

I was about to spring into action when the first rays of the sun peeked over the horizon.

And turned Ned to stone, freezing him in an angry roar. Well, fuck.

Our assailants grabbed their guns off the pavement.

I huddled behind Ned, bits of him covering me in dust as the bullets ripped through him. Dammit, there was going to be nothing left of him if these assholes kept it up.

I peeked between his legs. The trenchies stalked forward.

I snatched a piece of Ned that had broken off by my feet. I didn't like using him as a weapon but at least it wasn't his dick or anything.

I vaulted over his wing and hurled the stone at one goon. It smacked him in the head, toppling him over.

I flung a vial from my pocket into the other idiot. It cracked open, spilling its contents all over his face.

He screamed and clutched his ugly mug, knocking his fedora off. A goblin. I had already surmised as much. While the Goblin King had many different kinds of supernats under his employ, the size and gait of these two losers gave them away. And the smell.

Speaking of which, my goblin buddy wasn't enjoying the scent I just doused him with: elf sweat. Goblins hated elves and couldn't stand having anything that reeked of the lithe creatures on them. I didn't know what they were talking about. All the elves I knew smelled like a spring meadow dotted with lavender. But that was goblins for you.

How did I get elf sweat? Um, that's one of those stories Ned doesn't want to hear about. Let's just say it's really difficult to make an elf sweat. They have crazy endurance, so I had to work my ass off.

Gobby #1 struggled to his feet. I roundhouse kicked the gun out of his hand and rammed my knee under his chin. His head snapped back and he collapsed like a falling tree.

Gobby #2 leaped onto my back, clawing at me wildly. Apparently, he was really pissed off about the elf sweat.

I shielded my eyes from getting gouged, twirling my body around, trying to dislodge him.

I rammed him backward against Ned, knocking the air out of him, then smashed my elbow into his cheek, sending his gross head ricocheting off Ned's chest. He collapsed in a heap, probably dreaming about cute goblin chicks.

I leaned against Ned, catching my breath.

"Thanks for the assist, partner." He didn't reply. He was always the strong, silent type in the morning.

Now I just needed to figure out how to get him out of here.

Hauling a huge gargoyle statue back to our office wasn't the easiest trick. Fortunately, Cassia offered to help. She could be very sweet that way. Though, not so sweet when she said I owed her another debt. Geez, couldn't she find other humans to be her tasty snack?

I lounged on our tattered couch, taking multiple cat naps while waiting for my buddy to get over being stoned.

My eyelids drooped, and I was about to doze off for the tenth time when huge chunks of rock fell to the floor. Followed by a big gargoyle butt heading right for me.

I rolled off the cushions, barely avoiding Ned's large posterior. He collapsed onto the couch, shaking the entire apartment. No wonder our furniture was in such bad shape.

I was trapped under his meaty legs on the floor, laying in gargoyle dust, but at least I hadn't been squished. "Um, Ned?"

"Elena?" It always took him a minute to get his bearings after changing back to his animated form.

"Hi."

"Where are you?"

"Stuck under your legs, you big lunk."

He raised his tree trunks, and I scrambled up. "My apologies. You're so small I didn't see you."

"Hey, I'm a perfectly normal size. Everyone looks small compared to a gargoyle."

"Yes, we are quite impressive."

"And so modest too."

"Look who's talking."

He tried to stand. I put my hands on his chest. "You're not going anywhere. I need to dress your wounds." Now that he was back in his non-stone form, the bruises and cuts from where he'd been shot were evident.

"It's nothing."

I rifled through our huge case of first aid items. "Oh, stop being such a tough guy."

I stood behind him, pressing gauze to his wounds to stem the bleeding. "Man, those assholes really shot you up."

"Yes, goblins can be quite annoying."

"And stinky!"

"Indeed. Even worse than humans."

"Hey!" I sniffed my shirt.

He patted my hand. "It's a scent I've gotten very accustomed to and would surely miss if you weren't around."

I threw my arms around his neck, giving him a teary-eyed hug. "Yes! I knew you loved me. I'm the most amazing human in the universe!"

"That's not saying much, but very well." He clutched my hand. It disappeared in his massive paw.

I kissed him on the cheek. "Oh, and thanks for saving my life. You were pretty amazing yourself."

Gargoyles didn't blush, but if they did, I bet his cheeks would be rosy as hell right now.

"Yes, well...it would have been very difficult to find a new partner."

"Shush. You're ruining the moment."

He shushed. I rested my head on his broad shoulder, continuing to embrace him. I didn't get a lot of heartfelt moments with my gargoyle buddy, so I was going to really soak this one up.

I finished bandaging him, and he grunted in approval.

I scooped up the leftover first aid items, but he caught my arm before I could return them.

"Elena...thank you for protecting me when I was in my stone state. I owe you a great debt."

I blinked. Holy shit, when did grumpy pants turn into the gushy gargoyle?

"Someone wants another hug, don't they?"

"No, that is not nece-"

"Too late!"

He winced. I should probably have saved the super-hug for after he healed up.

"Oops, sorry!"

"It's all right. I appreciate the sentiment. But let's return our attention to the case."

I sighed. Sappy, emotional time was over. But it's the most I'd ever gotten out of him. I'd have him reading romance novels in no time.

"Okay, fiiine." I paced, trying to come up with a clever plan. "We could go see the Goblin King."

"No one gets in to see him," Ned replied. "Unless you're invited. And that's not an invitation you want to get."

That was true. I wasn't sure even my irresistible charm would work on King Gobby.

Okay, time for more ingenious thinking!

My eyes lit up mid-pace. "I've got it!"

"Oh no."

"You haven't even heard the idea yet."

"I don't need to."

"Oh, yes you do. We'll go undercover and enter the Monster Mash!" I thrust my hand up in a pop-star power pose and waited for the amazing applause.

I got crickets instead. Ned stared at me with one of his classic, "Oh, Elena" faces.

"Please tell me you're joking."

"I never joke about dancing. Or food."

"You can't enter the competition. It's only for supernats, I mean, supernatural creatures."

I jumped up and down. "Yes! I knew supernats would catch on. You're so hip, Ned."

"Elena," he sighed, putting a hand on my shoulder to stop my pogo stick movement.

"Okay, I know I'm not a supernat. But I can disguise myself as one."

"This is a terrible idea. Do you know how much trouble you'll get in if you're caught?"

"Um, of course not. Like, I study all your arcane supernat dance rules."

His whole body sagged as he let out a long sigh. "Even if that works, you'll need a dance partner."

I smiled. "I'm looking at him."

Ned's eyes got big, which was saying something for a gargoyle. "Absolutely not."

I clutched his arm, hopping up and down again. "C'mon, you said you're a great dancer."

"It's too dangerous."

"Ned, our whole job is dangerous. We just got shot at by stupid goblins."

He harrumphed. He hated it when I made sense.

"Plus, we promised Kaly. We never give up on a case. That's the rule, remember?"

Louder harrumphing. "I hope Miss Kaly appreciates this."

I leaped onto him, wrapping my arms and legs around his huge torso. "Yes! I knew you'd see the amazingness of my plan. Oh, and of course Kaly will appreciate it. And she can show it by providing me some nymphy naked time!"

He set me on the floor. "Is that all you think about?"

"No. I think about food, too. Ooh, is there any leftover takeout?"

He rolled his eyes and handed me a cardboard container, which I noisily slurped up.

"How do you plan to pass for one of us?"

"Leave that to me!"

THE MONSTER MASH WAS held in a gorgeous Gothic manor. I marveled at the decor as I strolled in with Ned.

"This is so exciting!" I exclaimed, clutching his arm.

"You're not acting very vampire-like," he scolded me.

I passed a large baroque mirror and admired my ensemble: a lovely ballroom dancing dress, black on the torso and crimson below my hips.

Cass had picked it out and helped me look like the hottest vampire ever. Well, next to her.

"Haven't you ever heard of super-peppy vampires?"

"No."

"Well, you have now!"

Before he could retort, we reached the sign-in table.

"Welcome to the 583rd Monster Mash!" a friendly ogre greeted us. "Name and species please."

"Hi! We're thrilled to be here. I'm Elena, a sexy vampire. Check out these awesome fangs!" I bared my teeth, showing off the extended incisors Cass had fitted me with.

"Oh, yes, they're, um, very nice," the ogre replied, apparently not used to vampires showing off their teeth.

Ned elbowed me, apparently also thinking I wasn't being a very good denizen of the night.

"Oh, and this is Ned the gargoyle."

He bowed. "It's an honor to be part of such a prestigious competition."

I rolled my eyes. Suck up.

"I can't wait to see your moves on the dance floor," the ogre replied, batting her eyes at him.

Ooh, Ned had an admirer. He needed to get laid something fierce, so, hopefully, he and this ogre lady could have some rock-hard fun later.

She gave us each a piece of paper with a number, which we attached to our costumes. Ned looked super-swanky in his dance tuxedo: black over white with tails streaming behind him. A crimson rose stuck out of his lapel, matching my dress perfectly. No wonder the lady ogre wanted to jump his bones.

"You look really hot, Ned."

"Er..." He hated getting compliments. "Thank you, Elena. You're...very beautiful."

I beamed. "Aw, thanks."

"Especially when you don't have spaghetti sauce running down your chin."

I frowned. He had to ruin it. "Let's snoop around and see what we can find out."

We went in opposite directions, mingling through the crowds of sparkly dressed supernats. It seemed like every species was represented. And I was the only human getting to see this. So cool!

I'd strolled by a gigantic cake and squeezed my way between two werewolves when a goddess appeared, dressed in a shimmering light blue dress.

Our nymphtastic client rushed over and yanked me into an alcove, giving us a modicum of privacy.

"Elena, what are you doing here?" Kaly asked in a cute whisper.

"Shhh. I'm undercover as a super-hot vampire. See?" I displayed my fangs.

THE ADVENTURES OF ELENA AND NED,... 365

She clasped her hands together. "Ooh, they're so nice. Please bite me!" She covered her mouth, blushing. "I mean, you have to get out of here. You'll be in so much trouble if you're caught."

"No way. We promised we'd help you." I loved being this close to her. Her light brown strands danced across her shoulders, making her look even more beautiful.

"You're such a sweetie!" She hugged me, turning my knees to putty. She smelled like cinnamon and lilies. And I wanted to keep my face buried in her hair forever. But I realized continually sniffing her lovely locks was kind of another creepy stalker thing.

"One of the judges hasn't shown up," she said, still holding me close.

"Oh yeah, we stowed him away somewhere safe so Head Gobby can't get to him."

"Ooh, he gets real grumpy when you call him that."

"I should introduce him to Ned. They can be grumpy together."

She bit her lip, which somehow made her look even cuter. "But what does the Goblin King have to do with it?"

Before I could tell her, my number was called over the magic PA system, which sent the audio directly into my ear. "Oh shit! Ned and I are up. Time for some Supernat Samba!"

"Elena, wait..."

I scampered off, the rest of her words getting lost in the noise of the crowd. Hey, I wasn't going to pass up an opportunity to dance in the Monster Mash. If we won, maybe they'd let humans enter every year. Or, maybe they'd put me in supernat jail. I'm sure Ned would visit me every day.

I found my partner by the entrance to the dance floor, tapping his foot impatiently. "Where have you been?"

"Flirting with Kaly. I mean, doing important detective stuff."

He ignored my sass. He was good at doing that. "I overheard they found a last-minute replacement for our leprechaun friend."

"Excellent! That means the Gobster probably hasn't had a chance to influence the new judge."

"Exactly. But he may have other nefarious plans to affect the competition."

"Oh no! Nefarious people are the worst."

"Please be serious. We're supposed to dance after the current couple finishes."

"Hey, I'm super-serious. Wait till you see my amazing moves!"

"Well, you're about to get your chance. We're up."

He proffered his huge hand. I took it and smiled. My gargoyle buddy could be quite the gentleman.

He escorted me onto the dance floor. We passed a gorgeous elf lady and super-hairy sasquatch, who had just finished a crazy-intense routine. The elf glistened with sweat, which somehow radiated her beauty even more. The sasquatch was probably really sweaty too, but who could tell under all that hair?

Ned spun me into the center of the dance floor, where I struck a sexy pose. He got into position, looking very debonair.

The spotlight bathed us in golden light. I took a deep breath, steadying myself right before the music began.

A colorful Latin beat sent us into motion. I twirled into Ned's arms and went into a backward basic samba. My

Brazilian roots made me very familiar with the dance, and I loved shaking my tush to the vibrant music. But who would've guessed Ned was so light on his huge feet?

He sashayed back and forth like he was walking on air, matching my movements perfectly. He twirled me away and back into his strong chest, my dress swirling around my legs and almost giving the audience a peek at my derrière.

We threw in some voltas and bota fogo combinations. The crowd hooted and hollered, which spurred us on even faster.

We were like whirling dervishes, moving perfectly in time with each other. When we briefly separated, I shook my hips like Shakira, which I hoped made Kaly soak her pretty fairy panties.

I was feeding off the energy of the crowd. Holy crap, we could actually win this thing.

"Throw me!" I said as I spun into Ned. He hurled me over his head like I was weightless. I soared high above the dance floor, tucking my arms against my chest and twirling like a corkscrew. It was exhilarating! Ned was taking me dancing every week from now on.

My hulking buddy caught me and immediately swung me by my legs so my head almost touched the floor. The crowd oohed and ahhed as we did even more impressive aerial maneuvers. I had always been crazy flexible, and it was certainly paying off here.

The roar from the audience was deafening. Yes! We were so going to win.

And then a huge chandelier plummeted right at us. No! We were so going to die.

The light refracted off the white crystal, creating a dazzling display. A dazzling display that was about to crush me.

"Ned!" I screamed, drawing his attention to the imminent danger.

He threw me upward at an angle. I twisted my body, the crystals cutting wisps of my hair and just barely missing the rest of me.

He launched himself in the opposite direction, the chandelier smashing into the floor a split second later. He shielded himself with his muscular wings, the glass shards bouncing off them.

He zipped upward, catching me in mid-air.

"Ned, you're amazing!"

"Naturally," he replied. Okay, I'll admit it: gargoyles were pretty awesome.

"Look! Up there!" I spotted a shadowy figure leaping through the rafters. "Fastball special!"

He hurled me like a dart at the fleeing fugitive. I felt like Supergirl, able to leap Gothic manors in a single bound.

I crashed into the sneaky fiend, tackling him off the wooden beam he was traversing.

And then we were falling. Crap.

Fortunately, there was something below us: the huge cake. The creative confection was almost the size of Ned.

I twisted my quarry around, so he would take the brunt of the blow. We splatted into the gooey goodness, sending frosting flying everywhere and silverware clattering to the floor.

The table holding the cake split in half, depositing us on the floor, completely covered in frosting and fluffy goodness. I licked some off my finger. Yum! Supernats sure knew how to make delicious desserts.

I straddled the baddie, wiping enough cream off his face to see he was a goblin.

"Okay, you stinky jerkface. Why were you trying to take us out of the competition?"

"Your dancing sucked!" he spat. What?! That was it. It was one thing to try to kill me. But criticizing my sweet moves was going too far.

I spotted the elf girl from before. "Gorgeous elf lady! C'mere!" I dragged her down into the frosty mess. "I need your sweat!"

She looked at me, bewildered. What? Like she didn't get that request all the time.

I squeezed some perspiration out of her golden locks, and they splattered jerkface's, well, face.

"Ahh!" he yelped. "Okay, okay, I'll tell you."

Yes! Elf sweat was the solution to everything.

"You will tell them nothing," a voice boomed.

The crowd parted. And there stood the Goblin King.

He was taller and wider than most goblins. He wore a three-piece suit with a top hat adorning his grayish-green head and carried a walking stick.

He also exuded authority. The crowd fell into a hush as soon as he spoke.

His cane click-clacked against the floor as he slowly approached me and the cake goblin.

Ned landed beside me, ready for action. I smiled at him, grateful for his support.

Head Gobby towered over me.

I proffered a handful of confection. "Hi, Sir Goblin King. Would you like some cake?"

His eyes narrowed as they flicked between me and the mess in my palm.

"Oh, um, cake's not your thing? Okay!" I shoved it in my mouth. Sooo good!

"What are you doing to my minion?" His voice brooked no shenanigans. Unfortunately, shenanigans were my specialty.

"Your stupid minion just tried to kill us. Admit it, you were trying to take us out because you were afraid we would win. You've been trying to rig the whole competition!" I finished with a dramatic, accusatory finger jab like I was a prosecutor on Law & Order: Supernats. Frosting flung off my hand onto the King's suit.

The crowd gasped. Though I wasn't sure if it was at my accusation or the fact that I had soiled his fancy clothes.

I smiled sheepishly, wondering if I was about to be carted off to the goblin dungeon.

"Your claims are meaningless, human."

Ohhh shit. "Wh... What? I'm not some stinky human. I'm a super-cool vampire. See?"

I exhibited my fake fangs. And he promptly ripped them right out of my mouth.

"Son of a bitch!" Fuck, that hurt!

A collective gasp echoed through the hall. I hopped to my feet, glancing around nervously. I was so screwed.

"Do you know the penalty for violating the sanctity of the Monster Mash?"

"No! Why does everyone think I know these things?"

Ned stepped in front of me. "Your Majesty, I have no quarrel with you, but I cannot let you harm my partner."

I sighed. Aw, Ned. He was getting the biggest hug ever after this. Assuming we survived.

"You dare defy the Goblin King?"

I scooted next to Ned. "Yeah, we dare! And stop talking about yourself in the third person."

He glared at me. I thought laser beams were about to shoot from his eyes.

A flash of blue and the scent of a spring overloaded my senses. I blinked and Kaly stood before us, hands on her hips, staring up at the King.

"Don't you dare hurt Elena. She's super-sweet and smart. And really cute!"

Okay, it was official. I was totally smitten with this girl.

"She has no business being here," Chief Gobster retorted.

"I hired her and Ned to figure out who was being a big cheating meanie. I can't believe it's you."

I couldn't believe the Goblin King was letting a tiny nymph talk back to him. Kaly was so brave!

He stared at her. Then sighed, his shoulders hunching. "I did it to make sure you would win."

Kaly stomped her foot. "Daaad! Why do you always have to be such a poophead? I want to win on my own."

Dad? Ohhh fuck. How the heck was a big grouch like the Goblin King the father of such a beautiful and super-sweet naiad like Kaly?

"I'm sorry, jellybean. I just want you to be happy."

"I'll be happy if you butt out, stinky breath!"

I suppressed a giggle. She sounded like an angsty teen, even though she was probably way older than me. Nymphs lived very long lives, though looked eternally young. Not a bad gig.

The Goblin King looked away, stung by her words. She immediately hugged him. "Ah! I'm sorry Dad. I didn't mean it. Your breath isn't stinky at all. Well, sometimes it is, but I still love you!"

He embraced her, patting her delicate head. "I love you too, jellybean."

I clutched Ned's arm. "Aw, isn't it sweet?"

"You realize he was just about to severely punish you."

"Well, yeah, but now everything's cool."

"I wouldn't go that far," the gushy goblin intoned.

Crap. I thought I was going to get away scot-free. "Haha, let's just chalk this up to me being a weird, zany human and call it a day, okay?"

"It's true," Ned added. "She's the weirdest human I've ever met."

I wrinkled my nose at him. Gee, thanks. But in this case, maybe my weirdness would help.

"I will let you go unpunished," the Goblin King announced.

I jumped up and down. "Yes! You are so wise and benevolent, Kingster."

"However," he continued. "You must come dance for me every week for the next two months."

"Hey! I'm not a stripper!"

Ned elbowed me. "He means you and me ballroom dancing."

"Ohhh. That's totally different. Sure thing! Will we get paid? Ow!"

I received another gargoyle elbow. "We would be honored, your Majesty." Ned bowed, yanking me down to imitate his gesture. Okay, fine, I guess we could put on free performances. Especially if it meant my cute, human butt wasn't thrown in supernat jail, or something worse. Plus, I'd get to see Kaly every week. That alone was worth it.

"Now, let us continue the Monster Mash!" the Goblin King proclaimed.

Ned and I watched the fantastic displays on the dance floor, impressed by how talented all the different creatures were. We were disqualified for me being a human. Which was totally stupid and unfair. I was going to write several strongly-worded e-mails. After a romp in the supernatural hay with Kaly.

Speaking of... She and her lady gnome dance partner got second place. And with no interference from King Gobby. The lovely elf lass and her sasquatch buddy scored first. They were really amazing, so they deserved it. I mean, Ned and I totally deserved it, but, you know, stupid supernat rules.

The most important thing was we had solved another case. We were the most amazing detective agency in town. And now I needed to reap the rewards.

"UHHH, KALY, NOT SO hard," I groaned.

"Oh, I'm sorry Elena, am I not using the right technique?"

I panted, sweat running down my body. "N... no, you're amazing at it. Can... can you just go a little slower?"

"Sure thing, sweetie!"

"Ohhh yeah, that's the spot!"

The door crashed open. Ned stalked in, his mouth agape. "What in the underworld is going on?"

Kaly and I stopped our gyrating, glancing at him.

"Um, what does it look like?" I replied.

I turned to face him, dressed as my favorite Chibibibi character. Kaly wore another costume of one of the cute critters. We were in mid-hip bump, practicing the famous Chibibibi Cha Cha.

"I don't want to know," Ned huffed.

"Ooh, did you remember the extra soy sauce?"

He sighed. "I'll be right back."

As soon as the door closed, Kaly clutched me. "Now can we have super-fun kinky sex?"

"Oh my God, yes! But really fast before Ned gets back."

"Yay!"

She threw me onto the desk and leaped on top of me, ripping my clothes off.

Fuck. Nymphs were the best.

Jeff Burns loves writing sci-fi/fantasy, and this is his second anthology story after contributing to *Dragons of a Different Tail*. He's the writer/director of online superhero comedy series *Super Knocked Up*, which he's currently turning into a novel. He's also continuing the shenanigans of Elena and Ned as a full-length book, so look for that soon! On the spicy side of things, he writes humorous geeky erotica as Riley Rose and has over 30 published books. Jeff geeks out every week hosting online improv comedy show *Super Geeked Up*, which he also performs live on stage at comic cons throughout North America. He secretly wishes he could live with Ewoks or travel the galaxy with Spike Spiegel and Faye Valentine. Check out all his work at supergeekedup.com and rileyroseerotica.com

THE GREATEST OF ALL TIME

By Francis Fernandez

Los Angeles, where dreams were made and fantasies became reality. This was my city, and I knew it like the back of my hand. Who hadn't heard of this place, the home of movie stars, fast cars, dirty bars, and Hedy Lamarr.

And then there was me, Hugh Marron Richard, Private Investigator. No one knew of my exploits, no matter how many cases I had solved. I preferred it that way. The cops got the glory, and I got the paycheck.

As I walked down the dirty streets of downtown, my head was on a swivel. I eyeballed a man in a long, crocodile leather trench coat that eerily looked like mine, minus the croc skin. He was probably a fellow private investigator, or more likely a flasher. Those were the only two types of idiots I could think of who would wear any kind of coat in the middle of LA.

Then there was this handsome gentleman, in a pin-striped suit, hailing a cab. The first thing I noticed was his hair. It looked darker than burnt toast, which was then again toasted. He was probably an actor or a model who'd rather dye than look old.

Then there's the woman in the red dress strutting toward me. A looker to the nth degree. She had legs that went up to her thighs and eyes you'd dot with a heart. She smiled at me coyly and I smiled back. My head told me we could be a good couple, my brain told me otherwise. These were the people this city called out to. These people are why I was there.

"What was that?" asked a burly officer, a look of disinterest painted all over his face. Apparently, I had arrived.

"I'm here to see Chuck," was all I needed to say. He nodded toward the open door past crisscrossed lines of LAPD caution tape.

I tugged at the front of my trilby in greeting to every officer I passed by as I made my way into the apartment complex. It wasn't until I got to the staircase that I needed to steel myself for what was to come.

I found myself in front of an open doorway that lit the dark hall in a sad, yellow light, like the kind you saw as a kid on those long car rides home.

The crime scene smelled of pizza, vodka, and vomit. The kind you'd find underneath your car's passenger seat after a long night of drinking and peeing in a bush. I could tell that LA's finest, Detective Chuck Boulevard, wasn't happy with what he was seeing. But of course, who would be? The body of a young woman was splayed on the floor, her face pale, her lips puffy, and her eyes blissfully closed. It was almost as if she was happy to be off her feet for a little while.

"Goddammit, Hugh... You're mumblin' your inner monologue!" Chuck grumbled, his comically thick mustache rustling as he took down notes on his pad. His rotund features made him look jolly, like a homicide Saint Nick. "I can still hear you!"

"Sorry, Chuck," I lied. "So, who was she?" I slipped my calabash pipe between my chapped lips. It felt good to take a few long puffs from the old pipe. The smoke was like a silky embrace on my lungs.

Chuck stood up from the body and looked at me with that ridiculous mustache. It was like a push broom made love to his upper lip. Wait. Why was he growling? Was I talking out loud again? Thankfully, Chuck broke the silence.

"We have Cassandra Jewel Teagen. Age 27. Probably seen her in the papers." Chuck waved his hand over the sea of framed newspaper clippings and magazine covers lining the walls of the small, modest office. "She was a world-renowned neurobiologist who discovered the cure for gallstones and athlete's foot." I was locked onto every word Chuck said, watching his mustache dance the cancan as he talked.

"Wish she was my doc," I said, directing my eyes to the body. "What happened?"

"The medical examiner says she bled to death." Don't look back at the mustache. "But we couldn't find any blood on the body, except for a little drop we found on her lips. There's no knife wounds, no bullet holes, no bruisin'." Chuck frowned even deeper at the woman on the ground. "I kinda wish there were fang holes on her neck, then maybe it'd make a little more sense."

"It does kind of look like the work of a vampire," I said, taking a few more puffs from my fancy pipe. "I could see how it could've happened. Vampire comes to the door, seduces the woman, gets invited in, they have a little pizza, some vodka, and..." I look around the room. It's immaculate. "Where's the pizza and vodka and vomit? This room smells like it's bathed in it."

Chuck shrugged. "We looked everywhere. That's why I called you, Hugh! You're like the Sherlock Holmes of this kind of thing."

I couldn't deny what Chuck was saying. I was like Sherlock Holmes. He was the greatest detective of all time! But, what did he mean "of this kind of thing?" Women? Homicide? Vomit? I prided myself on solving so many mysterious crimes over the years, but have I been wrong all this time?

"Jesus, Hugh, of homicides! You've helped us solve murders!" Chuck's mustache looked exceptionally angry. "Look Hugh, I had to call you because none of this makes sense. Was hopin' you'd give us some of your magic and help us figure out what happened here."

I rubbed my chin in thought, looking around desperately for some clues. The crime scene was surprisingly tidy, with furniture and knick-knacks still intact. The only thing that seemed out of sorts, other than the dead body of the young woman lying on the floor, were two glasses of red wine sitting on a side table. I knelt in front of them, looking at the Jackson Pollock painting of smudged fingerprints on one of the glasses. "This isn't vodka," I said to no one in particular, "No sign of pizza or vomit, either." There was only one set of fingerprints on one glass. That didn't mean someone else wasn't there. The body itself was unremarkable. If I didn't know she was dead, I'd have thought she was taking a nap on the floor. Her oversized t-shirt and shorts made it seem like she was settling in for the night, so the other person could have been someone familiar.

Pipe firmly between my lips, I took a stroll around the apartment. I looked at everything. The door, the windows, the furniture. My eyes scanned it all, my brain processing every inch of the place. The office itself, despite the smell, was clean and well-maintained. I looked over the wall of compliments that made her out to be amazing, with some articles calling her a legend, the greatest of all time, and the best of the best. So why would someone want to kill Miss "Cass Jewel T." as some magazines named her?

"Who found her?" I asked, blowing rings of smoke toward the detective.

"Neighbor was going out for a walk and saw the door wide open. Thought he saw someone hit the stairs. Saw Cass here and immediately called us." Chuck's mustache seemed to sag a little in defeat.

"Can you email me what you find, Chuck? I need a good think on this one."

"You got it, Hugh," Chuck said. I tipped my trilby and left.

I DON'T KNOW WHY I had Smashmouth as my ringtone, but that harsh, scratchy baritone was the sound I needed to wake me from my slumber. I answered my phone and saw the oversized caterpillar known as Chuck's mustache on the screen. "What happened?"

Chuck looked annoyed, from what I could see past his fence of facial hair, which probably meant I was saying my inner monologues out loud again.

"Hugh," Chuck replied, in what sounded like exasperation, "we got another three."

"Three?" I asked.

"Yeah. Santa Monica e-sports center." Chuck hung up. No goodbye. No see you there. How do people end calls so willy-nilly?

I didn't know what to expect when I got to the e-sports center, but it was definitely not what I saw. The center was a vast, dank, and deep cave of neon, plastic, cheesy snacks, and energy drinks.

The computers were hulking behemoths of light and glass next to screens larger than a breadbasket. Through the translucent side paneling, I could see the coveted RTX graphics cards, liquid cooling systems, and LED strip lighting that gave players a next-generation experience.

"I didn't know you were a gamer, Hugh," Chuck said from behind me. I jumped in surprise.

"Chuck!" I said, trying to regain my composure. "No, not a gamer. Just reading the little description card here." I pointed to the card that said the exact same thing. "So, where are the victims?"

He led me to a set of computers grouped together where two women and a man lay headfirst on their keyboards. On their screens was a game I knew was popular with the "fellow kids." They were playing LoL. Laugh out Loud, I think. A game that beckoned to the youths like a siren's song.

Pipe in mouth, I looked around the crime scene, taking in every detail I could find. The victims were young, fairly attractive twenty-somethings. The kind you'd see on a TV show about adult teenagers in a fancy high school that could never exist in real life.

Sniffing the air like a psychopath, I got the distinct scent of vodka, pizza, and vomit slightly mixed with potato chips and Red Bull. I felt like I was going to throw up. "Blergh!"

THE GREATEST OF ALL TIME

Chuck kindly handed me a trash can, which I not so kindly pushed away.

In front of each of the gamers was a glass of red wine. A bit too posh for a place like this. I turned to Chuck. "Any witnesses on this one?"

"You'd think so," Chuck chuckled chuffily, his facial fur fanning frantically. "Nah. These kids had their eyes glued to their screens. No one saw nothin'! No security cameras, either. Apparently, no one saw anyone come in or leave that wasn't playin'. It's bonkers!"

"Yeah, totally nuts," I agreed, looking back at the screens. There was a chat room open with people talking about what had happened and lamenting the loss of the greatest LoL players of all time. That's when I saw it. The webcam!

"Anyone got access to these webcams? Can we see what they were streaming?" I called out to no one in particular.

In moments, the staff got the latest stream up and running for me. The gamers were playing their LoL with the intensity of an accountant working on a spreadsheet. The furious mouse clicking and keyboard typing practically gave me carpal tunnel.

Then a figure came in from behind them like a hockey-masked, unkillable death machine in the night. Moving with the grace of an interpretive dancer, the figure reached out with a gloved hand and placed a glass of red wine at each of their desks. The face itself was hidden under the hood of a hoodie, and the dim lighting was not helping. I stared intently at the screen as I watched the gamers sipping idly at the glasses placed before them. It took each one a second before they realized what was happening. They each turned around at different times, probably trying to figure out who would treat them to this fine vintage of delectable spirit. Ominously, the figure came into view.

To my dismay, all I could see was the alligator skin hoodie the person wore. The way they were hunched over, I couldn't tell if it was a man or a woman. Whoever this was, they were clever. And just like that, the reptile-clothed perpetrator pressed their face to the first gamer, then the second, then the third. I couldn't see any resistance from the three of them as each one was methodically found face-to-face with the mystery person. And then one by one, they were turned back around and left to fall on their keyboards.

"That's some forked up shirt," Chuck said, his mustache rustling in disgust.

I nodded, lifting up my signature trilby to run my hands through my luxurious hair.

There was obviously something significant here I wasn't seeing. I had to take a few puffs from my pipe to get my head straight. Why was reptile skin clothing so popular? Did I miss the memo? And what of the wine? Was it just a parting gift? An appetizer to a meal of blood?

A sharp elbow poked my rib cage, and I turned to Chuck. "What do you think?" he asked.

"I don't know. I thought it could have been a succubus, but there wasn't anything sexual about this attack. Maybe a draugr or a fairy? Did you rule out vampires, detective?"

Chuck nodded slowly, stroking his furry lip monstrosity. "Look, I don't know anythin' about this supernatural mumbo jumbo you keep going on about, but I talked to my buddy, Vlad the Pimp Tailor. He says they only cosplay as vampires, and apparently it's hard out there. He also says that they don't actually drink blood. Unless it's a Bloody Mary, am I right?" Chuck chuckled.

"Right..." It was supernatural. It always was. It's too bad the LAPD always chalked it up to something more grounded in reality. But that's why they called me in for these cases. For the unusual. And looking at this reptilian-dressed killer, it was unusual indeed.

THE FIFTH VICTIM LIVED in Malibu. I loved Malibu. The city, not the rum. Coconut. Gross. Approaching the property, I was a little taken aback by what I saw. I'd never seen a mansion so large before. I could barely see an end to it. It could probably fit all of the residents of Rhode Island. Apparently, it had thirty bedrooms and fifty bathrooms, which didn't make sense to me at all. Why would a house need that many more bathrooms than bedrooms? Does the one man who lives here sleep in every bedroom and use every bathroom in rotation?

The gravel walkway was satisfying to listen to as I made my way up to the front door. The sentient fur beast known as Chuck's mustache greeted me. "Detective Boulevard," I nodded, tipping my trilby. "Mustache," I said, greeting the facial hair. "This is a nice house."

"Yeah! How does anyone live in a house this big? Do you think the man just sleeps in every room and uses every bathroom in rotation?"

I laughed. "What a silly idea, detective. No one would think that." I pulled down my trilby just a little bit more before taking out my pipe.

We walked into the main room to see the body of the latest victim on the floor. All the usual signs were there, the smell, the wine, the blood on the lip, and, based on the security camera footage, a shadowy figure in a turtle skin dress. The killer was clever to attack at night. All we could see were shadows and a hint of the scaly clothing. So, we knew that the murderer could potentially be a woman. A shapeshifter perhaps?

In another room, I could hear the distinct voice of one of the greatest actors of all time. Considered the sexiest man twenty years in a row, he spoke with an accent you could hear from a mile away. I made my way into the entertainment room where the movie *Dragonliver* was playing. It was about a medieval dragon who gave part of his liver to a drunken prince. The TV played my favorite scene.

The animated dragon bent down to the young man in front of him, looking so real. The music began to soar, and after a brief silence, roaring words came from its mouth, "Ushe my liver well, young prinshe. For it ish noble and true. Shave our kingdom, Prinshe Shamshon ShilverShpoon, sho it may proshper and grow into greatnesh." I would've shed a tear had I known what the dragon was saying.

"So, Bond Connery is the deceased," I said, as I walked back into the main room.

"It's a cryin' shame. Right after he was named 'Greatest of All Time' on the ole magazine. He will be missed," Chuck said, looking down at the body.

My brain kicked me as the pieces started falling into place.

"Sounds like that hurts," Chuck said.

I just stared at the man, but I couldn't see him past his upper lipholstery. Puffing on my pipe, I felt like this was all coming together. The thing the LAPD couldn't fathom was that this was once again a cryptid kill.

"What?" Chuck replied. I really needed to stop talking out loud.

"I need to go. This is going to take some time to mull over, but I feel like I'm close to solving this case."

"Whatever you say, Hugh. If you figure this out, you'll be the greatest LA PI of all time." Chuck grinned, his dirt-squirrel seemed to fidget in agreement, which gave me an idea.

Los Angeles wasn't short on its trendy, hipster, dive bars. The Night Thong happened to be themed to old 60's TV shows like the *Munsters* and *The Addams Family*, but with a sexy twist. Someone didn't get the memo, because the back wall was painted with an evening-time backdrop in the shape of a sandal.

The waitress stopped by my table and dropped off their signature drink, the Freffrisa. A blue, tropical concoction that was the bar's specialty. It tasted of improvisational comedy and bad impersonations. Luckily, that didn't take away from the sweet, sweet taste.

I ran through the murders in my head. People of renown dead before their time. I could only deduce that the killer wanted to be infamous, so they targeted people with a reputation. But not just any reputation. They had to be the absolute best, which should make it easy to find out who their next target would be.

I flipped through the images on my phone, scanning every pixel of every crime scene. The pictures taunted me, as if it was sticking out its tongue and teasing that I'd never be able to catch them. I just wanted to scream, "Who are you?! Are you a creepy step-uncle trying to get revenge on everyone for stealing his special interest literature? A dissatisfied Tinder date kissing people to death in hopes of winning a world record?" In all the years I'd been doing this job, I'd never seen anything like this.

I placed my trusty pipe in my mouth. It helped me think. And it also made me look cool. Now, if I could get Chuck's insane mustache, I'd be in business. A few good drags and I was in a good place. The cogs in my brain were finally turning.

What was I missing? There's obviously someone there! Maybe I had to think outside the box. It's a ghost. But how did that account for the blood loss? A zombie? A tapeworm? This was ridiculous. I didn't think I could playfully call myself Sherlock Holmes anymore.

"Is that what you call yourself?" a sexy accent asked from across the table.

"Sherlock Holmes..." My eyes climbed from my phone to see a petite woman sitting in front of me in what looked to be a white, dragon-scale dress. Her dark green eyes looked me up and down like a snake, ready to eat its dinner. I cleared my throat. "Was I talking this whole time?" I asked, nonchalantly. I probably was. Why can't I inner monologue like normal people?

A smirk parted her thin lips as she leaned forward, resting her elbows on the table. She was far too comfortable and acting too familiar for my taste. Still, I couldn't help but be intrigued and a little aroused by her assertiveness.

"I was told to find you, Hugh Marron Richard, Private Investigator," she said, her curly blonde locks swinging in front of her face, hypnotizing me.

I took a sip of my tasty Freffrisa, buying myself time to think of something to say. All I knew was that this felt wrong. Very wrong. "Were you? And you are?"

"Lizette Bode, but you can call me Lizzie. I was hoping you could help me." Her voice was so sultry, it was hard to concentrate. I watched as she drew her finger along the table in front of us before stopping to rest her hand on mine. "I need your protection. Someone is trying to kill me."

Her hand was cold yet soft to the touch. I tried not to think about the way my skin tingled from the contact. Instead, I tried to figure out why my gut was screaming at me to run away.

The accent. I couldn't tell where it was from. Maybe Central or South America. It was slight, but alluring, and had the measured tone of someone who'd been living in Los Angeles for quite some time.

The woman's clothing appeared new and hugged her body like a second skin. She moved in it like it wasn't a skintight body glove, but an extension of herself. Maybe she was a model or a vampire! I quickly looked for a reflective surface and saw her looking back at me, bemused.

There I was, looking like an idiot for thinking outside the box.

Her small frame looked unassuming. She appeared comfortable. Any bystander would think we were two people having a casual date at an 80's themed monster bar named after an undergarment or a flipflop. She didn't look like a woman fearing a stalker.

"How did you know where to find me?"

The woman's lips turned up into a grin as she squeezed my hand. "You posted about your Freffrisa and tagged the bar." She took out her phone and showed me the picture of myself doing the peace sign while sticking my tongue out over the beverage. What was wrong with me?

"Well, Miss Bode, who told you I could help you?" I asked, apprehensively.

"Bond Connery."

"He's dead."

"I know, but his followers aren't." She tapped on her phone and showed me a chat room that had my name plastered all over it. You couldn't hide from the internet. "That's why I need your help. I think I'm next." She flashed me a coy smile.

This wasn't a woman afraid for her life. She wanted something.

"What makes you think that?" I asked.

My phone rang, and on the caller ID was detective Boulevard. "Sorry, I have to take this."

Finding a dark, quiet corner away from the woman, I answered the phone.

"Hugh!" Chuck screamed.

I made an incoherent sound, nearly dropping the phone.

Chuck called out again. "Hugh! We have another one! Same MO, near the Night Thong!"

I gasped aloud. It couldn't be.

"Hugh? Are you there? Did you hear me?"

I looked back at my table to find Lizzie gone. In her place was a now empty glass of Freffrisa and a strangely large note that said she'd call me soon.

I SAT IN MY office looking over the photos of the latest murder. The squeaking of the overhead fan was the only thing that kept me company. It was another hot summer day in the City of Angels. The kind of heat that made your pants stick to your cheeks.

I clicked through the pictures Chuck had sent me of the crime scene and sniffed the sample of the fabric with that familiar smell. I'm pretty sure I was starting to like the scent.

The sixth victim was a local basketball player. The pattern was more than obvious to me by then. A creature who either loved to wear—or was made of—reptilian skin, who sucked the blood from its victims using wine as a way to raise the blood pressure to get to said blood, leaving a distinct odor either naturally or as a result of feeding, and it only fed from the best of the best. They called him the greatest player of all time. Every person who's died was the greatest of all time in one thing or another. They were the GOAT, as the kids called them. So obviously, the killer was targeting these GOATs.

I was right about the supernatural angle. A killer with no murder weapon and no real motive. It was a creature of habit that was just trying to live. And only one creature sucked out the blood of goats. The Chupacabra. Which made much more sense than Chuck's theory, which he'd shared the night before, that the murderer was harvesting blood to make a GGOATOAT. The greatest, greatest of all time, of all time. Ridiculous.

It all made sense. Well, it didn't actually make sense, but I was all out of options.

My rotary phone rang, breaking the silence. Chuck sounded excited as he told me he could pull off my plan to catch the creature. The trap was set. It was time to lure this beast out into the open and let it know that I was the Greatest PI of All Time.

The next few days were embarrassing as I posed for photo shoots and was interviewed by late night talk show hosts about all the cases I'd solved over the years. I lov...hated every second of the attention. By the end of the month, I'd done every podcast, live stream, and Dungeons and Dragons actual plays known to man, sharing the exploits of my long and illustrious career. Newspapers, websites, and magazines had my face plastered all over them. "The Greatest Private Investigator of All Time!"

The word was getting out about how amazing I was. No longer could I hide behind my humble exterior. I had to let everyone know of my escapades and truly share the story of how awesome I was. The world needed to know I was an incredible Private Investigator. I mean, because, well, it was all to catch this murderous monster. Yeah!

Unfortunately, more bodies piled up as the Chupacabra did what it did best to survive. Sucking GOATs.

GOATs blood!

GOATs blood...

The cold air caressed my skin from the newly installed air conditioning unit, which was the best thing to come out of my little publicity tour. No longer sticking to my leather chair, I could move around freely and catch a cold as God intended.

My phone rang as if on cue. Maybe my crazy plan had actually worked.

"Hello?" I asked in the manliest way I could.

"Hi. It's me, Lizzie, from the bar," came the reply. Could it be? "I asked for your help a few weeks back. I need it now, more than ever." That accent was so damn attractive with just a hint of being sinister.

Lizzie gave me her address and told me she'd see me soon. When I hung up the phone, I debated whether I should stay in my cool, refreshing office a little longer. The trap had been set. Could it have also been sprung?

The Valley was a part of Los Angeles that people had forgotten. That was until some martial arts TV show reignited the nostalgia. Some of the wealthy and prominent called The Valley home, with its triple-digit temperatures and hoity-toity supermarkets. The house I found myself in front of could have easily been for a big-name actor or sports ball player.

Neither stood at the entrance of the small mansion. Lizzie, all five feet of her, in a long crocodile leather trench coat, had a grin on her face. I kept my cool, tipping my trilby in greeting.

Before I got to the door, Lizzie made her way in. Frowning slightly, I followed her.

The house was dark, with the blinds and curtains all drawn shut. I could barely see. But that wasn't the strange part. It was the familiar smell. Was I too late? It was stronger than before.

A light from a phone came on in the living room before dropping to the floor. The screen's light shown on a body that I could only assume was the homeowner strewn across the floor like a discarded toy. The home reeked of vodka, pizza, and vomit. "Lizzie? Are you okay?"

I picked up the phone from the floor and saw that it was on an article. "Hugh Marron Richard, the Greatest Private Investigator of All Time."

A hissing noise came from behind me and I spun around, turning the phone toward a smiling Lizzie.

The light illuminated her standing there licking her lips. The coat she wore shrank into her skin. Her face started to distort, and for a moment, she looked like a man I'd seen once before. The flasher! The face continued to stretch and bend until a lizard creature with kangaroo-like legs was standing before me.

"I thought you guys were dogs," I murmured. I had hoped for a dog because at least dogs were cute.

The lizard, Lizzie... Oh... I got it, spoke to me in that seductive tone. "You really thought you were Sherlock Holmes, didn't you?" She smiled. "I was afraid you'd figure me out and stop me. That's why I looked for you that night." Lizzie put her face to mine, and I could smell the noxious fumes that lingered at every crime scene. "But now I know you're a GOAT, and I bet you taste delicious." I was so torn. This was kind of a turn on!

I stifled a cough, the stench becoming unbearable. I didn't want my blood to be sucked. I threw the phone at Lizzie and sprinted for the door. In her final form, I guess she had superpowers, as she leaped in front of me and stopped me in my tracks.

Her raptor-like arms slammed the door shut in my face and she tried to grab for my head. My repulsion was more powerful as I found the strength to duck away from her clutches and blindly make my way up the dark and dreary stairs.

Lizzie the Chupacabra was not far behind me. I heard the powerful, large Chun Li legs pursuing me. I wasn't actually sure what I was going to do on the second floor of a small mansion, but hopefully, there was a way out of here and into safety.

Nope. I was living in a horror movie. It was pitch black and every door I tried to open happened to be locked. She couldn't have prepared for this. Who locks all the doors in their house?

"It wasn't me," the Chupacabra yelled from behind.

It didn't take long before I reached the end of the hallway. The end of the line. I turned around to see the shadow of Lizzie standing there at the top of the stairs, looking around and obviously annoyed. "You're going to make me work for this, aren't you?" she asked.

Trying not to make any big moves, I pulled out my phone and dialed Chuck's number for a video call. He was my only hope. Sadly, my careful movement didn't fool the cryptid, as Lizzie bound toward me like a rabid dog in the dark. Her legs sounded like the kick drum from a heavy metal concert. Before I could react, Lizzie returned to her human form and kissed me. It was a nice kiss, too. I think I even kissed her back. Maybe gave her a little tongue.

That was when I felt it. Her tongue slithered between my lips like a slippery eel. Her small arms held me in place as I felt the spikes at the tip of her tongue latch to every side of my mouth. She started drinking my life's blood. It felt so good and so terrible all at the same time. Despite all that, I couldn't put into words the level of disappointment I felt knowing that my trap could have worked. My goal in becoming a GOAT was to lure the Chupacabra to me, where Chuck and I could finally solve this case together. Instead, I was lured to her.

Clever girl.

I knew that I was dying. It didn't feel half bad. It definitely wasn't half good. I didn't even get a final meal. I think I had buttered toast for breakfast that morning and some orange juice. The breakfast of champions.

The last words I heard were of Chuck screaming at me through the video phone call I made. Hopefully, he saw everything. Lord knows, the last thing I saw was that ridiculous, yet glorious mustache.

"So that's my story," I said to my companions at the table before looking toward the crowded pavilion. Death was much better than LA. Definitely not as hot. And who knew you just popped into this little world full of nightmares when you died? What did the weird animal at my table call it? After Life? Pretty nice place either way, but honestly, I'd prefer Before Death.

THE GREATEST OF ALL TIME

The one thing that annoyed me about the place was that I had none of the things I died with. Just the clothes on my back. No pipe, no trilby, no copy of the magazine naming me the Greatest PI of All Time. They weren't kidding when they said you can't take it with you when you go. Still, I couldn't help but pat my pockets, hoping to find my pipe.

"You do know, my boy, that you're talking out loud," said the small creature with the ears of a dog and the head of an otter. I stared at it. Maybe I just went insane.

I reached for my pipe again.

"Give it a second, mister," said a young man in what looked like futuristic, space clothing. To my relief, there was not a thread of reptile skin on it.

"Sorry, old habits die hard," I replied.

"With a vengeance," the Otter Dog replied back, chuckling in a strange, melodic way, like birds playing a harp made of kitten purrs. Yeah. I'd gone insane.

Before I could berate the little creature, I realized that a pipe was materializing in my mouth. I took a few careful drags and sighed happily. That was the smell and taste of home.

The young man beside this Otter Dog looked at me with fascination. "You know, I've never heard of these Chupacabra or GOATs before. They sound awful."

Thinking back on the kiss, I chuckled. "They're not that bad." It wasn't a terrible way to go. "But what was this about dragons in space?"

That's when I felt it. My body no longer had that euphoric feeling. That bliss you felt when you were...uhh... Instead, it felt like my brain was being torn apart from the inside. Which I guess, is really the only way to get to my brain.

My eyes rolled back in my head, and I felt my body go weightless. Otter Dog said, nonchalantly, "I guess it's not his time yet after all." Moments felt like minutes. Minutes felt like miles. Miles felt like....

"THERE'S NO PLACE LIKE home... There's no place like home..."

My eyes felt heavy and my body felt weak, yet all my senses felt like they were on overdrive. I could sense people nearby as my hearing focused on the ruckus around me. It sounded like I was being revived in a zoo during a thunderstorm in the middle of an avalanche. Mustering what little energy I had, I opened my eyes, the dim light blinding me. When they could finally focus, I sighed. Why was I not surprised that the last thing I'd see would be the first?

Chuck's mustache greeted me with what I could only call relief. "You're back!" he said, before patting the shoulder of the paramedic who had a bag of blood attached to my arm. I could barely move.

"Chuck. I had the weirdest dream. And you were there, and you were there, and you were there," I said through cracked lips, pointing to Chuck, the paramedic, and a random police officer I'd never seen before. Yeah, my brain was fuzzy and murky, like a mud pit that two ladies would wrestle in.

"Shut up, Hugh! We're tryin' to save your life. Lay still," Chuck grumbled as he ushered in another paramedic to check my vitals. "We're just lucky we got here in time, otherwise you'd be D E A D. Gone. Also, good job thinkin' of bringin' in a bag of blood as bait. Didn't know we'd be usin' it to save your life. And, since you didn't drink that wine of hers, it took longer to kill ya."

I did my best to look around and saw the Chupacabra in handcuffs. She was in her Lizzie form. Her head slowly turned, like one of those creepy horror movie dolls, and she looked at me with surprise. She smiled softly and licked her lips. Yeah. Still kind of hot. My head felt like a boulder when I turned around to look back at Chuck. "How did you find me?"

"You took a selfie with the house. Not sure I agree with the caption, 'Gonna bust the bad guy.' But, you did tag the house." Chuck paused. "You really gotta work on your selfie skills there, Hugh." He showed me the phone and my angry-looking face while I pointed at the house. There was a second picture with me giving a thumbs down and sticking out my tongue. It took what little energy I had left to look away.

"Thanks, Chuck. For saving me." I smiled weakly.

"Don't worry about it, Hugh. I should be thankin' you! You caught us another slippery one." Chuck patted me on the shoulder and let the medical professionals work. I lay there closing my eyes, wondering if I had actually died and gone to the After Life. But that would have to be a mystery for another day.

Los Angeles had the prettiest sunrise, wrapped snugly in a blanket of smog. The air was crisp and cool, and the sounds of honking cars and feet on the streets were its morning melody. It was a concrete jungle, not suited for everyone. But it was suited for me. I was the dad bod Tarzan of LA.

I took a bite of my street dog. The delicious mixture of ingredients I couldn't comprehend tangoed on my taste buds. It was good to be alive. And, thankfully enough, life had gotten interesting since the case of the Chupacabra. Cue the wind! A newspaper with my face tumbled toward me and landed at my feet. "Hugh Marron Richard. The Greatest Private Investigator of All Time." This stunt made me the talk of the town. Everyone wanted and needed my help. Chuck even called me more, asking for my thoughts on cases.

So, I tucked up the collar of my leather trench coat, pulled down the trilby over my eyes, and placed that familiar pipe between my lips. I looked out toward the Hollywood sign, staring at it like it was a camera. Moby's, "Extreme Ways" started to play on my phone. I walked toward the Hollywood sign, cars honking at me as I did. This is it. I'm sure I'll need a catchphrase. "It's investigatin' time."

Roll credits.

Francis Fernandez is a podcaster by night and a writer also around night. With what some people call "his radio voice," Francis is the cohost of the geeky, improv comedy show Super Geeked Up on YouTube, and the most generic podcast on the internet, the Points of Interest Podcast. He is also host of the Is This Love Podcast. Happy that some people kind of liked his first published short story "A Friend Called Home" in the *Dragons of a Different Tail* anthology, he hopes that he will continue to evolve as an amateur author and just become a regular author with his latest work. Learn little at http://sinceresarcasm.net/

Hexpad Blog: A First-Timer's Guide to the Big City

By Colten Fisher

A^{PRIL 29} Hey everyone, this is OutFromTheRoc17, and you are reading the first entry of my blog documenting my Big Move to New Astoria. Now, I know plenty of people have been there, or even live there (it *is* the biggest city on the continent, after all), but when I told people in my tiny mountain town that I was moving there, it was all:

Gasp! "You know there are ogres there, right? Aren't you afraid of being eaten?"

"Aren't you a little concerned about going somewhere where so many people are…you know, not like you?" (Of course, what they meant is "not human.")

"Oh, you have to check out the Mycotower!" (As if it was some secret, and not the biggest tourist attraction in NA.)

"Make sure to keep three pennies in your pockets. Goblins don't like copper or odd numbers."

And my favorite: "Great, another kid off to get brainwashed to think like a fairy."

I know they all meant well, but, you know, *cringe*. If there's anything that my Internexus friends have taught me, it's that most of what I grew up hearing is just stereotypes. Old prejudices from when my great-grandparents first got here and thought goblins and raccoons were the same things.

Anyway, that's what inspired me to start this blog. Or guidebook, if you will. I want to document everything I learn about New Astoria's culture, its people, its *life*. Everything that a human like me from the capital of Nowhere needs to know if they hope to have any chance of surviving in the Big City.

May 1
Tip #1: Toll Trolls Are Apparently Normal

I'm writing this under a bench in Jotun Park. Since it's made for giants, it's like a shelter for human-sized folk from the rain that's been drizzling all afternoon. And judging by the graffiti and empty chip bags, I'm not the first person to use it as such.

I'm taking a break in the park from the dreadful experience that has been apartment hunting, but I'll touch on that in my next post. For now, I'll tell you all how I, your Honored and Adventuresome Guide, managed to royally mess up my VERY FIRST interaction here in New Astoria.

I honestly thought toll trolls were a legend. They featured in so many silly stories growing up that I figured they were just another example of human prejudice.

So here I was, thinking I'm all enlightened, and that I'm going to walk into New Astoria with the open-est of minds, when a troll stops me at the Gateway Bridge saying, "50 cents, please."

See, she didn't really have much of a uniform. I thought she was just a regular person making a joke. So I laughed and said, "Oh don't worry, my big brother's just behind me, he'll pay both our tolls." (Which is a "Three Billy Goats Gruff" reference, for people who didn't grow up with human bedtime stories.)

Readers, have you ever had someone narrow their eyes at you, and in that moment, as your face begins to burn, you wish you could turn into a puddle and drip away through the grates beneath your feet?

Because I have.

Turns out, referencing a story where a troll gets knocked off a bridge by a goat, *to* a troll? Not the most enlightened thing I've ever done.

I stammered an apology, paid the toll, and rushed off in embarrassment. I kept my eyes so glued to the ground that I didn't even remember to admire the Gateway Bridge until after I was all the way across it. And the worst part is, from the look on her face, I was far from the first person to make that joke.

Why are humans so *dumb*?

The rain's letting up, so I'll sign off for now. The good news: it can only get better from here.

<u>May 2</u>

Tip #2: Human, Hobbit, or Harpy, Housing Sucks

I'm small (for a human). I don't need much. I thought that, when I arrived in NA, I'd spend the morning looking at the places I'd found ahead on Willow, sign a lease, and be good to go with my more-expensive-than-normal-but-still-quaint-and-homey little apartment.

Not so!

I know those of you who are more worldly than me may laugh, but I honestly expected to get an apartment with some amenities. Like, you know, a window. Maybe a toilet if I was lucky.

Nay. The only place I could get with the money I have saved *and* that would let me move in the same day was a two-room, stone-floor flat in a building built for dwarves that's a 30-minute Char ride from downtown. Each floor has a shared bathroom (also sized for dwarves), and the stove is installed in what clearly used to be a coal-burning fireplace, complete with a brick chimney. The stove is the homiest thing about the place, but I'll make do.

At least I have my sleeping bag to soften the floor until I get a bed.

May 4
Tip #3: I. Love. The Chariot

I'd only heard bad things about it before coming here. "It's crowded," "It smells," "It's never on time," and okay, all those things are true. But you guys...

It's also *beautiful*. It lets you travel nearly anywhere in the city for cheap, its wooden carriages are so quaint despite the smudges and stains, and the way it rattles on its tracks is like music. *And,* nowhere else can you see so many different kinds of people! A hobbit man in a tweed jacket holding hands with a brownie woman in a denim punk shirt. A dozen sprites sitting in the tiny row of seats near the roof built just for them (I'm jealous they can fly, but I guess it would be exhausting to fly all over the city, especially when you're that small). A leprechaun busking between stops by coming up with off-the-cuff satirical limericks. It's never-ending entertainment. I could people-watch there for hours.

Of course, staring bug-eyed at everyone didn't exactly make me seem like a local.

"Hey, kid." A particularly grumpy-looking elf caught me looking at him. Actually, I was looking at his nose, both because it was HUGE, and because I was trying to decide if the golden bar piercing straight through it was real, or just a clip-on. Anyway, he caught me looking and said, "Hey, kid. You new in town or somethin'?"

"Uh... yeah. Just moved here this week."

"Neat."

I thought the conversation was over, and then he said, "You ever been to Gal's?"

"Excuse me?"

"Gal's. You know, Galidan's. Best food this side of the river. It's elvish food. If that's not your thing, whatever, but hey, I'm an elf. I should know good elvish food. If you're gonna live in New Astoria, you gotta try Galidan's. It's up on 4th, two blocks west of Tremaine Ave."

"Uh, thanks. Yeah, I'll try it out."

I looked it up later that day. The full 7 stars. Only two dollar signs. Guess I know where I'm going out to eat. ...As soon as I get some money.

May 5
Tip #4: In New Astoria, Not Everything's Built for You

That may have been obvious from my earlier post about my apartment, but I fell a full half-story today because of this, so I figured it would make a good tip on its own.

Sometimes, you might have an appointment, like I did, in a building that was originally built for gnomes. And when they altered it to be more accommodating to general NA citizenry, they had to knock out every other floor, essentially making every story two floors tall. It makes for some interesting, if trippy, interior designs. Gives a human a sense of what it's like to be a giant.

But here's the weird part: when they took out the floors, they still had to keep the doors up to code. Which code, I don't know, but apparently there are laws against removing doors. So, you might find yourself stooping through three different doorways and taking the stairs six at a time up to floor 4 (8), only to realize you miscounted when you squeeze through a gnome-sized door and the floor that used to be there isn't there anymore, and you fall on your face in the foyer a full four feet down.

Free advice I received from a nearby gnome: if the door's too small, you're probably on the wrong floor.

PS: The appointment I was there for? It was with a recruiter (gotta get a job to pay rent, etc., right?). It went all right once he got me an ice pack. But if any of you readers know of jobs that would take a human with a big heart and a zest for meeting people, let me know!

May 8
Tip #5: Do Not Accept Free Samples From Fair Folk

Do you want to lose a day? Because that's how I lost a day. And apparently I'm lucky it wasn't more.

Three blocks east of my apartment there's a neat local coffee shop and bakery called Seelie Day that I've been wanting to try out. I had a job interview at 10, so I went in at 8 for some breakfast and coffee and to use the Wi-Fi since I still don't have any in my apartment. (You don't realize just how important an Internexus connection is until you're without one. That will be one of the *first* things I do when I get a paycheck.)

Anyway, I put in my order (one cherry scone and a large tir-na-ccino, with a shot of fairy dust for luck), paid, and while the distractingly attractive barista was preparing my drink, another fairy held out a tray to me and said, "Free sample?"

(Quick aside for my readers at home: by fairy, I mean fey person. Same size as a human, ancestors came from across the shimmering sea at some point, pointy ears, etc. I know a lot of people where I come from hear "fairy" and picture small, flying sprites, but they're different.)

Anyway, like a fool, I said, "Sure!" and took one.

See, in New Astoria, everyone's laws are upheld. That includes the fey's ancient laws about food. The ones where eating fey food can get you trapped in fairyland or make you dance until you die. Transactional purchases are fine and safe. You give me food, I give you money, we all walk away happy. But accepting food from the fey, with no *clear* price? No no.

The free sample was a two-bite custard tart, with a little dollop of something darkly saccharine, like molasses boba, on top. And I've never had anything so good in my life. As soon as it touched my mouth, I did the thing where

I closed my eyes and just let the flavor wash over my tongue. I savored the crumbling of the crust, the delectable creaminess of the custard, the never-endingness of the way the flavors combined. Dimly I was aware of the fairy worker taking my hand and moving me out of the way of the customers behind me. Dimly I was aware of music, of laughter, of a party, of maybe more food, and then—

"Hey, you all right?"

"Mmph." I opened my eyes. It felt like it had only been a second, but I had no idea where I was. It felt kind of like a basement, except where one of the walls should have been, the room opened onto a little terrace garden with bell-shaped flowers that hung from tall green stems, and in the distance, I could see the Mycotower and the New Astoria skyline. And beyond it, the sun against the sea.

"Wait." I sat up. "How is the sun—? What time is it?" Because the sea is to the east. Which meant it was dawn, and I definitely went into that coffee shop after dawn.

The guy who had woken me up was a young-looking minotaur. He wore a loose vest that barely counted as a shirt and his horns were just the right size to frame his unexpectedly handsome face.

"What?" I said, realizing he'd spoken and I'd completely blanked.

"I said, it's 6:30 in the morning. You partied all night. You were pretty awesome, actually. But you came in with fey, so I figured I'd keep an eye on you to make sure you were clear-headed when you woke up."

"Wow, that's...really nice, actually." Readers, I will not hide from you: I barely kept myself from crying. I had been in New Astoria for a week at this point, and this was the nicest thing anyone had said to or done for me.

And then his words registered.
All night?! I'd missed my interview!
"Fuck!"

May 9: 1,000 Daily Readers!!!!!

You guys! That's incredible! No tip today because I wanted to devote my whole post to saying how grateful I am to each and every one of you, and that I hope at least some of you are finding these tips and stories helpful. And, to those of you who commented asking if I was okay after my last post: Yes. Absolutely. Even though this city is way more... *more*, than I expected, it's still everything I wanted.

Here's to New Astoria, new journeys, and learning new things.

P.S. I got another interview. I'll let you know how it went in a future post.

May 10

Tip #6: ... I Don't Know

I'm not sure how to label this post. I'm not even sure if I have a tip. I haven't figured out yet what to think of my night.

I got mugged. That's the short of it.

Don't worry, I'm fine. Here's how it went down:

I'd just gotten off at my Chariot stop and was walking home. It was late. I was looking at my phone. I passed by an alley. And in the alley, there was a group of goblins.

Here's the first part of why I'm conflicted. We all have our internal biases. Our learned prejudices. Our "goblins will steal and eat your children" stories, or whatever your version is. Part of why I wanted to come to NA is so that I could get over all that human shit that I grew up with and try and figure out what's *real*. And so even though I utterly hated myself for it, the first thing I felt when I suddenly saw that group in the alley was fear.

And yet, in this case, fear was apparently the right response.

Because even though New Astoria isn't a death trap like my grandma warned me, that doesn't mean it's always *safe*.

"Hey, kid," one of the goblins said when he saw me. He wore a torn denim jacket and had the butt of a cigarette dangling from his lips. Its ember was the only light in the alley. "What're you lookin' so scared for?"

"I... I'm not—" The epitome of coherence, I know.

The goblin pushed off of the wall he was leaning on. His buddies came a little closer. "Whaaat?" he said. "I'm a goblin, not a ghost." He smiled. It did not put me at ease.

"Looks like this one's new on the block," another goblin said. "Maybe we should set down some rules."

"Yeah, I like that," denim-jacket said. He flicked his cigarette into a puddle. "Tell you what, kid. It's your first time. We'll let you off easy. Just empty your pockets, and you can be on your way."

"Wha-, I—"

"Did he fuckin' stutter? Hurry up!" One of the other goblins grabbed my wrist.

And without thinking, I punched him in the nose.

"AAAAHH, you little...!"

I don't know what would have happened then. I saw knives coming out, I saw teeth bared, and then:

"Hey!"

A voice called from the direction of the street. Another goblin, a woman, youngish, was glaring at the denim-jacket goblin. She started yelling at him in what I assume was Gobbish and he responded in kind. They screeched at each other for about 30 seconds, and then she grabbed my wrist and pulled me away, periodically looking over her shoulder to make sure the gang wasn't following us.

"Uh, thanks," I said when we were at least a block away.

"Don't mention it. Craft and his gang are just the local troublemakers. That was pretty stupid though, punching Garl. They're normally all bark and no bite, but you could have got yourself real hurt."

"Yeah," I said, "I wasn't thinking. It just kind of...happened."

She grunted, and then we were at my apartment building. She pulled out a key.

Apparently, she's one of my neighbors. She introduced herself as Nibs. "Short for Nibula." She said she's seen me a couple of times, which is how she recognized me on the street. "You look as un-local as a highland cow. You should work on that. Makes you seem like an easy target."

"Uh, thanks. I'll try."

And that was it. An almost-mugging. A rescue. And then I was back in my apartment, heart still pounding, adrenaline making my brain buzz.

So...yeah. Maybe my tip for this post is: People are complicated. And different. Some goblins are nice enough to rescue you from a fight. And some...

Well, not everyone's nice just because I don't want to assume ill of them.

It's a lesson that left me with a knot in my stomach.

May 12

Tip #7: Yes, Dragons are Banks. No, You Probably Won't See One

First things first: Your humble Guide has gotten a job! For secrecy, I won't say just where, but it deals with food, and I feel like I know about 5% as much as I need to, so, yeah, I'm terrified. But! Signing the paperwork led to a small adventure and the source of today's tip!

For those who come from places like I did, where jobs are just things that need getting done and wages are agreed on with a handshake, the bureaucracy of New Astoria can seem... arcane. And that's partially because it is. A consortium of very particular wizards (or did the lady say "lizards?") runs the Department of Labor, Service, and Wages, and they mandate that all paperwork be filed correctly, on time, and with the right people. So, before I could start working, I needed a bank number. And to get a bank number, I needed to go to the bank.

I went to the nearest branch of First Golden Bank and Lending. And I, like many of you, had heard the rumors. That all the banks in New Astoria were controlled by dragons, who lent out portions of their hoards in order to grow them with interest. Though I tried to hide it, what I expected to see when I walked through the heavy glass doors was a massive, six-story room containing a giant pile of gold and an equally giant dragon atop it.

Instead, I saw a long row of stalls, each one housing a teller, and that was it. The only sign of the dragon who owned the bank was a bronze medallion hanging on the wall that had the profile of a dragon etched on it.

It was, to put it bluntly, extremely disappointing.

The teller who helped me open my account—a thin, green-haired troll woman—must have seen me staring at the medallion because she looked over her shoulder and said, "Ah. Yeah, a lot of out-of-towners come in here hoping to see the Big Boss herself. But she spends most of her time in her office a few floors down, or flying off to meetings at the money-lenders guild." She stamped my forms with a big red "Approved," and carried on. "New Astoria's big, but even it's not quite big enough for dragons. It's easier for them to stay either in the tunnels below or the skies above. But keep your eyes out. Maybe you'll see one flying on their way to work."

I thanked her and took my paperwork. Outside, I looked up at the sky, then down at the ground.

TUNNELS?

This city gets cooler every day.

May 15
Tip #8: Visit the Mycotower!
Well, I'd been here for over two weeks. It was time to go. We've all seen it in movies. And on postcards and in schoolbooks. And we've all heard someone say, "It's nothing compared to seeing it in person."

Readers, let me add my voice to the chorus.

I knew what the Mycotower was *in premise*. A 300-foot, magically maintained, KING of a mushroom, containing a shopping complex, a restaurant with a long balcony just under the cap, so you can look out over the city and the sea, and even an art gallery! Admission to the tower is free (though they do limit the number and weight of the occupants, so I had to wait in line for half an hour), and I spent the whole day there! The shopping center has a few tiny food stands, most of which are mushroom-themed. I got strips of battered and fried shiitake with a little cheese crumbled over it, and wow. Well worth the $8.

Honestly, guys, I expected this to be a cynical tip. A "yeah it's cool but it's a total tourist trap; none of the locals go here" type of thing. But I am happily wrong. They're changing out the art exhibit in three weeks, so you can bet I'll be back.

Overall rating: 7 stars.

<u>May 18</u>
<u>Tip #9: All Those "Welcome, Come In" Signs? For Vampires!</u>

I had no idea! I thought it was just shop owners being nice or trying to get business. In a way it is, I suppose; don't want to have an entire demographic cut out of your customer base because you didn't invite them in. Because vampires *can't* enter a dwelling or shop without being invited in. So rather than hire someone to stand at the door and welcome everyone, most shops and bodegas just have those signs hanging at the door.

My boss told me all this when I forgot to hang our sign back up after cleaning the windows. He's a really nice guy, but he kinda leans into the leprechaun stereotype of maximizing profits.

But I learned something else from one of my coworkers: the signs are also a tacit political statement. It's pretty much assumed now that stores that *don't* have such a sign are anti-vampire. That might not always be the case of course, but since vamp folks have been getting more and more awareness lately, it's turned into one of those things where everyone either picks a side or ends up on the "anti" side through silence.

To all my vamp readers: I'm glad you're being welcomed into more and more places! Here's to that continuing.

May 20
Tip #10: I Gotta Recommend Galidan's

I'll get to that restaurant review in a second, but first: remember the minotaur guy from the fey food post? (I'll call him Hector here; privacy and whatnot.) Apparently, I'd given him my number at the party, and he reached out about meeting up again. I'd been meaning to try Galidan's, so I told him sure and that we could meet there.

I... think it might have been a date? I don't know. He didn't specify and I didn't ask, and we split the bill. The ambiguity helped, actually. I could tell myself I was just making new friends, and that let me tune out my mom's voice in my head saying, "No child of *mine* will go on a date with a minotaur!"

He wore a real shirt this time, which was disappointing, but he made me laugh a lot. He's lived in New Astoria all his life and gave me a ton of tips and recommendations. But he'd never been to Galidan's (said he'd hardly tried elvish food, actually), so we got to experience it for the first time together.

And It. Was. Delicious.

I didn't know what to expect. I didn't even know what elvish cuisine *was*, and the menu may as well have been written in elvish for all I understood what the dishes were. We basically just took our waiter's recommendations for the entire meal.

Galidan's is apparently forest elf cuisine (which is different than sea elf cuisine, I think), and so it was heavily plant and small animal-based, with a lot of small dishes meant to be shared. So, Hector and I started with a creamy, brothy snail soup; a salad of arugula, fried mushrooms, tree nuts, and crumbly cheese; and a board of dried fruits and thin wafer crackers drizzled in honey.

For our main course, I had a butternut squash ravioli that had butter, cinnamon, and a bit of spiciness in *just* the right combination. Hector, out of sheer curiosity, ordered the squirrel stew. I'd eaten rabbit once back home and thought it was tough and gamey, but the meat in this stew was as tender as sirloin and as juicy as the perfect fried chicken thigh. It came with bread to dip in the broth, which was thin and perfectly combined the flavors of the meat, tomatoes, thyme, and whatever else Galidan threw in there to make it magical.

Dessert was spiced, baked apples with caramelized custard in their core, and I think I may have cried they were so good.

Hector and I both left stuffed and not as much poorer as I expected given how good the food was. We agreed to meet up again sometime, maybe to try a different elvish place. I doubt any will be as good as Gal's, but you never know. Maybe all elvish restaurants are this good.

In summary: I gotta agree with the guy on the Char. 7 stars.

May 22
Tip #11: After a While, You Forget You're Different

Nibs told me today that I was finally starting to seem like a local, which was a nice validation of how I've been feeling. I've mastered the art of getting to the Char station exactly 2 minutes before it leaves (even though it's always running late), I've learned where to buy groceries without getting scalped for prices, and I'm even starting to be recognized by people in my neighborhood (most of them don't wave back when I say hi, but that's New Astorians for you).

On top of all that, another thing that's happened is that I don't notice my humanness so much anymore. Yeah there are still some purists in NA, but for the most part, no one cares if you're human or fey or chimeric or whatever. And that means I don't really have to think about it either. I don't have to worry if people will judge me or fear me because of things other humans did, or do, or say. I can just be me.

But that's sort of created a new dilemma. With everyone being so unique, uniqueness feels less remarkable. If enough parts get washed out in the melting pot, what does being "me" even mean?

May 26
Tip #12: Sportsball!
Sorry for the delay lately. Work is getting busier, and I'm starting to make friends with my coworkers. In fact, two of them invited me to go with them to a Nixies game!

I've never been a big sports person myself, but my brother is a huge hurling fan so I've seen my fair share of games just from him having them on. This was my first in-person game, though, as well as my first time visiting Argent Stadium. The place is *huge*, with different seat sizes for different folk, level upon level of merchandise stores and concession stands, and everyone is just so excited to cheer on the team! The Nixies were playing the Trollocks, so everyone was extra invested because I guess there's a big rivalry there.

My work friends got decent seats about one-third down the pitch from the Nixies' side. We were too high up to see anyone's numbers, but that didn't stop me from paying five bucks for a program to try and figure out who everyone was.

Things I learned:

- Our star player is a sea elf who grew up in a town just down the river from my hometown.

- Half of the Trollocks team really is made up of trolls.

- Hurling was a game invented when the first fey folk and humans met each other. Apparently, the sport was a better way of settling disputes than killing each other.

The game was great, we won, and I would say going at least once is definitely worth it if you can afford it.

The thing I loved most about it? All differences really do get left by the wayside. For two glorious hours of cheering and sports food, everyone in that stadium is a New Astorian, and nothing else matters.

May 30

Tip #13: New Astorians Are Fiercely Protective of Their Identities, But Don't Assume You Know What Those Are

It's a well-worn stereotype: New Astorians are extremely proud of being from New Astoria (even while they complain about it constantly). There's definitely some truth to that, but it goes deeper than just city pride. While for many the city that they call home is a deeply important part of their identity, it's only one part of their identity.

Yesterday I was sitting next to a dryad on the Char. I was wondering where she was going, whether she was from the city, and then, like with the elf, she caught me looking and cocked an eyebrow.

"This is the fastest way to travel to a place without trees," she said, as if answering my unasked question. Was she smirking? I couldn't tell.

"Oh, sorry, I didn't mean—"

"It's all right. We don't leave the gardens very much."

"You're from here then? Your tree is in one of the city gardens?"

"It was."

I waited for her to go on, but when she didn't, curiosity got the better of me and I said, "Was? Did it...get cut down?"

She shook her head, and it sounded like leaves being tussled by the wind. "No, it's still there. But the garden I'm from is...reclusive. The dryad community is deeply traditional. We hardly ever interact with other people. When we do, it's frowned upon, and we're never allowed to spend the night away from our trees."

"Allowed?" I said. "I thought going back to your tree was necessary for dryads. To live, or something."

She smiled. "That's a myth that came from the fact that we so rarely *don't* go back to our trees."

We were quiet for a bit while the Chariot clacked along its rails. Then I said, "Where do you live now, if not in your tree?"

"There's a place in the Iron Garden—far north of the city, two stops before the end of the line—that's an apartment complex for...transitory...folks like myself. And artists. I'm in charge of the gardens; I get a thousand plants now, instead of just one."

"Oh," I said, "I thought, what with the leaving your tree and what you said about your people, you were done with plants."

She laughed. "Not at all. I'm still a dryad. I always will be. I'm just...a different kind."

I had to get off then to switch lines, but before I did, she told me to come by the apartment sometime if I ever wanted to see her garden. Then for the rest of my Char ride home, I thought about what she'd said.

Her story was a lot like mine. She'd left a stifling community to seek a new purpose on her own. But she seemed so sure of herself, whereas I still feel like I hardly know what I'm doing. And, while she seemed proud of who she was, I realized that, at times (okay, a *lot* of times), I was ashamed even to be a human. That was part of what upset my parents about my wanting to move here. "You should feel proud to be a human," they'd said.

But I *wasn't*. So, I came here. To New Astoria, where I had *hoped* no one would see me as human. Would instead see me as just another New Astorian. And so what the dryad said really struck deep. It got me thinking. I *am* a human. I never won't be.

And so, maybe, instead of trying *not* to be a human because I'm ashamed of it, I can be...a different kind of human. A human who respects people who aren't like me. Who works hard to make the world a better place. Maybe...maybe I can be proud of that. Of being a different kind of human.

My kind of human.

Colten Fisher is a writer and narrative designer in Minneapolis, Minnesota. He likes gardening and exploring all good restaurants in the Twin Cities, as well as traveling to his friends and family across the country.

He's an avid D&D player and both runs and plays in several campaigns. After all, little is better for the author who writes for an audience than the instant gratification of a D&D table. Colten also burns some of his free time playing video games, and his favorites are the ones with narratives that leave you thinking about them for months after you've reached the end. And when it comes to books, he's a huge lover of fantasy—if it has dragons or gods in it, he'll probably like it—and more examples of his writing can be found on his website at coltenfisher.com

THE TIGER'S GIFT

By G.K. White

WATER FLOWED OUT OF the tilted jug onto Reshe's hands, warm and constant. It poured over her skin before dripping into the stone basin and sinking into the drain. She rubbed her palms together slowly, enjoying the heat.

She'd gotten into the second stage of selection. Only ten girls left.

Chills ran up her back.

She traced the rough patches of the hide-like skin that covered her arm and ran a hand through her short white hair.

A flash of color drew her gaze to the mirror. Her blood-red eyes shone in the low-lit chamber. the deep purple of her gown clashed with her chalk-white, pockmarked skin. Her natural armor. Her blessing.

Her hands glistened. Clean, but for how long?

"Lady?" A scratchy female voice called from the other side of the door. "Lady? Are you presentable?"

Oh, crap. She grabbed the lock of black hair on the edge of the sink and scrambled for her magic.

Be still.

The White Tiger's warm presence descended on her.

She stilled. Then she closed her eyes and pictured a raven. Its soft, dark feathers grew into elongated strands, flowing downward over peach-colored shoulders. She molded the warmth in her chest and reached out with it toward the picture like a hand. Grabbed hold of the picture. Made it real.

A warm feeling filled her chest. Love, the Tiger, and... Sadness.

No, ignore that.

She squeezed the river of magic inside her, lessening it to a drop. Two small drips that bloomed white, one in each eye. They did that uncomfortable roll in her head like they were reversing. Eventually, the hum of her magic, still warm and sad, faded. She gave her head a shake. Waves of raven-colored hair fell over her shoulders. It was warm against her skin. Good.

"Lady Reshe?"

She opened her eyes. Her skin was a rosy shade of peach. "Come in."

The door opened and an old woman stepped inside. She wore a simple brown tunic and a dark shawl that wrapped around part of her face. "Is the dressing room to your liking, Lady?"

Reshe forced a smile onto the new face her magic had supplied her. The palace's dressing room was beautiful, but it didn't make up for being taken off the street two years before along with every other eligible woman in the city. The palace was a cage no matter how pretty. But, when the king wanted a new queen from the land he'd just conquered...

Her thoughts drifted.

Two figures with half-white skin popped into her mind. One held her. The other ran a hand through her short white hair.

Pain blossomed behind her ribs. She shook the memory loose, letting it fall back into the hole she'd dug for it.

Focus on the servant, Reshe. She throttled her mind into submission. "The palace is wonderful. The king is very generous."

The old woman stiffened and then nodded, causing her shawl to shift off her face slightly. "It is as you say, Lady."

Reshe caught a flash of white skin. "Are you half-blessed?"

The old woman's head snapped up, and her hands gripped her shawl.

"Sorry, I was just—"

The old woman pulled the cloth back, revealing patches of rough, white skin. "It is fine, Lady. My name is Tella. And I am, as you say, half-blessed. Do not be scared."

Reshe looked closely at the woman. She was from Gotra, like herself. She had sharp features, and the downturn of her mouth suggested a dour edge to her personality. She probably would've been considered quite attractive when she was young, if not for discoloration of the left side of her face. Blessed by the Tiger's bloodline but not his magic. Half-blessed.

"I'm not scared, Tella." Reshe tapped her hand against her thigh. She shouldn't be questioning the king's servants. Drawing attention to herself. "I'm just…"

The old woman raised an eyebrow. "We have only a short time before…" She wrung her hands together. "Your turn."

Reshe swallowed. Her turn with the monster had come.

She clenched her hand to stop reaching toward her thigh. Toward the knife strapped there.

The guards searched them every three days, but when you could look like anyone given a bit of time and a lock of hair, well...

She shoved her nervousness to the back of her mind and did her best not to sound strained. "How wonderful, Tella."

The old woman turned to the door, stopped, and looked back at her.

One might've called the look suspicious.

"Yes, well. Come with me, Lady Reshe."

Reshe checked her reflection in the mirror. A woman with peach-colored skin, long black hair, and eyes the color of copper stared back. "Very well."

The old woman led her out of the room and into the lavish palace hall.

Anything not made of stone in the palace was made of gold. It ringed every pillar, doorway, and pot. The large corridors were painted with sprawling mosaics depicting the king's conquests.

"So..." the old woman glanced back at Reshe over her shoulder. "Why did you want to get ready by yourself? Most of the girls have stuck together."

Reshe gritted her teeth. Because of her condition, she'd chosen to prepare separately. Separate, story of her life since her parents had died. "I like my privacy."

"Hmmm, and where were you living before the palace?"

Before? Before the king banished his wife? Before he'd conquered all of Gotra for no reason at all? She tapped her freshly washed nails against her thigh and pushed down the burning sensation in her gut, lest it rise and find purchase on her tongue. "With my—" A flash of spears. Red mist. Screams. "Family."

"Mmhm." The old woman nodded. "Me too. My husband died in the invasion, so I had to come here."

Tell her.

She ignored the voice, her magic, the Tiger inside urging connection. Tella might want to share, but Reshe was better off alone. Besides, sharing might ease the fire in her gut. and she needed that to make things right.

"Here we are."

Without her notice, they had arrived at a large wooden door. A meshwork of gold and silver wove an intricate pattern across the frame.

This was not the door to the king's throne room. It was much too small.

Smile, Resh. Just smile. She widened her mouth in what she hoped was a sincere way. "Where are we?"

"The king's bed chambers." The old woman shifted her weight, looking at the floor. The disgust was clear on her face. "Where you will see him."

Reshe's heart spasmed, a strange gallop across her chest. Chills ran down her head into her arms like she'd just dove into cold water. "In his bed chamber?"

The old woman opened her mouth then closed it.

"Where are the other girls? The others he picked."

"They...the king...he's been seeing each alone."

Tiger save her. She would've noticed this if she'd been with the others. The squirming feeling in her chest multiplied. Alone with the king. Good. Great. Her hand shook against her thigh. Tiger's heart, why was she so nervous?

"They aren't seen again. I think he..." The old woman's frail voice was soft but filled with hate. "He's a monster."

The burning returned. The heat traveled up to her chest. Memories of screams and blood and soldiers drove it.

Clang.

The old woman ran back down the hall at the sound of the gong.

Reshe paid her no mind. Fire filled her whole body.

She had a king to kill.

THE DOOR TO THE bedroom swung open.

A tall man wearing a black tunic and sword stood just inside. "Raise your arms, lady."

A guard. A search. This was bad. "We were searched coming into the palace, and have been searched every three days."

The guard's hand rested on his sword. "Raise your arms, Lady."

Slowly, she raised her arms.

He patted her down, clumsily.

She stiffened as he reached around her lower thighs. Any higher and— "Do you plan to despoil me before the king? Should I strip as well?"

"No." The guard flushed.

A deep voice called out from within the room. "That is enough, Daro."

Her hands shook.

The guard hastily stepped passed her into the hallway, holding the door open. "You may pass."

The voice rang out again. "Come."

She walked inside.

The guard shut the door behind her.

Dozens of candles on a few small tables lit the room. The far side lay in darkness, but the edge of a bed frame was just visible. She shivered. Fear crept up from her gut into that empty cavity in her chest.

The scent of sweet lavender washed over her. She closed her eyes and breathed in. Her heart ceased its squirming.

Something soft brushed her foot. She opened her eyes. Sheep furs blanketed the floor. Shelves full of scrolls dominated the right wall. Two intricately carved stone chairs and a small table had been set just in front of them. A golden plate filled with various cooked meats rested on the table. Just beside it was a similarly furnished bowl filled with plums, grapes, and peaches.

The same deep voice spoke from her left. "Sit."

She did her best not to jump.

He had been so quiet.

She sat in the chair closest to the wall. The fur on top of the stone was soft and warm. She hadn't realized how cold she'd gotten in the hallway.

The man who had spoken sat bent over a table on the left side of the room. A clay tablet and a few scrolls lay open on the marble before him. He stared at the scrolls for a while, flipping between them quickly. The more he read, the less time he spent on each scroll, and the more his shoulders sagged.

He was tall with long black hair tied into a bun and a goatee. Gold trimmed the outside edge of the purple robe that hung from his broad frame. But what drew her attention was his skin. It was the color of desert sand.

She waited for him to speak, a tradition in the Serpan Empire.

He refilled his glass of wine, emptying the wineskin resting on his desk, and then studied on in silence.

She frowned. After a long while, she cleared her throat. Nothing.

The little spark began to burn inside her. "Sire—"

"Silence."

The word practically slapped her. The spark in her chest transformed into a roaring flame. How dare he? She had been getting splattered with spices and oils every day for twelve months just so her skin would have a natural aroma. All to please him. She shook her head. "Sire, I—"

He rose to his feet slowly. "You will be quiet."

He hadn't yelled, but the command rang in her ears. Heat rose to her face. Her chest heaved as she breathed heavily through her nose. Her hands fell to her sides, shaking. One of them bumped something beneath her dress. Her dagger. No servants or guards.

She was alone with the king.

She rose from her chair, heart hammering in her chest.

The king sat back down at his table, his head hanging. Then he sighed, pushed a few papers aside, and grabbed another wineskin that lay on the floor beside the table.

She slipped a hand through the secret slit in the cloth at her waist and fingered the leather-wrapped handle of her dagger.

Clang.

She jumped back as the door to the room swung inward.

The tall guard, Daro, entered and bowed to the king. "Sire, Magistrate Hecatet is here."

Reshe held still, her heartbeat drowning out all other noise save the mantra in her head. Send them away. Send them away.

The king stood with his wineskin still in hand. "Show him in."

Curse him.

A man in a fine green tunic swept into the room and knelt before the king. His dirty-blonde hair rested delicately across his wide shoulders. Though he knelt, he was so tall his head was nearly at the king's chest.

"Sire, you called for me," he said, with a smoothness that was at odds with his size.

The king gathered up the scrolls at his desk. "Yes, you may take these back."

"They confirmed what I have told you didn't they, my king? The growing discontentment of the people."

Reshe bristled. Of course, the people were unhappy. No one enjoyed being conquered. Before she realized it, the two men had stopped talking and were staring at her.

Unease spread like wildfire inside her. She gripped the handle of her dagger before realizing how odd she must look with a hand partway in her dress.

Hecatet raised an eyebrow from his position on the ground. "Perhaps, the lady is so nervous she didn't hear my question."

The words were almost lyrical. If she weren't having a heart attack, the melody might have been nice. She smiled. "Ah, yes, the lady misheard."

Hecatet nodded.

The king spoke from beside him in his deep timbre and a tone of indifference. "Have you been searched?"

She stilled. This was not good. "Of course, sire. The servants search me every three days and the guard did as I came into the room."

Hecatet ran a large hand through a wave of his hair. "The servants are useless at it, and the tall one is new. With the rumors of an assassination attempt, one can't be too—"

The king sighed. "Do as you wish, Hecatet. Just be quick about it."

Hecatet bowed his mountainous body low once more to the king and stood. He stalked toward her, practically gliding across the furs.

A chill stole over her. She turned to hide pulling her hand from within her dress. But then, Hecatet's massive hands were on her.

He started with the golden pins in her hair, then moved on to her neck, then each limb. His hands glided over her right thigh and nudged the hilt of the dagger.

Every muscle in her body stiffened. Her fingers clenched into a fist against her will.

Hecatet frowned and moved his hands over the area again.

The hilt pressed into her thigh as he felt around its edges. She readied herself to pull the blade. The king had turned his back to her, reading the clay tablet that lay on his worktable. If she was fast enough...

A large hand enclosed her right wrist. It was over.

The large man deftly reached beneath the outside of her dress and pulled the dagger from its sheath.

"Well?" the king said from his seat on the other side of the room without lifting his head. "Is it safe?"

A hundred thoughts flashed through her mind. They'd behead her. One of the court guards would use a saber. At least there was no one to miss her.

Hecatet released her hand. "Perfectly safe, sire. I apologize for my caution."

Reshe stared blankly at the large man.

He smiled at her like they'd shared a secret.

"You may go, Hecatet," the king said as he sank into his chair. "You give the orders to the generals. Do what you feel you must to make sure the people's fears are eased. I'm too tired to deal with it."

"Yes, sire. I will take care of it." Hecatet stuffed her dagger inside his tunic and leaned in next to her. "You are a bold one, but I need you to behave. If the king dies tonight...I will find you."

Reshe shivered.

With a chuckle, he swept out of the room as quickly as he had entered. The door slammed shut behind him. She was left alone with the king yet again, but this time without a weapon.

"NOW, THEN," THE KING said, coming to sit in the chair opposite the one she'd chosen by the shelves. "Sit. I'd like to talk."

She sat back down. Black spots dotted her vision. She released the breath she'd been holding. The spots faded.

The king held up two burnished cups, one of which he offered to her.

She took it and drank. The liquid was cold with a sharp tang. Wine. She drained the cup and wiped the sweat off her forehead with her sleeve. Someone had ripped open a crack in her chest, and all her fears poured out. Energy coursed through her, making her limbs shake.

Hecatet knew she'd tried to kill the king. How long would he hold his tongue? Yet, he'd left them alone. Should she try without the knife? Would she be able to overpower the king? What of her escape? The man would know it was her. She could switch forms. Maybe become a servant. Maybe—

Be still.

The Tiger's voice was soft and loving. His presence descended like a gentle rain putting out the fires in her mind.

She took a deep breath. Calm down, girl. Just relax and talk for a while. Wait for your moment. She placed the cup back on the table. "What would you like to discuss, sire?"

The king plucked a red grape from the bowl and pressed it between his fingers. His gaze seemed distant. "What is your name?"

She rested her hands together in her lap and straightened her posture. If she wanted to stay in his presence, she had to maintain his interest. Enthrall him. "My name is Reshe, sire."

He sighed. "Ask me a question, Reshe."

She blinked. "What kind of questio—"

"Think for yourself, Reshe," the king said flatly, pouring himself more wine. "I have no desire to do it for you."

She stiffened. Fine, she'd give him a question. "What are you doing here?"

The desert-colored skin at the corners of his eyes scrunched as he squinted, and he sat up straight. "What is your meaning?"

For the first time since she'd entered, his focus was on her. Something in her was greatly satisfied by the surprised look on his face. But the fire that had disappeared when her dagger was taken had found its way back, and it was in full control of her tongue. "Why are you in Gotra? Why did you take this province? A place that never threatened Serpa or gave any provocation. Why did you conquer a peaceful neighboring province? What are you doing here, king?"

The king's eyes widened.

Tiger take her. She'd practically yelled at him. The words had gotten away from her so quickly. According to her father, stating the truth as she saw it was her gift and curse.

"Well," the king said in his deep way. "That is a question." He raised his cup to his lips and gulped his wine. He set it back down hard. "Gotra was controlled by Libania. A country as chaotic and volatile as any that exists. *They* did threaten my people, and now they belong to the Serpan Empire. As does Gotra. So, there is peace."

Images flashed through her mind. Men with spears and horrified faces. Blood, pain, and tears followed. Peace at the cost of violence, of war. She clamped her teeth together to keep her tongue from spewing the swirling hatred boiling in her gut.

The king sat back. "Now, I ask a question. Have you heard of the curse of Gotra?"

A burst of ice in her veins froze the vitriol working its way up her throat. Her tongue teetered between self-preservation and a desire to scream her anguish at the man's face.

The king sagged slightly in his chair. "I speak of a race. 'The Ka,' they are called by the locals. Skin half-white with bumps and whitened hair. Do you know?"

The ice cracked as he spoke the name of her race. He couldn't know what she was. He'd just heard the rumors. "Yes, I know of them."

He grunted. "What being cursed them so?"

She rolled her eyes. All the misconceptions. "They are not cursed. They are blessed with the bloodline of the White Tiger. A being as fierce in his love of his children as he is in the destruction of his enemies."

"A powerful creature?"

"The Tiger is both terrifying and beautiful to behold."

"And they follow this Tiger without question? Obey him above all else?"

"Some of them, yes, to their dying breath."

"Hmmm." The king stroked his goatee, shaking his head. "I am told they have monsters among them. Evil creatures that can steal your face and wear it as their own. Is such a thing real?"

She focused all her energy on not reacting. Measured and slow words. Don't deny. Don't confirm. "There are myths of such things."

"Do you believe them?"

An image of the king cowering in his room, scared of the big bad Ka sorcerers, floated into her mind. A sickly-sweet sensation warmed the fire in her heart. "Oh yes. His strongest people are blessed not only with his blood but magic as well. They are the Ka's protectors."

"Mmh." The king nodded and turned his gaze on her. "You have beautiful eyes, Reshe. Not unlike Andorra's."

"Your banished queen?"

His lips pulled tight, and his brow furrowed. Every feature displayed pain. Then the shine came to his eyes. The heat. He jumped to his feet and jabbed a finger toward the door. "Your rooms are across the hall. The guards will show you."

As soon as the word "guards" left his mouth, two men entered the room from the hallway. One was Daro, the one tall guard who'd searched her. The other was a short, stocky man wearing a white sash.

The king waved a dismissive hand. "Agba, Daro, take her to her room."

Before she could do anything, the guards shuffled her out of the king's bedroom, across the hallway, and through a small wooden door painted with red circles. They slammed it shut behind her.

She shook herself, catching her breath. The bedroom was much smaller but similarly decorated to the king's, with furs, gold trappings, and lit candles. She sat down on the bed. Soft white cloth hung from the frame. Her heart slowly returned to its normal rhythm. A cold feeling sank into her stomach like a stone. She'd missed her chance. She dropped her head into her hands. Curse her for a fool.

The door to her room swung open, and a large, dirty-blonde head peeked through. Hecatet's smile was a gruesome, crooked thing.

"Hello, girl."

Unsure of what to do, she stayed perfectly still. "What do you want?"

The broad-shouldered man widened his hands. "There will be a feast tomorrow, a celebration banquet."

She rubbed her eyes, suddenly tired. Feasts were not uncommon, and girls from the king's chosen were occasionally invited. But she couldn't recall being told about a feast. "What are we celebrating?"

"Why, you, of course. You've been chosen."

She shook her head, trying to make sense of his words. This was a sick joke or some kind of power play. Or was this just part of a game she didn't understand? "Chosen for what?"

"To be the next queen. The king just gave the decree. He'll see no other girl."

She waited for the smile on his face to turn into a laugh. It didn't. "The king wants me as his queen?"

"Yes, he does." Hecatet's smile grew wider, baring all his teeth. He pulled her knife out of his tunic. "And tomorrow, you, my queen, will do exactly as I say."

A cold sliver of dread crept up her spine.

Hecatet tapped the knife against the gold frame of the door as he exited. "Welcome to the palace, Queen Reshe."

The door shut with a soft thump as the wood hit stone.

What had she gotten herself into?

THE FOOD FOR THE feast took all day to prepare. She'd kept to her room, Hecatet's words echoing in her ears. But by the sheer amount of decoration, servants must have been preparing for months for the new queen to be chosen. Several dozen low tables and fur seats had been laid out in the many large halls of the palace. The perfect place to host several hundred people.

Getting lost in the sea of guests out there would've been wonderful. Instead, she dined in the throne room. It was decadent beyond anything she had seen. Large golden double doors barred the entrance. Red velvet and inky gold decorated every surface. The floor was a painted mosaic depicting the king leading his great army across the land. Marble pillars ran around the edge of the room. Each bore a carved image of the king that sat at its top. But all of it was put to shame by the large golden chair on a red velvet-covered dais that dominated the back wall.

The artists and decorators must have worked endlessly to get it all done in the four years since Gotra was conquered. Probably against their will.

"More wine, lady?" Tella stood behind her, holding a ladle over her wine jar. "It is quite strong."

She smiled. Having the half-blessed old woman nearby comforted her. At least the king had allowed her to pick her handmaiden. "I'm fine, thank you."

Tella wasn't the only servant present. Several stood around the large stone table that had been set in the middle of the room. Some held trays full of food of every kind. Some stood over wine jars.

All around the table sat eunuchs, satraps, royal inquirers, and the distinguished ladies of the king's court. Fifty or so people in all. All very important, yet she sat in a fur-topped marble chair in the middle of the table. A place of honor with a wonderful view of the monster.

The king sat at a small ornate table on the raised dais, positioned to be directly in front of his throne.

She hadn't seen him since the night before. He'd spent the day in his room and saw no one but Hecatet.

The feast had just started, and the king was already on his second cup of wine. He had eaten little. He'd looked at her several times but had so far been swarmed by inquirers demanding his attention. Even in his high-backed chair, his shoulders sagged as the feast progressed.

The large golden doors burst open. Six of the king's courtiers strode through. Their long blue robes fluttered around them, and they wore tall, pointed caps of different colors. A booming laugh echoed from behind them. They parted, and Hecatet shoved his way among them, shaking hands with each man. He smiled and joked as he did so. Many laughed as he talked.

Hecatet caught Reshe's gaze from across the room and walked her way.

She sat straight in her chair. What did he want? She dug her nails into her leg. Hecatet smoothly grabbed a cup of wine out of a servant's hand and took the seat beside her. The dignitary sitting there scrambled out of his way, falling to the ground. Hecatet didn't even look down.

"Queen Reshe, so good to see you again."

Even sitting he towered over her. It was like looking up at a mountain. Then suddenly, the mountain was out of his chair and kneeling. The profound silence struck her. Every person in the room had gone quiet. Hecatet was no longer staring at her but over her shoulder. She turned.

"Hello, Queen Reshe," the king said in his rumbling tone. He seemed brighter somehow than he had looked sitting on the dais. "Come sit with me for a moment."

Her heart pounded in her ears, drowning out the silence of the room. The king always stayed on the dais during feasts. Courtiers and officials were invited by a servant to join him, never by the king himself.

She splayed her hands over her green satin dress, stilling the small jitter in her leg. "I'd be delighted."

Hecatet smiled. A fake thing plastered on his face. "I'll escort her, sire."

The king hummed in affirmation, a pleasant noise for a monster to make, and then walked back to his throne.

Both she and Hecatet rose. He grabbed her arm rather firmly. She swallowed her repulsion at the touch of his hand as he led her around the stone table and toward the dais where the king was retaking his seat.

Hecatet whispered in her ear. "He'll ask if this place is dangerous. Tell him Gotran is not safe for him, and I'll forget the blade I found between your legs."

Her hands itched. She fought the compulsion to grab the nearest eating utensil and stab him in the face. *Play along, Resh. Just play along. Tell the king that the Gotrans are dangerous.* If she was any example, it wasn't even a lie. But what did Hecatet gain from—

He released her arm as a servant pulled out a stool at the small table for him. She sat in the chair directly across from the king. Hecatet sat between them.

The king stared. His eyes were bright, and he was sitting up and forward in his chair, more alert than he'd seemed the entire feast. "Queen Reshe."

She bowed her head slightly. "Sire."

The king spread his hands. "What do you do for enjoyment?"

Surprised, she laughed. Oh, the irony. Plotting his murder. That's what she did for enjoyment.

The king's mouth pulled up at the edges in a soft smile that touched his eyes. She'd never seen him smile. It was a nice smile, innocent. If only it belonged to someone decent.

"Sorry, Sire. Your question took me off guard."

The king held his hand in the air. "Don't apologize. You have a beautiful laugh."

A sincere warmth filled her. Her voice was one of the few things about herself that she couldn't change with magic. The only real thing about her. "Uh, thank you. And I mostly spend my time planning...events."

To her left, Hecatet's face soured.

She squeezed her hand into a fist in her lap. The warmth in her face faded, replaced by a nagging feeling at the back of her neck that she was quickly learning to associate with Hecatet.

He coughed and eyed the king.

The king gave him an annoyed look. Then he put down his wine cup and steepled his fingers.

"Reshe." He hummed in his deep tone. "Last night, you said there are things here that are dangerous, monsters."

She nodded slowly.

"You are from here. Do you believe this place is too dangerous for us to stay? Are there some among the people likely to try and take back the city?"

She glanced at Hecatet.

His face was stone with cold eyes and a fierce gaze. What did he gain by this? There must be more—but it didn't matter. Spears. Bloody spears had popped into her mind. Her mother's screams rang in her ears, gnawing at her sanity.

Give Hecatet whatever he wants. Then bring justice.

"Many Gotrans lost loved ones in your conquest of Libania. To us, you are an invader, a hostile false ruler. Yes, this place is dangerous for you. You should leave and take your court with you...sire."

"Mmh," the king hunched over the table. His hand found his wine cup again.

An impatient huff came from Hecatet. "There have already been reports of violence, sire. They will not obey. They are a threat to your reign, which means they are a threat to every citizen of the Serpan Empire."

The king nodded.

A smile spread across Hecatet's face. "We should start immediately. The courtiers—"

The king waved his hand in surrender. "You deal with them." He pulled a golden ring from his forefinger and placed it into Hecatet's hands. "Do what you feel is necessary to protect the kingdom."

Hecatet's eyes lit with satisfaction as his hand closed over the ring. "Thank you, sire."

He rose from the table and left, leaving Reshe alone with the king.

Normally, she'd have questions about their cold-blooded exchange. But fury had taken over. She stayed quiet and watched the king's guards instead. Agba, the white-sashed guard, was sneaking drinks to Daro, the tall one, who was getting quite drunk.

She kept her eye on Agba's dark brown hair, a plan forming in her mind.

The king breathed in deeply and rubbed his eyes. "Thank you, Queen Reshe. For your honesty."

The words just slipped out. "Regret invading a peaceful province now, my King?"

The king's eyes were dead. "I am sworn to protect the innocents. How long should I wait to take up my sword? How many children of Serpa must die?"

A scathing reply formed in her mind, but the deep sadness in his eyes muted it. Without the heat in her gut to guide her, she stumbled over her words. "There are innocents everywhere, king."

He sagged back into his chair. A servant refilled his cup with wine. "You are dismissed, Queen Reshe."

She stood, gave the king a short bow, and left, happy to get away. He kept saying things...acting...differently than she expected. It disarmed her rage. And she wasn't anything without that.

She took a deep breath and focused on the thought she'd had before the king had spoken. Hecatet had all he wanted. So, if she wanted to kill the king, it had to be that night.

She looked to the dais. The king was drinking. And Agba was still getting Daro drunk.

Beards itched something fierce. Not to mention everything going on below her belt.

She could barely walk twenty paces without scratching. How did men get anything done?

A few well-placed words to Tella were all it had taken to spark a drunken brawl between two royal messengers. Once the chaos spread to everyone, Reshe had plucked a lock of Agba's hair while he was wrestling a courtier to the ground.

After the king retired for the night, she found a quiet spot to transform and headed to his bedroom. Only Daro guarded the king's door, and he was slumped against the wall. He barely looked at her as she strode past and grabbed the door handle. It wasn't even locked. She smiled at her luck and entered. Thank the heavens for wine and fools.

The room was dark, but the king's figure was outlined. He lay on his bed in the dim light of a single candle.

Her heart sped up. Heat boiled from the pit in her stomach. Slowly, she let her magic fade. Her skin loosened, becoming baggy, then twisted inward on itself not unlike swirling water. Her manly, short brown hair became black, long, and flowing.

She probably should've stayed a guard, but this form felt good. The anger, the rage was more real in this body, an avenging angel taking its countenance from the old queen. Besides—her hands clenched—she wanted him to know it was her.

She crept toward the bed. Something glinted in the light. A dagger lay beside the candle. Her dagger. The one Hecatet had taken from her.

She grinned and picked it up. Gently, like a lover, she rolled the king to his back. Soft sighs left his full lips as she positioned the dagger over his heart. He yawned. The fruity scent of wine filled the space between them. One of his arms rolled to the side. He had a sealed scroll clasped in one hand.

Be Still

"No." She shook her head. "No, this is my chance to make things right."

The Tiger wouldn't take this from her. No one would.

"Reshe?"

Her heart seized. The king stared at her with drooping bloodshot eyes. Panic took over. She sat on top of him, pinning his arms with her body. She slid the knife up his chest and pressed the blade against his throat. "Do not call out."

He stiffened against the cold steel, but the relief in his eyes surprised her.

Hatred burned in her limbs so hot that they trembled. Anger she could understand, but he looked... The king's voice was without tremor. "So, you are the one helping the Ka. How many in the palace will die tonight?"

She ignored him. "Be quiet."

He lay still, but the downturn of his mouth and his bent brows said volumes.

"Don't you dare pity me, king."

Nagging thoughts scurried around the edge of her consciousness. Something was wrong. Only one sleeping guard, her dagger by his bed, the unlocked door. Assassinating a king shouldn't be this easy. She kept her blade against his throat. "What do you mean I am the one?"

The king tilted his head away from the blade. "Hecatet has feared an uprising from a sect of Gotran revolutionists, the Ka." The king's gaze drifted down to her dagger. "He found the blade in the palace, one of their make and proof of a spy. It's why I gave him my sigil, so he could craft a decree."

The words were like a shadowy hand crawling up her back. She didn't want to know, but she had to. "What decree?"

The king carefully gestured with his head to the scroll in his hand.

She grabbed it, breached the seal with her finger, and held the open scroll up to the light. It was hard to make out every word, but four stood out. *Kill all the cursed.* The Ka.

Hecatet had sealed her people's fate.

A sinking feeling pulled her back to herself. She stared at the king. "What would happen if I killed you now?"

The king's dark blue eyes held so much pain. "I have no heirs. The royal courtiers would be forced to vote for a new king."

Hecatet at the feast, shaking hands and laughing with the courtiers. The picture was a burning coal in her memory.

Kill the king, then blame it on the people you don't like. Petty and power-hungry.

But she would live. She could change into anything. Be anyone. Only the half-blessed would be killed by the decree. Their lives were worth her parents' peace—

The pain pierced her heart. She had stood there. Done nothing while they died. There was only one way to atone—

Let it go.

Bloody spears and her mother's screams battled the Tiger's voice in her head. The fire of rage versus the warmth of his presence. It was tearing her apart.

The king breathed deeply, lifting her slightly, distracting her. There was pain in the scrunch of his nose and the tilt of his head. The pain she'd been seeing in him and finally recognized. Grief.

They asked the question together. "Who have you lost?"

She answered before he could before the pain strangled the words in her throat. "My parents. In the invasion."

"I'm so sorry. They were soldiers?"

She shook her head, trying to keep the tears at bay. "Farmers. Slaughtered in their house."

His brows furrowed at that.

Her hand still held the knife, but her grip was looser, less certain. "And you?"

"A boy. My boy." His voice cracked, and a tear rolled down his cheek. "He liked to sleep on my chest. There had been threats, but I didn't think...he took the blade meant for me."

"Is that why...with Queen Andorra?"

"I lost myself in grief, and she in bitterness. When it became unbearable, I banished her."

Reshe's hands shook. The last vestiges of anger sparked in her gut. "Why torture each other? Why stay together so long?"

She knew before he spoke. The answer was written on her heart, hidden by her anger.

"I didn't want to be alone."

Her heart felt heavy as the anger fled. She didn't want to kill him. She just wanted her parents back.

Tears flowed freely down her cheeks. Her mind was exhausted from going in circles. Every limb in her body was a sack of bricks. She slumped onto the bed beside the king. He didn't reach for the dagger nor call for his guards.

She wouldn't have cared if he did.

S HE COULDN'T REMEMBER THE last time she slept through the night.

When she woke, the king was putting on his regalia beside the bed. The decree was in his hands.

In the light of morning, things were clear. Hecatet had used her anger the same way he'd been using the King's grief for years. She'd nearly given him the throne and gotten her people killed.

He had to be stopped.

There was no anger in the thought. Just a sense of purpose. A desire to protect, but she'd need the king. And something had changed between them last night.

She took a chance. "Sire, I am not a spy for the Ka."

He nodded. "I believe you, Reshe. But that doesn't make them innocent."

Okay, different tack. "Yes, it's just…it was too easy to get in here last night, and I didn't ask anyone for help."

His look hardened. "You are saying someone else in the palace perhaps wanted you to…"

Soft touch, Reshe. "Maybe."

The sadness touched his eyes again, and he gripped the decree tighter in his hands. "Understood." He reached for the wineskin next to his bed.

She gently lay her hand on his. "It wasn't your fault. You have the strength to face this."

Something in his eyes lightened a little. He pursed his lips. "Yes," he said, leaving the wineskin where it was. "Perhaps you are right."

Good. That was progress, but she needed more time with him.

"King, I would like to talk again. Like we did last night." She pressed her hands together. Push, but not too hard. "We have much leftover food. Perhaps a second feast for the people. That will lighten your duties, and after, we could meet here."

He slowly rubbed his goatee. Though it didn't show on his face, his tone was light. "Celebrating the queen is worth at least two days of feasting."

She lowered her head. "Thank you, sire."

The king opened the door to the hallway. "Thank *you*, my queen. And you may call me by my name, Mahdi."

And with that, he left.

A small hatchling of trust had formed between them. It was...different, nice. But how far it went, she didn't know. It seemed enough to quell her anger and his depression. Maybe it could do more.

After the eating and drinking of the second feast had died down, she headed to the King's bedroom. Six guards stood outside, led by Agba. It seemed the king was taking no chances. She wondered how many of them Hecatet controlled, remembering how Agba had sneaked Daro drink after drink.

Agba smiled at her with a nasty glint in his eyes. They searched her and then let her in.

The king sat at the small stone table in front of the shelves, drinking water from a small golden cup. Hecatet sat across from the king.

The king raised his drink. "My queen, come."

She sat next to him as her mind sped through the possibilities: How much had Hecatet discovered? How much had the king told him? His presence meant he suspected something was wrong. After all, the king was still alive. So last night had been a setup.

"Have some wine." Hecatet offered her a cup. "We were just discussing the threats from Libania that led to the invasion of Gotran."

She mimed drinking from her cup, being careful not to get the liquid too near her mouth. Somehow, she doubted it was just wine.

The king shook his head. "Hecatet, I'm more interested in why innocents far from the field of battle were slain during the invasion."

Hecatet stiffened but quickly smiled. "Casualties of war, my king. There are bound to be a few with every invasion."

"I plan to know the exact number." The king stared at the water in his cup. "I'll be meeting with the generals tomorrow. It's time for a review of our army. Our soldiers will account for their actions, as will any who instructed them to do such things."

Hecatet's smile became tighter at the corners. "Of course, my king."

Reshe rejoiced. Hecatet was losing his grip on the king, and by the look on the man's face, he knew it.

But Hecatet talked for the next hour, telling one story after another spouting their shared triumphs. And as the candles burned lower her heart began to sink. In the morning, the decree would be announced to the city. The half-blessed Ka would be rounded up one by one and killed. Even if the king decided to free himself from Hecatet, it would be too late.

A chill stole through her as a horrible realization dawned. Hecatet had wanted the king dead last night. With the decree already sealed and delivered, he didn't need to wait till the morning. But his plan had a problem. He needed someone to blame for the murder, and she hadn't killed the king. He needed time to frame her.

The guard, Agba. The smile he'd given her. He could be in her room, planting the evidence as they sat.

She drummed her fingers against her thigh. The cold feeling slipped down into her chest, freezing it from the outside in. Her ribs were an icy tomb that tightened with every drip of wax from the candle on the table in front of her.

She couldn't wait till Hecatet left. It'd be too late. She had no time left. Panic built in her throat and tumbled out of her mouth, startling both men. "King!"

The king smiled. "I told you, you may call me Mahdi, my queen." He carefully placed his cup on the table. "What is on your mind, Reshe?"

She took a steadying breath. "I would like you to reconsider the decree about the Ka." The words came out too fast, too eager. "They aren't hostile. They're just people. Regular people."

The king tilted his head. "*You* said they were dangerous. That they would not obey our land's laws and may even attack my people. That Gotran was not safe for us with them here."

"Yes, but I didn't know exactly what—"

"Sire," Hecatet interrupted. "My family has run into the Ka before. They have always proven to be resistant to authority at every step. We've found evidence of monsters among them, shape-changers."

The cold squeezed her chest tighter. "They won't try to overthrow you. They just want to live in peace."

The king looked toward Hecatet and back to her. "Reshe, what of these shape-changing monsters? They are too great a threat to let live. Hecatet has reports from every inquisitor in the city. He has my trust. He knows how important my people are to me. And he serves me with his very life." The king touched her hand lightly. "He would never hurt something I love."

Hecatet faked a yawn, victory in his eyes. "It is very late, and the queen is upset. Perhaps we should all get some rest."

The king frowned. "Perhaps you are right, Hecatet. Time we all slept. Have a guard escort the queen to her room."

Hecatet's voice dripped with victorious mirth. "Don't worry, king. I'll have Agba take care of her."

She stood, frozen. If she walked out with Agba, she and the king were dead. And in the morning, all the half-blessed would be rounded up one by one and killed. A deep burning ache spread through her chest. The weight of her failure was like a stone slab slowly crushing her.

Be you.

The Tiger's words sparked an idea. A terrifying idea. Be herself. She'd never shown anyone. She'd spent her life hiding. Even her people feared her. She looked at the king. Fear melted the ice and boiled it until she was burning all over.

He wouldn't understand.

Be you.

She took a deep breath and focused on the Tiger's warm presence. Then she let her magic fade, all of it. "Mahdi, my king."

He stared at her. They both did. Their eyes grew wide, bodies shifting backward as the soft brown color of her arms slowly drained away, revealing the coarse white skin beneath.

The black stripped away from her hair layer by layer until all that was left were waves of brilliant white. She held the king's gaze and the words came unburdened to her lips. "If you are killing the Ka tomorrow, then you will have to kill me, too."

Hecatet drew his short sword.

Shock dominated the tilt of the king's brow and the slant of his mouth. But that small thing was still between them. That little bit of trust. The understanding of two lonely people. She put her hope in it.

The king's lips tightened. "Put away your sword, Hecatet."

Hecatet glared at her. "Sire, she's a monster, a killer—"

"Put it away," The king said in the calm voice of someone who expected to be obeyed. "She is no killer nor a monster. She's a light. I know it. I have seen it."

Warmth flooded into her, lightening the fear and melting what little failure remained. Gratefulness was all she knew. This was being trusted. This was being known. Praise the Tiger.

Hecatet kicked over his chair, his sword still in hand. "Sire, she's a—we have evidence that these people, that their evil magic is a threat to—"

"And I have evidence that they aren't." The king stalked around the table toward Hecatet. "So, we will delay and reconsider."

Hecatet hunched over, almost like he was in pain. His voice dropped from indignation to annoyance in the blink of an eye. "Well, then. I guess the Ka killed you both."

The sword was so fast that she saw only the blood spray across the shelves.

A shout rang out. The king clutched his arm and fell toward the bed. Hecatet loomed over him. Pure instinct shoved her forward. She drove her foot up between Hecatet's legs. Her sandaled foot hit padded hide. He was wearing protective underclothes.

A large fist hit her square in the throat. She grabbed at his arm as she collapsed to the ground, tearing some of his skin and hair. Pain lanced up her shoulder where she landed on it, but she couldn't make a sound. Her throat convulsed.

The blurred form of Hecatet wrestled with the king on the bed. He shoved a cloth in the king's mouth. The sword glinted between them.

"Sire?" A voice called out from beyond the closed door. "Are you all right?"

Hecatet shouted back while pressing down on the king. "His highness is fine, just dropped a cup."

A fever coursed through her veins. A single clear line of thought came through the pain: Do something or he's dead. She stumbled to her feet. She couldn't yell, but...

"With me, Tiger."

The magic descended on her. Waves of dark brown skin folded over her. She focused on her face. Her black hair shortened, growing into a lighter blonde. She rose a few inches as her muscles puffed out. Her head pounded, and her shoulder and throat were on fire, but she'd transformed a thousand times. She pooled the magic, then let it slow to a drip.

The king gave a muffled grunt. More blood pooled onto the goat skin bed.

Reshe grabbed a feather pen from the work table and jumped onto the bed beside Hecatet.

He turned, bringing his sword to bear, but stopped short from the shock of looking into his own face.

That slight hesitation was all she needed.

The pen made a squelching sound as she stabbed it through his left eye. Hecatet screamed and shoved her backward. She careened off the bed, tipping over the end table as she went. She landed hard on her knee but ignored the pain and rose to face Hecatet.

He clutched his eye with one hand and reached for her.

Blood spattered her face. A bronze sword tip emerged from the middle of his throat. The man gurgled once, fell to his knees, then slumped forward off the bed and onto the floor.

The king stood behind and above Hecatet's corpse, still on the bed. He wiped Hecatet's sword clean of its owner's blood. The king himself was covered in the stuff. It flowed both from a large gash on his bicep and a deep cut in his thigh.

Relief flooded through her. She let her magic fade. Her skin slowly returned to its normal white.

The king shouted. "Guards!"

Two heavy thumps sounded from outside, then three royal guards burst into the room, looking haggard with several small flesh wounds between them.

Daro was among them and spoke first. "Sire, are you—"

"I'm fine." The king pointed his sword at Hecatet's corpse. "Hecatet tried to murder me. There may have been others with him."

Daro nodded. "Agba and two others attacked us when we heard the shouts."

Reshe sucked in a painful breath and coughed. As the adrenaline faded, pain blossomed in her shoulder and knee. She stumbled to the bed and collapsed.

"Fetch a healer!" The king yelled and sat down hard on the bed beside her.

Exhaustion took over each of her limbs. Her brain retreated from the growing pain. Yes, pass out. Fine by her. Her people were safe. She was fully seen and accepted. The king's body was warm. His soft murmured words gave her comfort as darkness overtook her.

"It's all right, Reshe. I'm here. You're not alone."

MAHDI'S WHITE TUNIC FLOWED beautifully in the wind. His cinnamon scent wafted over her. They sat on fur-covered stone chairs carved to resemble the sun. The courtyard of the palace was gorgeous in the summer.

The courtiers, the retainers, all the royal officials, and many Ka, had gathered to watch King Mahdi's new edict be put into law. The one that stated that the Ka would be protected in the empire of Serpa.

The sun was up, but a lovely breeze kept her nice and cool. She ran a hand over the white skin on her arm. It felt so strange to be in her natural form, especially outside, where others could see.

"You look lovely, Reshe," Mahdi said as a long procession of Ka walked past, thanking them.

"Thank you," she said, fiddling with the hem of her green dress. The one she'd worn the night of the first feast.

"Lady Reshe." Tella stood before her. "I knew what you were the moment you called me half-blessed." Fire burned in the old woman's eyes. "You were supposed to avenge our people. My husband...You were supposed to be our warrior."

The accusation stung. "Tella—"

"How dare you? How dare you forgive him." The old woman's frame shook. "He hasn't earned it. He hasn't earned any redemption."

A guard beside her grabbed Tella by the arm, but Reshe waved him away. Sadness welled in her heart.

She took the old woman's hand and spoke softly. "I'm so tired of earning things from others, Tella. Of making them earn things from me." She pictured Mahdi. When she revealed what she was, he saw beyond her past and her skin. He'd trusted in her heart. "Redemption isn't something you earn. It's a gift you're given."

Tella made a noise of disgust and ripped her hand free. "You failed us, blessed one." She turned and walked away. "You failed us."

The words itched at Reshe's heart, forming a small fear. Fear would lead back into shame. And shame back into anger. The same anger festering within Tella, and no doubt many more Gotrans. They'd want Mahdi to pay for lives that were taken. To prove he had changed. To earn it.

Mahdi took one of Reshe's clean white hands in his. His touch was warm.

Be free.

The itch faded, and the soft embrace of the Tiger's presence filled her. They'd changed. Both of them. He didn't need to prove it to her.

G.K. WHITE WAS BORN in Texas in 1991 and raised by two amazing parents who, by reading to him, created a love for stories and myths. As a kid, they had to work hard to pry his hands off the latest *Redwall* novel or a video game controller and convince him to eat dinner. Both obsessions carried over into his adulthood and were vital parts of his procrastination as he matriculated at the University of Houston-Clear Lake with a BA in English. He lived in western China for a few years, where he taught both English and Writing. It was there he met his better seven-eighths, his amazing wife Holly. They currently live in Houston where he works as a freelance author and editor.

Four

BEHIND THE SCENES & SOUNDTRACK

BEHIND EL CUCUY

By Scott A. Johnson

WHEN I TEACH CLASSES on monsters, there's always one assignment that my students both love and dread. In it, I tell them to look outside their own cultures for monsters that aren't well known. To further complicate matters, I often give them the stipulation that the creature can't be one I've heard of (a task that gets harder and harder as time goes by). Through this assignment, students are forced to enrich their world-views and to research other cultures, the goal being to develop an appreciation and respect for the folklore of other countries. In researching other cultures, one discovers that every culture has common monsters. Every culture has vampires, ghosts, and, oddly, clowns. But one more thing that every culture shares is a boogeyman that feasts on naughty boys and girls and drags them into the dark. In Mexican culture, this creature is the shadow-walking El Cucuy.

I first came to know about El Cucuy from my wife, Katie, herself proud of this Mexican heritage. I found the story fascinating, so I asked her to tell me about it. She remembered stories of her youth and her eyes sparkled with childhood mischief when she told them. So, when this opportunity came about, I decided to write this story as a tribute to my wife, to her heritage, and to show respect to the folklore of the Mexican people.

SAJ

BEHIND GORE VELLYE (THE AUTUMN TUMULT)

By Anne C. Lynch

WHEN I WAS ASKED to contribute a story to Monster Mash, I eagerly took the ~~bait~~ offer. Sure, horror is outside my genre, but I teach middle schoolers by day—I thrive on chaos. And, anyway, I love horror. I love monsters. I love ghosts and goblins and all things supernatural. Gimme a good scare and I'm happy. (Again, middle school teacher...it's very on-brand.)

I launched myself head-first into my laptop, waived a quick hello to Dr. Google, and went in search of my beast. I wanted a monster that I knew nothing about; a thing that sank its claws into my hide and yanked. It needed to live in a particular type of place; isolated, remote, insular. Lovely on the surface but creepy underneath. Islands—but not tropical—it had to be cold. What I wanted was the Orkneys. What I chose was Sanday.

On the island of Sanday, native folklorist, Walter Traill Dennison, transcribed the tale of a man who claimed to have survived an encounter with the Nuckelavee, the Devil of the Sea. Obviously, this was the place and the monster I had been seeking. Sanday became my new obsession. (By the end of my research, I swear I could run tours of the place. So. Much. Googling.)

All the places in my story exist on Sanday—Kettletoft Harbor, The Belsair, the Lady Kirkyard Cemetery, the Quoyayre (the inspiration for Petyr Rendall's cottage on the beach), and the Neolithic Quoyness Chambered Cairn. I truly hope to be able to visit someday. The place got under my skin...and yanked.

So, I'd found the place, I'd found the creature, but I needed a twist on the tale. In the original, the Nuckelavee had always existed. It was not a curse that passed from one victim to the next. In considering the plot, the obvious path was to have the protagonist search for the beast, be chased by it, and then either die or escape. Predictable. So, I did something I never do: I wrote the story without an outline. I am a dedicated 'planner' when it comes to writing. But in this case, I just started.

I had my protagonist in mind, and I knew where she was headed. *Okay. Dive in, waive to Dr. Google in passing, look at maps, find universities with advanced degrees in Scottish/Celtic folklore, look into ferries from Aberdeen to Sanday, answer the question of why she was going there, etc...* And at the end of all those questions and answers, I still got stuck on the whole "die, escape, what's the damn twist?!" problem. I kept writing.

I knew I wanted the Lady Kirkyard Cemetery in there and the Quoyness Cairn (because, "duh!"). It wasn't until she was in the Cairn with the creepy dude that it hit me...he was the Nuckelavee. After that, it was easy. You know the rest.

Thanks for reading! Below I've added the story of the Mither o' the Sea and Teran. It helps explain the title "Gore Vellye."

The Mither o' the Sea, Teran, Vore Tullye, and Gore Vellye:

Off the north coast of Scotland are the Orkneys, with a rich culture and mythology that stretches back into prehistory. Their stories often revolve around the character of the sea and how it rules their lives, day after day, season after season, year after year. The Mither o' the Sea and Teran are a foundational story:

The Mither o' the Sea (Sea Mother) rules the benevolent months of Summer. She brings days of sun and gentle seas that provide full nets, green fields, fat livestock, and abundant harvests. But, the Mither has a mortal enemy—Teran, the spirit of winter whose shrieks of rage are heard on the winds of violent storms.

During the spring and autumn, these enemies war for control. During the Spring Struggle (Vore Tullye), the Sea Mither defeats Teran and binds him at the bottom of the sea. But, during the Autumn Tumult (Gore Vellye), the Sea

Mither's strength fades. Teran breaks free and tethers the Mither to the seabed. The stormy seas of winter follow as his reign begins. And with that reign come his minions. The most gruesome and heartless beast in Teran's ranks is the Nuckelavee—the Devil of the Sea.

BEHIND PREY ANIMALS

By Sen R. L. Scherb

I'VE ALWAYS FELT THAT horses were an untapped potential in horror. Most people have been around horses, and those who haven't either didn't feel the need or knew there was a purpose in staying away—and for good reason. Even a little pony could cause some serious damage if they wanted to. We've always been lucky that horses are flighty prey animals rather than predators.

Yet, it seems that more than anything else that can be considered just as dangerous, we are attracted to them in a way that is unlike any other animal of its caliber. Children are given horses every day, and someone who has suffered a horrific injury at the hooves of a horse gets back on their back the first chance they can.

Mythology and folklore usually paints horses as peaceful, benevolent creatures. There are unicorns that can heal any disease or sickness, pegasi that showcase beauty and grace, and hippogriffs that demonstrate power. Quite honestly though, I think Scottish mythology got it the most correct with the introduction of kelpies.

I originally wrote "Prey Animals" for a Monsters class in my graduate program headed by none other than Scott Johnson (Hi Scott!). The initial spark to the assignment was to discover a monster that was not well known or common knowledge, and essentially introduce it to the class. I think I went with another monster for my "discovery," but I couldn't resist adding in the background of kelpies—and was immensely surprised to find out that kelpies, in fact, *weren't* common knowledge.

I mean, the murderous, shapeshifting, water-dwelling creature that would lure people onto its back and then drown and eat them? How was something so cool and terrifying not common knowledge, especially since I had been obsessed with them since I was a child?

But they weren't—and I jumped on the chance.

The actual start to "Prey Animals" was a writing exercise I did with a couple girls I tutored in creative writing. We all began with the same sentence, and I wrote a very short few sentences about this black oil that began spreading and no one noticed. The girls were obsessed, and wanted to know more, so I filed it away for later.

For the actual assignment and story, I like to describe it as how I wrote it on "half an idea." I had no idea what it was going to turn into, and I was going off a vague aesthetic and premise—and, of course, imbuing the horror with horses.

As I continued writing, letting the story unfold, letting the narrator of Lif tell their story, I started getting more and more the concept of what was going on—until it culminated into the story that you see today. It became a tale of the side effects of money and power, and what those things can make someone ignore. The final piece of the puzzle lay in perhaps what might be the coolest idea I had for it, even if I'm not sure it completely came across in the piece: the idea that the entire story is taking place in just a few minutes.

The dream-like sequences that we follow through Lif's eyes, watching as an outsider, everyone disappear and no one remember, occurs while all of the characters are being drowned by these kelpie-like creatures. Every time someone disappears, it is when they have died in the real world and no longer have a consciousness to be kept in this idealistic dream by the kelpies wanting to keep their prey subdued.

Did this idea come across? I'm not sure. I'd certainly like to think so, and I especially think it does in subsequent reads, picking up on the smaller details.

It should be mentioned that I am more of a fantasy writer—in fact, I am usually *only* a fantasy writer, with this being my first foray into real horror. I'd like to think that I fulfilled my own expectations. The scene with the horses staring through the window still chills me. I want to see more horses being used as elements of horror.

I suppose it should also be mentioned that I'm a horse owner, too. I'm not scared of horses—but I recognize their power, their ability, and am grateful every day that they aren't predators after all.

BEHIND THE DEVIL AND SCOTT

By W. H. Horner

HAD ELLERSLIE MANSION NOT been surrounded by DuPont's secretive Chemours Edge Moor Plant, if it hadn't been torn down in 1973, and if I-495 had not been constructed in that decade, I'd have had a clear view of the old house from the back windows of my parents' home. Growing up, I didn't even know it had existed or that the Fitzgeralds lived there briefly in the late 1920s.

The families that lived and vacationed in the long-gone houses along the bank of the Delaware River would hike up the sloped terrain to have picnics and watch the water and the distant banks of New Jersey from a slightly higher vantage point. The neighborhood I grew up in was built in the '40s, and in the middle of the '80s, my mom found a literal silver spoon buried in our backyard. When we learned the Fitzgeralds lived within a few minutes' walking distance, we started joking that maybe it had belonged to them.

My mom grew up in Salem County, NJ, and was often terrified by stories of the Jersey Devil. She gave me a well-worn book about the creature, and I was fascinated by it in junior high and high school, so much that I nearly applied to universities with folklore programs because of it. A literal legend that close!

When my weird Jersey Devil book and obsession became a topic of discussion one day at school, my English teacher, who had never heard of the creature before, told a story about staying in a cabin in the Pine Barrens. She was alone one late afternoon, and a huge shadow darkened the window. She assumed it was a turkey, but her dog freaked out, and she was left uneasy—I borrowed from that for Scott's initial brush with the creature in my story.

Despite the fact that everyone says how horrible and dangerous a creature the Leeds Devil is, I always felt bad for it, being cursed as a baby and all. I settled on the Devil as my subject pretty quickly, wanting to pay homage to a lifelong interest, but I also wanted to do something different and a little unexpected (while staying truer to the source material than that totally disappointing episode of *The X-Files*—yes, I'm still bitter after nearly thirty years—a recent episode of *What We Do in the Shadows* mocked the Jersey Devil, but at least it was a little more "accurate"). I'm not even sure when my brain decided to mash up the Jersey Devil and F. Scott Fitzgerald, but once it did, scenes began flashing to life. I realized I had a fun opportunity to play with themes of being an outsider, longing, and frustration at life not living up to hopes, dreams, or simply what is deserved. I could mirror Fitzgerald and the Devil and throw in a tiny bit of Gatsby as well (not that hard, considering that Scott—I can't think of him any other way now—modeled Gatsby, in part, on himself).

I'm no Fitzgerald scholar, but I read as much as I could about his life as I wrote, focusing on the time he and Zelda and Scottie lived in Delaware, and I tried my best to bring to life a larger-than-life literary figure, with all his insecurities and contradictions, and I peppered the story with as many historically accurate details as I could. He evidently did celebrate his thirtieth birthday in the big house on the Delaware by lying in a coffin.

I owe many thanks to Sen, J.C., and Victoria, who all left fingerprints on this tale. Special thanks to my wife Michelle, who pushed me to toss what wasn't working in earlier drafts and to take a more difficult route with the story, and to Garrett, who provided two enthusiastic critiques with great suggestions for delving more deeply into the psychology of both the Jersey Devil and Scott.

BEHIND A THING OF HOPE

By Carrie Gessner

I CHOSE THE DOVER Demon for this anthology because the story has fascinated me since I first heard of it a few years ago. If you're not familiar with the urban legend, over the course of two nights in April 1977, three separate teenagers in Dover, Massachusetts, saw a mysterious creature. One of them, Bill Bartlett, made a sketch of it. Interestingly, if you trace out the sightings on a map, the creature appeared to have been going in a relatively straight line.

The prevailing theory was that it was a young animal of some kind—a horse, elk, or moose. Police mostly viewed it as a teenage hoax, but the story persisted, and the creature became known as "the Dover Demon." One of the reasons this intrigues me so much is that we'll never have a definitive answer.

Shortly after I sat down to write this story, despite my enthusiasm, I realized I had put myself into a corner. Writing an account of those two nights would be...fine. Maybe even a little boring to readers familiar with the Dover Demon already. I also had reservations about writing about real people who still live. Moreover, to tell a story that had already been told wasn't the point of this anthology.

The more I brainstormed, the more two things stood out—unlike a cryptid like Bigfoot, the Dover Demon had been seen by a handful of people over the course of two nights in one small area. And the witnesses had seen only one creature. To me, this was evidence that the creature was solitary.

But what if it wasn't solitary by choice? And what if I didn't simply retell what happened in 1977, but added new context? Once I reached that conclusion, everything fell into place and Starlight's journey came alive. And, of course, where else would Starlight go to scour for evidence that he's not the last of his kind but the library? Patronize your local library if you're able to, folks! If you want to know more about the Dover Demon sightings, that would be a great place to start. In the meantime, I hope you enjoy my take on this classic cryptid.

BEHIND THE GNOMIES

By Kevin Plybon

THE GERM OF THIS story was "from the perspective of a garden gnome." I'm pretty sure that the inspiration was a commercial for a certain travel website. A monster rarely understood, and even more rarely investigated. I thought that a twist ending would be good, revealing a second type of monster in addition to the gnomes, so kept an eye out for that newcomer while I started writing. I like to draft short stories with only a vague idea of where they're going.

I searched for a conflict to get things started. Since gnomes can't really walk about, I wondered what sort of trouble they could possibly have, other than arguing about whose robes were shinier. Being unable to move sounded like an awful situation, especially when attacked—and that's when I hit on a gnome's natural enemy: a cat. Entitled and merciless. I had my inciting incident, and I was off.

I knew that I wanted the story to be whimsical, even as it took its gnome protagonists seriously. They had experiences and opinions, after all, that I needed to respect. But I discovered early on in drafting that the gnomes were trapped souls, so I knew the story had to take a dark turn. What souls-in-gnomes story is complete without a new soul in a new gnome? Then I realized that whoever created that new gnome would be a murderer, and my second monster, the Overlord, made her entrance after some quick revision.

From there, I just followed threads. Who owned the cat? What would the Overlord think about that person? What rules of gnomic immobility could I break? What happened if a gnome cracked? And so on. The vagaries of magic systems came into play, too, as I tried to strike a balance between explaining too much and keeping things mysterious. I decided not to delve too deeply into the Overlord's powers or motivations, for example. I figured I should devote my limited word count to the gnomies instead.

I hope readers liked the ending. I like to imagine that our resourceful heroes will escape the Overlord at some point. Until then: peace out, my gnomies.

BEHIND DON'T FEED THE TROLL

By Katharine Dow

I LOVE SATIRE AND humorous speculative fiction. For that reason, when I decided to write a monster story, my first instinct was to find the most ridiculous monster I could and create a story inspired by it.

I initially found a promising candidate in some poor creature that grows out of the end of a plant. If I remember correctly, it's a Welsh monster, and it doesn't appear to do much more than live its life stuck in a field, surrounded by regular plants, totally unable to move. I imagine small children find it terrifying, but it's likely that no one else does.

It's difficult to weave both despair and laughter into a story in such a way that one doesn't accidently overpower the other. But I thought I might have found that delicate balance in that sad, possibly Welsh, excuse for a monster.

In the end, I instead found my monster after reading a nonfiction book about online misinformation called *How to Lose the Information War*, by Nina Jankowicz. After finishing it, I decided that a troll who lands a job as an internet troll should be my monster.

I typically think of monsters as scary looking, malevolent creatures. Pure evil. Nothing like us humans, right? But as I created my monster, I wondered, what does my troll think of himself? What are his values? What are his moral blind spots? How does he see his place in the world, and what does my troll think of humans? Because of the way he earns his living, I also thought about how ordinary people are manipulated, sometimes very willingly, by the forces of capitalism and power. I will admit, I struggled while writing this story to feel any optimism about human—or monster—nature.

Online misinformation and hate—even if it's presented in this story with a heavy dose of absurdity—is a nightmare. So is revenge. But even though I struggled to balance the forces of despair and laughter in "Don't Feed the Troll," I still had a lot of fun writing it. I love my morally ambiguous troll. I adored creating his mess of a boss. I hope whoever finds this story has as much fun reading it as I had writing it.

BEHIND DON'T LOSE YOUR HEAD

By Victoria L. Scott

I WISH I COULD say that this quirky little story about a cephalophore finding true love came from a lengthy pre-writing process, a great deal of research, and an eye toward a tale 'full of meaning.' Instead, I learned the anthology was about lesser-known monsters in unusual situations, and the following sentence popped in my head:

"Washington Irving was a son of a bitch."

Now, I have no personal beef with the guy, and I've no idea where the line came from, but it was that...uh...flounder slap to the face? I guess? That was the genesis of the story. It's not exactly a "process," but I often find ideas for stories from these kinds of eructation from the background processing of my very odd brain.

I really liked that sentence. If only I could start every story with "So-and-So was a son of a bitch."

Heavy sigh.

I read some of Irving's yarn about Ichabod Crane—who seemed to be more 'on the make' with the local gals than I recall seeing in the cartoon/film versions of the story—and was shocked by how overly '19th century' the prose was. I mean, it's even more Nathaniel Hawthorne-esque than Hawthorne, and that's saying something.

Yeah, yeah, I know the guy wrote *in* the 19th century, so it isn't really his fault, blah blah blah...but as a short story, "The Legend of Sleepy Hollow" was drudgery to read. (True confession: I didn't finish it. Even worse: I had no desire to finish it.)

I wanted my story to be fun and light-hearted with a happy ending where the bully doesn't get the girl. First step, cool first line. Check. Get rid of bully element of the story. Check. Channel some of my inner Molly Harper for the appropriate 'snark' versus 'sweet/funny' ratio. Check.

After that, I had to figure out how online dating sites worked. *shudder*

Checking out eharmony and match.com was...awkward. I found the process of creating fictional, research-based profiles to be mildly disturbing. Once I finished, I immediately deleted my profiles, but not before my spam folder erupted with a few 'here are some men who might interest you' emails, which was...creepy? The fact that eharmony charges people to find partners was mind-blowing to me. I get it...it's a business, but still...a year-long subscription? I know there are people for whom such websites have been successful—hell, my MC ends up with a partner due to my fabricated dating site—but nothing about online dating appeals to me.

That being said, writing a story that was sort-of romantic where the MC gets the girl was a departure from my usual story plots, which range from men consuming cremated remains in hopes of receiving eternal life, to a dementia patient and her robot dog facing a drug addict holding a gun, to a few middle schoolers trying to rescue a large pig from an excrement-filled basement. Not exactly Hallmark Movie material.

It was a fun story to write, though. I hope you enjoy it.

BEHIND EYES LIKE BURNING COAL

By Jeremiah Dylan Cook

I LOVE WRITING ABOUT monsters, so I jumped at the chance to contribute to this anthology. The story kernel that popped into "Eyes Like Burning Coal" started when I wrote and submitted a work for the Humans are the Problem anthology released by Weird Little Worlds in 2021. My tale for that collection concerned a government agency called the Monster Bureau. That story was rejected, but I loved the idea of an agency dedicated to monsters. Thus, I decided to recycle the idea for "Eyes Like Burning Coal." Perhaps one day that rejected work will see the light of day, and I'll canonize the Monster Bureau as the second evolution of the Department of Cryptid Collection.

For this tale, I originally wanted to focus on the Headless Horseman and call this "The Headless Horseman Rides

Again," but since the Headless Horseman was already taken by another writer, I decided to give the story's central villainous role to Spring-Heeled Jack. I tried to keep my Jack close to his historical descriptions, but I removed all references to the idea that he might be a human in disguise because I wanted him to be a cryptid. Hence why I changed his metal springs into "fleshy...appendage(s)." Hopefully, Spring-Heeled Jack purists can look past that and still enjoy my work.

Since I'm a nerd, I couldn't help leaving a few horror easter eggs in "Eyes Like Burning Coal." First, Jill, my main character, takes her name from Jill Valentine in the Resident Evil franchise. Second, when I wrote the capture of Spring-Heeled Jack, I was partially drawing on memories of the opening for the 2001 film Thirteen Ghosts. Third, I tried to describe the Department of Cryptid Collection's underground tunnels in a way that would remind readers of the Nostromo hallways that Ripley navigated with her cat, Jonesy, at the end of Alien. Fourth, in another nod to a film Sigourney Weaver appears in, I tried to craft a climax that was reminiscent of the ending to the 2011 classic Cabin in the Woods. Fifth, and related to four, the character Gary Hadly's name is a combination of two characters from Cabin in the Woods. Lastly, Dr. Zarka takes his last name from Dr. Emily Zarka, the host of PBS's Monstrum.

If you enjoyed "Eyes Like Burning Coal," which I very much hope you did, you can find links to all my other publications on the "Read My Work" subpage of my website, www.jeremiahdylancook.com. I'd also be glad for your friendship on Twitter. You can find me @JeremiahCook1.

BEHIND THE MAGICLAND MISCHIEF

By J.C. Mastro

AH, MAGICLAND... THE MOST obvious parody of the greatest amusement park in the world. Such was my intention, as not only a huge lifelong fan of the entertainment company represented by a cartoon rodent, but as a perfect location to ramp up a certain character's special type of magic and tell a fun tale. "Magicland Mischief" is not only a monster story featuring a troll and the trope of possessed animatronic creatures, a continuation of the Boatman character from my *Dragons of a Different Tail* story, but a fan service homage to a real-life magical place and beloved characters found within.

As was the case with the *Dragons* anthology, I had no idea at first what to write about. This time, any monster was open to us, so long as it wasn't one of the overdone classics and we twisted its tropes. Any tone was also acceptable, from horror to comedy. I love monsters, especially the mythical kind from around the world. I was excited to write for this...but where to begin?

In my story, "Spirit of the Dragon," everyone who read it loved the Boatman character. If you haven't read that anthology, please do! In it, he is an enigmatic wizard of sorts who guides the heavy metal band DragonFraggen to summon the spirit of a dragon back from the abyss. He's so much fun to write as a mischievous trickster, mysterious being with unknown power and purpose, and a great voice. I had to bring him back.

This led me to create something of an origin for him, which I refuse to tell you now as his story will continue eventually. But that origin, in part, came from the Anglo Saxon, Nordic Invasion period of Britain. And one of their best mythical beasties was the ettin, jotunn, or troll. Given the Boatman's actions in "Spirit," it didn't take long to reach the plan that he'd be bringing back the spirit of a troll.

But where might he find a troll to reanimate? Why, at a fantasy-themed amusement park, of course. And then my fandom of that park and company took hold and wouldn't let go, and I set out to write what might be the most fun story I've ever written.

First, a bit on the monsters within this story. Our troll, Harry, is a bit of a mash-up of the Anglo Saxon and Nordic myths. Giant, hulking, purely evil supernatural beasts that were feared and avoided. Far from the spikey haired little dolls people like today. In Nordic mythology, the Jotunn were ice giants from a land of the gods. For Saxons, a creature like Grendel from Beowulf is considered a troll and a representation of evil. It's quite a mixed up, complicated mythos, but however you spin it, Harry the Troll was a destructive, bombastic menace.

The other monster in this story would be the possessed animatronic. Made famous in recent years by the Five Nights at Freddie's games. I also took influence, albeit very minimal influence, from a Nicolas Cage movie titled *Willy's Wonderland*. But, as the Boatman/Druid Guy had done before, we couldn't have him in Magicland without summoning the spirits of olde to inhabit some of our beloved characters! Harry, intentionally. The others, not so much, thanks to our heroine's interference. Some are malevolent, others kind. Some are ancient spirits, others simply animated character personas. And all a lot of fun.

"Magicland" is a harrowing journey through that famous park, albeit so utterly abridged as it nearly hurt my heart that I couldn't include more. As someone who has been there enough times that I could navigate it blindfolded, I was able to visualize our heroine's trip through to get the help she needed and stop the Boatman, now renamed Druid Guy by her. I knew instantly I wanted to include a few favorite (and obscure) spots, and two of my favorite characters.

I had an absolute blast writing Abe Lincoln and John Arrow. Not only trying to capture their likeness, but twist reader expectations of them and have them be an integral part to saving the day. Especially for Abe. Arrow... I just wanted to write his dialogue! The dinosaurs were an unexpected writing surprise, but fun. And, if you know they're there in the park, you know what I was talking about. If you didn't, there's a new discovery waiting for you on your next visit. And the geese... yeah, they creep me out, too.

Ghost Manor, one of the only rides we actually enter during the story, is a personal favorite... And it's resident mystic character a great foil to Druid Guy's plans. With Mistress Leona, we get a bit more of the history of our strange antagonist. He's been around a long time, caused magical troubles in the past by summoning these spirits, and there are others who've dealt with him before. As a writer, I do hope you're trying to deduce more of his origin, but lacking just enough insight that you'll watch for future stories about him.

This story, when it comes down to it, was an opportunity for me to have fun and play as a writer in a world I know well and love. To tie it into the mythology and world I'm creating through these stories. And to hopefully give readers a few laughs, thrills, intriguing questions, and nostalgic feels. I hope you enjoyed reading it as much as I did writing it. Stay tuned, my friends, for the world has not seen the end of our trickster wizard.

BEHIND THE GHOULY GIRL

By Sophia DeSensi

THOUGH FICTION IS JUST that, for me, writing is always a deeply personal and vulnerable act. As a writer, I filter my experiences through the lens of fabricated characters and settings, often with speculative, romantic, and comedic themes. In my previous short story, TINY HEARTS, in the anthology DRAGONS OF A DIFFERENT TAIL, the protagonist searched for familial love after loss, though unwillingly at the start, and went through many comedic conflicts as a result. I believe the best stories are those that provoke a sense of heartbreak, love, comedy, fear, and strength, because life gives us all. I hope GHOULY GIRL invites readers to feel all the latter in the comfort of Ever's fictional tale.

As an avid fan of both speculative fiction and romantic comedies, GHOULY GIRL came to me after a binge watch of NEW GIRL. I've always loved sitcoms and I thought, "how can I make this comedic dynamic speculative?" That's when I came up with the idea to cast the protagonist as a ghoul. What would that look like if a ghoul moved in with two male human roommates? I loved the added layer of, not just the juxtaposition of feminine and male energy cohabitation, but her ghoulish tendencies as well. From there, I continued to brainstorm who Ever was as a character, her interests, her mythology, and her limitations.

I needed a reason for a ghoul to be forced to live with humans in the first place. I believe when writing paranormal, even contemporary paranormal, one of the most fun aspects of mythology is the character limitations. I wanted my ghoul to be different from other interpretations, so I came up with the idea for her to need warmth as a source of energy. I also, really liked the folk lore around ghosts and how homes were built with odd shaped windows and sharp angles to keep ghosts out. But Ever isn't a ghost. Ever finds comforts in the architecture meant to keep her out. In the story, I refer to this as her "tether," which keeps her anchored to out physical world.

In other works of ghoul fiction, the monsters typically want to consume humans in order to gain strength. Ever simply wants to live amongst humans and be included in our physical world. She's wandered alone for hundreds of years, and decided to finally "move in" the right way, rather than continue to watch life pass her by as a shadow haunt. When she does, she finds she's accepted by her young roommates despite her differences. And she finds a sense of home and belonging. Though Ever will live for*ever* as an immortal spirit, long past her roommates, I believe she's found a renewed love of life through the bonds of human companionship.

BEHIND THE WORST VACATION EVER

By Jeannie Rivera

MIDDLE-GRADE MONSTER HUNTERS FRED and Cindy are characters from a larger work—*Frederick Moody and the Secrets of Six Summit Lake*—which is planned to release in late 2022.

Frederick Moody and The Secrets of Six Summit Lake is one of two middle-grade novels completed for the M.F.A. in Writing Popular Fiction program from Seton Hill University. It is the story of a socially awkward, Bigfoot-obsessed sixth grader living in the Adirondack Mountains of NY, on a mission to win back his best friend, Cindy, by proving the creature is real.

"The Manananggal" takes place two years after the friend's adventures with Bigfoot. The idea for the story about Fred and Cindy visiting the Philippines was birthed while taking a genre class, "Monsters," during my first semester at Seton Hill. The final exam was an assignment to write a short story either about an obscure monster, or one from another culture. I must credit my sister-in-law, Rachel Davide, who was born in the Philippines for her help with folklore and ideas about monsters from her culture.

The protagonist, Frederick Moody, in my MG novel went through many transformations since I originally wrote "The Manananggal." He changed from demon hunter to monster hunter to amateur supernatural sleuth in his small hometown. One thing, however, that always stayed the same is Fred's social awkwardness, his affection for his best friend, Cindy (hints of romantic jealously two years later, anyone?), his knowledge of all things weird, and his brilliance with scientific gadgets that oftentimes go awry.

Although not stated outright in the manuscript, the protagonist is on the autism spectrum—his traits are more pronounced in the novel than in the short story. My intention is neurodiverse characters as heroes without the stories being about disability or autism. This allows children to see themselves and their friends—both their similarities and differences—in stories without labels. It is my hope that these au-some kiddos go on to write their own heroic stories in life, and see their uniqueness as their superpowers.

BEHIND THE BRAZEN SKULL

By Michael La Ronn

NECROMANCERS DON'T HAVE A good reputation in fantasy or pop culture, generally.

I can't say that I blame readers for this. I'd be suspicious of anyone who deals in skulls, dead bodies, and spirits, too.

But what if a necromancer used his powers for good? What kind of man would he be? What if he embraced darkness to create light in the world? What would have to happen to someone for them to embrace this decidedly dark skillset?

This concept inspired *The Good Necromancer,* the urban fantasy series that "The Brazen Skull" is set in. Lester Broussard became a necromancer to save his dying wife from cancer; a deal with a demon went south, and the demon killed both his wife and son, leaving him alone and forever giving up the dark art. When the demon murderer comes knocking, Lester has to rekindle the dark art, this time to save his soul—and the world.

If you think about it, necromancy is quite a valuable supernatural skill that often goes unnoticed because necromancers are usually villains. A guy like Lester would always be in-demand. Everyone wants to know about the great beyond. Everyone has a reason to communicate with the dead. ("Where'd you leave that will, Grandpa?")

If you could go to a good necromancer, get secret information to solve your problems, and leave without him double-crossing you, would you do it? That's a winning supernatural character type if you ask me.

In Lester's case, help from the dead doesn't come easily. The dead are unreliable, and the demons that gallivant in the spirit world are murderous. It takes a certain personality type to succeed as a *good* necromancer—one who is street savvy. Mess up, and you're dead. Succeed, and you can truly change people's lives.

I am styled out of the old pulp writers. Pulp fiction is how I see the world. As I was writing this story, the brazen skull spoke to me. Pun fully intended. It was the perfect item for a necromancer to be seeking. Everything flowed from there.

Thanks for reading "The Brazen Skull." I hope you will check out *Shadow Deal* (Book 1 in *The Good Necromancer* series). If you liked this story, you'll love the rest of Lester's escapades.

BEHIND THE REBEL WITH A CAUSE

By Marx Pyle

"REBEL WITH A CAUSE" started with a question: what are the fae doing in the Obsidian Archives world? I had written *Obsidian Monsters*, and although it contained a few fae characters, I didn't really ask my creative self how the fae fully fit into this shadowy urban fantasy world of secret agents and monsters. At least, not in the same way that I did the other major species.

So I decided to write a short story taking place in a different corner of the Obsidian Archives-verse. Where *Obsidian Monsters* was *Mission Impossible* meets urban fantasy, "Rebel with a Cause" was going to be *John Wick* meets urban fantasy. I made Rebel a púca, because ever since I read *War for the Oaks* (considered by many to be one of the earliest urban fantasy books), I've been curious about the phouka fae (another of many spellings). I researched these Irish folklore fae, then asked myself how (in my story world) human interpretation could have got it so wrong, and what the "truth" is in the *Obsidian Archives* world.

I enjoyed imagining all the ways that a shapeshifter could use their powers—not just for disguise, but also for combat. It was entertaining to envision his favorite shapes for different situations, and who these shapes are modeled after. I found Rebel's voice pretty fast, and loved his dynamic with Oz. Hopefully you do, too.

Rebel has a complicated background. Raised in a multiracial human family, he learned the hard way about his changeling fae identity. So I guess I cheated, in a way—I really told a story about a púca and changling combo, two for the price of one! Plus, lots of action and jokes.

If you wondered why he wasn't raised by an Irish family or speak with an Irish accent (since the púca are from Irish folklore), it's because, like all of us, the "monsters" and Otherworlders in *Obsidian Archives* have adapted to the culture in which they were immersed. (And as someone who is multi-ethnic, I've found personal identity an interesting theme to explore.) Technically a shapeshifter can look like anyone or anything, which would seem to complicate things. Plus, Rebel was raised by humans, so he thinks like them more than he does a fae. Heck, one of his favorite shapes is a female elf gun fighter, so does that effect how he sees gender? He has some complex identity themes to work out...between heists and beating up bad guys, of course.

This story made me take a hard look at how the fae fit into the world, and I was surprised by some of the answers.

I realized quickly that there was another story that needed to be told, and this short story is a start.

Yup, lots of secrets to reveal in future adventures of Rebel and Oz. What else would you expect from a trickster fae named Rebel?

Until then, I hope you enjoyed this first installment, and that a púca/phouka/pooka (whatever your favorite spelling) is now one of your favorite shapeshifters.

BEHIND AN OLD FAVOR

By Marisa Wolf

Usually with a story, I get the characters first. Their voice, their general attitude about the shenanigans they've found themselves in, and/or an archetype they're determined to twist to their own ends. For this story, I had a general idea—Gorgon PI—and a handful of names—adapted from the scientific names of the poisonous snakes of Greece—and so I did what any super-sane Serious Author would do and posted an informal survey on my Facebook page. "Here are two names," I wrote, along with a fun gif. "Here are three bullets about the character. Vote."

People voted, and—again, like a very structured and analytical Serious Author might do—as I read over their brilliant opinions, I realized I already knew the answer and retreated to my writing hole. Because it wasn't name A or name B, it was a pair of sisters and their complicated backstory, and the life one sister pieced together to survive when her more monstrous sibling left.

Then, Ochia existed entirely in my head. Her look: floppy hat (to hide the snakes), dark sunglasses (to keep from turning innocent passerby to stone), and long coat (because PI). Her attitude: a general 'no thank you' to the world. Her fun skill: she can talk to statues, or at least, the kind that were once living creatures before they got on the wrong side of a Gorgon's eyeline.

She had strong opinions of how she Did Not Get Involved, and so I had to come up with something to trump that. That part was surprisingly easy. I already had a world for my Gorgon PI, one I've thought a lot about for a few other stories. And in that world is an even more ferociously stubborn character who played pretty well off Ochia.

So while I'm not—as you may have gathered—a Very Serious Author, I do take my characters very seriously. Everything Ochia does in her story is rooted in her core belief/question of herself. She's not a monster, not anymore. Is she? To what lengths will she go to preserve that view of herself? What will she ignore?

From there the story mostly came together, especially after some key feedback from some of my fellow authors. There are also some little easter eggs in there—you may notice a certain drink appears in various stories in the anthology, for example—and I have a feeling it's not the last we've seen of Ochia and her crew.

BEHIND THE ADVENTURES OF ELENA AND NED, GARGOYLE P.I.

By Jeff Burns

HI! DO YOU NEED amazing private eyes to help you with your monster situation? Well, I have the duo for you! I hope you enjoyed the first of Elena and Ned's wacky detective adventures. That's right, this won't be the last time you see them. I had so much fun writing this story that I decided to write a full book comprised of their various cases. And they'll be just as zany as the Monster Mash caper you read about in this anthology.

This story was inspired by the *Gargoyles* animated series made by Disney in the 90s. I was a huge fan of that show and the two main characters – gargoyle leader Goliath and

NYPD police detective Elisa Maza – were loose inspirations for Ned and Elena. Though I took them in a much zanier direction, something I love doing in all my stories.

I liked the idea of doing a gargoyle story because it's not a type of monster I see very often in books or other media. But I think they're really cool! I decided to make Ned the main monster character in the story but also worked in a bevy of beasties to establish this was a world where you could find virtually every monster imaginable.

I also wanted to make the detective duo polar opposites. I love writing energetic, quirky characters, so Elena's effervescent, sex-obsessed character has been a joy to write. Ned's voice was a little tougher for me to nail down initially. I knew he needed to be more serious than Elena. But I also liked the idea of doing the opposite of what you might expect of a large gargoyle: having Ned eat very daintily while Elena shoves food in her mouth like a slob. More than one person who read this story in advance said Ned was their favorite character, so I guess whatever I did worked fairly well. I hope it did for you too, and you enjoyed him, Elena, and all the other characters.

I strive for fun, humorous stories in everything I write. That led to me coming up with the case the intrepid duo had to solve. I wanted to have them be hired for something that you would never think of in a noir-style detective story. And trying to figure out who wanted to rig a monster dance competition seemed perfect to accomplish that goal. Plus, I got to work in a fun dance number!

You may have noticed me and a few of the other authors mention a *freffrisa* drink. The origins of that comes from the *Super Geeked Up* comedy show I co-host with Francis Fernandez. Our amazing viewers came up with the name

Freff, which is a ship of Francis and Jeff. And we've had fellow author Marisa Wolf on our show so often, our viewers added her name to the mix. Thus, it became Freffrisa. We thought that sounded like the name of a drink, and it would be cool to include it as an easter egg in our stories. Marx Pyle got in on the fun too by having the super-sized *freffrisa-x* in his tale. So, ask for that drink next time you go out to eat!

If you read the first book in this anthology series – *Dragons of a Different Tail* – you'll know I'm a big fan of martial arts. I included a lot of kung fu in my "Wei Ling and the Water Dragon" story. While this one isn't as fight-oriented, I wanted to work in a little martial arts. Part of Elena's backstory is that she's trained in Muay Thai: in the alley fight scene with the two goblins, I have Elena using elbows, knees, and feet to do most of her fighting.

For Ned, I wrote in my character notes that he uses gargoyle grappling as a fighting style. To be honest, I'm not exactly sure what that is, but I'll probably work it into one of their future cases. For this story, I thought it'd be cool if he used a sonic scream to attack baddies, something unique among gargoyles in this world.

The most important part of the story for me, though, is Elena and Ned's relationship. They may seem like total opposites and get on each other's nerves, but they really care about each other. Which I hope I got across in the scene where Elena tends to Ned's wounds and they have a heart to heart. Amid all the goofiness, I felt it was very important to have a tender scene like that. And their relationship is what drives all the other cases they'll tackle (some of which I've already written). I hope you'll continue to follow their shenanigans when that book comes out!

Before I fly on out of here carried by my gargoyle buddy, I want to give a big shout-out to Marx Pyle for inviting me to be part of this anthology and all the other awesome authors I get to share the pages with. But, mostly, I wanted to thank all of you for picking up this book and reading all the stories. I can't tell you how much I appreciate it. I hope you enjoyed them and that you're inspired to form a detective agency with your favorite monster and have lots of sex. Wait, what? Um, Marx just pretend I didn't say that last part.

If you dug my story, please consider checking out my other work as well as the comedic, geeky erotica I do under my pen name Riley Rose Erotica. Thanks so much! Don't forget to practice for next year's Monster Mash!

BEHIND THE GREATEST OF ALL TIME

By Francis Fernandez

IN PREPARATION FOR WRITING this, I read the behind the scenes from *Dragons of a Different Tail*, the first anthology I was honored to be a part of. I decided not to write a behind the scenes for that book because it would have been three lines. I came up with the premise on the spot when I was told about the book. I thought about it constantly until it was time to write the final draft, so I wrote the story out based on critiques and as things came to mind.

I wanted to write about things that people may not have thought of before. There was no grand inspiration from stories I've read in the past (though I happen to be a fan of fantasy/sci-fi novels like Piers Anthony's *Apprentice Adept* series and *Ender's Game*), nor was it in honor of anyone I knew or for whom I looked up to. The entire story writing process was impulsive. I had no idea how it was going to end. I just typed because I had a deadline. I had never written anything like this before. It was my first published work.

I learned a lot from writing that first short story, "A Friend Called Home." The people who read it and critiqued it helped me a lot in learning how to actually write well and how to approach story telling. With my newfound knowledge, I promised myself that I would approach this next anthology with thoughtfulness in mind. So, when I was told what our next short stories would be about, I blurted out the first thing that came to my brain. And of course, it was a joke. Thus "The Greatest of All Time" was born.

Fighting the urge to be impulsive is hard. Especially when you're a procrastinator. I'm sharing ink and paper with accomplished authors who weave amazing, imaginative tales, and here I am, shooting from the hip, just throwing ideas around like confetti. I wanted to do things differently. I didn't just want to write things as they came to mind. I wanted to write something with more personality than my last story.

So, I took a moment and actually planned out (in my head) how I wanted it to end, and built the story around that. The most important thing to me was some kind of payoff to the punchline of my joke. Now, I'm no comedian, but I hope I built a narrative where you never quite know why things are happening until you get to the gag. It's like the joke, how do you fit two elephants into a Safeway bag? You take the f out of safe and the f out of way. If you didn't say out loud, "but there is no 'f' in way," then I need a better joke.

I also thought more about the focal character, the private investigator Hugh Marron Richard. I wanted him to have a personality and characteristics that made him stand out like Otter Dog, from "A Friend Called Home," but who actually did something. I wanted Hugh to be good at his job, but also kind of scatterbrained and weird. I wanted a setting I was unfamiliar with, like noir. I've seen *Bladerunner*, but I didn't want the story to be dark and brooding. I wanted things to happen and for people not to be bored with the narrative. I wanted there to be a little levity like Dixon Hill in *Star Trek: The Next Generation*. I understood what the tropes were, I knew what was expected, and I wanted to make them comical.

In the end, I just hope I'm improving as a writer. I hope that I was able to create something that was fun, different, and sticks with you like corn between your teeth. And who knows? Maybe the adventures of Hugh Marron Richard will continue. All I know is that I would like to build more of this little world I've made.

So, thank you for reading this behind the scenes and reading my story, "The Greatest of All Time." I hope you found it funny, or at least entertaining. Thank you to Marx Pyle for allowing me to be among such awesome writers who actually know what they're doing. And to anyone saying thank you back? Maybe the real "you're welcome" are the friends we made along the way.

BEHIND THE HEXPAD BLOG

By Colten Fisher

"Fantasy is hardly an escape from reality. It's a way to understand it." - Lloyd Alexander

I PULLED THE INSPIRATION for this story from numerous sources: mythology books I read as a kid, tv shows, even Pinterest posts (internet wanderers might have recognized the fae café). I wanted to write a story that dealt with very real-word concepts—like moving to a new city or growing up sheltered—while at the same time exploring all the crazy ways life would be different (or the same) if the fantastical was layered on top of the real and modern. I didn't write the story to be any kind of allegory, nor do I think it really functions as one. Nothing in New Astoria is meant to *represent* anything from our world. The dragons are included because dragons are cool and known for hoarding gold. Elves are included because I wanted to play with the various depictions of elves that we have in our culture. Nevertheless, I *did* set out to explore the blending of real-world issues with fantastical ingredients.

Humans have enough difficulty finding common ground between our own groups; how much harder would it be if they got thrown in with dozens of other races, creatures, and magical forces? One of the greatest uses for fantasy is to take something serious from our world, add in some whimsy, shake it up, and see what chemical reactions happen.

Writing this story was also a great exercise in considering accessibility. For example, I never got to mention it in the story, but the chariot doesn't run on iron rails in order to make it accessible to the iron-averse fae folk. I got to consider things like building sizes, green spaces, some things that even humans need for accessibility, and some things that would only matter if your population contains dragons. New Astoria still has its issues (any city will), but it was fun crafting a setting that had so many different types of people to try to accommodate.

In regard to my protagonist, I aimed to make a character who was at once a broad, open canvas onto whom each reader could project their view of what *this* type of person would be like, but who still had a very specific and unique voice. I let OutFromTheRoc17, our bold blogger, be whatever gender each reader might picture, while still possessing an immutable curiosity and dauntlessness.

One thing that I'm most proud of is that, much like New Astoria, I think our protagonist defies being pigeonholed into any specific box. We've got the clueless country kid *and* the politically correct activist, the genuine learner, *and* the misguided ally. Of course, there was probably a bit of a self-insert quality as well, with our protagonist exhibiting all the joy and wonderment of getting to see a magical place like New Astoria that *I* wish I could feel.

BEHIND THE TIGER'S GIFT

By G.K. White

AND NOW A PEEK behind the scenes! Some stories come out nice and smooth. You get inspired, you do some research, you sit down to write, and out pops a story. Sure, there are challenges, but nothing you can't hurdle with a bit of elbow grease and a red pen. Then there are other stories. Hard stories. And pulling these stories out is like performing a root canal with a hacksaw...guess which one this story was.

My initial plan for an exciting thriller about soldiers fell flat on its face. When I sat down to write...nothing. It just didn't feel right. Not that anyone asked, but my purpose for writing is to honor God and the love He has brought to my life. I just couldn't see how to do that with this story. When I asked Him what was going on, He said, "If you want to honor me, why not ask me what you should write?"

Yeah, big facepalm moment for me. But I then asked Him what I should write, and He brought up the story of Esther. Perfect, smooth sailing from here on, I thought. Then I sat down to write. For those who don't know, writing a first draft that you know is bad is like having a stomach bug that causes you to violently explode from both ends. You know you're not making anything pretty, and your spouse will never look at you the same, but you gotta get it out.

Pretty quickly, I realized I didn't want to do a direct re-telling of the story. It is only inspired by Esther's story. The characters are quite different in personality, and the cultural aspects and situations were changed. That being said, the structure of the story remained largely the same, though shortened. All of that felt good. My struggle (the exploding from both ends part) was with the through line, the theme that would tie it all together.

The theme of the first draft was on the definition of what made a "powerful" person. I wanted to present a powerful person as someone who had flaws but overcame them, dealt with their emotions and hurt instead of making them other people's problem. That failed pretty fantastically. The theme was messy and preachy, the plot was cliché in many areas, and overall, the characterization just didn't fit within the backdrop/inspiration that I was going with.

Then one of my critique partners mentioned that the king hadn't earned his redemption by the end. That line struck me. It struck me because of a situation I'd been recently experiencing. I won't go into details for the sake of those involved, but I had been approaching a relationship with a very performance-based mindset. Trying to earn trust and love. Requiring others to do the same for me. It left me feeling a lot of fear. Fear of what would happen when I failed to earn it. God led me through the situation, helping me realize that I was letting other people's opinions about whether I was trustworthy or loving determine whether I saw myself as those things. And I wasn't trusting others to trust me without that performance.

In short, I had been learning that I just needed to be who God said I was and trust others to do the same. When my critique partner told me the king hadn't earned his redemption, he had unwittingly birthed the theme of my story. For me, the story is about how a performance-based mindset and making people earn forgiveness results in fear, anger, and loneliness. It's about the freedom that offering love and trust as free gifts brings, and treating/speaking to people based on the good in them. Writing it helped re-inspire me. I'd like to be a person who calls out the gold inside others. Those people change the world.

TALES OF MONSTROSITY: THE SOUNDTRACK

T HANKS TO THE SUPPORT of our backers, we have created a playlist for your listening pleasure.

(*El Cucuy*)
El Cucuy - John 5

(*The Devil and Scott*)
Jersey Devil - Kieran Kane, Kevin Welch (feat. Fats Kaplin)

(*Eyes Like Burning Coal*)
Lost Themes III: Alive After Death album by John Carpenter

(*Don't Feed the Troll*)

TALES OF MONSTROSITY: THE SOUNDTRACK

Werewolves: Wolf Like Me – TV On The Radio
I'm A Werewolf, Baby – The Tragically Hip
Vampires: Transylvanian Concubine – Rasputina
Zombies: Astro Zombies – by the Misfits
Zombie – Fela Kuti, Afrika 70
Monster Mash – Misfits, John Cafiero
Famous Monsters album by the Misfits
Ghost of Stephen Foster – Squirrel Nut Zippers
Little Ghost - The White Stripes
Whistling Past the Graveyard - Screamin' Jay Hawkins
Dead Souls - Nine Inch Nails
Spellbound - Siouxsie and the Banshees

(*Magicland Mischief*)
Magic Carpet Ride - Steppenwolf
Magic - The Cars
A Kind of Magic - Queen
The Wizard - Black Sabbath
The Magic of the Wizard's Dream - Rhapsody & Christopher Lee
Hall of the Mountain King – Performed by Apocalyptica

(*Ghouly Girl*)
Zombie - Natalia Kills
Metling Waltz - Abel Korzeniowski
Mustang Sally - The Commitments, Andrew Strong
Love Me Dead - Ludo
everything sucks - vaultboy
Ghost - Confetti
Who Knows? - Natasha Bedingfield
Higher - Michale Bublé
this is what heartbreak feels like - JVKE

Vienna - Billy Joel
Achilles Come Down - Gang of Youths
11:11 - Ben Barnes
Haunted House - Mckenna Grace
Underground - Cody Fry
Give Me One Reason - Tracy Chapman

(The Brazen Skull)
The Gods of Yoruba - Horace Silver
Valley of the Shadows - Bob James
Good Guys, Bad Guys - Jean-Luc Ponty

(Rebel with a Cause)
Outlaws & Outsiders - Cory Marks, Travis Tritt, Ivan Moody, Mick Mars
Sweet Oblivion - Jimbo Mathus, Andrew Bird
Rebels - Call Me Karizma
Monsters – Run River North

(The Adventures of Elena and Ned, Gargoyle P.I.)
Thriller - Michael Jackson
Monster Mash – Performed by Bobby "Boris" Pickett, The Crypt-Kickers

(The Greatest of All Time)
Walking in LA - Missing Persons
Enemy - Imagine Dragons
Dragonheart theme
All Star - Smashmouth
Closing Time - Semisonic
G.O.A.T - Performed by Theory of a Deadman
Extreme Ways - Moby

ABOUT THE EDITORS

Marx Pyle is an author, screenwriter, filmmaker, podcaster, adjunct professor, and martial artist whose journey has been as complex as his characters and the worlds in which they live. His first degree was to save the world (Psychology), and the next to pay the bills (Computer Information Systems). His third degree (Film Production) helped him follow his storytelling dreams, but his final (Master of Fine Arts in Writing Popular Fiction) allowed him to do so without budget constraints. In addition to urban fantasy, he dabbles in science fiction, fantasy, and horror because he can't filter that "what if" voice in his head. Marx's urban fantasy/thriller, *Obsidian Monsters* was recently released. He enjoys relaxing at home with his supportive wife, their two cats (Veronica & Teddy Bear). He can be found online at marxpyle.com and on Twitter as @MrMarx.

J.C. Mastro grew up in California in the 1980's. As a child, he enjoyed science fiction and fantasy, spending sunny days outside battling invisible aliens and flying through space in oversized, cardboard ships. Evenings and lazy afternoons were spent consuming 1980's TV and movie favorites like reruns of *Star Trek*, and *Star Wars* on worn-down VHS tapes. In his teens, J.C. discovered a love of reading sci-fi and fantasy novels by authors such as Frank Herbert, Michael Crichton, and Timothy Zahn. Nowadays, he's a huge fan of authors like Brandon Sanderson, John Scalzi, and Andy Weir.

J.C. is a graduate of the Master of Fine Arts in Writing Popular Fiction program at Seton Hill University and a visually impaired author. His debut young adult science fiction novel, *Academy Bound*, released in 2022, and his short story "Spirit of the Dragon" appears in the Outstanding Creator Award winning anthology, *Dragons of a Different Tail*, where he also served as an editor. He lives in sunny southern California with a bunch of kids and dogs—and wouldn't want it any other way.

Website: www.jcmastroauthor.com Instagram: @jcmastroauthor Twitter: @JCMastroAuthor

ABOUT THE EDITORS

FIVE WORDS DESCRIBE **Victoria Scott**'s knowledge base: "How hard can it be?" This can-do attitude inspired her to learn to speak Latin, to quilt, and to operate a blueprint machine. Sometimes what she tries can be damn hard, like learning Ancient Greek, studying karate, and taking Calculus. Those...were not as successful.

Victoria writes Contemporary Fantasy and Science Fiction usually while hanging out with her dog Red the Wonder Husky. She teaches Social Studies and Latin by day and earned her MFA at Seton Hill University. Her bucket list is simple: drive a Zamboni, cruise down the Nile River, and get a book published. How hard can it be?

Anne C. Lynch teaches magic—the magic of books and the world of ideas. Words have power. Stories can change the world. So, yeah, she's an English teacher. She is also a writer of historical fiction with degrees from The University of Texas-Austin and an MFA in Writing Popular Fiction from Seton Hill University. She is a closet lover of all things horror; books, short stories, and movies. (Not the bloody stuff. That's gross.) Anne lives in Austin, Texas with her husband and two dogs, Penny-the-slightly-defective beagle and Luna-the-delightfully-derpy ~~house pony~~ Great Dane. Her debut novel is *The Mercenary's Son*. She is currently completing her second novel, *Gold Star Pilgrims*.

ABOUT THE PUBLISHER

Tales of Monstrosity: Monsters, Myths, and Miscreants
Published by Cabbit Crossing Publishing LLC

Signup for news and special offers!

https://www.subscribepage.com/cabbitcrossing

At Cabbit Crossing Publishing, we started as readers who love urban fantasy, epic fantasy, science-fiction, superheroes, and more. Now we are writing what we love and sharing it with the world! Like the urban legend of the cabbit (a cat rabbit hybrid) our stories are often blends of genres.

Also By Cabbit Crossing Publishing:

The Crossing Genre Collection:

Dragons of a Different Tail: 17 Unusual Dragon Tales
Tales of Monstrosity: Monsters, Myths, and Miscreants

Obsidian Archives:
Obsidian Monsters (Book 1 of the Obsidian Archives) - Coming Soon

WHAT NEXT?

Thank you for reading our anthology!
Please consider leaving a review.

If you liked this, then you will probably enjoy our previous anthology, *Dragons of a Different Tail: 17 Unique Dragon Tales*
https://books2read.com/dragonstail

"*Dragons of a Different Tail was one of the most creative and entertaining anthologies I've had the pleasure of reading.*" - Witty & Sarcastic Book Club

"If you're a fan of dragons, I highly recommend picking yourself up a copy of Dragons of a Different Tail. Hell, if you're a fan of anthologies, regardless of the subject matter, I would recommend it." - W.A. Stanley

CPSIA information can be obtained
at www.ICGtesting.com
Printed in the USA
BVHW040456110423
662089BV00005B/22